THE
SEVERED STREETS

By Paul Cornell

London Falling
The Severed Streets

THE
SEVERED
STREETS

PAUL CORNELL

TOR

First published 2014 by Tor
an imprint of Pan Macmillan, a division of Macmillan Publishers Limited
Pan Macmillan, 20 New Wharf Road, London N1 9RR
Basingstoke and Oxford
Associated companies throughout the world
www.panmacmillan.com

ISBN 978-1-4472-6206-0

1 3 5 7 9 8 6 4 2

A CIP catalogue record for this book is available from the British Library.

Typeset by Palimpsest Book Production Ltd, Falkirk, Stirlingshire

Printed and bound by CPI Group (UK) Ltd, Croydon, CR0 4YY

For Neil, with love and thanks

PROLOGUE

London in the summer.

One fine day and don't the English go mad? Every square of grass suddenly acquires a PA with a sandwich and a book about bondage. Sound seems to carry further. Music and news catch you unawares.

'Police marching in Trafalgar Square, in advance of the forth-coming vote, chanting they want the right to strike . . .'

White-legged men in ridiculous shorts. Socks under sandals.

'In the shadow of that fucking ridiculous— . . . You know what we need down here? Not an "Olympic Velodrome"! What's it for now?'

Pimm's with the sun shining off the pitcher. Furrowed brows are now white lines on pink.

'Cuts in front-line policing, never mind the specialist units. If the riots continue, if the Summer of Blood arrives, there will be areas where there are riots, where the police will not be able to go!'

In the evenings, crowds spill out of the pubs onto the warm pavement. At six in the evening, you can hear the number drone of cricket scores on the radio.

'They are expecting us to work for free, when they've sold this country . . .'

Wimbledon and Glastonbury and the Proms . . .

'Sieg heil! Sieg heil! Sieg heil!'

There's something about the blank summer sky – when the endless dog day, global-warming, tufty storm clouds part and unseasonal shivers give way to proper hay fever – that demands fire. Sparks in the blue black. But sparks sink back to the ground. Where the sparks land, there is fire.

There's a car going past the ends of streets. The car is polished so the sun reflects off it. There are pools of shadow at the end of every street. In every corner that stays dark there's a beggar now, an addict or a whore.

This is my car. I'm in it. It's polished like this because of me. It's a big rich car because of me.

What? Is that me? Is this me now, in this big car?! How did that happen? Who does this summer belong to? Who's coming?

Michael Spatley MP, chief secretary to the Treasury, woke with a gasp. He was in the back of his official air-conditioned car, but he was sweating. Light was sliding across his face. He looked out through the tinted windows, and there were the reassuring streets of London. He must have fallen asleep almost immediately when they'd left the House of Commons. They hadn't even reached Green Park yet. The traffic on Victoria Street was heavy this evening. Spatley loosened his tie and let out a long breath. He'd been having such terrible dreams lately. He always woke up feeling as if he was being accused of something.

He really should find a weekday flat closer than Kensington. Now he was in the Cabinet, he could afford it, just about. His title sounded so grand, but the pay was actually painfully less than he could have earned in industry. The general public just didn't get that. An unexpected smell came to him, from outside the car. He hit the button to lower the window. It didn't work.

'Sorry, sir,' said Tunstall. Tunstall was Spatley's regular driver from the Ministerial Car Service. He had a finger to his communication earpiece. 'I've switched on the security features. There's a problem up ahead. We'll be turning off in a sec and going the pretty way.'

'Thanks, Brian.' The smell was of smoke. A big fire – not just wood, but tyres and that stench of hot tar, way beyond the scent of baking streets. 'What's going on?'

'You know – the protests. Okay, here we go.' He swung the wheel, the angle of light changed across the car interior, and they were off down a side street where shops lined the lower floor of the surrounding tall buildings.

It was good to be on first-name terms with one's driver. Spatley liked the way Tunstall dealt with whatever got in their way, as if life in the capital was one big traffic jam to be slipped around. Spatley took his iPad from his bag and checked Sky News.

'. . . *incidents in Peckham, where police have yet to arrive, report residents. Shop owners are taking to the streets in an effort to protect their property, some armed with makeshift weapons. Meanwhile, unscheduled anti-cuts protests by flash mobs have slowed traffic to a halt in parts of central London . . .*'

That was new: 'flash mob' now an offhand part of the news vocabulary. A month ago that would have been 'so-called'. He watched the images for a while: kids in Peckham in hoods or with scarves over their faces, running, in the sunshine, which looked odd, to see all that energy while it was still light. Cut to a mass of kids who looked much more middle class, bushy beards and skinny shirts, rushing into the foyer of some big corporation. Spatley watched the protestors; many of them were holding their phone cameras in the air, like crosses to repel evil, as they upended a vat of what looked like blood but was surely some sort of dye onto the PA's chair. That imagery wouldn't play well for them: a scared black PA, chubby, *nice*, furious at them. The problem was that you couldn't see their faces, with the front row of the protestors wearing those aristocrat masks with top hats, some of them sporting the little capes.

To him, those masks just looked like giving in. As if revealing who you were these days was not just dangerous, as they wanted to imply, but actually impossible. Face coverings weren't allowed at certain protests now; he'd voted for that legislation. He'd thought of Muslim women as he did it, and hoped for some care to be taken in the specifics, but, well, the debate just hadn't gone in that direction.

He noted that there was long brunette hair spilling out of the back of one of the masks in the news clip, small, youthful breasts filling out the crisp white shirt. No silver-topped walking canes this time, though, not since the first of these protests, when the police had classed the canes as weapons and charged right in, and several of the protestors had suddenly understood what they'd got into. 'Protestors' – was that the right word, even? I mean, come on, they talked about being against 'the cuts' – that was all he ever heard from them, 'cut cut cut' – but could many of them even sum up the economic case against? *'What do we want?' 'It's complicated!'* That had got a laugh and a groan of annoyance at the same time from the audience on *Have I Got News for You* the other night, as if a satirical show should only have a go at the government and not at a bunch of bloody students. He wished he could sit them down and try to persuade them that he and his colleagues on the Liberal Democrat side of the Coalition were actually doing their best to hold the fucking Tories back.

Or . . . well, that was what they kept saying to other people and to each other. It was more that the presence of him and his colleagues made the fucking Tories even more like the fucking Tories, because they had to keep proving themselves to be so damned hardcore. He kept finding the images coming unbidden into his head: people dragged out of shops and put into vans; Orwellian signs about reporting illegal immigrants; reporters being told that they had no right to know. Wasn't this exactly what he'd campaigned *against*, not very long ago?

He wasn't going to let himself give in to hopelessness. If he could reveal what he'd discovered in the last few weeks, those 'Toff' protestors in the masks would be glad he was still in government. Then maybe the Coalition would mean something. Then maybe *he* would mean something. Because he was actually on the point of demonstrating that there was something much, much worse just under the surface – something he could root out and bring into the light.

Yes, in the last few days he'd made up his mind about this. He was going to act, and he was going to do it *soon*. He found his hand going to the inside pocket of his jacket, as it reflexively did when he needed to be reassured about what he had there. He stopped it. He knew what he had. Now he had to act on it.

They had turned left and were now heading slowly along a backstreet: residential, nice window boxes. That smell was getting stronger, and now he could hear something in the distance: drums and rhythmic shouting. They passed a crowd outside a pub with people in suits enjoying the sunshine, all looking in one direction – the direction they were headed, towards where the sound and the smell were coming from. They weren't looking nervous, but interested, laughing, raising their glasses. Here it comes, say the British, we love a comfy disaster, spices things up, doesn't it? The fuckers. Why was it so hard to get any of them to believe in anything positive?

'Brian?'

'We're heading towards the demo now, but we're going to turn off down Horseferry in a second.'

'Okay.'

How would it be if he told Tunstall to stop and open the door, and if he got out and followed the sound of the drums and the smell of the smoke and went and joined in with the protest? Or he could find a box and stand on it and orate to the crowd and say, *We're actually* you, *we're the opposition and the government at the same time! Can't you see that?*

The car moved forwards again. Suddenly, the volume of noise from ahead grew, as if a mass of people had turned a corner. Oh, here came – God, was this them? There were people moving back down the street. Ordinary people, not protestors, trotting out of the way. Then the first of the kids in those costumes, running hard, not after them, but away from something.

The main body of the protest had presumably run into police efforts to contain it somewhere up ahead.

'What the hell, Brian?'

'Sorry.' Tunstall looked over his shoulder, wondering about reversing, but they were stuck among cars that were all frantically honking their horns.

Spatley looked round. Protestors were running the other way up the street now too, appearing behind them, meeting up with those from the other direction, all desperately looking around. Oh, don't say that the police had kettled them in here, right in this street! In moments the car was surrounded: kids dressed in that Toff costume; kids with placards; kids just looking excited and sweaty, bare chested in shorts, sunburned from the day out, sparkling with factor fifty, scarves ready to be wrapped around their faces, those masks and capes and hats scattered among them.

A placard slammed against the side window, then the window opposite, then bodies swiftly started to surround the car. His view became obscured as more and more of the kids started thumping against the side of the vehicle. Those masked faces loomed as they tried to peer in, rather intimidating, especially when up close. Those things were such a mistake on their part. They should be trying to make people love them, not be scared of them. They couldn't see in through the darkened windows. They were just assuming someone important or rich was in here, probably a 'banker'. Some of them would know what a banker was: Mummy or Daddy. That was maybe why they hated them so much. Tunstall was muttering at them, annoyed. He hit the horn, held onto it. 'I've called for backup; we should have you out of here in a bit. Don't worry, it's not as if they can get in.'

The car started to rock from the weight of bodies against both sides. Then the protestors must have felt the movement, and a cheer went up, and they started to synchronize, to do it deliberately. The ends of placards started to hammer against the windows. There was one of those canes thumping at the glass beside his head. But Spatley knew the glass would hold.

'Little shites,' called Tunstall. 'Wish I could reverse into 'em.'

'We can't, I'm afraid.' Just for the record. 'How long until that backup gets here?' He glanced at the window beside him and didn't hear Tunstall's reply, because suddenly his attention was caught by what he saw there.

It was another of those masks, but shoved right up against the glass. Even like that, you still couldn't see anything behind the eye slits. Was someone just holding it there? No, there was clearly a body out there too. Spatley leaned closer to examine it. They sold these outfits online; some of them were the proper ones, so called, and some of them were cheap knock-offs. The Chinese were shipping them over. Capitalism in action, on the back of the anti-capitalist movement, straight from the Communists. Anything could mean anything nowadays. The top hat this figure wore was pushed up against the window too. Whoever wore it was almost acting as if he could push his way into the car.

No, wait, was that . . . ? This wasn't possible. Was he dreaming again?

The mask was somehow . . . forcing the glass inwards around it, the brow of the hat pushing ahead of it, bending only slightly with the pressure, the window becoming a viscous liquid. Was it some sort of chemical?

There might be genuine danger here. Spatley looked quickly to Tunstall, but he was oblivious, hitting the horn again. 'Brian!'

The man looked over his shoulder, looked right at the face slowly pushing through the glass, and it was suddenly, horribly evident to Spatley that the driver couldn't see anything unusual. 'They'll get bored. You hold on.' He sounded less certain now, nervous even.

'But . . .' Spatley looked between the two faces. He didn't know how to say that he could see something that Tunstall couldn't.

Oh. This must be what having a stress hallucination was like.

He turned back, trying to control himself, to watch as the face shoved itself through the glass, the head almost completely here now. He was thinking about Ann giving birth to Jocelyn, he realized. Was this some sort of dream sign, that he should accept this protest movement or whatever it was into his . . . his *car* . . . ? No, no. That was weakness.

Below the head, something was pushing through the material of the door itself. Of course. If glass could do that, so could metal. Spatley watched it form. It was going to become a hand, he saw. It was holding something, metal flowing all around it. Then the object heaved its way right through the door and into clear view.

The hand was holding a cut-throat razor.

Spatley yelled and ripped off his seatbelt. He shoved himself across the seats, scrambling to get his back to the far door. 'Brian!' *I'm awake*, he wanted to yell, *I'm awake!* 'Let me out!'

'What is it?' The driver had turned to look again. He was looking right at where a second hand had pushed its way through the door. The thing's upper body was now joining the head as it snaked into the car.

'Can't you see it?! You have to let me out! They're . . . they're getting in!'

'What are you talking about?'

Spatley closed his eyes tightly, opened them again, and the figure was still there. It slowly and carefully pulled its knees out of the door to kneel on the seat; that mask of a face was looking at him, the razor raised so that the blade was a line in his gaze, the other hand resting on the upholstery. Its meniscus method of entry sealed behind it and now it was entirely in the car with him. Its posture was that of a dancer, of someone playing a part in a mime show. Spatley grasped that feeling desperately to himself – that whatever else this was, there must be a person inside there. He still couldn't make himself demand that Tunstall see it. 'I . . . I . . .' Even trying to talk to it felt terrible, as if he was making it real by acknowledging it. 'What do you want?' he asked, as quietly as he could. 'Who are—?'

It leaped at him.

He flung up a hand to protect himself, but the hardest punch he'd ever felt hit him in his neck. He screamed at the force of it and threw himself forward to fight. But, as he moved, he realized that something wasn't right in his throat. Okay, he was injured. He got his fingers to the mask. He tried to prise it from the thing's face. His other hand grabbed the hand with the razor, but it was as if he was trying to force his fingers into the cracks of a wall. He suddenly felt how huge this thing was, how strong. How . . . old. The razor hand wasn't yet moving, but – his throat . . . he had to look down. Blood was somehow now flowing freely down his chest. He felt the weakness of the blood loss in that moment, the darkness thundering into his head, as if he was suddenly up a mountain and needed desperately to breathe. He tried and couldn't. The hand wrenched itself out of his weak baby grip. That hard pointed punch landed again, now in his torso. In that moment, Spatley knew he was terribly wounded, knew that the second blow had punctured something far inside him.

Michael Spatley bellowed with pain. Instead of sound, what burst from his throat was a deluge of blood.

Brian Tunstall looked round at the sudden sound from behind him. In the back seat, Spatley was thrashing around. It was just him in there. It took the driver a moment to take in what he was seeing, to be sure there was nobody else in the car. 'Medical emergency,' he shouted into his headset. 'Ambulance required on scene.' He was unclipping his seatbelt as he said it, turning to – to do what, exactly?

Now he could see how much blood there was. In an instant there was more of it, out of the man's abdomen and groin. Tunstall could see the fabric ripping apart. Suddenly the man's trousers burst open, and there was a great gout of blood as—

Just like that, the screams stopped.

Tunstall stared at the flesh that spiralled up into a sort of swaying pillar, a snake of . . . oh, God . . . what was this? How could this be happening? He'd never imagined—

With a slap like meat hitting a slab, everything he was looking at suddenly blurred sideways and, with a concussive splatter of blood, something sped through the side of the car.

Across the rear seats lay the remains of Michael Spatley, his neck and abdomen and groin split open and empty, his mouth lolling. The thumping and swaying against the car continued. For a moment, Tunstall could only stare. Then he made himself clamber into the back seats and did what he had to do.

ONE

Detective Inspector James Quill liked his sleep. He liked it especially on these short summer nights when he was woken by the dawn and had had to leave the window open to get cool, and then it rained on the carpet. He would only willingly give up his sleep for his daughter, Jessica, who would on occasion wander into his and Sarah's bedroom at 3 a.m. with something very important to tell them. These days Quill, having once been made to *forget* Jessica through occult means, would listen to that important thing with a bit more patience. Now once again there was an unusual noise in his bedroom, and he found a smile coming to his face, sure it was her.

He blinked awake, realizing that this time the noise wasn't the voice of his child, but of his phone on the bedside table, ringing.

He lay there for a moment. There was a lovely pre-dawn light through the curtains.

'Would you please answer that,' said Sarah, 'and tell them to fuck off?'

Quill saw who was calling and answered the phone. 'Lisa Ross,' he said, 'my wife sends you her fondest regards.'

'If it's her, I actually do,' amended Sarah.

'It's the Michael Spatley murder, Jimmy.' The intelligence analyst's voice on the other end of the line sounded excited.

'Please don't tell me—?'

'Yeah. It looks like this is one of ours.'

Quill took a deep breath as he always did before quietly opening the door of his semi-detached in Enfield and stepping out into the world. He looked around cautiously as he approached his car in the driveway. This morning there didn't seem to be anything horrifying—

'Morning,' said a voice from nearby.

Quill jumped. He looked round, his heart racing.

It was the newspaper delivery guy, with a bag over his shoulder. He'd parked his van at the end of the close. Quill tried to make himself give the bloke a smile, but he'd already seen what was with him. The delivery guy was followed by a trail of small figures, giggling and nudging each other. They looked like tiny monks and wore robes that hid their faces. As Quill watched, one of them, seemingly unnoticed by the man, leaped up like a monkey onto his shoulder and whispered something in his ear. The man's expression remained unchanged. But now Quill thought he could see a burden in the eyes, something being gnawed at. 'Don't like the look of the news this morning,' said the man, his voice a monotone.

Quill nodded and went swiftly to unlock his car.

He headed for the A10, but, as always, couldn't help but look up into the sky ahead of him as he did so. Towards the reservoir, something horrifying loomed in the air. It was there every day. It had taken him a while to notice it, as was the way with the Sight – the ability to see and feel the hidden things of London that he and his team of police officers had acquired by accident less than six months ago. Once he had seen the thing, it had become more and more obvious, to the point where he now wished he could ignore it.

But, being a copper, every time he had to look.

It was a vortex of smashed crockery, broken furniture, all the cared-for items of a home, whirling and breaking above a particular house somewhere over there, over and over again, each beloved thing impossibly fixing itself only to be smashed again. He could never see such detail from the car, obviously, but as he'd become aware of it, he'd gained the emotional context, the feeling of rage and betrayal, the horrible intimacy of it. Those feelings were also part of what the Sight did. The detail of what he was seeing had come when he'd looked into the matter and found out about a poltergeist case that dated back to the seventies. Once he knew what he was looking at, the Sight had filled in the gaps, and now every time he drove this way he was therefore burdened by something that looked like a distant weather phenomenon but also shouted pain into his face.

The worst thing of all was that there was nothing he could do about it. The participants no longer lived around here. No crime that he was aware of had been committed. It might not even have really happened. But in some way, via some mechanism that he and his team had not yet got to grips with, London *remembered* it. Being *remembered* was one of the two ways one could gain power from some intrinsic property of the metropolis itself; the other being to make an awful sacrifice to . . . well, they didn't know what the sacrifice was made to, really, though they had made some worrying guesses. Quill sometimes thought that living here with the Sight was like continually wearing those Google glasses he'd read about – always seeing notations about the world. Except in this case the notes were all about ancient pain and horror.

Those little buggers in the hoods were another example. As far as he and the others could tell, they were some sort of . . . well, they were either a metaphorical representation of various psychiatric disorders – of human misery, basically – or they actually *were* that misery, and psychiatry was the metaphor. They were as common as rats, and Quill's team had quickly stopped trying to deal with every instance of them they saw in the street. They could be chased away, or the person they were tormenting could be taken away from them, but they always came back. Quill could swear that, as the summer came on, he was seeing more and more of them. At least he didn't have any following him. Yet.

He turned the car onto the A10, thankful not to have the weight of that poltergeist thing in the sky right in front of him any more. The familiar lit-up suburban bulk of the lightbulb factory loomed ahead; a few early cars were on the road. He took comfort in the ordinary these days. He switched on the radio, found some music on Radio 2. He felt guilty every time he thought about it, but he often found himself wondering if life would have been so bad had he and his team actually accepted the offer that had been made to them. That terrifying bastard whom they called the 'Smiling Man', who was almost certainly not a man at all, had used a proxy to tell them that he was willing to take away the Sight. They, being coppers, being aware that if they did that they'd spend the rest of their lives wondering what they were missing when they came across a crime scene with some hidden dimension, being aware that that smiling bastard who had been behind their first case had something enormous planned . . . like mugs they had all, for their differing reasons, said no.

It didn't help that the awful things they could all now see were confined to London. You could get away from it by going on a day trip to Reading. Quill and Sarah had taken Jessica to a theme park in the Midlands a couple of weekends ago, and had had what had felt like the best sleep of their lives. Sarah didn't share the Sight. She hadn't been there when Quill had touched that pile of soil in the house of serial killer – and, as it turned out, *wicked witch* – Mora Losley. In some way that they still didn't understand, it had been that action that activated this ability in himself and his three nearby colleagues. Sarah only knew what Quill told her, which was just about everything. On the drive back to London from their weekend break, Quill had seen Sarah's expression, how complicated it was. She was trying to hide the fact that she admired Quill's need to do his duty . . . but hated it too.

Quill realized that the radio was playing 'London Calling' by the Clash and angrily changed the channel to Classic FM. He didn't need his situation underlining, thank you very much. He wound down the window and immediately regretted it, but left it open for the cool air on his face. The air brought with it the smell of burning. The smell was of last night's riots and lootings, of some borough or other going up in smoke. Thanks to an interesting series of interactions between this government and certain classes of the general public, it was shaping up to be one of those summers. He and his team had been told that the Smiling Man had a 'process' that he was 'putting together', and Quill kept wondering if he was somewhere behind the violence. He could imagine a reality where the coalition in power had done a lot of the same shit, but without a response that included Londoners burning down their own communities. Really, it was down to how the initial outbreaks of violence had been mismanaged and a strained relationship between government and the Met that was leaving him increasingly incredulous.

The news came on the radio, and he made himself listen. Sporadic looting, protests against the cuts and austerity measures. Cars on fire and bottles being thrown at police. *The postal ballot on strike action by the Police Federation—'*

Quill told the radio to piss off as he changed the channel again. He could understand the frustration felt by his fellow officers, really he could. Every move, every sensible decision that the Met made to get to the cause of the unrest and damp it down seemed to be instantly overturned and criticized by either the mayor's office or the Home Office. To the 'lid', the uniformed police officer on the street, what that meant was that you got spit in your face and then found out that you were going back the next night for more of exactly the same, when it was obvious to you and your mates – spread out and targets for missiles as you were – that the situation wasn't going to get any better. The other police forces of Britain had their own difficult relations with this government, knew where the Met was coming from and wanted to support their colleagues.

But strike action? His old police dad, Marty, had been on the phone from Essex, making sure Quill wasn't having any of that. It was against all the traditions of the Met. Against the law, even

– coppers didn't have the right. Besides, Quill's team's speciality, standing against the powers of darkness, seemed a bit too urgent to allow for industrial action.

He realized he was passing the cemetery on his right. He always tried not to glance over there, and always failed. Graveyards were usually, in his team's experience, a bad idea. This one was full of greenish lights that danced between the graves, and there were a couple of swaying figures, one an emaciated husk with glowing eyes who had taken to . . . yes, there he was again this morning, like every morning.

Quill tiredly raised his hand to return the wave.

Forty minutes later, Quill got out of his car at Belgravia police station. The sky was getting properly light now. He found Ross standing under one of the big fluorescent car park lights, moths fluttering around it. She had been watching the first batch of last night's Toff protestors, the ones whom the police presumably had no legal reason to keep, stumbling from the building. They had those Halloween-style costumes of theirs bundled under their arms. A few of them were, even now, giving each other high fives and laughing. But most of them looked grim. Quill looked at their emotion and again felt distant copper annoyance at bloody *people*. He used to joke that without people his job would be a lot easier. But now he supposed he couldn't even say that. 'What have we got?' he asked.

She looked round at him. Maybe she was his team's intelligence analyst, a civilian, but what they'd been through together had brought them as close as Quill had ever felt to any fellow officer. He owed her the life of his child. There was something about the paleness of Ross' left eye compared to her right, about the broken angle of her nose, that made it always look as if she'd just been in a fight. Her hair was cut short to the point where sometimes it looked as if she'd just taken a razor to it. She was biting her bottom lip in that skewed smile of hers, which only appeared once in a blue moon, and which Quill had started to associate with the game, as they say, being afoot. 'Maybe just the op we've been looking for,' she said.

Quill had caught up with the Spatley case before he'd left the house. The headline on the first edition of the *Herald* had read, 'Murdered by the Mob'. Michael Spatley, chief secretary to the Treasury, had been cornered in his car by anti-government protestors, who had forced their way in and eviscerated him. The story had been the lead on the BBC ten o'clock bulletin last night, but Quill had gone to bed thinking, ironically, that he was glad that it wasn't his problem.

'Why is it one of ours?'

Ross led him towards the doors of the nick. 'I have search strings set up in the Crime Reporting Information System, and I check them four times a day. A locked report came through on my page of results late last night, with the heading directing me to the extension of one DCI Jason Forrest. I couldn't read it, but if it set off my searches it must contain some extreme words, like "impossible". Around 2 a.m. it showed up on the Home Office Large Major Enquiry System too, so it's a murder. I checked where this bloke Forrest works, and it's this nick, which is also the obvious one for a suspect in the Spatley case to be brought back to. I got excited and called you.'

Quill wanted to slap her on the shoulder or fist-bump her or something, but the very urge was against his copper nature. His was a squad created within the budget of a detective superintendent, its objectives hidden from the mainstream of the Metropolitan Police while cut after cut reduced the operational capacity of every other Met department, and the riots and the protests and the outbursts of dissent in the force's own ranks were pushing the system to breaking point. His team needed a new target nominal – a new operation – before people in senior positions started asking questions about why they existed.

'And you were awake at 2 a.m. because . . . ?'

Her poker face was immediately back. Quill sighed to see it. After they'd defeated Mora Losley and thus solved the mystery that had loomed over Ross for her whole life, the analyst had opened up for a few weeks, become more talkative, cracked a few jokes, even. It had been wonderful to see. But now the cloud was back. 'I'm still working through those documents we found in the ruins in Docklands.'

She was also, thought Quill, probably still considering the plight of her deceased dad, who, in the course of the team's first – and so far only – op, she'd discovered to be residing in Hell. Whatever Hell was. Quill was pretty sure it didn't map onto conventional thoughts about damnation. Ross had told them that she was aiming, in the fullness of time, to do something about getting her dad out of there, if they ever found a mechanism to do so. Whether or not she'd made any progress on that was between her and her copious notebooks. 'Okay, but—'

'That's my own time, Jimmy.'

Quill raised his hands in surrender, and indicated for her to proceed.

'Witnesses are saying to the press that the doors of the car weren't opened at any point, meaning that the government service driver, whom I've discovered was one Brian Tunstall, must be the only suspect, presumably the "thirty-eight-year-old male" the Major Investigation Team have announced they've arrested in connection. The words that set off my searches might well be contained in his interview statement.'

'Terrific.' Quill took out his phone. 'You get our two comrades over here. I am about to wake a detective superintendent.'

The first result of Quill's call to his superior was that a hassled-looking lid came out of the nick, found Quill and Ross, and checked them through into the canteen. As in any nick, the canteen smelt of comforting grease and echoed with the clatter of cutlery and the sound of music radio from the kitchens. To venture any further into this bureaucracy, they were going to need their polit-ical muscle here with them. The food hall was full of uniforms looking pissed off, having just come off a shift where half of them would have been beaten on by protestors and rioters. Ross kept looking at her phone. 'Now they've made an arrest, I'm waiting for those "the mob did it" stories on the news websites to change. They might give us more information to go on.'

'In the meantime,' said Quill, 'there exist in this world bacon sarnies.'

Forty-five minutes later, Kev Sefton arrived, dressed like his under-cover self, in hoodie and trainers, but with the holdall he now carried everywhere. Quill suspected that, given the riots, the detec-tive constable must have been stopped a few times lately and searched for the crime of being black in the wrong suburb. Quill just hoped Sefton flashed his warrant card before the uniforms found the collection of occult, or what they'd taken to simply calling 'London', items that he now regularly carried in that holdall. In their line of work, as Sefton had discovered, some ancient horse brass with a provenance in the metropolis could be much handier in terms of repelling evil than garlic. If Ross had a boxer's nose, Sefton had the rest of that body shape, compact and hard. As Quill had discovered, what went with that physique was a detec-tive's intellect that was willing to believe in extraordinary possi-bilities, which could lead Sefton to think about the horrifying reality they'd discovered – to a degree that the rest of the team, Quill included, weren't yet capable of. It was as if he had an undercover officer's adaptability that could extend itself beyond reality. Quill had started to think of him as his weird-London-shit officer. He got the feeling that that role was letting Sefton breathe, that all his life he'd been waiting for a chance like this.

'I thought this might be one of ours,' he said, sitting down.

'Do you mean that you did some sort of . . . ?' Quill still didn't have the language to form that kind of question, so he contented himself with spreading his hands like a stage illusionist, indicating the sort of occult London thing that he supposed Sefton now did.

'I wish I *had* some sort of . . .' Sefton returned the gesture with a smile.

Quill was pleased to see that. He knew that Sefton liked to try and keep a positive surface going, but that being the one to deal with the London shit, especially when they'd made relatively little progress, weighed heavily on him. He had had adventures on his own that, while he'd described them to the team in every possible detail, he'd added had been like 'something out of a dream'. Which wasn't your normal copper description of encountering a potential informant.

'Right then!' That was Tony Costain, marching in as if he owned the place as always, dressed to the nines as always, in a retro leather coat that emphasized his tall, slim loomingness. The detective sergeant was the other black former undercover police officer on the team. If Costain smiled at you, and you knew who he really was, you wondered what he was hiding, because here was a copper who'd been willing to sell on drugs and guns he'd nicked from the gang he'd been undercover in. Still, Quill felt he'd treated Costain too roughly on occasion. He had felt for Costain when he'd developed a desperate desire not to go to Hell and had decided that from now on he was going to clean up his act, having caught a glimpse of the Hell he was certain was waiting for him. It felt like something that didn't sit well with the man, though: an abstinence that chafed on him every day. Costain, basically, didn't *want* to be a good boy. Quill had never said it out loud, but he'd started to think of this consummate actor's ability to step in and out of the dark side, to bring on the dodgy stuff, as a positive asset to the team. He had found himself hoping that, should push come to shove, Costain could find it in himself to do, perhaps, extreme violence and leave redemption until later. 'You look like you got some sleep,' he said.

'The sleep of the just,' Costain nodded.

'The just what?'

Costain gave Quill exactly the sort of smile he'd been anticipating.

'There you are, James, with the bacon sarnies.' Detective Superintendent Lofthouse had entered. The smart, angular middle-aged woman looked exhausted, as always, while never actually seeming tired. 'Someone's fetching one for me, and a gallon of coffee to go with it.' She sat down with them and lowered her voice. 'I've had a word with the senior investigating officer on the Spatley case, Jason Forrest, and he, despite his puzzlement, you will be pleased to hear, has expressed his trust in his old mate, me, by asking to talk to you at the earliest opportunity. You and I are to take the lift to the third floor.'

'Thank you, ma'am.' Quill found himself sitting straighter in his chair and glanced around at his team to see them all reacting similarly. None of them quite knew how to deal with their boss these days.

Three months ago, Quill's team had used a pair of 'vanes' that had been employed to attack Quill with some sort of weaponized poltergeist but could also be utilized as dowsing equipment. With these they had found a ruined building in London's Docklands. It was something like a temple, the remains standing absurdly on an open space between office blocks by the river. There had been ornate chairs and a big marble table that had been cracked in two. A pentagram had been inscribed on both that table and the ground underneath. Quill had swiftly realized that only they could see this building, that passers-by were looking at his team searching the ruins as if they were performing some sort of avant-garde mime. They'd discovered a few details of a group that called itself the Continuing Projects Team, people who, they'd been startled to find, showed up not at all on internet searches. Quill's team had already seen what a huge amount of energy it took to make one person be forgotten by a handful of people. The idea that a group of prominent people could be made to vanish so completely from public memory was staggering. They had found an empty personnel file that these people had kept, and on the cover of it had been the name 'Detective Superintendent Lofthouse', and then she had stepped from the shadows, holding an ancient key that Quill had recognized as having been on her charm bracelet. '*This*,' she had said, 'explains a *lot*.'

Quill and the others had been bursting with questions. She'd shaken her head in answer to all of them.

'I know you lot are doing something . . . impossible,' she'd said finally. 'I realized that a while back.'

Quill had pointed at the key. 'What does that have to do with this? Did you know the people who worked here?'

She had raised her hands to shut him down. 'It's only because you say so that I know there *is* something here. I can't tell you anything more, James. I know less than you do.' She'd asked for a detailed description of the ruins, walking through them with a look on her face that said she was willing herself to sense something there, but couldn't. There was pain in that expression, Quill had realized. She'd handled the key as she'd looked around at what to her was just an empty area of Docklands pavement, reflexively toying with the object. Then, when she'd been satisfied that she'd been told everything, she'd looked once more to Quill. Her expression drew on their old friendship, hoping he'd understand. 'I'm sorry,' she'd said. 'I know you want more from me. For now, please, just accept. Be certain you can always rely on me. From now on, tell me about your operations. I'll believe you. But I can't tell you why.'

Before they could say anything more, she'd marched off into the night.

Quill had understood at that moment that Ross had had that expression on her face that he'd come to associate with some immediate deduction or revelation. 'Oh,' she'd said. 'Oh.'

'That, from her,' Costain said, 'always ends with us getting told something true but deeply shitty.'

'Even with the Sight,' said Ross, 'Jimmy still forgot his daughter. He couldn't process any of the clues to her presence in the physical world. He just ignored them. So how come we can see that document listing the people who worked here, who otherwise have been completely forgotten?' She hadn't given them a moment to think about an answer. 'For the same reason that these ruins have been left. Deliberately. For people like us, who can see things like this, to notice.'

'As a sign, a warning,' said Sefton, nodding urgently. 'That's why all we've found is a list of those people and nothing else. Having found that document, we now know it's possible for people like these, people like *us*, to be not just killed, not just wiped out, but actually erased from everyone's memories.'

'It's a display of power,' said Costain.

'She –' Ross indicated where Lofthouse had gone – 'knows more about that situation than we do. But if we want to keep this unit going, we can't ask her about it.'

'"Just accept",' repeated Quill, sighing. 'Does she *know* any coppers, do you think?'

In the three months since, they hadn't found out anything further. DeSouza and Raymonde, the firm of architects that owned the land upon which the temple stood, when interviewed, had no more knowledge of the Continuing Projects Team than anyone else. Ross' examination of the documents found at the scene revealed them to be mostly about architecture. She had shown the others what looked to be learned debates about how 'the side of a building does turn the water' written in a brown and curly hand that looked like something from the seventeenth century, and printed pamphlets from before that arguing lost causes in dense language. Those who'd curated this material seemed not to have understood it much more than Quill's group did. There were only gestures in the direction of a filing system or index. Nor could they find any useful occult objects in the ruins. On closer examination it had become clear that, as Ross had speculated, scavengers had been through the place and taken anything useful.

Lofthouse had set up regular meetings between herself and Quill, and had listened with great interest to his reports of things which she should think impossible. True to his word, he had not asked her any questions. It meant that he left every such meeting feeling exactly as tense around her as he was feeling now.

He picked up his bacon sandwich for a last bite before they had to go and meet the man in charge of the Spatley case and glanced to his team, trying to keep the wryness out of his voice. 'Good to have you onboard, ma'am,' he said, 'as always.'

Detective Chief Inspector Jason Forrest had a body like a rugby player's, wore a bespoke suit and had an old scar down his left cheek. He looked as if he'd been persuaded at gunpoint to let Quill and Lofthouse into his office this morning. He asked a lot of questions about the exact purpose of Quill's 'special squad' and rolled his eyes at the imprecise answers he received. 'Come on, why should I ask you lot to help with my investigation?'

'Because if there are features you find hard to explain—' began Lofthouse.

'How do you know that?' He sounded bemused to the point of anger.

Lofthouse looked to Quill. Quill told him about Ross' search strings.

The DCI's expression grew even more nonplussed. 'Why are you interested in words like "impossible"?'

Quill had his explanation prepared. 'Following the Losley case, we've been specializing in crimes with an occult element to the motive.' The look on Forrest's face suggested that Quill was barking up the right tree. 'We've been given access to . . . advanced sensor . . . techniques, the details of which we can't go into. It gives us a bit of an edge.'

'You jammy buggers. We could do with that technology for the riots.'

'We're trying it out. Maybe other units will get it soon.' *'Cos you'd really enjoy that.*

Forrest considered for a moment longer, looked again to Lofthouse and finally gave in. 'All right, I'll formally request that your team assist in the investigation. You'll get access to the crime scene after it's been forensicated, and to witness statements and evidence. I'll be overjoyed for you to help out my very stretched staff by interviewing persons of interest. I've already lined up searches at Spatley's offices, both in Whitehall and the Commons, but if you can think of anywhere else to search, I'll okay that too.'

'Thank you, sir,' said Quill. It was already occurring to him that his lot would not need just to find different places to search, but to go over the same places, given their advantage of having the Sight.

'So, here's the problem.' Forrest opened the file on his desk and placed some gruesome crime scene photos in front of Quill and Lofthouse. 'We have a car surrounded by witnesses for the whole time frame in which a murder could have been committed. We have CCTV footage of that car throughout. We have enormous coverage of the incident on Twitter, loads of social media photos. No one gets in, no one gets out. One of the two men in the car is brutally murdered. The other maintains he didn't do it. Incredibly, we have some reason to believe his account – because we can't find the weapon. The driver, Tunstall, has some of Spatley's DNA on him, but only what you'd expect from him getting in the back to try and help Spatley after the attack, as he told us he did. I suspect,' he finished, looking up from the photos, 'this may well be how the word "impossible" popped up.'

Quill was making a determined effort not to smile; his target nominal had appeared on the horizon. There was something in the photos that was literally shining out at him, which Forrest and Lofthouse could not see. His team had, brilliantly, finally, a case of their own. 'Is there any chance, sir,' he said, 'that my team could take a look at that CCTV footage?'

'This lot can't work out what we're about,' said Costain, as a young female detective constable closed the door of an office behind Quill's team and left them to it. 'We could be an elite squad, we might be irrelevant. I got halfway to convincing that young officer of the former.'

'You didn't say a word to her,' said Ross, switching on a PC.

'It was how I walked.'

'Oh, I'd let myself forget that for just a second. You're such a people person.'

Costain's front remained intact. 'One of us has to be. But, being serious, thank you for noting that.'

Ross didn't make eye contact with him as she set up the PC to view the footage. That holier-than-thou carefulness that Costain often adopted these days in his fear of going to Hell seemed to annoy her more than it did Quill and Sefton.

When it appeared onscreen, Quill's team moved in close to see the images that might give them new purpose. Only Lofthouse held back. They were looking down on a car caught in a traffic jam, protestors swarming around it, some of them looking up at the camera and covering their faces further. A couple of bricks were thrown towards it, but nothing hit it, thank God. Many of the protestors were done up in that Toff mask and cape.

Then something different came walking through the crowd, approaching the car from the left. Quill's team all leaned forward at the same moment.

The figure flowed past the protestors, its presence pushing them aside, its passing going unfelt.

'That's also someone in a Toff outfit,' said Sefton.

It was. But it was blazing white, obviously a thing of the Sight. It was like watching an infrared image of a warm body in a cold room.

'The trouble is,' said Ross, 'you can't see much detail.'

Quill looked over his shoulder to check with Lofthouse.

'I can't see anything,' she said. 'Which I suppose is good news.'

He looked back to the image. The figure was pushing itself up against the side of the car, still getting no reaction from those around it. It started easing its way into the vehicle, until it had completely vanished inside. They watched for a few moments as nothing much happened, horribly aware of what had been reported, but seeing nothing through the tinted windows.

Suddenly, the figure burst out from the right-hand side of the car. It left a spatter of silver as it went. Quill recognized that stuff, whatever it was, as what he'd seen shining out of the car crime scene photos, a liquid that had been deposited all over the seats.

With the grace of a dancer, the figure leaped onto the heads of the crowd, and then it was jumping into the air—

It was literally gone in a flash.

Quill's team all looked at each other, excitement in their expressions.

'Well?' asked Lofthouse.

'We have set eyes on our target nominal, ma'am.'

'Excellent. I want to be kept in touch with all developments. As soon as possible, I want your proposed terms of reference for a new operation.'

Quill was sure his team would have applauded, if that was the sort of thing coppers did. For the first time in weeks, there was an eager look about them.

'Game on,' he said.

TWO

The torso of Michael Spatley MP was a horrifying mass of wounds, including an awful washed stump of pale, open blood vessels where his genitals had been hacked at.

'He seems to have been slashed across the throat,' said the pathologist, 'and then multiple incisions across the abdomen, by a very sharp blade, probably that of a razor. The weapon was not found at the scene. His testicles were cut at their base and the subsequent shock and swift large loss of blood was the cause of death. Time of death tallies with the clock on the CCTV camera, which indicates between eighteen-thirty-two and eighteen-thirty-nine. Direction of blood splatter –' she held up a photo of the interior of the car from the files they'd all been given by DCI Forrest's office – 'is consistent with the assailant kneeling across the rear seats. No arterial blood was tracked back to the front seats. The driver appears, and I stress appears, to have stayed put in the front during the attack.'

'From other CCTV cameras,' Ross noted, 'it's clear that the brake lights come on at several points during the time the car was stuck there, meaning that someone's foot was still on the brake pedal, until a point which may coincide with the driver going to help the victim after the attack, as per his story.'

Quill knew from what only his team could see that that was actually precisely true.

'How interesting,' said the pathologist. 'Not my department.'

What she wasn't talking about, because she couldn't see it, was what Quill could see the others glancing at too. All over the corpse, from the grimace on his face to the ripped-up abdomen, there lay traces of the same shining silver substance they'd seen earlier. It looked like spiders' webs on a dewy morning, or, and Quill stifled an awkward smile at the thought, cum. As the pathologist went into a more vigorous description of how the wounds had been inflicted – frantic slashing and then precise surgical cuts – he gave Costain the nod.

Costain suddenly spasmed in the direction of the pathologist, knocking her clipboard from her hands, as if he was on the verge of vomiting.

Sefton quickly took a phial from his bag and, while the pathologist was fussing over Costain, managed to get enough of the silver stuff into it. He screwed the top closed and dropped it back into the bag.

The pathologist was helping Costain straighten up. 'If you're going to do that, we need to get you out of here,' she was saying.

'No, no,' Costain waved her away and abruptly straightened up, smiling at her as he handed her back the clipboard. 'Thanks, but I think I can hold it.'

They went to the custody suite and arranged an interview with Spatley's driver. Brian Tunstall looked stunned, Quill thought, stressed out beyond the ability to show it, as if at any moment this would all be revealed as an enormous practical joke at his expense. He must be somewhere on the lower end of the Sighted spectrum – there were degrees to this stuff – because he hadn't mentally translated what he'd seen into something explicable. But Quill supposed that, in the circumstances, doing that would have been quite an ask. There were still traces of the shiny substance on his shirt. It was odd to see an adult standing with such mess on him, not seeing it, and therefore not having attempted to clean himself up.

'Listen,' Tunstall said immediately. 'I want to change my statement.'

'Now, wait—' began Quill.

'What I said happened was impossible. It couldn't have gone like that, could it? One of the protestors must have got into the car—'

'Mate,' said Costain, 'we believe you.'

Tunstall stopped short. 'You what?' Then he slumped, a tremendous weight on him again. 'Oh, right, I get it: you're the good cop.'

Costain pointed to himself, looking surprised. 'Bad cop.'

'Surreal cop,' said Sefton, also pointing to himself.

'Good cop,' admitted Quill. 'Relatively. Which is weird.'

Ross just raised an eyebrow.

Tunstall looked between them, unsure if they were taking the piss.

Being interviewed by this unit, thought Quill, must sometimes seem like being interrogated by Monty Python's Flying Circus. At least they had his attention. 'Why don't you tell us all of it,' he said gently, 'just the truth, as you saw it, and don't edit yourself for something that's too mad, because mad is what we do.'

Tunstall sat down at the interview table. 'What does that mean?'

'We have access to . . . certain abilities that other units don't. Which means that, as Detective Sergeant Costain says, we are indeed willing to believe you. We know there are more things in heaven and earth, Horatio. So telling the whole truth now might really do you a favour.'

The man looked more scared than ever.

It took until lunchtime to complete the interview and sort out the paperwork. Tunstall's story was indeed impossible, and confirmed all the physical evidence. The man finally said he couldn't remember anything else and needed to get some sleep. Quill ended the interview. He found his own attention starting to wander and baulked at the prospect of going back to the team's nick for maybe only an hour or two of bleary discussion, so he sent his team home for the day and went back to his bed. Only to find that Jessica was home and wanted to play with trains. So that was what they did, until Quill lay his head down on top of the toy station and started snoring.

Kev Sefton felt that he was finally getting somewhere. Being the officer who'd become most interested in the London occult and who'd started to read up on it had given him some extra responsibilities, okay. But now, instead of being second undercover, he was first . . . whatever his new job title was. Doing that well made him feel better about being out of the mainstream of policing while London was going up in flames.

He'd kept the phial with the silver goo in it in his fridge at home overnight, next to the beer, with a Post-it note on it that told Joe not to touch it. That summed up, he thought, the make-do way his team did things. He was used to having odd dreams now, as his brain dealt with all that he'd had to stuff into it, but those of last night were particularly weird. He felt as if he'd been rifled through and shaken out, as if large things were moving inside him. That phrase had brought a smile to his face as he drove through the gate that led onto the waste ground across the road from Gipsy Hill police station, the mud baked into dust by the early sunshine. *No change there, then.* He'd stopped on the steps of the Portakabin that served the team, exiled from the mainstream as they were, as an ops room and looked out across London. There was that smell on the warm air . . . smoke. Well, now they might be doing something to help restore order. He'd taken a deep breath and headed inside.

Now, as the others watched, wearing oven gloves he'd stolen from the canteen across the way, he was using a pencil to encourage the silver goo out of the phial and onto a saucer. He was hoping that graphite and tea-stained china didn't react with whatever this silver stuff was. Maybe it would tell them something if it did. He was trying to take a scientific approach to his London occultism.

Sometimes that made him feel like Isaac bloody Newton, and sometimes as if he was barking up completely the wrong tree. It felt as if this London business only submitted to science *sometimes*, when it felt like it. The goo dropped onto the saucer. The others leaned closer. Sefton thought he could hear a faint sizzling. He took the thermometer he'd bought at the chemist's and held it as close to the gel as he dared. He nodded and put on his most serious expression. 'It's . . . really cold,' he said.

'Like the insides of every ghost we've encountered,' said Quill.

'Only this is much more extreme, and, because we're pretty sure that what we've seen aren't exactly ghosts in the usual sense of the word, inverted commas around the g-word, please,' said Sefton.

'Is that it's "really cold" the full extent of your analysis?' asked Quill.

'If we can get hold of some specialist tools, like maybe a temperature sensor that I could actually risk inside this stuff, then I'd do better. But that'd only get us so far. Only we can see this material. It's too plastic for mercury, too metallic for some sort of oil by-product, and it's keeping itself and the things around it cold, like a fridge, but without being plugged into a socket. If it's an element, it's one we've discovered.'

'Seftonium,' said Costain.

Sefton used a teaspoon to put the goo back in the phial. 'So-called spirit mediums used to pretend to be able to project something they called ectoplasm, which usually turned out to be glue and other gunk. Maybe the original idea for that came from this.'

'Like in *Ghostbusters*,' said Costain.

'It reminds me of what I saw inside those "ghost ships" on the Thames,' said Ross. 'They had a sort of silver skeleton inside.'

Quill went to the corkboard which served this team as an Ops Board. 'All right,' he said, 'we've got enough to start building the board, to list the objectives and to name this mother.' All the board still had on it – the artefacts of the other half-arsed would-be operations they'd considered lately having already been consigned carefully to drawers – was the PRO-FIT facial description picture of the Smiling Man and the concepts list, which now was just a series of headings referring to files on their ancient computer (and the phone number of the Smiling Man, which Quill had labelled 'the number of the Beast'). At the very top of the board was a card with a question mark on it, over which Quill now pinned a new blank card because the name of the operation was about to be decided. Beneath all that Quill added a picture cut from a newspaper. 'The victim: Michael Anthony Spatley, Liberal Democrat MP for the constituency of Cheadle. Chief secretary to the Treasury, which is a cabinet position. Jewish by birth, atheist by inclination. Forty-six years old. Wife: Ann. Daughter: Jocelyn. Son: Arthur. I've put in a request for us to search his home and offices too, which, judging by the tone of voice of the PA I spoke to, will be regarded with incredulity by those who've already had the main op through. But we shall persist.' He attached a red victim thread upwards from the picture and pinned a sheet of white paper above it, on which he drew a very rough cartoon of the Toff figure.

Ross took a new square of paper and added 'Brian Tunstall' to the suspect area, also attaching a victim thread between him and Spatley. She drew a dotted line beside both threads, indicating uncertainty. 'Two suspects,' she said.

'Despite the fact that only one of these "suspects" was observed fleeing the scene,' noted Costain.

'Yeah, because we make assumptions only when the specialized nature of our work forces us to. And then we take care to note them.'

Sefton looked between the two of them. Costain had always been the sort of officer who'd insisted on the importance of first-hand street experience, and Ross' intelligence-based approach always felt that that procedure was missing the wood for the trees, but now . . . He knew that Costain, when Ross had been unconscious in hospital after the Losley case, had stayed by her bed, had slept in a chair. Sefton had wondered, during those few weeks when Ross had been full of the joys of spring, if they were going to get together. That looked impossible now, which was tough on these two, because he and Quill had someone to talk to about the impossible stresses this team were under, and they didn't.

Costain picked up a card of his own and drew a squiggly mass of people on it, then he attached it to Spatley with a dotted thread too. 'Maybe it's the "spirit" of the riots? Losley said there were two ways to power in London: to "make sacrifice" or "be remembered", and it's not like it's only the old or famous stuff that gets remembered. We hadn't heard of that green monster thing Kev met. Maybe this is the sort of collective will of those protestors made solid, or something.'

Quill nodded. 'Good. But I hope that doesn't bloody turn out to be the case, 'cos it's going to be hard to nick a manifestation of the collective unconscious.'

Sefton had something to add. 'All the "ghosts"' – he made the speech marks gesture – 'we've seen have been really passive. Everything "remembered" as part of what seems to be a sort of collective memory on the part of London just kind of hangs around, in classic haunting fashion. They didn't hurt anyone. Not even the remembered versions of Losley.'

'So maybe one of the protestors has made a sacrifice and is deliberately making this happen,' said Costain.

'Absolutely.' Sefton was glad to hear Costain making deductions like that about his world. Sefton couldn't do this bit alone, and it always pleased him when the others had a go. He was the opposite to Ross in that respect because his speciality was bloody terrifying and hers wasn't. 'But Losley was very set in her ways and didn't acknowledge things she didn't approve of or know about. She didn't mention various powerful items, for instance, like the vanes that were used to attack Jimmy. I don't think we should imagine she knew or was telling us about every mechanism that exists to do . . . the sort of stuff we know objects that are *very London* can do. Speaking of which . . .' He stepped forward and added, down the left-hand side of the board, in the space which their team and only their team used for concepts, 'Cold residuals. Meaning that silver goo.'

'But which now sounds like something you'd need to talk to your agent about,' said Quill.

'Nobody outside the car saw anything,' said Ross. 'Nobody felt the suspect move through or above the crowd. Tunstall's testimony is what you'd expect of someone who was watching an attack by an invisible assailant. And I should add . . .' She used her own pen to write 'Can walk through walls (slowly)' under the cartoon of the prime suspect.

'Like Losley,' said Costain.

She also added 'Can vanish'.

'And again.'

'Remind me to cover that up at the end of the day,' said Quill. 'We don't want to terrify the cleaners.' He paused as he stepped back from what was once again a blankness. 'We need to do proper police work on what's up there,' he said. 'We need to find meaning, a narrative. We work our three suspects: in the real world and in what, horribly, I'm starting to think of as *our* world.'

Sefton saw that now was the time to announce the plan he'd been putting together. He was a bit proud of this, the sort of cross-discipline package that, in normal police work, would have been a boost to his CV. Now Lofthouse had made it obvious that she was aware of what they did – whatever the implications of that were – it might still be a good career move. 'I've been assembling a list of people who seem to be on the fringes of the subculture we encountered at that New Age fair. I know a few places where they hang out. I could start to attempt undercover contact, get some sources for general background on all this stuff and work towards specifics concerning the Spatley case, if you think it's time to risk all that.'

'I do.' Quill nodded. 'Go forth and make it so, my son.' He turned back to the wall and began pinning up a big sheet of paper on the right of the board. 'And now, ladies and gentlemen, it's time for . . . operational objectives!' He picked up a marker and began to write.

1. *Ensure the safety of the public.*
2. *Gather evidence of offences.*
3. *Identify and trace subject or subjects involved (if any).*
4. *Identify means to arrest subject or subjects.*
5. *Arrest subject or subjects.*
6. *Bring to trial/destroy.*
7. *Clear those not involved of all charges.*

'Maybe it's a bit vague,' he admitted, standing back to admire his work, 'but for us it's always going to be. Even writing the word "destroy" . . .' He let himself trail off. 'But that's how it is for us. And, of course, this list mirrors the objectives of Forrest's SCD 1 murder inquiry, which, if we're not careful, may lead to conflict and ire. Now, instead of drawing the names from the central register, I say we continue to name our own ops because that's how we roll and I like it. So for this one, where we might well be venturing into Gothic and clichéd portrayals of our fair metropolis, how about . . .'

He wrote on the card at the top of the Ops Board:

OPERATION FOG

The rest of the day was spent assembling all the evidence they had and building their initial Ops Board to the point where they all felt they were looking at everything they knew. They kept the news on in the background, but no fresh details came to light in the press. Ross had set up a bunch of hashtag searches on Twitter, but, as the day went on, they only revealed that London was panicking and gossiping in many different ways about the murder; no one signal was poking up out of the terrified noise.

All in all, Sefton was glad to have put in such a productive day and, with the Portakabin getting stuffy, he was pleased when Quill sent everyone home. Home was now a tiny flat above a shop in Walthamstow with, on good nights, a parking space outside. Tonight he was lucky. The flat was half the size of the place he'd used as an undercover. It was like suddenly being a student again. Joe, who lived in a bigger place, had started coming over and staying most nights, which neither of them had commented on, so that was probably okay. Tonight he found Joe had just got in, using the key Sefton had had made for him two weeks ago, and was planning on heading straight out to the chippy. 'Best news all day,' Sefton said, after kissing him, and they headed off.

The streets of Walthamstow were full of people, loads of office workers coming out of the tube in shirtsleeves, jackets slung over their shoulder, women pulling their straps down to get some sun. They looked as if they were deliberately trying to be relaxed, despite the smell of smoke always on the air, even out here. But even the sunshine had felt sick this summer, never quite burning through the clouds, instead shafting through gaps in them. It felt as if the whole summer was going to be dog days. Or perhaps all that was just the perspective of the Sight. It was impossible for Sefton to separate himself from it now. Every day in the street he saw the same horrors the others did, startling adjuncts to reality. 'The opposite of miracles,' he'd called them when Joe had asked for a description. There was a homeless person begging at the tube entrance as the two of them passed, an addict by the look of him, thin hair in patches, his head on his chest, filthy blankets around his legs. He was newly arrived with the 'austerity measures'.

'So,' said Joe, 'what did you do at work today?'

'Can't tell you.'

'I thought you told me everything.'

'Everything about the . . . you know, the weird shit. Nothing about operational stuff.'

'Ah, so now there *is* operational stuff.'

'Yeah. Kind of big, actually.'

'Oh. *Oh!* You mean like what everyone's been talking about all day?'

Sefton sighed. Why had he been so obvious? 'And now *I'm* shagging a detective.'

Joe worked in PR for an academic publishing house and was now doing the job of what had been a whole department. *His* work stories were about dull professors who couldn't be made interesting.

He lowered his voice. 'I saw about the murder on telly and thought the same as everyone else is saying, that it had to be the driver—'

'I can't—'

'—which means it must really be something only you lot can see, like, bloody hell, another witch or something, like maybe there's one for every football club? The witch of Woolwich Arsenal? The witch of Wolves? It can only be the alliterative ones. Liverpool doesn't have one. Liverpool has a . . . lich. Whatever one of those is.'

Sefton put a hand on his arm and actually stopped him. 'Could we just get those chips?'

They sat on the low wall of the car park outside the chippy and breathed in the smell of frying. The old woman in a hijab they always saw around here trod slowly past, selling the *Big Issue*. Sefton bought one.

'How are your team getting on now?'

'I can't talk about the case.'

'Which is why I'm asking about the people.'

'I think there's something up with Ross.'

'Really?' Joe followed the people Sefton talked about as if they were characters on TV, never having met them, and Sefton almost laughed at the interest in his voice.

'Ever since she got into the Docklands documents, she's kind of suddenly gone back to how she was: all curled up against the world. Maybe it's that she's found something terrible and doesn't want the rest of us to have to deal. Maybe she's waiting until she's got all the details.'

'Like what?'

'I don't know. I don't even know if she and Costain are rubbing each other up the wrong way or . . .'

'Just rubbing each other?'

'I hope it's that. It's weird when I get a feeling about a person now. I'm trying to let myself be aware of the Sight all the time, to listen to something whispering in my ear, but, doing that, you start to wonder what's the Sight and what's just you. If I'm not careful I'm going to start being like one of those toddlers that notices a bit of gum on the pavement and hasn't seen that before, so he squats down and keeps looking at it until his mum goes, "Erm, no – big wide world, more important." The others want me to keep looking into the London occult shit, to be that specialist, and, you know, I like that responsibility, but they don't really get that that kind of leads you away from being a police officer. Crime stories: all about getting everything back to normal. This stuff: there *is* no normal.'

'Crime stories say the centre *can* hold; in reality, it's going to fall apart any minute. Maybe all this chaos lately is something to do with the sort of thing you lot investigate.'

'Yeah, we're all wondering about that: that maybe the shittiness of life right now is all down to the Smiler and how he's "moved the goalposts" and changed London. That'd be a comforting thought, eh?'

'Only for you is that comforting.' Joe, having finished his own, took one of Sefton's chips. 'I think the riots and protests would have happened anyway. The protestors are the only people left who give a shit. You just *expect* a sort of . . . self-serving hypocrisy from politicians now. You'd be amazed what the guys in my office said about Spatley. Nobody was like, "He deserved it," but . . .' He let the sentence fall away with a shrug.

Sefton let his gaze drift along the street full of people. 'Bloody general public. Even with London falling apart in the world they *can* see, all they talk about is the royal baby and *The X Factor* and all that shit—'

'You *like The X Factor.*'

'—while my lot are involved with . . . the secret of eternal life, making space out of nothing, extra "boroughs" that don't seem to be in this universe. You know what'd be really good?'

'Go on.'

'You remember when I caught that "ghost bus" and went . . . somewhere else, somewhere away from this world, and talked to . . . whatever that being was, that called himself Brutus and dressed like a Roman?'

'You really told your workmates about this?'

'I really did, but even when I did it sounded like something I'd dreamed or made up. Anyway, just having met some sort of . . . big London being . . . that the others hadn't, I felt like I'd started to get a handle on this stuff. But as time goes on I'm starting to feel more and more that I *did* dream him. It's not as if he gave me much in the way of solid advice, a path I could follow. He didn't leave me with anything *certain*, with any mission in life. And without that certainty, there's this . . . *gap*. There's all sorts of stuff I want to ask him about. I've made an actual list, and today I added the silver goo to that list.' He rubbed the bridge of his nose and then had to brush away the salt from his chips he'd deposited there. 'Sometimes I feel like he might just show up, that I might sit down on a park bench and there he'd be. And then there are times when I *know* he isn't real. You can sort of feel something like him in the air, sometimes.' He was very aware of Joe's arched eyebrow. 'You can. That's a proper Sighted feeling. That seemed to be getting easier as summer came on, but now . . .'

'When Ross got her Tarot cards read, she was promised "hope in summer", wasn't she, and "in autumn" too, just those sentences? And it had something to do with that card called "The Sacrifice of Tyburn Tree" which you all thought was about her dad—'

'You remember all the details, don't you? You're such a fanboy of us lot. Just don't go on the internet with this stuff.'

'I'm saying, maybe good stuff is about to happen. Maybe you'll find Brutus.'

Sefton sighed, had to look away from that smile. 'But it's summer *now*, and it's just this . . . burdened heat.'

'Is there anything you can do to, you know, summon him or something?'

'Nothing in any of the books I've found. *He's* not in the books. If I can't find him, I need to find . . . something.' Sefton suddenly felt the need to get rid of all this shit. 'Fuck it, I need a pint. And you're not going to let me go on about the Hogwarts stuff any more tonight. Deal?'

'No,' said Joe, smiling at him.

As always, Lisa Ross was awake into the early hours. Hers was one of many lights still on in her Catford housing block. There were people who kept a light on at all hours, no matter what the bills were, as if that offered some protection against the shrieks of the urban foxes and the drunken yelling outside. She barely registered that stuff. She would get the three hours' sleep she found necessary sometime around 3 a.m.

Tonight, like every night, she was about her secret work. She was sure that the others thought she was nobly sacrificing her spare time to make a database of the documents they'd found in the Docklands ruins. She had let them think that. It was safer. Quill had stars in his eyes about her, about her having saved his daughter. She was letting him and the rest of the team down so badly.

But she had no choice. After the ruins had been looted for so long, there hadn't been much of interest left, so she wasn't actually keeping the team from anything that could help them. She wasn't telling them the whole truth either. The document she spent all her time on now was about her own needs. It had probably been spared the scavenging that had emptied that building because it was written in an indecipherable language in a hand that didn't invite study. That obscurity had spoken to her of something being deliberately hidden. She had found something like the script on a visit to the British Library archives. It turned out that it had been noted on only one tomb in Iran, but the inscriptions on that tomb had been written in several other languages also. So there was, it had turned out, printed only in one issue of one archaeological journal, and still not available online, a working alphabet for the document she had before her. It hadn't taken her long to translate the document, and thus understand what she was looking at. The document was a description of an object that had arrived in Britain in the last five years, just before the destruction of the Docklands site, in fact. Now she was looking on her laptop at a series of objects that might prove to be that thing. She had been doing this for the last week of long nights. She was on the fiftieth page of the third such catalogue site she had visited, and she was still absolutely certain, because she made herself stay awake and alert at every page load, that she hadn't yet seen the object she was after. She was starting to wonder if the tomb in question really had, as the document alleged, been empty. If there really was an object that would do what the document said it did.

There was a noise from beside her. A text message. She was startled to see it was from Costain. He was wondering if she 'had five minutes'.

What? At this time in the morning? He'd never texted her before. He was probably drunk. Or was this meaningful? Was this the start of the sort of activity on his part that she'd told herself to watch out for? Whatever. She put the phone back down without replying.

Costain was the one from whom she especially needed to keep this work secret.

Quill was once again hauled awake by the sound of his phone. His dreams had been full of something reaching towards him, reaching into him. But he couldn't remember it now. Jessica, unwoken by the sound of the phone, was lying across his head.

'Would you please answer that,' said Sarah, 'and tell them to –' she looked at her daughter and gritted her teeth – 'go away?'

Quill saw that the call was again from Ross, and said so.

'Getting over her now,' said Sarah.

He picked it up. After listening for a few moments, he quickly got out of bed and started getting dressed.

'What?' moaned Sarah.

'Another one. It's police.'

The slightly portly middle-aged man lay across the sofa. He was still dressed in a blue towelling robe, the now-familiar silver fluid splattered across him and all over the room. The robe was open, and so was he. A livid red trail led from what remained of his abdomen, across the polished wooden floor, and finished in an explosion of blood against the far wall, next to a Jack Vettriano. The expression on the victim's face was an almost comical extreme of horror and incredulity. His eyes were open, glassy.

Quill's team stood in the doorway, feeling – if Quill himself was anything to go by – like anything but an elite unit at this hour of the morning. Forensics had just finished with the crime scene and were packing up. Uniforms were filling just about every available inch of the building.

What they were staring at was enormous. Bigger, even, than the death of a cabinet minister.

'Sir Geoffrey Staunce, KCBE, commissioner of the Metropolitan Police,' said Ross, keeping her voice low as a uniform made her way past.

'They got him,' said Quill. 'That's what the papers are going to say tomorrow. With a strike looming, the protestors killed London's most senior copper at his home in Piccadilly.'

'There were indeed Toffs in the area last night, making a nuisance of themselves,' said Ross, looking up from the report she'd been given on entering. 'For this sort of address that's pretty incredible.'

'The connection is also the locked room and the MO,' said Quill.

'Plus, from our point of view, the silver goo,' added Sefton.

'And,' said Costain, 'the wife is talking about an invisible assailant.'

They paused for a moment, taking in the scene. Quill's team's speciality was now being tested against a *very* mainstream, *very* high-profile, *series* of murders.

'This is going to set London on fire,' said Costain. 'I mean literally.'

'Where's this message they were talking about?' Stepping carefully, Ross followed the trail of blood across the room. She got to the enormous splatter of it across the far wall and stopped. Quill and the others joined her. She was pointing at the fine detail that the chaotic enormity of the splatter concealed. Among the blood was written, in awkward, blocky characters:

THE JEWS ARE THE MEN WHO WILL NOT
BE BLAMED FOR ANYTHING.

'What is that?' said Sefton. 'I recognize that.' He started to tap at his phone.

'So this is almost certainly from the killer,' said Costain, 'but—'

'Making assumptions,' said Ross.

'You said we could—'

'Only when we remember to mark them as such. This is me doing that. Yes, it could be from the killer, but there might also have been person or persons unknown here, associated with the killer or otherwise, who might have left what they regarded as a useful, or just anti-Semitic, message for the many Londoners who will read it when they get a news camera in here.'

'Next time you make an assumption, I'll make sure I mark it.'

'I hope you will.'

'Would you just bloody finish the sentence you originally started?' Quill asked Costain.

'Just that it's really weird,' said Costain, 'to use "are the men" in what's otherwise a natural-sounding phrase. It feels like . . . pretence to me. A front.'

'You'd know,' said Ross.

'I would. There's the fingerprint.' He pointed to the very end of the words, where the fingers that had daubed the message had paused for just a moment, leaving a single smeared print.

Ross took a photograph of it. 'I'll ask to hear from the

investigation about the comparison of that to the prints found in Spatley's car.'

'Oh, my God,' said Sefton. '"The Jews are the men"!' He held up his phone as the others clustered around. He read from it, keeping his voice down so the uniforms all around couldn't hear. 'Those words, or something like them, were what was written on a wall in a place called Goulston Street in Whitechapel, in 1888.'

'So?'

'It's the message left by Jack the Ripper.'

THREE

'Jack . . . the Ripper?' Sarah Quill slowly lowered her cup of coffee to the kitchen table.

'Such is my glamorous existence,' said Quill. 'Celebrate my diversity.'

'What does that even mean?'

'I don't know, I just say these things.'

'I mean, is it that the Ripper's . . . *ghost* has started to attack people?'

'We don't know anything beyond the message, not yet. But it makes sense of the shape of the attacker. That Toff image of the protestors is also very like the archetypal image of the Ripper. And, thanks to the press—'

'Ahem.'

'Present company excepted. Thanks to them, everyone thinks the protestors have now started murdering people, though they can't quite work out how. The original version of what's become the Toff mask was, so the people at the factory tell us, part of their "Jolly King" costume. That costume company have gone from employing a publicity person for the first time, and neither condoning nor condemning the protestors, to slamming the doors and hiding behind press releases.'

'Royalty? Like in some of the mad Ripper theories? Could that be a thing? One of your lot will have said that, right?'

Quill loved it when she deduced something. She didn't do analysis exactly in the way his team did, but like the news editor she was, always casting around for a lead. 'Sefton. He's been reading up on this stuff. Ross said that when she first got the Sight, she felt a certain gravity from the direction of Buckingham Palace. I bloody hope this Ripper business doesn't take us there.'

'Jack the Ripper. God, Quill, I wish I could have this story. *Can* I have this story?'

'No. Because you and I have a deal—'

'I know, I know: you all need to have someone you can talk to about this stuff. But, bloody hell, of all journalists, only I know that there's a connection between these two incredibly high-profile murder cases. Only I know about the message on the wall. And I'm going to go back into my office this afternoon, and my editor's going to ask how you are, and I'm going to say, "He's fine, he expressed sympathy about the ongoing decline of the *Enfield Leader* and the redundancies that are bound to start happening soon—"'

'Love—'

'Fuck, I could string this story to the *Mail* or the *Herald* or something. I could make a fortune. They still give people who dob in for them serious money.' She made grim eye contact with him again. 'I'm only having you on. Really. No, I am.'

The media were, of course, even with the little they knew, going apeshit about the killings. The *Independent* was calling this second murder 'the final failure of authority' and the *Sun* had gone with 'Day of the Mob'. The *Herald* was still very much implying that the Toff protestors must somehow be to blame, and that the CCTV footage from the car attack had somehow been tampered with. Quill wondered how many news stories over the years had been influenced by stuff from what was now his area of expertise, and how much impossibility, before the blinkers had been taken off, he'd seen euphemized or made 'sense' of. That paper, and a couple of others, had long since wandered away from facts into what Sarah called 'opinion leads' – meaning, so far as Quill could see, fiction – which the *Herald* usually used to cover half the front page with furious wordage that led up to a big headline. 'People don't buy newspapers for the news now,' she'd said. 'They buy a voice that agrees with them. The *Herald* knows that best of all and is angling itself towards a future when all the papers will be like that.' Quill hoped that by that point some kind soul might have put him out of his misery. The *Herald* regarded the Coalition government, incredibly, as far too middle of the road and wishy-washy, and it wanted a crackdown on, well, everything, as far as he could tell. Every now and then, someone on the news would opine that the paper might soon declare its support for some other, currently minor, party further to the right. That would, people said, be a game-changer. Quill wasn't sure and didn't care very much at the moment. To him it was all bloody people doing what bloody people did.

'At the end of all this,' he said, 'when I retire, maybe you can write the book.'

'By then we'll be living in a land where what you lot deal with is accepted, will we? I don't know if I'm looking forward to that. I keep thinking that we should send Jessica to school somewhere outside London when she's old enough.'

'But—'

'I mean boarding school. You have to stay here to fight this stuff.'

'But—'

'And we can talk about this sometime in the next five years.' She picked up her iPad. 'I'm just checking on the headlines. Not contributing to them. At all. Just looking. Shit.'

Quill didn't like how her expression had changed. 'What?'

She held up the front page of the *Herald* site so he could see the headline. This time it was short and to the point:

YOURS TRULY, JACK THE RIPPER

Quill grabbed the tablet off her. 'How the fuck did they get that?'

'Well, this is the *Herald*, the cleanest newspaper in Britain, as they proudly state. So they'll just have been looking through the window of that house with a long lens. Or had an anonymous photo emailed to them. Or something equally ethical. Dear God, I could have beaten the *Herald* to what's turned out to be an exclusive for them. By about a minute. It's an exquisite form of torture.' She gave him a deliberately manic grin, threw back her tea and banged the mug down on the table. 'Have a nice day at work, dear.'

Quill knew exactly what he was going to see when he entered Lofthouse's office at Gipsy Hill. Sure enough, there it was: the *Herald* on her desk.

'In case I hadn't heard,' he said.

She gave him a wry look and daintily dropped the newspaper into the wastebasket. 'Tell me.'

Quill paused for a moment, returning her calm expression. He wished he could ask her to tell him what *she* knew. But he had learned from their first few regular meetings that it wouldn't get him anywhere. He was still getting used to being able to talk to her about impossible things. 'We found traces of the silver liquid that you can't see on the exterior wall at what would have been the exit point of the assailant. There were a few drops of it in the garden, but no major deposits, and nothing had been disturbed, suggesting, once again, an airborne escape route.'

'You've talked to the wife?'

Quill recounted his interview with Jennifer Staunce. She had had a terrible expression on her face, not just the grief and horror Quill had seen so many times before, but a dubious and suspicious look that he was starting to recognize: she was shocked that her home, her security, had been violated, but her rational mind still couldn't see how it could be so. 'Geoff . . . had just turned down the sound on the television,' she'd said. 'He turned it down, and so we could hear the noise from those . . . Toffs they call them, outside, chanting from the street. So strange to have them here. Disturbing. He was about to make a phone call. To his brother. He's in property, in

Northampton. They talk about this time every week. That's what he said he was going to do. He's a creature of habit: nap every afternoon, he always likes the same things for his dinner. So I went into the kitchen to make some coffee. The percolator is quite loud, I didn't hear . . . I didn't even hear him scream or anything like that, I just heard . . . some odd noises, sounds of movement. So I went back in and . . . there he was. Being . . . hauled around. Already . . . already obviously . . . by something I couldn't see. I didn't get to see who was doing it. Geoff . . . must have been in the way. All I could think of was . . . they've got in. They're in here.'

'They?' Quill had asked.

'Those protestors. After what happened to Michael Spatley, I'd been thinking that Geoff wasn't safe on the streets. But in here . . .! I've been a copper's wife for thirty years, Mr Quill. I thought we were past him being in the line of fire. High office never suited him; he's had nightmares with every promotion in the last couple of years. I'm rambling. Sorry. I ran, I'm sorry – I just thought of what he'd want me to do, and I was such a coward!' She'd stopped and visibly steadied herself. She'd known what Quill needed from her. 'They . . . say there was . . . a message? Something about Jewish people?'

Quill had nodded. 'Is there anyone of Jewish ancestry in your or Mr Staunce's family, ma'am?'

'Not that I know of. We have some Jewish friends. Or I think we must do. It's not something you ask, is it?'

'Thinking back, was there any sign of an intruder?'

'No. They must have . . . I don't know. I didn't take more than two steps towards the . . . Geoff . . . the . . . I could see . . . I ran straight out of the room, not to the door, because I was thinking, If they're in here, if they're in here, I'm next, and I have to tell someone. So I ran into the downstairs toilet, because that's got a bolt on it, and I slammed it, and thank God I still had my phone on me, and I called Ben at the office. And that's where they found me.'

Lofthouse nodded in appreciation now. 'Good for her.'

'Very good, in the circumstances. The first unit on the scene broke a window to get in rather than try to batter down a front door that was still deadlocked and secure. If she'd gone to the body, if she'd got a single splash of blood on her, she might have already been arrested.'

'And she might still be, despite, once again, the lack of weapon at the scene.'

'She also doesn't seem a likely fit for daubing messages about the Jewish friends she might or might not have. There was CCTV in front of the building. My lot got a look at the recordings, and we saw the same glowing figure leaving the scene. But nothing new.'

'What about the wording of the message?'

'It's spelled differently to the original version and has better grammar, but the records of the time give three different versions of what that message actually said. So it might be that our Jack continues to write exactly the same thing he always did. Or perhaps he writes it in whatever the current vernacular is.'

Lofthouse stood up and went to the window, as if she needed to see some everyday reality. It wasn't as if, Quill thought, she was used to thinking like this. Whatever her mysterious knowledge was, it hadn't prepared her. 'So our . . . our . . . *suspect*: it looks like Jack the Ripper, it leaves the Ripper's message—'

'And it kills like Jack the Ripper. The single slash across the neck, followed by multiple incisions in the abdomen, done with some medical precision – that's pretty much the original Ripper's MO. Except that in this case the victims are male.'

'So is this actually what it looks like? Jack the Ripper is back, only this time he's killing rich white men?'

'Well, concerning the message, Spatley was Jewish, but Sir Geoffrey was not. But they were both indeed powerful, relatively but not grandiosely affluent, middle-aged white males. That's certainly the connection the media are making . . .'

'Because for them it's cake every day. Hey, Mr Typical *Herald* Reader, you could be next!'

'That seems to be about it. One was money, the other was law. They had met, but only at the times you might expect them to: cabinet meetings about security issues around the Olympics, official functions – that sort of thing. We're sifting through the related correspondence between them, but so far it's pretty anodyne. They share no schools, housing, jobs or friends outside government circles, at least not that we've been able to uncover yet.'

Lofthouse toyed with her charm bracelet for a moment, her fingers finding the key. That made Quill frown once again about what he wasn't being told.

FOUR

As Costain had driven to Whitechapel, he'd found himself changing channels on the radio a lot. He didn't like what he was hearing.

'If one of the biggest coppers in London isn't safe, then who is?! They should bring in the army! 'Cos the police are shitting themselves!'

'People are talking as if this is a copycat Jack the Ripper serial killer, but apart from one wrongly transcribed message and the nature of the attacks themselves . . . Listen, as a Ripper expert . . .'

'When you think Jack the Ripper, you think fog and prostitutes, don't you?'

'The Jewish community . . . I can't speak for a whole community, but "dismayed" would be the word. That someone who committed these unspeakable murders should seek to slander us in the process . . .'

'Attacks on two synagogues in the East End, but we're talking about a few youths daubing paint here; it might be part of the wider disturbances . . .'

'True British nationalists say it's time to stand up to these thugs that are on the streets looting every night, but the police are still obsessing over the content of one scrawled message, because it mentions ethnicity, rather than dealing with the death of their own most senior officer, rather than dealing with what's in front of their noses, which is that they have lost control and people are demanding a better solution!'

'Our protest has always been peaceful. We march against spending *cuts and corruption, which have killed many more people than Jack the Ripper. We do not condone the murder of anyone. However . . .'*

In the end, he plugged in his iPod to escape the news. He finally switched that off too, frustrated at having run away from what was real. As always now, he was wondering if that running away contributed to his own approaching damnation.

He parked in the first free space he saw in Whitechapel, put his logbook in the window to avoid getting a ticket and closed the car door gently, without slamming it. He would do *anything* to stay out of Hell. That thought went round his head so often it was like a mantra. He would do *anything*.

He found Ross looking at a lurid sign, a woman pictured lying in the gutter, blood dripping from her mouth, and a silhouetted caped figure running away. The sign was propped against a brick wall that looked as if it had been scrubbed clean of centuries of dock slime for the tourists. Or perhaps it was new, built in the old style.

She turned to look at him as if he was something on the Ops Board. 'Why'd you text me the other night?'

'And hello to you.'

She frowned at him, but at that point the tour guide arrived and took their money, and others who wanted to go on the tour started to arrive; he was relieved not to have to answer the question.

The tour was called, in dripping red letters, 'Jack the Ripper Extreme'. Their guide was a Mr Neville Fennix – probably his stage name. He was dressed in a top hat, opera cape and evening suit, and he carried a silver-tipped cane. There were a large party of Italians and their translator, and another group who were talking in what Costain thought might be Korean. There were also quite a few younger people, students, several of whom were wearing what had now become known as the Ripper mask on the back of their heads to shade their necks from the sun. That bloody thing was everywhere now. Previously only a fraction of protestors had worn it; now it was their uniform. He'd seen T-shirts and online banners with the Ripper mask portrayed in those Obama 'Change' campaign colours or like Che Guevara, with slogans underneath such as 'Occupy Hell'. The Ripper had put a face to the summer of blood. He had killed not just an MP, but now one of the most senior police officers in London, right at the point when the Met was creaking under the pressure of lack of resources and government meddling. *If they can get to him, they can get to any of us,* that's what a spokesman for the Police Federation had been quoted in the *Herald* as saying, *and the job cuts and the service cuts and every cut make every single one of us more vulnerable.* The driver, Tunstall, had been released at the end of his ninety-six hours in custody, the main investigation having convinced a judge that they needed the maximum period of detention. Tunstall hadn't changed his impossible story, though, and so now the media were also full of the news that he was 'back on the streets'.

As Fennix took cash from the other tourists, Costain found himself glancing at Ross again. She was still looking interrogatively at him. He wasn't going to be able to get away from her question.

On the night he'd sent the text message, he'd first been annoyed at her for not getting back to him, then at himself for sending it. It had been exactly the wrong step to take. He'd tried to get to sleep, despite the heat, but he'd kept waking up, not liking how vulnerable he felt in his dreams. So, without thinking about it as much as he should have, he'd reached out. He'd wanted to talk to someone. He told himself now that he'd had his overall objective in mind. He wasn't sure if that had been true.

Ross hadn't raised the matter of the text message the next day, and, relieved, he hadn't either. But Ross wasn't very good with social interaction and so had saved it up for now because . . . well, who knew?

'Well?' she said.

'Sorry. I was pissed. You know, you text your mates, ask if they're up for a pint—'

'You asked if I had five minutes.'

'But that was where it was going.'

'At 1 a.m.?'

'Like I said, I was pissed.'

'After last orders?'

'At home with some cans.'

'You drink at home alone?'

'Not often. I'd just got back from the pub.'

'Open late, was it?'

'Yeah.'

'You really thought I'd come over for a drink?'

'Like I said, pissed.'

'Okay.' She suddenly nodded as if it was the end of the interview and looked away.

The tour guide returned and began his spiel. 'Whitechapel today may look harmless, modern, charming even. But mentally replace the sunlight with darkness and fog, and follow me now as we go on the trail of the man who is now once more in all the headlines, the man of the moment . . . Jack the Ripper!'

He set off and they followed. Costain kept trying to make eye contact with Ross. But now she was having none of it. That was worrying.

'Mary Ann Nichols,' said Fennix, 'or "Polly" was her *trade* name.' He paused for a laugh, which, after a moment of delayed translation, he got. They were standing in a backstreet behind the station, flanked by fenced-off brownfield sites, but there were no vehicles or workers, and they could smell the scent of undisturbed mud baking in the summer heat, suggesting that nothing was actually being built. Costain associated that smell with his childhood because nothing really changed. There were school gates over there, and the map he was looking at on his phone showed a sports centre down the road. House prices would have been shooting up before this latest recession, *nice* people coming in . . . and then it had all fallen backwards, as it always did. He glanced over and saw Ross was looking at her phone too.

'Jewish cemetery round the corner,' she said under her breath.

'One thing we should be thinking about,' said Costain, also in a whisper, struck by a sudden thought, 'is, if the murders are about Jack the Ripper being *remembered*, why aren't they happening right here? Everything we've seen like this before – from Berkeley Square to when Losley got powered up – it all stayed put where it was. Or where it was most associated with, like your ships.'

'Yeah.' Ross took out one of her enormous rough books and wrote it down.

Costain found himself taking pleasure in that. 'Ever since we found those files in Docklands—'

She suddenly looked straight at him, as if he'd caught her out, then looked away again, as if she'd revealed too much of herself. *Interesting.* 'What?' she said, finding something else to write.

He drew closer to her and she closed the book, as if to stop him seeing inside it. 'The Continuing Projects Team were obsessed with architecture,' he said. 'Maybe our two victims were just in the wrong place, kind of like deadly feng shui.'

Ross nodded, but she didn't look convinced. Her face wasn't giving anything away.

'Perhaps you'd like to share with the class?' Fennix had stopped and, having realized that Ross and Costain weren't going to shut up, had decided to mock them for it. That had got a laugh too.

Get many tips, do you? Costain flashed the man his most generous grin. 'We're just fascinated with this stuff, mate. Tell us more. We were just saying there's a Jewish graveyard round the corner—'

'Ah, yes.' The actor nodded solemnly. 'We'll be visiting the site of the original eerie message implicating our Judaic friends, found over a piece of a victim's soiled clothing, later. Was there a Jewish conspiracy involved? Is that conspiracy still afoot in London today, behind two modern murders? Was Jack's original message a protest about the capitalist excesses of his own times, which resonates in the modern day? Or is it the other way round?' He quickly looked at his tour party, as if to gauge their sensibilities and/or ethnicities. 'Is it a conspiracy to *blame* these terrorist acts on the Jews?

Are they to be the fall guys for the New World Order yet again? Were these prostitutes – I mean, these proper young ladies –' he paused for the delayed laugh again – 'slaughtered according to secret religious ceremonies as per the request of the secret rulers of the world, the Illuminati? Perhaps we shall see. Perhaps. But let us begin at our starting point, the bloody scene before us. Imagine it!' With a sweep of his cape, he walked over to a wall. He pointed to the kerb beside it. 'How much scrubbing did it take to remove every trace of such a scrubber?' Perhaps knowing that the line wouldn't translate, he moved swiftly on. 'She'd been the wife of a printer's machinist.' Costain didn't know what that was, and suspected, given the ease with which the phrase had come out, neither did this bloke; it was just one of those things that got written down and repeated. It sounded as if Fennix had added his modern conspiracy rhetoric to an older script at the last minute. It was hardly convincing. But the crowd seemed to be lapping it up. He continued, 'But she was too fond of the bottle, and their marriage broke up when she started turning tricks to supplement her income.'

Costain realized, as he was looking at the spot the guide was pointing to, what he wasn't seeing here. He looked to Ross, and saw a puzzled expression on her face too. The two of them had started to anticipate seeing all sorts of terrors in London, visions associated with particular places, disconnected from current reality. Ross had taken the team to Vauxhall Bridge Road to see a weird house at the end of the bridge itself that had five chimneys and five coffins. They had all felt that the dust that rose from the coffins would be deadly should they venture inside and stay for any length of time. They hadn't found out what that was all about yet, despite all their research. But here, at one of the most famous murder sites of all time . . . Ross nudged him, and he looked around. Oh. There she was. As clear as daylight. But she was actually behind them, in the opposite direction from where Fennix was pointing. The Sight could sometimes be more accurate than history. It was a painful memory of what had really happened, before power had written over it. It wasn't that the Sight gave you the ability to see every murder victim, just the ones about whom there was . . . *story*, Costain supposed, was the way to put it. London seemed to remember the big stuff, the emotional stuff, the *memorable* stuff, whether or not its people did. But the metropolis also forgot most of what it saw. Otherwise they'd be tripping over phantom bodies with every step.

Here was a young woman in what were actually rags, with a strikingly colourful bonnet on her head. She was emaciated: her legs two bows of muscle, her face marked by disease, a vision of famine in Africa stamped into a British shape. She was looking hopefully at Costain and Ross, like any homeless addict, telling you the lightest generalizations about how great the world is in return for what they needed. What she needed was shockingly beyond their ability to give. She was holding her stomach, her hands pressed back into her skirts, trying to restrain a bloom of blood that actually hung in the air around her, as if she was caught in a single frame of a violent movie. Her need reached into them and made them feel the cold on this sunny afternoon. Her shadow looked like black ice.

'No silver goo on her,' Costain whispered to Ross.

'Noted.'

There was the Ripper himself, the archetypal figure, more of a shadow really: a silhouette that fluttered over all these buildings, like a misfiring advertising logo beamed down at them. His shape was diffuse, remembered hugely but not precisely, glamorously mysterious, while whenever anyone thought of his victims, it was all in the gory details.

'She left a pub in Brick Lane at half-past midnight, and, lacking four pennies for her lodging –' again, Costain heard the familiar lilt in the way the man said it, as if this was a song he'd sung many times, an inaccurate mantra – 'was thrown out of 18 Thrawl Street, the latest victim of merciless capitalism.' There was his new narrative, a new geological layer, flung on top for new money, with no thought as to what was underneath. This bloke didn't care if he contradicted himself; he had no idea, in the end, what he stood for or what he meant. That pricked Costain. These days, *he* had to be careful about his every action, about everything he said. He only hoped, and he glanced over at Ross again, that didn't extend to what he *thought*. He put all that from his mind and went back to listening to this man who had given up all such limitations.

'She said she'd go and find the money on the streets,' Fennix continued. 'It'd be easier that night . . . she'd just bought a new bonnet. We can only wonder if that was what caught the eye of the man who turned out to be the most important encounter of her life, the man who . . . made her famous. At 2.30 a.m. she had a conversation with one Nellie Holland at the Frying Pan pub, which is now a balti house. "Polly" told Nellie that she'd made the money she needed three times over, and then drank it all away again. This was late August, a warm, humid night, just like today, in fact. You can imagine "Polly", a few too many buttons undone, perhaps, beads of sweat on her young flesh, a bit merry, in her new bonnet, chancing down this backstreet, the rumble of the newly built railway station in the background – a station built so the middle classes could go on their holidays, flattening the slums to do so . . .' Fennix had spread his hands in the air, his leather gloves flexing like those of a mime artiste. 'She'd sacrificed herself on the altar of booze and cheap pleasure, turned herself into the perfect brazen victim. Or perhaps she'd been that from birth. And then out he stepped.' He took a sudden stride towards the crowd, and with a flourish drew a knife. The Italians and the Koreans obligingly gasped and leaped back. The students gave him the gift of their ironic laughter.

Ross was left looking calmly at the end of the weapon pointed at her face. She cocked her head to one side, examining it professionally, as if for traces of blood. Or silver. None was present.

'I call this my twanger,' said Fennix, and plunked the end of the rubber blade with his finger to make it vibrate. '"Polly" didn't meet with anything so harmless. She had her throat slit with one blow.' He turned away from Ross and took two steps forwards, going straight past Mary, who looked towards him with a sudden interest, as if he might be the one to give her money. He slashed across the air nowhere near her, and she looked sadly at him. Costain had half expected her to flinch. 'Then he lifted up her skirts, cut down her abdomen, and disembowelled her.' The young woman continued to watch him, oblivious to her own fate. 'Which shows that perhaps he was a medical man, that perhaps his instincts in this matter were not entirely . . . natural.'

With that hanging in the air, he led them off. Costain and Ross looked over their shoulders to see Mary continuing to stand there, gazing after them.

Fennix took them to the next murder site. 'The canonical five, they call them,' he said, 'their names writ in blood in the book of history.' They arrived in an indoor market, stall owners to either side managing clipped smiles or just avoiding eye contact. There had obviously been no financial arrangement to bring the tour through here, thought Costain, even with Fennix's increased cash flow. The butcher and pie-maker must feel their business suffering several times a day, with a discussion of human meat nearby, but what could they do about it?

He saw her from a distance this time: what he initially took to be an almost Madonna-like figure, some sort of shawl over one shoulder, her hands spread out. The shape of the Ripper was again a shadow cast all around her. 'Annie Chapman, slashed across the throat, then had her intestines hauled out and laid across her shoulder like the fur she could never afford.' Now they were close, Costain could see that she was indeed open, showing off her wounds in silent complaint. Again, there was no silver. 'Excuse the gynaecological detail, gents, but Jack cut out her uterus and part of her bladder, and took those with him, as well as the brass rings off her fingers.' Costain watched Ross' expression grow tremendously calm as she made eye contact with the revenant or recording or whatever you wanted to call it. 'This place was a yard behind a house then – lots of windows overlooking – brave of Jack to do his business here. Next to her was found a leather apron. Typical attire, as you'll know, sir,' Fennix said, looking to Costain, 'for Jewish tradesmen.'

Also for many other sorts of tradesman, surely? Were all blacksmiths or tanners Jewish? But Costain didn't give voice to his thoughts. He wasn't sure if this man would have answers that went any deeper than his script.

They left Annie and the butcher and pie-maker in their aprons behind them.

They walked to a pair of wooden gates in front of what seemed to be a schoolyard. Against the gates stood a tall washed-out woman with blood spilling down her dress. Her eyes were angry, insistent. '"Long Liz" Stride, only slashed across the throat, perhaps because Jack was disturbed.' There he was, a fleeting glimpse, running. 'One Israel Schwartz – note that name, sir – saw her having a row earlier with someone he described as "a gentleman". That is how we know that Jack was, or was pretending to be, a member of the ruling classes, perhaps even royalty. Now, days had separated the previous murders, but this time, perhaps frustrated at not having got what he was after, just forty-five minutes later . . .' Fennix let that sentence trail off as he led the party down the street to Mitre Square, where modern offices looked down on a group of benches, across which was sprawled the emaciated remains of a woman, her skirts and legs open, endlessly jerking and juddering, her arms windmilling as if she was in the act of falling, her head just a red lump. Costain wasn't sure he wanted to move closer, but found himself doing just that.

'Catherine Eddowes, again a drunk and a whore, again cut with a mighty blow across her throat, then systematically butchered, her intestines pulled out and laid over her shoulder, again her uterus and this time her left kidney taken by Jack. But this time he went further, which is odd, considering that these were all houses around here, and he could have been watched – perhaps was watched – from any one of these windows. He went further in what to us now looks almost like a demonstration, like a work of cruel performance art, like a protest at the conditions that had given birth to him. Her right ear lobe was sliced, a V shape was incised into each of her cheeks, and cuts made into her eyelids. Jack also snipped off the tip of her nose.' Costain looked into what remained of the woman's face, a mess of blood, and saw that her eyes, faint as they were, were again pleading. He wondered, not for the first time, what the connection was between what seemed to be people, preserved in time like this, and the Hell he'd glimpsed. Were these just images of people, as all the copies of Losley had been? Or were these somehow still the people themselves? Were they suffering? Was the history of London their Hell? Did they know that what had happened to them had started to happen again? Was this how he might end up, unless he played his cards *exactly* right?

There was the Ripper, standing all around, hands holding vague trophies.

'And he took her apron. With two groups of coppers after him, the Metropolitan Police and the City of London Police – because that was the case in those days, each police force having its own territory – Jack cannily hopped back and forth over the border between them, hue and cry all around!' Fennix led them off again, and this time Costain, following on his phone, knew where they were going.

Ross walked calmly beside him.

'Here is Goulston Street, ladies and gentlemen, these days, ironically, the location of Petticoat Lane Market, and –' he winked at Costain – 'yes, sir, there's a synagogue just round the corner.'

'Storks on roofs,' Ross whispered.

It took a moment for Costain to remember that that was a metaphor she'd used during the Losley case. There had been an exact correlation, he remembered, between the size of families in Holland and the number of storks that nested on the roofs of their houses. It wasn't because storks brought babies, but because rich people back then had both bigger roofs and more children.

She'd obviously seen that momentary look of consternation on his face. 'I mean, Jews were poor, so the slum landscape of the killings of course includes lots of Jewish references.'

'Are you sure that's all there is to it? Spatley was Jewish.'

Ross shook her head, as if now annoyed that she'd shared her thoughts. 'Don't know.'

'Here's where Jack dropped that apron, and then perhaps wrote, on this wall here, his famous message. Depending on whether you believe that any of the letters the police received were really from him, depending on if you believe he even wrote this – perhaps this is all we ever hear in the man's own voice. The message that calls out to us even now, which was written in blood in the house of a rich man only this week. Here it was written in chalk, and originally the message read . . .' Fennix held up a slate, on which was written:

The Juwes are the men that will not be blamed for nothing.

'One of the versions, anyway,' said Costain to Ross. They'd all been reading up on the history of this shit. She just nodded absently. She was looking up at the wall. Costain followed her gaze to where the original message still shone, for just the two of them, in all its different versions, frustratingly, with crossings out and some words faded and some reinforced, as if the memory of London was trying to accommodate all the possibilities, everything remembered, imagined or written about these words. This was merely testimony, Costain thought, as Ross took a photo of it. Not as solid as evidence. Not as reliable. The city continued to be their key witness. But what it told them was subjective.

If enough tour guides kept getting the precise positions of the bodies wrong, as Fennix did, the Ripper's victims would finally end up there.

The last murder turned out to have happened forty days after the previous one, in what was now a loading bay beside a multi-storey car park. This time Costain was prepared for his senses to find something terrible, but it took a while. When they finally did, as Fennix gestured wildly around the space, he initially had trouble recognizing what he saw at the foot of the bay as a person. He only got there when Ross stepped over to stare at it.

She was just a pile of meat, swaying like a mirage, her hands still flailing in the air, nothing else left of her able to communicate anything to the few who could see her. She looked like a ragged plant, fronds of blood and gore shifting at the bottom of an ocean of time. Not all of her was flesh. Some of what made up this knot was bedstead and blankets. This woman, Mary Kelly, had been killed at home, in her own bed. Costain slowly walked around her and saw her as an anatomy display, organs orbiting her, entrails endlessly wrapping around her. She was an explosion that continued: silent, hard to see. As with all the others, there was no sign of silver. Costain let himself look round, and nearly stepped back in shock when he found a solid cylinder of sheer Jack right in front of him, a knot of hatred and self-hatred and vomited sanity in the air.

'Her neighbours heard the cry of "Murder!", but they heard that every night! A lot of other cries too. Cries of stark passion. Cries of release. Because this was a notorious rookery, the bleak face of poverty and oppression. This time Jack had privacy, and he could take his time. She must have let him in. She must have teased him, tempted him, provoked him. He hacked away her entire face. He attacked her thighs. He opened up her abdomen. He cut out her uterus, her spleen, her liver and kidneys and her breasts and he left them here. But he also managed to do what no other man had done before, for he stole her heart away!' Fennix spread his arms wide for a theatrical finish. 'So who *was* Jack the Ripper? Someone *special*, that's for sure. Perhaps the artist, Walter Sickert, who used the case as a subject for his art, including a painting suggestively titled *Jack the Ripper's Bedroom*. Perhaps Sir John Williams, obstetrician to Queen Victoria's daughter, looking into the causes of infertility in all the wrong places. Or, the most shocking possibility of all . . . perhaps it was Prince Albert Victor, Duke of Clarence and Avondale, Queen Victoria's grandson, driven mad by syphilis, with an establishment around him willing to indulge in this rich man's . . . sport.'

Costain looked over to Ross. Now he could see, and perhaps it was only because he knew her, that she was shaking.

After the tour was over and Fennix had passed his top hat around to collect tips, and had signed some of the Toff masks, Costain and Ross got away and found a modern pub and a quiet table. The modernity of the establishment wasn't at all a guarantee that there'd be nothing horrible inside – as they'd just had re-emphasized to them, London was built on horror – but it was a gesture towards control that they both needed right now.

Costain waited silently as Ross updated her notebooks, stopping, flipping back, making tiny notes on different pages as if landing a stack of mental aircraft that had been circling in her head. He knew that feeling, but she did it on a much higher level than he did. It would be so hard to put on a front to her, to fool her. He also knew the comfort that came from translating the chaos of the world into the familiar patterns used by coppers. They shared that. Finally she put her palms on the table and took a last look at the page in front of her. Then she closed the book, picked up the pint so far unattended beside her and took a long drink. 'Fuck,' she said.

'How are you feeling?'

'Angry.'

He lowered his voice, indicating that he understood. 'Yeah.'

'Because that tour guide made so many baseless assumptions about connections between the killings. The Illuminati conspiracy, my arse. I actually don't think we *can* rule out a Jewish or anti-Semite angle, because the differences between the old message and the new are indicative of *something*. I don't know of what. But that twat had no idea. I don't think the message can have been left by the killer at the time. I mean, what, he's trying to blame the murder on the Jews while actually maintaining that he's the murderer? Maybe that's why the grammar got so awkward and there are crossings out. He's standing there going, "Wait a sec, haven't thought this through . . ." But in our case, like you said at the crime scene, it probably *is* the murderer who wrote it, so what does that mean?'

Costain laughed. 'When *I* said it, it was assumption.'

'It was. But we've labelled it as such now. So that's okay.'

'But what I meant was . . . you know, *I* started to feel pretty shitty about what that tour guide was saying—'

She was shaking her head, angry with him still. 'You want me to be all touchy feely? Sorry, I thought we were in law enforcement.'

'I'm just saying—'

'Right. Four points here, I think.' Now she was talking at high speed. 'Firstly, the Jack the Ripper case is a trap for analysts. It feels like there's a signal there that's right on the edge of being heard through all the noise. Suspect doesn't rape them when he has the chance. His interest doesn't seem sexual. He's clearly a misogynist, or wants us to think he's one, but he kills quickly; he doesn't want to torture them. He likes the thing with the intestines over the shoulder, and what does that mean? It's completely non-archetypal. Like he's just following his own ideas, not anything he's read. He takes organs sometimes, and which ones he takes varies, but, given all the time in the world, he leaves loads of them behind. There are genuine suggestions of medical ability, but also random violence. And all that *bollocks* is what's sucked in so many people over so many years. To *no* end. And it threatens to draw *us* in even more because, having the Sight, we think we have an advantage. But we haven't seen a single piece of new evidence today. If we are called upon to solve the Whitechapel murders in order to get traction in these new killings, we will be doing that *forever*. And I'm thus going to recommend that we concentrate on our new victims and the fresh trail and keep this squarely in the background, while of course being alert to the possibility of connections. Secondly –' she raised a finger before Costain could interrupt – 'my decision there is because I'm not sure there *is* a signal to be found. I researched the Whitechapel murders before we came here, but I didn't keep my parameters to anything "canonical" or "written in the book of history" and, you know what? This sort of shit was just business as usual for this neighbourhood. A tourist trail of "Whitechapel violence against women" would tend towards infinity. You get killings and assaults showing many of the "Ripper" aspects, both unsolved and stone-cold solved, culprits put away or hung, for decades before, even during and for quite a few years after. So maybe "Jack the Ripper" is just . . . a whole culture: blokes and a desperation for money. Maybe that means what we're dealing with in the modern version really is like those ghost ships I saw, something London thinks *should* be out there, not specifically created by the will of the protestors or by anyone else. Maybe our Ripper kills all the time, and people only notice when it has – and this is thirdly – changed its MO from killing poor helpless women to killing rich and powerful men. Having seen this end of the background, I'm sure *that* change is the single biggest data point. If we figure out what *that's* about, we can nick him. And the reason I'm sure that *is* a change, and that we haven't lost a few lords and dukes over the years without making the connection, is because, fourthly –' Ross took a breath and slowed down, and Costain now finally thought he saw, somewhere in the depths of her expression, the emotion – 'this whole process whereby the horrible deaths of five women get turned into a narrative, where they get pinned to a map of London and displayed . . . it's what I do, when I turn violence into evidence and stop feeling anything about it. And I have to do it – we all do. That tour made me start *thinking* about that process, and, yeah, okay, so I had a bit of a wobble and lost my objectivity for about a *minute*—'

'What? I wasn't saying you were . . . weak or anything. I felt that too.'

'Right. Great. Okay, then.'

Costain found himself looking intently at her face, wishing desperately that he knew what was going on underneath all that anger. But he wasn't going to find out now because he'd set off all her defences. He raised his hands in surrender. 'I'm really sorry.'

She just shook her head again. As if she was shaking him off her.

In the car heading back to the nick, Lisa Ross looked out of her side window and tried to keep her expression steady. Costain was an expert at hiding his intentions, at getting people talking. Had he tried today to get her to open up about herself? Right at the moment when she had something she wanted to hide, particularly from him? He'd seemed really awkward about that text message – *really* awkward, as if it had been an embarrassing mistake, the sort of mistake someone trying to put up a front shouldn't make.

Or maybe the sort of mistake someone trying to put up a front *wouldn't* make.

She sneaked a look across at him driving. Was it just that he fancied her? She was constantly taken by surprise when that happened. She never realized until it was too late. It was always difficult and complicated. She remembered him having stayed with her in the hospital. He'd shown a whole caring side to him that . . . or, even back then, was that what he'd wanted her to think?

Maybe she was being too hard on him. What had he done, today, really? Just tried to find in her some utterly understandable feelings of being shaken up. Maybe he really had felt the same way. He'd looked as if he had at the time. He'd hit one of her buttons: she could never live with any suggestion that she was being less than professional.

Maybe he'd hit that button deliberately to set her off, to see what it revealed. Had he any inkling what she was up to? Would she ever know, one way or the other? If he did, it was impossible that he wouldn't act on it, impossible that he wouldn't start trying to play her. He would have to know for himself what she was finding out. The object she was after was unique, too valuable for him just to ask her about it and risk warning her of any intentions he might have.

Was it just that he fancied her? She wondered if he'd ever do anything else about it, now that she'd behaved the way she had.

Those eyes of his were very useful for an undercover, she decided. He looked very trustworthy. Even when she knew he wasn't.

FIVE

Sefton finished his coffee. He was inside the usual pub, in his usual place, sitting looking towards the window but far enough back from it that he wouldn't be seen by anyone looking back from his target. He'd started to come here a few weeks ago and had previously treated this part of his duties reasonably casually. Now, though, he'd been asked to begin to make use of the progress he'd made in getting a look at people involved in London's occult community. So today was going to be a bit different and he was now in the mental space he associated with being undercover, lightly wearing a role which could basically be described as 'definitely not a policeman'. He'd always come here on Thursdays because that was the day when more of the particular sort of people he was interested in – the people who could make a little use of what his team called 'the London shit' to do impossible things, the people Losley had called Privileged – tended to go into the particular shop on Greek Street, across the road from the pub. In fact, there was one of them now, a bloke whom Sefton now knew well enough by sight to be able to follow him in a crowd: white male; early twenties; around six foot one; slim build; neatly trimmed beard; always wore a waistcoat and tie; a bit tweedy. Student, most likely. Straight. Whether or not everyone who made use of the power of London also had the Sight was an open question, one which Sefton had made a lot of notes about in his special

71

notebooks. More certain was the fact that neither those who had the Sight nor those who knew how to use the power necessarily stood out as being important to someone Sighted. The team hadn't been able to follow Losley just by feeling her presence. From his own studies, and this was something he was planning to share with the team soon, he suspected that he knew of at least one way in which those who understood how to use this stuff went into stealth mode.

The man was wandering over to the biggest branch of Quicksilver Dawn, the chain of occult shops that had sponsored one of the stalls at the New Age fair the team had attended when investigating the Losley case. All the meaningful customers that Sefton had identified seemed to dress slightly differently to the norm, but there had been very few in anything like the full-on Victorian dress seen at that fair. This, Sefton understood as he made his way to the door, was something J.K. Rowling had got right about the non-Muggle population: the askew dress sense. Maybe she knew more than she let on. He left the pub and sauntered across the street, enjoying the sunshine on his arms. Last night he'd had troubled dreams again. He had felt as if something was trying to get into his head, that the summer had got past his antihistamines and shoved its way right up into his sinuses and was rushing about in his brain, kicking down all the doors. He'd gone into the bathroom at 3 a.m. and splashed water on his face, and only slowly got back to sleep.

Now, in the distance, he could hear the drums of yet another protest march, heading for Parliament. The murders hadn't deflated that movement; if anything, they had actually increased the number of protestors. The public, he thought, had sensed blood, and now it was as if their ancient hatred of those in power had started to be set free. If there was going to be a Police Federation strike, Sefton had already decided that he wouldn't join in.

He went to look in the window of the shop. Just displays of completely ordinary Tarot cards and crystals on fake velvet in the window. There was an artificial spring that bubbled from a length of silvered tubing and twinkled as it fell delightfully into the limpid depths below. That might give his team an excuse to stroll in here one day this summer. 'Hosepipe ban, sir. We're searching the premises for free-flowing water.' Even Quill, open to leaving the rule book behind now that they were working in the wild extremes, might blanch at that. There was nothing of Sighted interest in the window, nothing weighty.

Sefton paused for a moment and found that he was quite calm. He was undercover, he was at home with this sort of tension. He went inside.

The shop smelt clean and airy. The shelves were white, and enormous posters and paintings decorated the walls. Gentle, tuneless music wafted past. No incense; it would be too hard for the staff to put up with all day. There were those staff, twenty-somethings in black T-shirts with the logo of the shop; two of them were laughing at the till, everyday-looking kids, divorced from the clientele he was after.

He wandered towards the back of the store and realized straight away that this was like walking uphill. There was a precise gradient. Every step he took, according to the Sight, got him into more serious territory. Checking the price tags on the items, he saw that they followed that index too: more expensive with every step. He stopped. That felt . . . wrong. Why? This shop, logically, attached a higher price tag to items that were genuinely powerful, that had the strength of London about them, that had the age so prized by the small portion of the clientele who knew what they were doing. Presumably, he was heading towards more valuable items that could accomplish things – like the Tarot of London or *Book of Changes* that Ross had encountered – unlike the jewellery in these halfway cases, which just shone through association, without the feeling that it might leap up and help him or hurt him. So what was the problem with any of that? He realized he was feeling that there was something wrong with linking occult power and money. Something almost . . . *gauche* about it. He could feel that embarrassment as a physical effect. It was like . . . being on a fairground ride, with each foot on a plank that rocked in a different direction . . . the power and the money were sort of . . . angry at being chained together. They were resisting each other. What the fuck was that about? He recalled the same feeling from the green thing that he'd run into in Soho when he first got the Sight – that same anger at money.

He shook off the feeling and glanced back to the staff. They hadn't even looked up. They must be used to people doing weird shit in here.

He kept moving.

There was an area right at the back with glass-fronted cases and narrow walkways between the shelves. It smelt mustier. The design of the shop identified it as the dull bit, for serious collectors only, but there were two security cameras up there, neatly covering everything. It seemed that the owners didn't find it profitable to bring much in the way of this genuine stuff to the New Age fairs. Sefton's target was looking into one of the display cases. Ignoring him, Sefton walked up to stand beside him, deciding to fix his eyes on something in there that shone brightly to the Sight: a brass bracelet that looked as if it had spent some time underwater, decorated with rough knotwork. There would be some serious London history to it. There was no label on it; if you were back here, you were supposed to know what this stuff was. There was a price tag, though: £1999.99. He could feel the object kind of itching at its attachment to such a value. He could feel its age. He could also feel that there was nothing scary about it; here was an item you could lean on in a crisis, an old friend that would always see you through. He'd seldom felt emotional detail like that with the Sight. Maybe that was because of the shop environment. If someone Sighted had stocked this place – and that was a conclusion he felt he could safely come to – they wouldn't put out anything that made their customers feel like shit. That'd be in the back, the higher slopes that he felt continued past this end wall, the special stuff for special people.

Sefton had picked the bloke he'd followed in here because he looked young and was in modern dress, unlike the serious practitioners they'd encountered at the New Age fair. Today was just about making sure that the guy saw him here, so that by the third or fourth encounter he'd think of him as a regular, and then maybe start talking to him. Sefton wasn't planning to begin a conversation himself. You didn't initiate contact. Doing this in a subcultural context couldn't help but remind Sefton of something he'd never done himself: cottaging. What would be just a small indicator that he and the man shared common predilections? There might well be a secret language here, but if there was an occult underworld in London, the sort of community that knew itself *as* a community, it stayed off the internet. With what Ross had reported about her fortune-teller's embrace of all that was old, maybe that wasn't surprising. What would be the obvious thing to do here?

He let himself smile at the warm feeling coming from the artefact, then glanced sidelong and saw that the young man was surely feeling the same way. But then he actually made eye contact with Sefton, and instead of any shared sentiment, as if they were both in an art gallery, the look on his face was grim. To Sefton's surprise, the man spoke. He kept his voice low and urgent. He had a slight stammer and an upper-class accent. 'Does you being here mean what I think it does?'

Sefton turned slowly to look at him, sizing him up.

'Does someone like you being here mean that the Keel brothers are about to make their move?'

Someone like him? In what sense? Sefton chose his West Indian gang accent. 'I don't feel you.' Suggesting that he really *did* know what was going on.

The man looked suddenly shocked. He lowered his voice even further. 'You're prepared to go that far? In the presence of all this?'

Sefton was now completely lost. But he didn't let his expression show it. It was vital that he continue to feed this man's assumption that he knew as much about what was going on as the man did. That was his way in. He smiled a very deliberate smile, and straightened his back from his gang slump, squared his shoulders, emanating basic dominance. Whatever this was, yeah, he was prepared to go that far. Feigning confidence had saved him in the past. Sometimes he thought that was all there was to life. He wished he found it as easy to do in the real world as when he was undercover.

The man seemed not to know what to do. He looked exasperated for a moment, then turned and walked quickly away. He looked back to Sefton from the end of the aisle, then he was off.

Well, that had been a come-hither look. So, here we go; the way in was opening up. Sefton gave it a moment of further window shopping, then went past the oblivious staff again, down something that was trying to slope both ways and out into the sunshine and onto the normal pavement. The man was loitering on the corner beside an ancient-looking cafe; when he saw that Sefton was following, he went inside. So Sefton did too.

The cafe was one of those you got on the corners of central London, unchanged in design and function since the fifties, apart from a microwave and a smoking ban. There were, now Sefton thought about it, quite a few businesses like this near the occult shop. The pub he'd been in hadn't even had a telly. Were the proprietors aware that some of their clientele were what might be called neophobic, culturally attached to the past? Or was this just an evolutionary process caused by the flow of cash: in the squeeze, anything that had smacked of modernity had just unknowingly suffered from those customers not showing up? Maybe not. It wasn't as if the individuals they'd met at the New Age fair were rolling in it. Exactly the opposite.

He went to join the man at a corner table, and now the bloke felt able to look up and acknowledge his presence. 'I'm on your side. I really am.'

Sefton kept looking stern. Let him talk. His aim here was to find out as much as possible about the culture this man belonged to, and perhaps get an invitation to move further in, to meet more of them. The now-urgent need the man had to express some sort of fellow feeling might be an excellent engine to power that along.

'But you can't just march across all the lines. You have to tread carefully.'

What lines? Costain always liked to say that Sefton asked too many questions when undercover. But, sod him, Sefton was in his own world now. 'Are you disrespecting me?'

From the wince on the man's face, that had been the wrong thing to say. 'Why do you keep doing that? Whatever the Keel brothers might want, speaking like that is going too far.'

As his training had taught him, Sefton did the opposite of what he wanted to, looking aside as if being accepted, being invited to become part of this community in some way, was nothing to him.

'I know it's hard, in your position—' the man started to say.

'You don't know anything, mate.'

'I'm only on the fringes myself. But when I'm in their places I do my best to talk their language. You know, to speak all old-fashioned London. All that *Mary Poppins* music-hall nonsense. It's just what they've always done.'

He meant how Ross' fortune-teller at the New Age fair had talked. So that was what this guy was worried about – his speech patterns. Just as well he hadn't gone total Peckham on him.

'I know the Keel brothers and others are trying to force changes now, that a generational thing of some kind is going on, and that suits me too . . .'

Sefton filed that one away for future reference.

'. . . but you can't get everything you want at once. Might as well work out which way the wind is going to end up blowing. I know I'm only in the very first stages. And I know it must be a lot worse for . . . for you . . .'

'For black people, you mean?'

He hesitated again, big time. 'I'm not one of the people who feel you're automatically too modern. There have been . . . people of African descent in London for centuries.'

So this was definitely about being seen as too *modern*. Something not from whatever 'golden age' people like that fortune-teller harked back to.

So, hey, entering that shop and heading into the serious stuff at the back must be something you didn't often see people of colour doing. To this bloke, encountering Sefton had been like getting onto the bus and having Rosa Parks sit down next to him. 'Right,' he said. 'It's time for a change.'

'Are you going to the Goat?' He had lowered his voice, so it seemed that mentioning it in public was dangerous. But he'd also said it as if it was obvious that Sefton would know what he was on about.

Sefton narrowed his eyes and made as if to get up, again doing the opposite of what the man wanted rather than reveal his own lack of knowledge. Again, it worked. The man leaped to his feet, obviously feeling that he'd offended Sefton in some way. 'Listen, I know about what they say is going to happen there this month. I'm a regular, just on the first level, not every Thursday, but at least on the first Thursday. People are saying that now that the Keel brothers have bought the place, it might get easier for me to, you know, get downstairs. That they're going to change the rules. You must know *something* about that.'

The man was obviously assuming that Sefton's skin colour automatically made him a radical in this subculture, and radicals knew about radical developments. The *Goat*? It might be a pub. On the first Thursday of the month. That explained why Thursdays brought this sort of person into town. He'd just found one of the meeting places of the London occult community. Job done. He didn't let that satisfaction show. He slowly sat back down, nodding as if appreciating this bloke's knowledge of the situation. 'I might.'

'Well, if you're there next Thursday . . . tread carefully, eh? They might announce new rules, but real change takes time. This might not be the moment. But, hey, if you do get anywhere, I'll be there to cheer you on. I'd benefit too. I've worked hard to get this far. Be nice to get down to the lower floors.'

Sefton considered. He really wanted to know this man's name and to be given a map of how to get to a location that might be supernaturally hard to find, but he couldn't risk asking for either. Names were a big deal in both undercover work and everything he'd read about the weird stuff. He waited for a long moment before answering. 'Let's see how it goes.'

'Okay. Great.'

Still taking care to look unsure about this guy, Sefton got to his feet again. He moved to the door like a wary beast on the edge of being tamed by Tarzan. He turned back and gave the man a long, significant look. Then he inclined his head to him. *You're cool, my white brother. I will think hard about what you've said here today.*

As soon as Sefton turned the corner beside the cafe he broke into his everyday stride, dropping the undercover from his shoulders with great relief. He hit the button on his mobile to call Quill. 'Jimmy,' he said, 'have I got juice for you!'

Quill listened to the description of the juice. He found it good. He took pleasure in the way his team all looked so engrossed as they stood around the main table in the Portakabin, gazing down at the Google map of London on Ross' phone. 'There's only one pub name with "goat" in it within five miles of that shop,' she said. 'The Goat and Compasses, on Manette Street.'

Quill looked it up on his own phone. 'Can't book it for the first Thursday,' he said, 'or any other Thursday. Private function. And it is indeed now owned by Keel Promotions PLC.'

'The Keel brothers,' said Ross, 'being Barry and Terry, both with form for burglary and attempted robbery, both single, both with addresses in Shoreditch. The company office for the Quicksilver Dawn chain of stores is the shop that Kev visited.'

'Interesting name, goat,' said Sefton, 'a bit Denis Wheatley, and compasses, a bit Masonic.'

'But,' added Costain, hitting buttons on his phone, 'it says here that the name's a corruption of "God encompasseth us". Wow. This is so the right place that it's even got a cover story.'

'We should get it checked out,' said Quill. 'With the aim of learning anything about the murders, and, incidentally, anything about the Sight.'

'I'll take a tube of the silver goo along,' said Sefton. 'In case there's someone I can show it to. Maybe indicate that I want to trade it.'

'We should also listen out for any mention of a thing or a person that can walk through walls and skip off like Peter Pan,' added Ross.

'If the Ripper turns out to be Peter Pan,' said Quill, 'I will have had the last of my illusions shattered.' He looked round the group for more input, and found none. 'Thus endeth the list of what we'll be listening out for.'

'We?' said Sefton.

Quill had thought hard about this. He had approached Lofthouse for authorization under the Regulation of Investigatory Powers Act and she'd got it for him, but she'd raised an eyebrow at what he'd told her he was planning to do. 'We all go,' he said. 'We may only get one chance to hear something important before this community is on to us. It seems to be all about who's in the know and who's not, and like some of the communities Kev and Tony have gone undercover in, it has its own forms of speech. Some of us may bounce down the steps and some may get invited into the back room for a hand of supernatural whist. Our two undercover officers might find themselves being bounced, given the racially challenged aspects of what we've heard. I'm also thinking that this could be the Losley house all over again. What we discovered there, and in Berkeley Square, was that we handle the really terrifying shit better as a team.'

'But you and I aren't undercovers,' said Ross. She had developed a serious frown.

'And you're not a police officer, which I wouldn't normally mention, except to say that I am absolutely not asking you to go undercover. It's a public space, the two of us will stay entirely within it. We just show up, off duty. We don't have an angle; we just watch and chat, and ask *no* questions. We do not use assumed names, but we don't volunteer our real names either. We thus stay outside the definition of a covert human intelligence source.'

She considered for a moment. 'Okay,' she said, finally.

Costain was looking worried too. 'From what we heard at the New Age fair, police officers are loathed and feared by this community—'

'If things get anywhere near serious, I'll walk out of there to the car I'll leave round the corner, and that'll be the signal for Ross to follow. Same the other way round. You two specialists, on the other hand, *will* be using constructed identities, and will be free to explore beyond the public areas, should you deem it safe to do so.'

'What if someone from the New Age fair is there?' asked Sefton. 'Me and Costain showed our warrant cards there.'

'You haven't seen anyone familiar in your investigations so far. If we do, we bug out immediately.'

'What if they can tell who we are?' said Costain. 'At the fair, Madame Osiris had some sort of supernatural tripwire set up, to detect coppers.'

Sefton suddenly grinned. 'I've been thinking about that,' he said. 'You remember when Losley scanned our bar codes and suddenly knew about my batting for the other team?'

'I'm so glad we all speak metaphor,' said Quill.

'She used gestures to do almost everything – apart from that destructive shout of hers – and it'd be hard to have everyone shouting in a social situation, so I think we have to watch out for hand movements.'

'It was when I said "Mora Losley" that Madame Osiris knew I was associated with the police,' said Ross. 'I felt that happen, like . . . a sort of pressure wave in the air. She kept her hands under the table much of the time, so she might have done something while I was there, or she could have made a gesture beforehand that set that up in advance.'

'So, we need a way to stop people checking out who we are

and discovering that we're coppers,' said Sefton, as if all the above had been an interruption to his grand announcement. 'Just as well I've been working on something for that very situation. This would, in fact, be only my second venture, after the vanes, into doing anything useful with this London shit.' He went to his holdall and brought out a file, out of which he took one of the browned and ancient documents from the Docklands ruins. These were manuscripts he'd found that night, and Quill recalled that Sefton had had to negotiate with Ross, once she'd begun her indexing process, to keep them for his own study after she'd given them a once-over. 'Since this was left there after years of the site being looted, I'd guess what's written here is kid's stuff, second nature to anyone starting out on the road of being *Privileged*, but of course it's new to us. I can't find anything about how actually to read a person—'

'Because that would be of enormous use in our job,' said Quill. 'And because we have the luck of coppers.'

'—but I have here what the document calls a "blanket". A way to hide one's identity from prying gestures.'

'Blanket, as in hide under one?' asked Quill.

'From some of the other language used, I think it's a corruption of "blank eek", "eek" being Palare, fairground language, for "face".'

'But if we use this "blanket", won't everyone get suspicious that we're the ones hiding our true selves?'

'If I've understood this . . . Jacobean English, I think it is . . . right, then keeping shtum about yourself when scanned is only *proper*, what the Privileged automatically do, a sign of belonging in itself. Assuming nothing's changed since the seventeenth century.'

'Given what we've seen of this lot,' said Ross, 'I think that's a safe assumption.'

'And labelled as such,' said Costain.

Quill noticed the glare she flung him about that.

'Of course,' said Sefton, 'someone could always bring a bigger gun to the party, use something to break through the blanket.'

'In which case,' said Quill, 'we revert to Plan B and run like fuck.'

Sefton read over the parchment once again, then turned to Quill. 'Okay,' he said. 'I think the only way to simulate being read is if I yell in your face. When I do, attempt the following . . .'

That was how they spent the afternoon.

At home that night, Ross found herself stopping in her researches, considering sleep, but also fearing the dreams that would come. Maybe they were guilty dreams, her searching her conscience. She went to make herself a cup of tea, then returned to her desk, staring out into the familiar orange light of the suburban night. She was eagerly anticipating the next day. Sefton had, without knowing it, moved her closer to her own, private, goal. Getting into the occult underworld of London could make all the difference. She'd had to appear to be against Quill's proposal at first, though, because if she'd grabbed at it, he might have known something was up.

Would he? No. That was her being paranoid about someone whose defences, as far as she was concerned, were completely absent. Damn it. Quill was definitely not trying to pry into her secrets in the way she was worried Costain might be. He was innocent of the idea that she might keep any such secrets from him.

She was going to go with her colleagues into a situation that was potentially as dangerous as Berkeley Square had been, and she was not going to be entirely on their side.

Costain volunteered to be the first of them to enter the pub, as was only right for his rank and experience. On Wednesday he walked past the Goat and Compasses, which looked to be a perfectly ordinary city-centre pub: on the classy side, hanging baskets outside, not averse to the odd tourist, colourful chalkboard outside advertising lunch.

On the Thursday night, the first of the month, at around seven, he entered the pub in character, in a suit that wasn't too flashy, as if he'd just come from work, but with the little flourishes of a tie pin and a pair of excellent shoes. It felt good to be back under-cover. The character he'd decided to play was well behaved, so as not to risk his soul, and because that fitted the operational require-ments, but it was an evening out of his own skin, a breathing space. There had been some debate about whether or not he should wear something symbolic, but he had ruled that out. 'This is a newbie,' he had said, 'who's trying very hard to not make a fuss, to play by the rules. Maybe he's come for the first time because he's heard this change is happening, whatever that's about, and feels for the first time that a dusky gentleman might be welcome. We don't know enough yet about what all these occult symbols mean for him – for *me* – to wear one. This bloke I'm playing knows enough not to rock the boat. He'll wear a symbol when he's seen what's what.'

The pub looked just as normal inside. Young blokes, a few suits, an old bloke alone with the newspaper, everyday-looking staff, some Eastern Europeans and some Aussies. None of the Hogwarts crowd, and none of that rough white vibe that said he wasn't welcome, either. He ordered a Diet Coke and carefully looked around, lost, wondering where the do was. A chalk sign by a stairwell at the back said 'private party' with a big, coloured-in arrow pointing downstairs. Did this place prefer to keep its monthly clientele out of sight of the regular punters? He considered asking whether he could go downstairs, but, no, newbie is worried about being told he's not allowed. He headed down the stairs. Nobody stopped him.

As he took his first step downwards, he noticed that, for the first time since he'd entered the pub, he could feel the gravity of the Sight. There was lots of important stuff down here, but it was a bit . . . muffled from the pub above. As if where he was going had the equivalent of a lead lining. At the bottom of the stairs, opposite the toilets, a pair of double doors led into a downstairs bar area. Careful not to walk in as if he owned the place, he pushed through them.

He was early. Only a couple of people around, and they were both looking at him. Newbie mistake to arrive so early. Exactly. There was a bouncer in the corner, which was weird – inside, and in a pub like this, and this early in the evening. But the bouncer was weird too: classically shaped as such, with a jutting chin and a bow tie even, but a bit of a caricature, like a comedian playing a bouncer. None of the door staff subculture vibe that you saw with the real thing, which usually shouted either extreme sports enthusiast or former gang member. Costain drained his drink as he looked at the punters. One of them was a middle-aged man in a tweed suit and waistcoat, bearded, a pint of dark ale in front of him. He was sitting in the far corner beside a stairwell that led down, in exactly the same place as the one in the room above. He looked as if he was guarding it. He was reading a volume bound in leather. He made eye contact with Costain, which seemed signif- icant for a moment, a slight pause – oh my goodness a person of colour – then back to his book. The other punter was in his twen- ties and looked like something out of an advert: stripy suit; bright yellow brogues; waistcoat with a fob watch dangling from it, and huge, neatly tended handlebar moustache, like Dali crossed with Bertie Wooster. He plucked his monocle from his eye and gave Costain a bow of greeting. He was a rich kid, a modern dandy. But still – so far, so friendly. The bar itself looked to be the kind you might find downstairs in any modern pub. Where was that sensation of weight coming from? Still under his feet. Spread out evenly, as he walked to the bar. Perhaps the Keel brothers, having bought the place, had put some of their more meaningful shop merchandise somewhere. Behind the bar a young woman in the same uniform as the one upstairs, but with a certain attitude about her, had appeared. She had wide open holes in her earlobes, goth decoration that might not be allowed in a mainstream bar.

'You can get your drinks here,' she said, 'you don't have to keep going back upstairs.'

'Okay,' he said, 'thanks.' If she'd been all old-fashioned with her speech, he'd have matched it.

He bought a vodka and Coke, and went to sit at a corner table, facing the door. A new-looking menu advertised cocktails. The Cemetery Jitters. The Last Rites. The Night Terror. He checked what the top-end champagne was. Blimey. Bollinger Blanc de Noirs Vieilles Vignes Françaises 1997, £400 a bottle. That was well at odds with what they'd encountered at that New Age fair. The poverty of the fortune-teller Ross had met there had been evident. The team had been working on the theory that the occult underworld, if it existed, was made by and for the disenfranchised. Maybe that wasn't always the case. He flipped to the back of the menu. You could, it seemed, 'order' The Damned to come to your table and perform 'Grimly Fiendish' for 'prices starting at £15,000'. Getting much pricier if they were away on tour or something, presumably.

He took a glance at his phone, to make sure Quill hadn't sent him a last-minute no-go message, then dropped it back into his pocket. No showing-off of modern devices. Of the four of them, only he and Sefton were even carrying their phones tonight, in case they went deep and needed a way to call for backup. He looked back to the young man at the bar, now chatting to the barmaid. So, okay, there was a lot of retro styling to him, but he was fundamentally a modern young man with some cash to spare, out on the town. Maybe the dude was on his way to a party, just a part-timer here. So how about the older one? Costain looked over to the corner. There was something of the unkempt about the man, the quality that they'd all glimpsed amongst the serious players at the New Age fair.

Neither of them had attempted to 'read' him. Or if they had made some sort of gesture, he hadn't felt or noticed it, and they now knew all about him. He hoped that his undercover experience meant they might read the role instead of the real bloke, but if they had they weren't acting on it. He had no cause to raise the alarm.

Costain took from his pocket the book that Sefton had given him, the small paperback edition of *The Stratagem and Other Stories* by Aleister Crowley, first published in 1929. It was something a newbie with possibilities might pick, both harmless and indicative. He held it so people could see it was old and crumbling. He started to read, glancing up every now and then. Over the next half-hour he noted a number of people entering, a few who seemed interesting. Soon his lot should start . . . yeah, there was Ross, entering with the look of a scared rabbit about her. Good acting. Or maybe she was just letting her usual poker face drop. Kind of disappointing, if so. She wore a colourful waistcoat, a big puffy shirt and tailored trousers, halfway between a waiter and a gunfighter, all a bit Nineties. Kind of lesbian. She'd put on some make-up, which looked so weird on her he couldn't tell if he liked it or not. But she looked good. A natural, in an eccentric get-up like that. As if she was about to walk into a spotlight and start singing, but obviously also someone who didn't quite know how to fit in here. So not playing a role, not doing anything she couldn't handle. It suddenly occurred to him that, ironically, it meant that he was possibly seeing something like the real Ross here. Or a guess on her part at what the real Ross might be. He was careful to keep watching her sidelong, not look straight at her. When she turned away, he realized he wanted to see her from behind. He did, and felt awkward at having done so; he went back to his book. Those trousers suited her. Good bit of tailoring there. Well cut.

He remembered how it had been when he'd last been under-cover. Some undercovers had wives waiting for them at home, who they went back to at weekends, on the other side of the country. Costain, with what he'd started to recognize had actually been an excessive sense of self-preservation, had always thought that sounded risky. It hadn't ever seemed an option for him. He'd never met anyone he was interested in while being himself. Or he'd never given himself the chance. What was 'being himself'? There wasn't anyone he'd ever properly opened up to. That had been how he was long before he'd become a copper. At school,

he'd dance with girls, make out with them . . . Beverley Cooper
. . . yeah . . . but when they started to want to go on dates, to
hang around, he'd back off. They always took that as him being
macho. But really . . . he had no idea what it really meant. He
didn't know why he was the way he was.

In the Toshack gang, he'd received enough attention, but on
nights out with the other gang soldiers he'd always acted boozy
and boorish, distancing himself from women while appearing to
be up for it. He'd got close to a couple of toms, actually, found
that paying them let him carry on playing the part of the gang
soldier while getting some . . . not sexual release, you could do
that with a wank, he never understood blokes who went on about
that . . . some emotion, some closeness. They'd laughed a lot in
bed, Sam and Jo, whichever of them had been around; he'd always
paid them well enough so they'd stay.

Why was he thinking about this now?

He had looked at Ross and felt guilt about what he was considering.

He realized he'd been staring at one page of Crowley's rather
too pompous writing without reading it. He looked over to Ross
again and saw that the bloke with the moustache was talking to
her at the bar, and she was delighted, taking in every detail of his
face, nodding along.

Costain closed his eyes for a moment, then made himself open
them again, and made sure he kept reading.

Ross had made notes on Costain's instructions about how they all
had to look, and she had taken them out when she'd sat down in
front of the bedroom mirror that evening. This took her back. She'd
been told, years ago, during her training, that police social functions
were quite expensive and entirely optional, not the sort of thing
analysts did, but she'd wanted to go to one. She'd created her new
life, she'd thought then. She had colleagues now, she wanted to do
the sort of things they did, to show, as part of her determination
to get Toshack, that she was on their team. She'd bought two

evening dresses, had taken bloody ages deciding which one to wear, and then in the end had spent a really boring evening trying to find anyone who wanted to talk about operations or methodology.

This time she wasn't playing a role: she was herself, off duty. But – and she'd known in advance this was going to be a problem – she had no idea how that was supposed to look. She was the one who'd pointed out that the persons of interest they'd met at the New Age fair had made statements with their clothing. She normally made none that she was aware of. Quill had agreed that, while still being themselves, he and Ross should both dress with the style of the 'occult underworld' in mind. Take care to not obsess about it, he'd added. So those had been mixed messages.

She'd last tried to dress to specific effect when she'd been persuading the Toshacks that she was a normal teenager, a credit to their family. This was going to be entirely different from that. She'd found the waistcoat in a market two days ago. She made herself up in the way she had when Toshack had expected her to 'go to discos', not with her adult eye. The results were . . . oh, God. But this would all help. She was both herself and a newcomer in this culture.

As she entered the downstairs bar she'd remembered that last time she'd moved amongst these people, at that New Age fair, she'd felt some kinship with them. She'd recognized a certain look about them, but not many of those people were here now, she saw as she entered. Instead it was mostly bloody hipsters, that weird 'oh I'm so awfully British' look that had come along around the time of the Olympics and the Jubilee and was probably supposed to be ironic. Beards that looked halfway between Edwardian and pirate. Great rolls of hair in mock Mohicans. She'd gone to the bar and let herself be chatted to by some bloke and did all the things that let him think this was worth continuing with, which was also the real her. At least it had been, sometimes. It meant that she didn't stand out by rebuffing him. She'd waited for that feeling of air pressure, of someone checking her credentials, but had felt none.

'So what made you interested in, you know, our jolly old sort of thing?'

Really? He'd said 'jolly old' and added distance and irony as he'd said it. The fortune-teller Ross had met had been desperate and honest about her use of dead speech patterns. If this man was typical, this place didn't look too promising for the operation or for her own aims tonight.

Ross laughed in a way that said she was laughing with him rather than at him. 'Oh, you know, you read a few books . . .' She realized she hadn't attempted, as Quill had advised them all, her own equivalent of 'jolly old'. But, okay, she was being herself.

'Did you see one of the fliers?'

'No.' Lying, she had been told, was entirely out.

He fished one of them out of the pocket of his waistcoat. 'Only given out to the right sort of people in the right sort of places.' He handed her one with a flourish. 'There you go.'

The flier looked like a music-hall poster. In that Victorian font it promised, in big letters, *The Secret Metropolitan Gathering of which you Have All Heard so Much.* Lesser attractions in boxes were noted as *Invitations to Further Delights, That which Dare Not Speak its Name* and *Rum.*

'That which dare not speak its name?' Oh. That had been a question, hadn't it? But surely she would ask *some?* If she was being herself. Playing a part.

He feigned shock. 'I dare not say. Obviously.'

'Only, that was what Oscar Wilde called being gay . . .'

'That's mainstream now. This is . . . truly blinkin' underground.'

She laughed again and carefully slipped the flier into her waist-coat pocket. 'Right.' The people from the New Age fair wouldn't have allowed themselves a flier. She looked around the room. Had they even got the right place? Maybe this was just a sort of . . . copy, a cargo cult, weekend punks. She saw Costain. He had been looking at her. He'd told her not to worry if she happened to look at him. Being herself, she would sometimes look at him. He looked weird, all buttoned up like that, his head bent over his book while all around him people were chatting. She saw one of his fingers resting on the words, and wondered if he was really reading them. He moved his fingers as if he was, and then he delicately turned a page.

She looked back to the bloke at the bar, because he'd started to look in the same direction, and then took her own gaze over to the bearded bloke by the stairs. He was still reading too, paying absolutely no attention to all the bright young things who were gathering around him. He looked up from his book, as if feeling her watching him . . . and, oh, that might actually be true . . . and made eye contact with her for a significant length of time. She tensed, expecting him to check her bar code. He didn't. He looked back to his book again.

Sefton had been tempted to ask Joe's opinion as to what might make him look the part tonight, but that would have only made Joe worry, without saying he was worried. In the end he'd chosen a battered leather jacket he'd had at the back of the wardrobe, which he'd got from a second-hand shop, so probably qualified as vintage. The inner pockets were thick enough that the flask containing silver goo didn't feel continually cold against his chest. He put the vanes the bloke at the New Age fair had attacked Quill with in the other one. He still had no idea how to use them as a weapon, but they might be a useful sensor. He put the jacket on over a bland polo shirt. He was meant to look as if he didn't give a damn. His character had been established as in your face at the shop, so in your face he would remain. It was quite crowded by the time he arrived. He didn't look for Costain and Ross, and didn't find them. He'd waited across the street until he'd seen beardy waistcoat, his mental shorthand for the bloke from the occult shop, enter, and followed. There he was now, at the bar, talking to a very severe-looking young woman. She was the real thing – the most interesting by far of all those who'd arrived. She wore a black dress so old that the seams and creases were white. Her hair was a black mop, tufts in all directions, completely unstyled. She couldn't have been more than twenty, but she looked sour, with great rings of sleeplessness under her eyes. Beardy waistcoat was looking shocked at her, shaking his head in mute astonishment at whatever she'd just said to him. Sefton went straight to them, but then made sure to stop when beardy saw him, as if registering only in that moment that the man had company. Beardy waved him over.

'Glad to see you,' he said. 'What are you having?' He wanted to get Sefton away from the woman, whom it seemed he'd just met, but was already having difficulties with.

'Who's the cunt with the sun tan?' she said. Her accent was full-on Eliza Doolittle, and Sefton actually had to restrain a laugh. *Wow.* That *sort of old-fashioned racism?* Was this how it was going to be tonight? He let the other half of what he felt hearing that, the sudden bleak anger, show on his face.

The man shook his head. 'Oh, for God's sake. She was like that with me, too. Would you please just—?'

'What?' The woman looked calm and empty as she said it. She was, weirdly, taking no pleasure in this. She seemed utterly sober. 'He's a fucking nigger.'

'What the fuck?' said Sefton.

'I-I think maybe it's—'

'You don't know shit, you look like shit, you're talking shit.' Again, precise, resigned to what she was saying. There were signs of old bruises about her throat. Was it likely that she was throttled on a regular basis? Maybe it was some sexual thing? It was as if she had Tourette's or something. There was a sense of harm about her, of harm that was done to her rather than what she'd do to others. But he couldn't let this go, could he? Every character he'd played before, especially he himself, the real him, would have shrugged this off, but this one—

He made his decision and stepped into her space. 'Are you asking for a beating?'

She closed her eyes, her teeth bared, wincing, preparing herself to be hurt. She took no pleasure in that anticipation, like some people Sefton had met, facing the prospect with a sort of grim determination. He saw that one tooth in two was missing, that there was weird bronze stuff screwed into some places there. She broadcast dental pain. When it was clear that he was hesitating, she spoke again. 'You know what wog stands for? Westernized Oriental Gentleman. That's what they say. That's what you are.'

'Oriental?'

Beardy tried to step between them. 'Listen, I think I know what you're doing. We all find our own path to studying the ways of London, but—'

Sefton let his body react. With a straight arm, he pushed beardy back. This was between her and him.

She opened her eyes, and now her gaze was dancing over his face, taking him in as she spoke quickly under her breath. 'Cockney rhyming slang: Berkshire Hunt, cunt. It should be "bark" for "Berkshire", but the meaning is only conveyed if you change the pronunciation.' It was as if she was reciting something to herself, a mantra or a prayer, while expecting to be beaten. If you didn't count the words, everything in her body language was pleading with him not to hurt her. What sort of character was he playing, who couldn't rise above it?

'*You're* a fucking berk,' he said. Which was slight. Not enough.

She let out a long, relieved breath.

'I think she's dedicated her speech to breaking off her every social relationship,' said beardy waistcoat. 'It's a sort of sacrifice. I've read about—'

'Fuck you,' said the woman, mildly, and then nodded to Sefton. 'And you and all, you fucking flid fucking nigger fucking twat.'

He let himself make understanding eye contact with her. 'Yeah,' he said. 'How nice for you.' He hoped she knew that was what the Queen was supposed to say when she didn't like someone.

She gave him a relieved smile and a nod of appreciation. Then she turned on her heel and was gone into the crowd.

*

Quill had never paid much attention to what he wore. Now he was feeling awkward, walking down the steps into a boozer in what felt to him like something his old man would have worn on a night out after nicking the Shantry gang in 1983. He'd stuffed those rather too well-upholstered abs of his into a waistcoat that was a bit too tight. He'd found some natty striped trousers of which he was rather proud, and a jacket that swung under its own weight, all poured into a pair of brothel creepers. 'Fancy dress party?' Sarah had asked, and so he'd told her. 'Just because you're going as Gene Hunt,' she'd said, 'don't act like him.'

It was sound advice. That Seventies TV copper was the part of his dad he sort of was but tried not to be. The place was rocking. He immediately clocked where his officers were, got a pint of something filthy and went to look at the paintings that lined the walls. Supernatural subjects: watercolours of graveyards; wood-cut prints of dancing skeletons; occult modernist pieces that were all clashing shades and angles. He checked out the juke box. It was the modern sort, millions of choices, probably downloaded from somewhere. The list of suggested tracks demonstrated an interest in the spooky, from mockery like 'The Monster Mash' to Black Sabbath and Led Zeppelin. He hit a button, and found . . . two pounds a play – bloody hell. It had been a while since he'd used one of these. The introduction to 'Don't Fear the Reaper' rang out under the noise of the crowd.

Costain had noted the arrival of the rest of his unit. It was getting too crowded in here to be doing what he was doing. Already all the other chairs had been taken from his table, on two occasions without asking, with just an annoyed glance in his direction. He put his book back in his pocket and stood. That bearded bloke across the way who was now obviously watching the stairs hadn't been disturbed similarly. He was still reading, a discreet space kept around him even now the bar was packed. He had been, for some minutes now, making eye contact with Costain every now and then. Now the undercover watched as a young woman approached the man directly and he looked up. He . . . oh, there we go, he'd done that checking thing Sefton had mentioned: there had been just a little hand gesture, a curl of the fingers in a sort of well-practised spiral, and then he'd nodded. The woman walked down the stairs and out of Costain's line of sight.

He turned to look at a noise from the bar. A group of lads, well dressed but very modern, in jackets and jeans, were suddenly laughing and whooping as if a goal had been scored. They were pointing in the direction of where the woman had just gone. 'Vanished!' he heard them yelling to each other. 'Right through the floor!'

Okay. Those were guys without the Sight, and the stairway downwards was something of the Sight, invisible to those without the ability. He looked back. The bearded man, who was obviously some sort of gatekeeper of that stairwell, was looking pained at the celebrations by the bar. Very gauche. They were letting the wrong sort of people in here nowadays. The man visibly sighed, then slowly and purposefully closed his book and looked expect-antly at the crowd, making eye contact once more with all those Costain had noticed earlier. They were the ones, Costain was sure now, who could see what he was sitting beside.

Costain stood. At the same moment, many others moved too. The people separating themselves from the throng formed not so much a queue, but an awkward spread, waiting for their turn. The ones who had wandered over . . . yeah, he could feel the sudden shift in gravity . . . you couldn't tell if an individual had the Sight, but when they all moved together . . . They were, largely, the ones who looked poor or wore older clothing. He looked back to the rest. There was a real anger in the room about what was happening now. A couple of the better-dressed people had marched over to insert themselves into this rough queue, and there was mocking laughter, rolling of eyes, people turning away in annoy-ance. Costain could feel the social forces in conflict here, a frustra-tion that, if it had been later in the evening, might have led to something kicking off. Hence the bouncer – he'd woken up a bit and was looking around.

Costain wished he knew more about the nature of the defences in this place, in case he had to make a sudden exit.

'See you later, then,' said Ross to the bloke at the bar, and she made to get up. She'd started a conversation about safety on the streets, in light of the riots, and had hoped the man might say something about the Ripper murders. But he hadn't.

He stopped her now. 'I didn't realize you were . . . one of them.'

She tried to look non-committal.

'We were told we were going to get to go down there too, sometime soon. You know, under the new proprietors.'

'Oh.'

'Obviously that message hasn't got through. I mean, I don't even know how we'd do that now, since it turns out to be true that we're not even able to see the bally stairs, but . . . could you remind those in charge? When you get down there?'

'Of course,' she said, and headed over. So, there was a whole other level to this place, and only people with the Sight were allowed down there. That was where juice for the operation might be found. Maybe juice that would help with her own plans too. She had to find some sources of information about occult objects, about one object in particular. She had to get down there. She wanted just to march over, but down there – given that it didn't exist as far as a lot of these people knew – surely counted, in the terms Quill had set out for the evening, as a private space. So to go down there would be to go against orders. She noted Quill nearby and walked past him, raising her eyebrows in a question.

Quill seemed to consider for a moment, then, just before he was gone out of her eyeline he nodded, which was a relief.

She headed for the stairs, and the man beside them met her gaze. He made a gesture so quick she couldn't follow it, a grab of nothing, and she felt the air flatten against her face . . . as she mentally recited the couple of lines of nonsense syllables that Sefton had taught them from the scroll he'd found in the Docklands ruins. She'd been repeating them to herself ever since so it was second nature.

He nodded her through.

Without looking back, she was aware of Quill doing the same and being allowed to follow.

She walked quickly down the stairs. At the bottom was another set of doors exactly like the ones that led into the bar on the floor above. Ross marched right in as if she belonged.

In the milling group waiting beside the stairs, Sefton had managed to strike up conversations with a few people, by just rudely butting in. It seemed to be the sort of interaction they were used to. He was being the classic undercover – not asking questions, but instead, annoyingly, moving the conversation away from the subject, making people focus on it again, while listening to what was said in the background. It turned out that what was most on the minds of these people was what was going to change about this venue. They mentioned a number of other pubs they might try, and Sefton made a mental note of them. Then there was the issue of whether or not the Ripper murders were going to be pinned on 'their lot'. These people were unsure if there was anyone aware enough of 'their lot' to be doing any such pinning. There was a little bit of a paranoid streak to them; they seemed pretty certain that soon enough bad things would happen. He caught whispers from people who'd look in his direction, and when he noticed and returned the gaze, look away: too many outsiders, too many changes. He heard someone refer to the Ripper as 'proper London', but there were urgent denunciations of that until the person who'd said it had to admit that they didn't know anything about what was going on now, that they'd been talking about the Ripper as part of London history.

The people who were doing the talking here, all in all, seemed to need to gossip about everything surrounding the Ripper murders but appeared not to have any idea how or why they were being committed. They were as scared and puzzled as any other slice of the general public. Like the general public, they were in general much more concerned about their own patch. But there were also those here who weren't talking. Sefton saw a couple of sighing expressions, a couple of looks that suggested that what might be the Sighted members of this community had seen what Quill's team had seen when they'd watched the news on television. Those were the ones who didn't gossip so easily.

He found himself making surprised eye contact with Costain when both the non-undercover members of his team suddenly took it upon themselves to do what they themselves had decided was beyond their operational parameters and move on down to the next level, without even consulting them. He lost the expression swiftly as he looked back to beardy waistcoat, who was beside him, now looking nervous.

'I can't see anything there,' he said, nodding towards the stairwell. 'Can you?'

Sefton didn't know how to answer him. Here was a surprise: beardy waistcoat was someone Privileged, who knew how to at least make a start at using the occult power of London, or so he'd indicated, but who wasn't himself one of the Sighted. Seeing that look on Sefton's face, he looked suddenly crestfallen. 'I know you're able to – I can tell when someone can; I mean, I pick up on the body language—'

'Mate, I'm just learning about this stuff too—'

'But there's nothing to stop me trying to go down there, is there? To support you, if nothing else. Whether or not change is coming to the Goat tonight, we ought to be allowed access to . . . whatever that man is guarding. Come on, we succeed or fail together.' Suddenly he was off, taking his place in the actual queue which was now forming out of the vague one, and Sefton could only feel he should go with him. The abusive woman had just gone down the stairs, and in front of them now was one of the angrier-looking young men of the hipster crowd. The man with the book invited him to step forward, making that checking gesture again with one hand. The youth did so, and walked straight over the top of the stairwell, his feet walking on what looked to Sefton like empty air, keeping going until he'd covered the space to the far wall. Then, furious, he whirled, looking back at the gatekeeper.

Who stared calmly back at him.

The bouncer took a concerned step from his corner.

After a moment of considering his options, the young man turned on his heel and marched for the door. The gatekeeper looked back to Sefton and beardy waistcoat, and visibly sighed when he saw Sefton. Here came more trouble.

Sefton's instinct as an undercover was to avoid confrontation. He really should just walk forward, deal with the man's gesture, get down the stairs, if being able to block the gesture and see the stairs was enough, if there wasn't actually full-on apartheid in place. But in character – maybe in reality too – he didn't feel like being *allowed* to go anywhere.

'What are you reading?' he asked the man. His first question of the night. Actually it was more of a challenge.

The gatekeeper looked surprised. He held up his book, which had a blank cover. Blue, tatty, like an ancient library book. Sefton had wondered if there was a list of people inside it, to go with the gesture and the ability to see what you were walking down. To get a look at that list might be valuable. He plucked the book out of the man's hands and opened it. He could feel beardy waistcoat behind him, going with it, craning to look at what was revealed inside these pages. Sefton realized, in that second, that he'd already handled books that could have done him considerable harm, that he'd just been unprofessionally reckless. That was where playing this character had led him. No, there was nothing inside this book to harm him. Indeed, there was nothing. The fine dusty pages were blank. Genuinely blank. It was just a prop, something to shore up this man's authority. If there were rules, they weren't written down. Sefton flicked all the way through to make sure, then he gave it back to the man, who was now smiling patronizingly at him. 'Thanks,' said Sefton, 'didn't like the ending.' The look on the man's face said that Sefton had really pushed it, that now it would be touch and go whether to let him in. Finally, the man made the gesture and Sefton bounced his silent question away and he was allowed to proceed.

He was about to go down the stairs, but from behind him came an odd, awkward laugh. 'A book of rules?' It was beardy waistcoat, looking baffled at Sefton. 'I could see they're written in a very tight hand, but I didn't get a good look at a single one of them. What was that you said about the ending? Come on, did you see how to do this?'

The gatekeeper looked despairingly at the young man. He didn't even bother to make the gesture. He just slowly shook his head.

'Oh, come on, this isn't fair. Tonight we were told we were going to be allowed . . .' Beardy waistcoat looked pleadingly to Sefton, who could only look steadily back in return. Anger made the young man's face suddenly flush. The oppressed minority he'd thought he was doing a favour to had progressed further than he had. 'I've worked so hard . . .'

The gatekeeper looked towards the diffuse, impatient queue that was standing all around, and by implication to the bouncer, who was even now sauntering over.

Beardy gave Sefton a look that could kill. A look like a mask falling that Sefton felt he would remember for a long time. Then he was pushing his way back through the crowd, heading for the door.

Sefton turned and calmly walked down the stairs.

Costain had noted the reaction to the bouncer from the guy who hadn't been allowed down the stairwell. So the bouncer could be seen by everyone, not just the Sighted. He wandered over and found himself casually standing next to the man. If this *was* a man, a real person. He looked real enough.

'Excuse me, kind sir,' he said, 'I was thinking I might head downstairs. May I?' Asking questions in this circumstance was something his character, the newbie, would certainly do.

The bouncer barely reacted. 'Depends,' he said. He sounded like a clichéd comedy bouncer too, brutal vowels and hardly opening his mouth. 'Are you on the list?'

'I'm not sure.'

'Then you're not on the list.'

'Where is this list?'

'You can't see the list.'

'Who else is on the list?'

'Are you on the list?'

'Possibly.'

'Then you can find out.'

'But not from you?'

'Depends.'

'On what?'

'Are you on the list?'

It was as if he was a character in a video game. Costain was pretty sure now that the bouncer wasn't a human being, but something made by someone. A sort of deliberately placed 'ghost'. But one that the non-Sighted were very much aware of. 'Is the list real? Or is it just some sort of metaphor? Does whether or not you're on the list change from moment to moment? Is it down to how confident you are or how you dress or who your parents were? Please, dear sir, enlighten me.'

The bouncer paused for a second. Processing. But no, there was nothing robotic about those quivering jowls. Whatever he was had been made of emotion and flesh. 'Depends,' he finally decided.

Costain sighed. His way out of this place, should he need it, was what it was. No advantage to be found here. It was time to share the risk his unit was taking. That was the right thing to do, and these days he always did the right thing.

Besides, Ross was down there. Among the powerful shit.

He headed for the stairs and patiently waited until it was his turn with the gatekeeper, who looked at him as if it was incredible that *two* black men had come his way this evening. He made the gesture and sighed at the result, letting him through as if the sky had fallen. Rules were rules, he seemed to be thinking, but he didn't have to like what the rules allowed.

Costain was about to walk past him with confidence, the star of this picture. Then he remembered the character he was playing. He stopped and made his body language submissive and dropped his gaze to the floor. 'Excuse me, sir,' he said.

The gatekeeper inclined his head, and Costain went down the stairs.

SIX

Quill noted Costain's arrival. Now all his unit were two floors below street level. Exactly what they had gone down into was another question. At first sight, this bar looked like the one immediately above it, but many of the details were different, and, with the Sight suddenly putting a queasy feeling of gravity in his gut, those details seemed drastically important. He felt as if he was already deep under the earth, as if rescue was a long way off, far above. When he first got down here he'd had to stop himself from going over to Ross and indicating they should both pull out immediately. But there was no operational reason for him to feel like that. Ross had walked straight over to a barwoman who looked a degree more specialized again than the one in the bar above, with a distinctly old-fashioned touch to her uniform, curls to her hair that looked to be from some era he couldn't pin down, and, startlingly, white pancake make-up that made her look like a mime artist. The dress code for those who'd got down here was clearly older, poorer, often specifically London in nature. There were remnants of uniform: London transport; real cavalry jackets; what Quill realized was a zookeeper, even. The look was distinctive, but hardly impressive in the way of a fashion show. They also showed signs of harm: the odd missing finger; bruises and cuts displayed proudly. There was something else about them now: their voices were hushed, they kept glancing towards the door. This lot were in their familiar place, obviously used to being here . . . but tonight they were afraid of what remained above. To get out of what had started to feel like a footie boozer with a bunch of away fans in it hadn't eased the pressure very much.

In the far corner, in the same place as on the floor above, was a different tweedy bloke with a beard, sitting guarding yet another downward stairwell. As above, so below. So there was another level beneath this. Of course.

Quill went over to the juke box, in exactly the same place as in the bar above. This one was an old-fashioned job with vinyl singles, and the selections were all songs about London: the Kinks; Blur; the Small Faces. To play one cost only twenty pence. But he didn't feel like being the first to select a track. He went to a table and picked up a menu. These cocktails had names like the Lambeth Walk, the Ally Sloper, the Black Shock. That last name made something echo in his head. Like déjà vu for something that hadn't yet happened. Quill didn't know one bottle of champers from another, but the top of the range down here was considerably cheaper than upstairs. He went to check out the paintings on the walls. These were all portraits of individuals, their names underneath, nothing spooky about them. Though, wait a sec, Aleister Crowley – there was a name he recognized: fat bloke, a sort of coked-up mania about him, half performance, half something a bit more worrying. Beside him: Dion Fortune; Austin Osman Spare; Gerald Gardner . . . There were many more – a complete circuit of them on the walls – and in between the portraits were what seemed to be action scenes, or at least metaphorical versions of such. Here were a group of figures under the searchlights and blimps of wartime London, their arms arranged in stark stick-figure angles, protesting against or attacking what was surely the threatening shape of a falling V2 rocket. Here was a parting of the ways, a splitting, as many figures walked many different paths, some falling off into nothingness, into a sunlit map of London.

So someone in this community knew at least a bit about the

history of it. Looking around, though, Quill decided that even the punters down here seemed about as useless as the general public he was used to.

Ross looked into the white face of the barmaid. 'What can I get you, my darling?' said the woman, her mask of make-up not equalling the welcome of her broad East End accent. The mask was extraordinary, now she was up close. Some of it, around the eyes, was obviously cosmetics on the surface of skin, but some of it was absolutely smooth, blank, as if there was only the artificial colour of the cosmetics and nothing underneath. If she wiped it all off, the woman looked as if she might be just eyes and what was around them and a mouth floating in mid-air.

Ross realized that she was staring and ordered a glass of red she had no intention of drinking. The barmaid gave it to her. Ross could see fine old cuts in almost every inch of the skin of her hands, making it look like a map on vellum. Her fingernails were cut to the quick. 'And how are you going to pay for that?'

Ross made a decision based on what she'd seen at the New Age fair. 'Not with money.'

'Good. Were they upstairs already? Are they going to come down here?'

'Who?'

'Well, that's even better, you going the right way about things without knowing what's going on. All right, what have you got to offer?'

What had the fortune-teller at the New Age fair lost? Fingers, teeth . . . 'Blood?'

The woman laughed. 'Bit much, my dear. Never met anyone before who *opened* with that. Tell you what, I'll start a slate for you, and eventually you can make a donation. Blimey, I can't get over it, a first-timer who actually wants to follow the form. You came here wanting something, I take it?'

Did she know?

The barmaid obviously read the expression on her face. 'I haven't just rifled through your drawers, love. It's why most people come here.'

Sefton followed the abusive young woman to a group of people seemingly familiar to her, hoping they'd take him for an acquaintance of hers and that would give him a way in. But the woman looked sidelong at him as soon as he got there, like a bird of prey needing to alter the angle of its vision to get perspective on its target. Perhaps, Sefton thought nervously, that was exactly what she was doing. He was among power, of varying degrees, and who knew who was hiding theirs? The users of it were all looking at him, and at Costain, now he turned to look, as if the two of them were a terrible development. He should think of this lot, as he did when he was in a gang, as being armed and dangerous. 'Fucking poser jacket,' said the abusive woman, actually raising her voice so he'd be sure to hear. 'How did you get down here, when you look like a complete fuckwit?'

Sefton was too intrigued now to get in her face again. Besides, a character shouldn't be one note. Her straightforward aggression was a relief after the chill coming from the rest of this lot. Also, she'd chosen a non-racial approach this time. Presumably she'd exhausted that material. 'I'm a complete fuckwit.'

Sudden mocking laughter erupted from behind Sefton. It sounded almost like a voice saying 'ha ha ha', in an extraordinarily cynical, almost self-critical way. 'At least *someone* here knows themselves.'

Sefton turned to see that an extraordinary figure had joined the group. He looked middle-aged, with a face that made him look as if he had some sort of wasting disease, a skull that, under a shock of bright red hair, boasted handsome cheekbones and eyes that seemed continuously challenging, rolling and staring. Those eyes knew everything about him, in a moment. Sefton found the undercover part of him reacting, certain he'd been recognized, that somehow this man he'd never seen before knew who he really was. He had to stop himself from marching for the door, telling himself there was no logical reason to do so, that this still might *just* be a feeling. Besides, the look of the man had stopped him in his tracks. His jacket was made of newspaper, from enormous edifices of Victoriana to brash red-top headlines, flowing and changing. The pattern on the man's trousers was a grid that resembled tartan, but it flexed like a topographical map. The man's grin was increasing as he took in what Sefton was now absolutely bloody certain he'd learned about him. Never mind walking out; in a moment, Sefton might have to sprint.

'Don't mind me,' the man said, 'I'm not real.'

'What do you mean?'

The man shook his head, impatient with the wrong tack being taken. 'Don't like that question. I'm going to answer a different one. Yes, I know *all* about *you*. Fortunately, I don't care.' Sefton kept his fear in check, making himself look calm once more. But still, this lot would now know there was *something* dodgy about him. 'I might know anything about anyone,' the man continued, 'with just one look. All the information of this world flows down to me.' He poked a finger into Sefton's jacket, and Sefton felt the vanes in his breast pocket jerk at the contact, trying to point towards the gravity of the man. The group had all turned to look at the new arrival, he realized, as if he was some sort of touchstone for them. 'You're all right, you are. He's all right, everybody!' That had been a call with no expectation that it would have any result, an irony at the man's own lack of influence, but Sefton could see that it had actually had some effect. 'Oh, it's all going pear-shaped tonight,' the man continued, looking back to Sefton. 'Our barmaid over there,' he indicated, 'I know her name but I will not share it; she made the mistake of continuing with the old ways, of not allowing coin to stay in her palm. The Keel brothers did not like that. The penalty was the loss of her face. *Les yeux sans visage*, as some pretender once said. The Keels would like her to continue working here, to please the old clientele even as they begin to fleece them. They have promised to give her face back if she's a good girl. But tonight we'll see.' He looked Sefton up and down, an arrogant and yet somehow self-mocking smirk on his face. 'We all love our masks, don't we? It's the only option when a circle has to fit inside a square. When one song has to be sung to the tune of another. The distortion continues. Ever feel you're being bent out of shape?' He whirled a finger in the air as if sampling the oppressive quality of the air, and then licked it, seeming to be entertained by the taste. He pointed downwards. 'The things I have to crawl up through to attend these soirées now. The things you people put up with. The things you *allow*.' Now his gaze was fixed again on Sefton. 'But still we get *new* arrivals. Oh, sorry, I said the N word –' he made a quick, scathing glance at the gathering – 'sorry.' He suddenly held out his hand to Sefton. 'I am John, and I was born in London. They call me the Rat King. When they call me anything at all.'

Sefton understood that that was a hell of a thing. In a company of people who kept their names like hoarded treasure, here he was being offered one for free. From someone who apparently knew who and what he was. He felt himself trusting this man with his own real identity because of that single surprising gesture. He shook the hand. 'The fuckers of this culture,' said the Rat King, 'are going to be troubled by what you might bring to their community.' He enunciated every syllable, underlining their meaning and put an entire landscape of irony between himself and that last word. 'So I am delighted to see you.' He leaned closer to whisper in Sefton's ear. 'But I am afraid I *don't* know the thing you most want to find out.'

His meaningful glance made Sefton certain that the Rat King was talking about the Ripper.

Costain, meanwhile, aware of the looks he was getting and not wanting to be seen as coming on too strong, had been looking for differences between this bar and the ones above. He was now inspecting one of several large cracks in the plaster of the walls. Were these walls under pressure from being underground? Pretty rubbish construction, if so. There was something . . . he leaned closer to the wall and saw something sparkling inside one of the cracks, something . . . silver. He could feel it on his face: the material in the crack was freezing cold. Yeah, here was that silver goo again. Only this time it seemed to be being used to hold this place together.

Quill managed to overhear a few conversations that expressed horror or wonder at the activities of the Ripper. Some of this lot had definitely, having seen the news on TV, noted the glowing figure leaving the crime scene, but apart from that, not a thing suggested that this community was better informed on the subject than the wider public. Also, nobody had said anything about a smiling man. He'd heard a couple of conversations where people had talked about making 'sacrifices to London', as if the metropolis was the thing this lot worshipped. Whatever plan the Smiling Man had used Rob Toshack to hint obliquely about to Quill's team, this group didn't seem to be in on it. Quill was backing up, trying to move round to join the fringes of another conversation, when he hit something with the back of his thighs.

He turned round and saw that he'd encountered the long legs of a man in black jeans, black T-shirt and black leather jacket who was sitting in a discreet corner of the bar, his mobile phone in his hand. He had a long face, caring, slightly sad, with a worried look around his mouth, and a shock of dark hair. He was looking as if Quill had disturbed him in the middle of a thought.

Quill realized, to his surprise, that he recognized this man. He didn't quite know from where, but he had a feeling that it wasn't in a police context.

'Can I help you?' said the man.

Quill became aware that he had been staring, and at the same moment knew where he'd seen this guy before. It had been on the inside flap of a book he'd read to Jessica, and on another that Sarah had been reading in bed, and he'd been surprised that the same bloke had written both. 'Here,' he said, 'aren't you that writer?'

'I'm *a* writer.'

'Children's books?'

'All sorts of books.'

'What are you doing here?'

'It's usually pretty quiet, and I can write, sometimes.'

'I mean, so you've got, I mean you must have . . . to get down those stairs . . .' Quill pointed to his own eyes.

'The Sight? Of course.'

'Of course. Of course. Myself, I got it when I touched a pile of soil. But of course it's not . . . always that. Is it?' *Arrgh.* Why couldn't he just talk normally to this bloke?

The man paused as if wondering whether or not he should answer, then went ahead, possibly thinking it was the quickest way out of the conversation. 'Someone handed me an object at a signing. They said they hoped it would give me "inspiration". It gave me a headache and a bunch of terrible visions on the way to the airport. And, as it turned out, every time I visited London. So the inspiration it gave me was mostly to live abroad.'

'And you got to the Goat . . . ?'

'When I got used to the idea of London being horrifying, I did a bit of exploring and found a few places. This bar has been relatively friendly, but I worry about the new management.'

'Have you been further downstairs?'

'No. But . . .' He considered for a moment and was absolutely silent, looking aside as if weighing up a few different possibilities. Quill found himself wanting to interrupt, but was too interested in what the man was about to say. 'No,' the man finally said again, as if it was a decision. Then he smiled broadly at Quill. 'Good to meet you.'

Quill understood he was being politely dismissed. 'And you. I'll let you get back to . . .' He gestured in the abstract direction of whatever the man had been looking at on his phone. 'Cheers.'

He headed off, kicking himself for asking a lot of bloody copper interview questions, completely ignoring his own rules, all because he'd run into someone who was, presumably, famous.

He realized there was something else he really should have said. He stopped. He headed back.

The man looked up again at his arrival, the look on his face now a little tired.

'My wife's a big fan of yours,' said Quill.

'Oh. Thank you.'

'Okay, bye.' He headed off again, knowing that for just a moment there he had sounded like Columbo and that his next move should really be to reveal the man's guilt in some extraordinary crime.

Then he realized again, stopped again. Damn it. He headed back.

This time the man looked up with only a slight raise of his eyebrows. *Oh, come on now.*

'Sorry, just checking, your name would in actual fact be . . . ?'

'Neil Gaiman.'

'Great. Thanks.'

'Okay.'

'Okay. Bye.' Quill walked quickly off into the crowd again, mentally rolling his eyes at his own gaucheness. When he told the others about it, it would be a tale of him getting loads of juice through his clever undercover teasing out of a conversation.

Something was happening ahead now: raised voices, people moving swiftly away from the doors. He made his way through the crowd to see as two powerfully built forty-something males, balding, pot bellies, facial hair, six foot one or so, marched into the room. They wore black vest-tops, shiny leather trousers and immaculate long black coats that didn't look like they'd be comfortable in summer. Lots of pockets, possibility of concealed weapons. The Keel brothers, Quill presumed, Barry and Terry. He recognized one of them from the New Age fair, but they hadn't spoken; he doubted the man had got a good look at him. He let out a breath of relief. Aggro he could handle. Famous people? Not so much.

Barry Keel was looking around the room as if he'd just walked in on an unexpected orgy. 'What the fuck,' he said, 'is going on here?'

Ross examined the new arrivals. No lieutenants in their wake, no entourage. Nobody in the crowd had stepped forward to answer them. The weird new bloke who'd been hanging around near Sefton was looking alternately angry and almost gleeful, anticipating trouble, scampering about, trying to get the best view. The barmaid had tensed and taken a step back from the bar.

'You!' Barry Keel went over to the bloke sitting by the stairs that led downwards. 'I'll say to you what I said to the one up there: You gatekeepers still aren't letting all our customers come down here. Today was the deadline. When are you lot going to get it?' He looked around, addressing the group in general. 'This is *our* place now. We *bought* it.' His accent, Ross noted, was a lot more modern London than the ones she'd heard from this crowd. 'So you lot *are* going to let paying customers enter, let the cleansing breath of the outside world clean up this outsider culture of yours a bit, and you –' he pointed to the barmaid – 'are going to take the coin of the realm, and stop with all this self-harming sacrifice barter shit. Or I'll take something else off you, right?' He made a gesture with his hand that had something showy and kung fu about it, but it was also obviously a genuine threat.

The barmaid stayed where she was, but Ross could see that she was breathing deeply, terrified. 'I thought I'd have a bit longer,' she said. 'But fuck it.' She raised her voice. 'You can keep my face,' she shouted. 'I've been here since before you were born, and I'm not keeping filthy *coin* in my hand.' She looked around the group, hoping desperately for support, and Ross could see a few nodding heads. But there were no voices raised in support. This lot didn't have it in them to stand up for anything. The woman looked suddenly, horribly, alone. Ross looked over to Costain and found that he was making eye contact with her. A tiny shake of the head.

Ross made herself step back from the bar.

Barry was looking at the barmaid with what seemed to be genuine sadness and frustration. 'You try and make a deal,' he said, 'you try and do this nicely.' He made his sudden gesture again, and this time Ross felt a slam of weight behind it.

The woman screamed. She slapped her palms to her face. She held them there for a moment as the crowd stared at her. Then, as if realizing she wasn't actually in any pain, she lowered them.

There were spaces where her eyes had been. Ross could see right through her head.

'I can't see,' she said, gently. She put a finger to where her eye had been . . . and then straight through it.

The Rat King stepped forwards, glaring, and put an arm around her shoulders. 'Come with me,' he said. He glowered as he led her towards the stairwell. 'You had your chance,' he said bleakly to the rest of the crowd, who were gaping in horror at what had been done to her. 'Well done. Love your "community". Turns out it's not a good idea to crowd surf when there isn't a safety net.'

Ross glanced back to Costain and was surprised to find that he had stepped behind the bar. As she watched, he stepped back out again, without looking at her. He'd obviously taken a quick look to see if there was anything important back there. She was the only one who'd thought to look in that direction.

'Wait,' said the barmaid, 'the new girl.' Ross realized she meant her. She looked back and saw that the barmaid had blindly stretched out a hand and the Rat King had paused to let her do this. Ross went to her, let her take her hand. The barmaid, with surprising strength, pulled her close, almost into an embrace that smelt of lavender and mothballs. Keeping hold of Ross' hand, she quickly felt for her own pocket, concealed somewhere inside her uniform, and shoved something into Ross' grasp. It was a business card. 'You followed the traditions,' she said. 'You wanted to barter. You deserve something in return. Listen. I got a strong feeling about you and what you were after. Whatever it is, I think it's going to be there, at the next auction.'

Ross looked at the card. There was just a bare date, and a map that seemed to swirl before her gaze, like a view down through a hole in the middle of the card. 'Thank you,' she said.

'You stay alive,' said the barmaid.

Then the Rat King hustled her off and led her carefully down the stairwell. The gatekeeper there stood up, glaring at the Keel brothers, as if daring them to interfere.

Costain had seen Ross take something from the barmaid. Now he noted which pocket she put it into. *Interesting.* Then he turned back to observe the Keel brothers. He was in an enclosed space with deadly weapons, and these two were between him and the door; otherwise he'd have already given the signal for everyone to abort.

'From now on,' Barry was saying to the crowd, 'no exceptions. Money will be taken. You may have noticed we've started to advertise this pub, only in the right places. We have produced actual fliers. The new punters, the people who've got interested in this stuff in the last few years, they're young and have spare cash, they have certain expectations about their social occasions. You will follow the dress code.' He grabbed a young woman near him and threw her to the ground. 'Smart! Casual! The weird fashions don't *add* anything, you stupid fuckers – they just mean nobody normal's going to want to hang around in a bar with you and drink our premium lager while you sip on your glasses of warm tap water!'

Terry, in contrast, had his hands raised, trying to be the voice of reason. 'Ever since whatever changed a few years back to make it easier for us all to openly use the power that comes from a deep knowledge of the shape of London . . .' He seemed to react to mutterings from the crowd. 'Yes, I'm saying all this out loud. Look. No bolt of lightning from above. No punishment for talking *clearly*, not in gobbledegook. Me and the bro, in modern gear, speaking like real people, paying hard cash for objects with London history' – and stealing some of them, thought Costain, if their convictions were anything to go by – 'we have got ourselves a lot of knowledge and a lot of power. We didn't need to do all the accents and costumes, we didn't see ourselves as poor noble outsiders, we didn't need to wait for some gatekeeper to give us the nod and say we were *allowed*. We proved that money can be used to shape the power of London too, whether London *likes* it or not.' Costain remembered what Sefton had said about the price tags feeling weirdly out of place on those objects in the shop. 'Still, we played nice with the culture we found: you lot, who assumed you owned this town, just because you did all the things that had always been done. We were cajoling, we extended the hand of friendship. You paid no bloody attention. But now we are in the middle of what we modern people call a *double-dip recession*. We need to *monetize* this place. So you lot will be dragged, kicking and screaming, into the eighteenth century.' No voices were raised to contradict him, but Costain saw people looking angry, heard whispers. 'Listen, a lot of you at least keep a toe in the real world; you know it doesn't have to be so hard for us now. When the big change – whatever it was – happened, it was like the people who can do what we do . . . it was like we *won*. So why are you lot still *hiding*?'

'Cut to the chase, Tezzer,' said Barry.

'The point is, whatever you think of us, *we* are like *you*. Our brand identity for this pub will embrace the essentials of what the Goat and Compasses has always been about. But from now on, on the special nights, for downstairs, we'll be charging admission.'

There were yells of protest from the crowd. 'This is the last night of the Goat, then,' someone said.

'Pair of fucking faggots,' said a woman with dark hair whom Costain had seen with Sefton. She meant the Keel brothers.

Terry turned to her, and flicked a sudden gesture that he seemed to think better of before it did her harm. The crowd flinched anyway. 'I am also fed up with you insulting our customers. You're barred.'

'*Who's* barred?'

'. . . whoever you are!'

'You don't even know my name! Your brand doesn't have much hold over someone without a brand of her own, cocksucker!'

'I'll brand you—!' He raised a hand to do it.

Ross stepped in front of her.

Costain saw Sefton react, minutely. The two of them had a responsibility to their non-undercover colleagues. They had to do something to move this conflict around and let themselves and their colleagues head for the door. But before either of them could do anything, Terry Keel lowered his hand.

'You tell her, love,' he said to Ross. 'She can stay tonight, but she'd better not come back.' He turned to the others and deliberately didn't hear the woman's next comment. 'Look,' he said, 'it'll just be a fiver or something. It's not like you lot have actual rules that you need to vote on or something. You just have traditions. An unwritten constitution, not worth the paper it's printed on. It's not as if you're institutionally racist, for instance.' He underlined the words with irony. 'But your "we like old-timey stuff" policy has successfully kept away potential *customers*.'

Barry took up the narration, nodding pleasantly to Costain and Sefton. 'Like these two modern and affluent-looking young gentlemen. Who are entirely conversant with a bit of the old—' He made the checking hand gesture, and Costain automatically now threw what Sefton had called a blanket over his thoughts. Even as he did so, he noticed something very worrying: that gesture . . . hadn't it been just a tiny bit . . . different?

Costain heard his phone beep at the same instant Sefton's did. The two undercovers looked at each other. Well, okay, Costain reasoned, so they were carrying modern tech, they could just say sorry and—

But a look of horror had come over the face of Barry Keel. An expression that Costain recognized from his nightmares of being caught while undercover. 'You fuckers,' he said. 'You're—'

Costain leaped forward and punched the man in the stomach.

*

Terry Keel lunged at Sefton. The man looked as if he knew how to fight. Low centre of gravity. He was probably packing gestures like his brother's, which could cause harm above and beyond whatever he could do with his fists. Barry had somehow used that gesture to read their phones. Their own phones, which were full of police-related numbers.

Sefton ducked the first two blows, then hit Terry one-two on the body, and winced at the pain in his knuckles as the man fell. He wasn't used to doing this without gloves. He took a moment to look around, to try to find Quill and Ross, to see if they could get to the door.

He could only find where Barry Keel was lying near Costain, clutching his abdomen. He was craning his neck painfully to bellow at the ceiling. 'Marlon!'

Something fell from the roof.

It was a figure, Sefton saw in that second. He managed to leap out of the way, and it landed with a crash where he had been. Sefton turned to see that it was the bouncer from upstairs, who was even now looking to Barry Keel for orders. The leather-coated man gestured to both Sefton and Costain. 'Rip them apart.'

As both Barry and Terry got to their feet, Sefton looked to Costain, found only a shared disinclination to be here, looked back. The bouncer was advancing swiftly.

There were screams and shouts from the crowd, many of whom – with Quill and Ross among them, he hoped – were now finding the space to run for the door.

The bouncer was herding himself and Costain, Sefton realized, back towards a corner, away from the door and the stairwell. Sefton reached into his pocket, and pulled out the vanes. He waved them purposefully towards the bouncer, as if he had any idea how to use them to attack, in the way their last owner had used them on Quill. But the bouncer paid no attention. He made little grasping movements with his hands, waiting for his chance to grab and rend. As soon as they reached the corner, neither of them would be able to get away.

This was the sort of moment, thought Sefton, where, in his former life, there would have been a horde of uniforms outside, ready to race in and bust heads on his behalf.

Now there was nobody. He and Costain were just going to have to run at the same moment and hope desperately that one or both would make it out. Sefton prepared himself to sprint for his life.

'Hoi! Mush!' The bouncer turned at the shout.

Quill leaped from the crowd and smashed the bouncer across the head with a champagne bottle he must have nicked from the bar.

The bouncer spun as if to grab Quill. Quill jumped away from him. Sefton and Costain ran for the stairs. Sefton had the feeling that Quill had started running at that moment too.

Ahead of them was a mass of people falling over each other to get upstairs. They were going to have to push their way through. Sefton glimpsed Ross up ahead, shoving to stay out of the crowd as it tried to take her with it.

Something grabbed Sefton from behind and threw him backwards. He was aware, in that second, of the same thing happening to Costain.

Barry and Terry Keel stood over them, Barry in front of Terry. He made a complicated gesture and suddenly something bright was burning in his hand. The bar was emptying. Sefton couldn't see where his colleagues had gone. He hoped they'd got out. He scrambled backwards and managed to get to his feet. Costain did the same, putting the length of the room between himself and the Keels. The bouncer moved to join the brothers, flexing its fingers once more. Sefton remembered it had been ordered to rip them apart.

Barry Keel drew back his hand, ready to throw his fire.

Sefton had a sudden thought. Just playground stuff: rock, paper, scissors. They had fire but *he* had—

He grabbed the freezing phial from his pocket. At the instant Barry Keel threw his heat, Sefton threw what he only thought of as pure cold.

Sefton didn't understand what happened next. He was somehow in the air. Heat was all around. He was breathing in heat. Then suddenly a wall came flying up behind him and it was going to hit him so hard—

Someone was yelling at him.

Sefton opened his eyes. He couldn't breathe. The weight on his chest. There was nothing on his chest! No, no, he could breathe, just little breaths. Control it. Just little breaths. What was he looking at? He was looking at the tweedy man who'd been sitting by the stairs leading downwards. The tweedy man was walking quickly down those same stairs, which, a moment later, vanished, leaving a smooth wooden floor.

Oh. What was this stuff all over him? He looked down. That was . . . silver goo. But now it wasn't cold. It was sizzling, evaporating. There were gold bits too, streamers of them. Amongst it . . . the remains of a bouncer's bow tie.

The bouncer had exploded. Why had the bouncer exploded?

There was a smell of smoke. It was everywhere. There was heat, there was fire . . . all around him there was fire.

'Kev!' That's who was yelling at him, that was Quill's voice. 'Kev, don't move!'

He slowly got to his feet. His head was ringing. His body ached everywhere. He took a step forward . . .

With a yell, Costain grabbed him and hauled him back, inches from a dirty great hole in the floor of the bar. A chasm. On the other side of it were Quill and Ross, and there was . . .

A pile of ashes. A pile of ashes and bones with fragments of a leather coat. The remains of Barry Keel.

He'd done that. He'd had the offhand thought that the cold of the silver he'd thrown would somehow counteract the heat of what Keel was about to throw. But he'd been wrong. He'd been horribly, horribly wrong. What if the silver goo was like . . . fuel? Something you could store to make the power of London work if you didn't want to keep on making hand gestures, something that could keep things in place without continual work. The remains of the bouncer, which he was now covered with, were full of it. Presumably the killer they were looking for ran on it, was leaking it.

If that was the case, then Barry Keel had used one of his gestures to call up destructive fire into his hand, and Sefton had literally thrown petrol onto it. The resulting explosion, which had killed Keel, had made the bouncer combust too. Sefton could only hope that, since it had been made of something other than flesh, it couldn't actually be called a person, that he wasn't responsible for *two* deaths tonight.

That felt too big to cope with right now. He put it aside and let himself deal instead with his current situation.

He was standing on the edge of an abyss. The floor of the bar had largely vanished. All that remained of it, apart from the corner where they stood, were . . . scraps . . . not the jutting planks and disintegrating concrete you might expect, but ragged edges of wood, sticking out into space from the walls. A couple of narrow ragged strips of carpet still lay, impossibly, across the gap. It was like the aftermath not of a real-world explosion, but of something that had happened in a video game. Sefton supposed that this floor of the bar hadn't been made of real-world materials any more than the bouncer had been, that they'd disintegrated for the same reason. What Sefton assumed had been lower floors were gone completely. He could only imagine that the gatekeeper he'd seen walking calmly down into them had . . . somehow taken them away with him. Those thoughts was pushed immediately from his mind by what he saw down there in the void.

What had been revealed beneath it all was wondrous, horrifying, something of passion, not some part of a game designer's pixelated imagination.

He was looking into a pit of absolute darkness, at the bottom of which . . . Sefton's eyes struggled to understand it. Even with the Sight, it was difficult. He dropped to his knees, half to take a closer look, half in awe. He was aware that, beside him, Costain was looking downwards too.

It was a contortion of twisting silver, like the aurora borealis. It was a river of silver, and Sefton instantly understood that this was the same silver as at the Ripper crime scenes, the same silver that was covering him. It shone. The silver was dotted with tiny golden lights, and now Sefton looked closer he could see that they were threads, golden traceries that were spun all through the silver, as they were through the remains of the bouncer. The whole ribbon flexed in silence. He could feel an enormous coldness radiating from it. If he and Costain fell, they would fall into it, and the cold alone would be enough to destroy them. He glanced up at Costain. 'Can you see . . . ?'

'Yeah.' His voice held as much wonder as Sefton had ever heard from Costain.

Sefton sniffed. A smell was rising from the river of silver. It was very subtle. You'd need that much of this stuff together in order for the smell to register at all. It reminded him of . . . something very old, something ungraspable, always just out of reach, as one's own earliest experiences were out of reach. It was immensely beautiful, epic, touching him in ways familiar and grand that made him immediately love it. He wondered if Costain felt the same way about what he was seeing. You could just as easily fear this thing. It was outside their time and space, maybe in an 'outer borough' like the London of Brutus that he'd visited had been. It was . . . what was underneath everything, where the power was, the source, the great river. The void it was in . . . He wondered if this is what they would have seen if, when they'd been in the tunnels Losley had made between all her different houses, they'd knocked a hole in the wall. This void was what everything was sitting in, the bigger cosmos, again outside normal time and space.

Beside his foot, a bit of floor detached itself and fell away into that darkness.

Costain suddenly grabbed him and wrenched him to his feet, dragging him back from the brink.

Sefton gasped. He'd been . . . kind of transfixed by this thing. He made himself wake up and looked to the room again. The dirty great hole in the middle of the floor had slowly started to increase in size, the floor crumbling away into it on the other side too, the paths across the middle getting thinner by the second. Quill and Ross were stepping back from their edge.

'What happened to the other Keel brother?' Costain yelled to them.

'Escaped,' called Quill, moving away as another bit of floor dropped away. 'You two get over here! Now!'

Sefton forced himself not to hesitate, ignored the tightness in his lungs, the bruises and the injuries, and stepped quickly out onto one of the strips of carpet that lay across the gap, didn't think of what was below, aware the floor might give way under him at any moment. He clung to the thought of Joe, of getting home to him. Costain had taken the other strip of carpet, moving quickly beside him.

'It's going!' yelled Ross.

Sefton broke into a run. He felt the material falling away at his heels. It was crumbling to the left. He ran right, veering away from Quill and Ross. He leaped and in the same moment he heard Costain yell too. He daren't look to see what had happened to him.

Sefton hit the far wall at a corner by the crumbling edge where Ross and Quill stood. His hands scrabbled desperately. He just got one hand around the frame of one of the paintings, then swung to grab it with the other. He managed to hang on.

The picture held, impossibly. He swung in the void, his forearms in agony, his legs scrambling for a purchase they couldn't find.

Ross had Costain, he saw. She'd thrown herself to the edge of the crumbling floor, had grabbed Costain's hands. Quill had taken a step back, realizing that in a moment he might have to try and haul both of them back at once. Wondering if he could, if he was going to have to leave Costain to fall.

Sefton knew he had to do this or die. With one huge effort, all he had, he hauled himself up the painting. There was something extraordinary holding this thing on to the wall. The mad-looking fat man depicted in the portrait glared balefully at him. He started to swing from side to side, wondering about making the leap. 'Jimmy!' he shouted. 'It has to be now!'

'Okay!' bellowed Quill. He got to the edge of the remaining carpet, squatting, his hands out awkwardly.

Sefton flung himself sideways. He hit something. Quill had missed him! His hands grasped air. He was going to fall! He got about half his body onto the crumbling edge. He felt it giving beneath him. He'd got so far—

Quill grabbed him under the armpits and heaved and rolled. He was up, and out. They were on solid ground and both stumbling quickly to their feet as they felt it start to give way too.

'Don't bloody let go!' Costain bellowed at Ross.

'Like I'd do that!' She only had a few seconds before her arms gave out, a few seconds until the crumbling edge in front of her broke away and his weight dragged her with him. She *should* let him go. But she wouldn't.

She heaved upwards, thinking only that she was giving her life for no good reason when she couldn't actually save a colleague.

Then she felt Quill and Sefton join in. They grabbed Costain around the wrists and pulled too. The three of them managed to haul him up. They staggered upright. They dashed for the doors as the floor continued to vanish from under their feet. They burst through them together and the carpeted hallway disintegrated as they ran. They raced up the stairs, which fell away behind them too, until they were standing once more, safe, in an empty, evacuated, normal bar. They all looked back to the entrance to the staircase. It all suddenly fell away in one moment, leaving a gap in the floor which, with a slam, replaced itself with the same wooden flooring as the bar had.

They stood there, panting.

'This level must be the last one that's, you know, real,' said Costain.

'I think everyone else got out,' said Quill, 'including Neil Gaiman.'

'Neil Gaiman was down there?' said Ross. 'The writer?'

'Yeah,' said Quill. He looked around. He found a sign that said 'private function'. He put it where the stairwell had been. 'Nice guy.'

There was nobody in the bar upstairs either. Ross felt tremendous relief. 'I think Terry Keel must have got everyone out,' she said. 'I don't think he knew where the damage would stop.'

'Hell of a lawsuit,' said Quill, 'collapse of reality.'

'Shall we put out the call for him?' asked Ross. She found she had to sit down, and dropped onto a bar stool. She looked at the floor and concentrated on the conversation. She sensed them all doing that, all willing each other to come up with the next useful sentence.

'Complicated. Do you fancy lying to a court about the exact circumstances of him assaulting a police officer?'

'Or his brother being assaulted by a police officer,' said Costain.

'You what?!' said Sefton. Ross glanced up at him. He had a pent-up, angry look on his face.

'I meant me,' said Costain quickly, 'I meant me thumping him, all right? I wasn't thinking of—'

'In the circumstances,' said Quill quickly, stepping between them, 'I think you were acting to protect yourself and your colleagues, Tony. And you, Kev . . . well, I don't know what happened down there. Did you know that was going to happen?'

Sefton shook his head.

'As your superior officer, I'm not going to be calling any of that to anyone's attention, not even Lofthouse's, so the fault's now mine, all right?'

Sefton remained silent.

'So, no, I don't think we should send the hue and cry after him. The other reason is that he still doesn't know who me and Ross are, and he might well assume that you two died down there, and – unless his brother somehow got the word to him before he copped it – he still doesn't know anyone there was a police officer.

He could just go back to his normal routine. We know where to find him. We know he's a good source of juice and we might need him later. Let's not give him a reason to run.' He moved a touch unsteadily towards the door. 'Now, given all that's happened, may I suggest a pint or two on the way home? Only not here, eh?'

Outside, breathing deeply of an evening that was still light, with curious passers-by looking at their charred clothes and obvious injuries, Ross felt a hand on her shoulder. She looked up to see Costain looking seriously at her, holding her back a little distance from the other two.

'Hey,' he said, 'listen—'

'It's okay.'

'What?'

'I know what you're going to say. I saved your life—'

'Well, yeah, and thank you, but so did those two, that's not what I was . . . Listen, do you want to go out for a drink?'

'Yeah, bloody right now—'

'No, I mean . . . I . . . think . . . okay *this* is what I texted you about.' His gaze was darting all over her face. He looked so shaken. He was determined to get the words out. 'Would you like to go out for a . . . drink. For dinner, maybe. With me. Tomorrow. That being Friday.'

Oh.

Oh no. Oh no. Absolutely not.

He was looking so seriously at her. There was something lost about it, something honest, as if he'd been shaken to the core and needed to tell her this. She knew she couldn't trust how he looked.

But she found that she was smiling. On the verge of a laugh. Against her will. Sort of. She was shaken too. She was still, actually, shaking. This was the worst possible thing that she could do. She was laughing at herself.

But . . . she could still hold on to her secrets, couldn't she? What, did she think she'd just tell him all he *might* want to know, just because they were on a date? She didn't even know if he *did* want anything from her, besides the obvious. To think that was to think the worst of him.

Damn it. She wanted to hear what he had to say. She wanted to hear him in private. She wanted to hear him try to get close to her. She wanted to have some closeness in her life, wanted to be able to choose whether or not to hold it off.

She was flattered. He was beautiful. She would stay in control. She would not tell him those things it would be disastrous for him to hear.

She would find out if he was indeed hoping to discover those things.

'Yeah,' she said. 'Okay.'

SEVEN

Quill stood at the Ops Board, a marker pen in his hand. He'd slept badly the night before, with terrible dreams about being pierced, penetrated. Not so surprising, considering his closeness to a major explosion. Perhaps he was still in shock. He wondered whether people who did what his lot did could ever get a good kip, whether being in shock was his life now. 'So,' he said, 'what have we discovered?'

'That silver stuff,' said Sefton, who looked like Quill felt. He took a pen and added to the concepts list, which had already gained several new entries this morning. 'That's the major connection to Operation Fog. It's not just something that occurs at the Ripper crime scenes, but, I'd speculate, and note that I'm speculating—'

'Noted,' said Ross.

'—that it's the fuel which powers occult London.'

'It was in the cracks of the made-up levels of the bar,' said Costain. 'Like the surface had fallen off and you could see the real power underneath.'

'Right,' said Sefton. 'I don't think, when everything's working as it's meant to, that you're supposed to be able to see this goo. Like with blood in a human body.'

'So, applying that to the Ripper case,' said Ross, 'I think it's possible that it means that our supernatural assailant got wounded in the struggle with either the first or both of the victims.'

Quill nodded. 'What the hell,' he asked, looking to Sefton again, 'was that enormous river of the stuff?'

'Maybe the source of all this power? I have no idea what it is, or where it is, or even if there . . . *is* a where . . .'

Quill saw the sleeplessness around Sefton's eyes, the burden on his shoulders. He'd never killed anyone himself. He'd known a couple of coppers in firearms units who had; it had never left them. He wished he could help Sefton with that burden. He hoped that maybe there was something in his philosophy, in the fact that he was the one who looked more deeply into the occult stuff, that could help him, but Quill suspected there couldn't be. 'Did you see the gold stuff threaded through it?'

'Yeah,' said Ross, and held up a page in her notebook. 'It looked like what was on the walls of Losley's house, on her pile of soil—'

'On what we thought was a sort of hyperlink in that book in her lock-up,' said Costain.

Sefton went back to the concepts section of the board. 'If the silver goo is the power source, the fuel . . .' He wrote two headings in the concepts column. 'Then maybe the gold thread is the software, the instructions.'

'So that could be what we touched when we touched the soil?'

'Maybe. And perhaps if we'd looked at that soil at a microscopic level once we had the Sight, we'd have seen silver goo in it too. The software and the power source.'

'Perhaps. But that still doesn't tell us why it was just us four, does it?'

There was silence for a moment. Quill supposed the others felt like he did about that central question of their existence. They all needed to know, at heart, if they'd been chosen for some grand quest or had been the victims of an accident. He wondered again if Lofthouse knew at least that much.

'John, the Rat King,' said Sefton, starting a new topic, 'seemed to me to be . . . not actually a real human being – he said so himself – something like that bouncer, but with . . . consciousness, ideas of his own, a character, not limited like they were in the bouncer – more like Brutus.'

'He went away downstairs,' said Ross. 'The bearded gatekeeper seemed calm enough to evacuate that way, so I think we can assume any lower floors just detached themselves and weren't destroyed in the explosion.'

'The Rat King had several features of interest. I'm pretty sure he knew I was a police officer as soon as he saw me. He had that kind of . . . greater power that Brutus had too. But he said he wouldn't give me away, and didn't.'

'So he knows about someone just by looking?' said Costain. 'He'd be the ultimate source, the fount of all info.'

'He indicated he didn't know who the Ripper was,' said Sefton, 'so his knowledge has limits, but, yeah. I just wish I knew how to find him.'

'That's still brilliant work,' said Quill. 'I asked you to find us background, and you got us tons of it.' He turned back to the board, knowing he wouldn't get an answering smile out of Sefton right now. 'Now, I asked a favour of some mates at West End Central and had a couple of uniforms take a turn past the Goat and Compasses and the Keels' biggest shop. The Goat has opened as usual today, and a car belonging to Terry Keel is parked round the back of his store in a parking place with his name over it. In short, it doesn't look as if he's scarpered.'

'There seems to be some sort of generational conflict going on in what I think we can now call the occult underworld of London,' said Ross. 'The Keel brothers, or now just Terry—' She stopped, realizing she might have said the wrong thing.

'It's okay,' said Sefton.

Ross nodded. 'They're on one side, the newer side, happy to use money in transactions. A lot of the regulars at the Goat seemed against that, wanted to keep with older laws about the use of barter.'

'Losley,' said Quill, 'if you remember, went apeshit when we dared to suggest she might be "employed".'

'Terry Keel,' said Costain, 'talked about a feeling that everything changed for this lot a few years back, but that the new generation have taken a while to take advantage of it.'

'Maybe that's about what destroyed the temple in Docklands,' said Sefton. 'If the Continuing Projects Team were the old law, and there's been nothing to replace them, then this lot found themselves free to do what they liked, only they didn't know it. I wonder why.'

'Maybe the Continuing Projects Team worked more like under-covers than beat coppers,' suggested Costain. 'Perhaps you only knew they were there when they nicked you.'

'I do wish,' said Quill, 'that we could find some good old-fashioned good and evil in this generational conflict, that we could say the barter people are the good guys and the money lot are bad. Because in my copper heart I have been waiting with baited breath to discover supernatural good and evil and the simple joy that would bring. But the barter people included Losley, and the money lot included your beardy waistcoat mate. So nuts to that.'

'That would be good,' agreed Sefton.

'I expected one side or the other to be all about the Smiling Man,' said Quill. 'But from either of them I only heard references to sacrifices being made "to London".'

They compared notes and found that was true for all of them.

'I don't think they know about the Smiling Man,' said Ross. 'Maybe he stays behind the scenes in that community too.' She found the relevant page in one of her notebooks. 'We still know almost nothing about him.'

'Things we did learn,' said Sefton, finding a page in one of his own scrawled notebooks and reading from it. 'Losley needed a line of sight on her victims, but nobody else seems to. I kind of thought that might be unique to her after that threat against us that was written on a note when we were at the New Age fair. Whoever wrote that could "smell death" near people, which is not a line-of-sight thing.' He obviously saw the slight smile on Quill's face. 'This is the sort of detail I keep track of.'

'What about Neil Gaiman?' asked Quill. 'Him we can find, presumably, and he seemed in the know. We ought to get a statement.'

'I've put a call in to his agent,' said Ross. 'Let's hope he hasn't flown back to the States.'

'Yeah,' said Costain, 'it'd be awkward to have to bring this up on his blog.'

Sefton realized that there was something he'd expected Ross to have mentioned by now, yet she hadn't. 'The barmaid gave you something,' he said to her.

'Yeah.' Ross raised a finger, wait a sec, as if she'd forgotten. Sefton was pretty sure she hadn't. She found it in her bag and pinned it to the board. It was a colourful flier for the pub evening. 'I think that was her way of saying that, no matter what had happened to her, I was welcome in that pub.'

Sefton didn't know why he felt worried at her poker face. An alert went off on Ross' phone. She looked at it. 'DCI Forrest's office. The fingerprint results have been checked between both crime scenes. And . . . we have a match.'

'Excellent,' said Quill.

'The smeared one at the Staunce scene, by the message on the wall, is the same as one found inside the Spatley car. So, since Tunstall was in custody for the Spatley murder when Staunce was killed—'

'That should clear Tunstall of suspicion.' Quill indicated the objectives list. 'I'd say we've achieved objective seven there.'

'—but said fingerprint doesn't appear in any criminal database, so Forrest's office is asking us to help build a case against Tunstall by looking into the possibility that he may have had an accomplice.'

'This is what happens,' sighed Quill, 'when only one suspect is *visible*.'

An hour later, Ross found Costain alone by the tea kettle. She made sure she was calm, and then she walked over to him. 'I've changed my mind,' she said.

'About what?'

'About tonight.'

'Too late,' said Costain, slurping his tea as he moved off. 'I booked the table.'

Ross stood there for a moment after he'd left, annoyed at how easily he'd shrugged that off, and at how it turned out she didn't mind that.

That evening, Sefton put the Xbox controller down on the table and closed his eyes. 'I killed someone,' he said.

Joe took a deep breath and slowly lowered his own controller. 'I wondered what you hadn't been saying,' he said.

Sefton told him everything.

Joe held on to him. Finally he said, 'You killed someone by accident, someone who was trying to kill you.'

'I know that.'

'You lot would normally get counselling and compassionate leave—'

'And be investigated and interviewed and all that, and I could do with that and all.'

'Because that would end up with you being *officially* told you hadn't done anything wrong.'

'Probably.'

'Well, you haven't.'

Sefton considered for a moment, and realized that, as always, Joe had helped him frame how he really felt. 'No,' he said finally, 'I have.'

'Russell Vincent bought our paper,' said Sarah, dropping her bag onto the kitchen table.

Quill motioned for her to be quiet. He'd just got Jessica to sleep. He went and closed the door of her room. 'And that's a good thing?'

'It's a great thing. We get to keep our jobs.'

'Then that's a brilliant thing. Russell Vincent is . . . that media tycoon who's on telly all the time, the one who—?'

'He's the owner of the *Herald*. Opinion leads, long lenses, that one.'

'Oh.'

'Oh indeed. He's personally famous for taking on the Bussard Inquiry into phone hacking. He told them his firm had once used it to get celebrity gossip, but that when he found out, he'd fired everyone involved. He gave the inquiry access to his entire communications network and told them to go fuck themselves.'

'I remember.'

'But, hey, whoever owns my paper, I am still, thank God, employed as a journalist.'

'Excellent.' Quill rooted around at the back of a cupboard and found a dusty bottle of cava, which he uncorked and poured into two glasses, after giving them a quick rinse under the tap.

'He actually bought our whole group. Seven local papers in all. There's a reception on Sunday night for all the employees. You're invited too – there's a plus one.'

'Sure. Depending.' He clinked glasses with her. 'I can ask him how he got the inside track on the Ripper murders.'

'Yeah, don't do that.'

'Like he'd tell me.'

Costain parked outside Ross' housing block in Catford half an hour early. This he never did. It felt as if he was conducting surveillance. He was only early because he was nervous. He knew he looked good and smelt good. He'd prepared. But still he was nervous.

He waited, enjoying the late evening sunshine. He put the radio on, but all he could find were news stories about it all kicking off in Wandsworth now, about how people were throwing bricks and setting light to shops across London, Toff masks everywhere, taken up by rioters as being an easily available way to hide their faces. He switched off the radio and tried to put it all out of his head.

He had one clear aim in mind for this evening, and he had to focus on it.

Ross had interrogated her wardrobe until it failed completely. Neither of her dresses was useful. But it was either those or something she'd wear to work.

Why shouldn't it be something she'd wear to work? She wanted to find out what he was after, not to make herself more attractive to him.

It was a pity about her and Costain. Everyone else had someone to talk to. Someone they got to go home to at the end of the day. The two of them had nobody, and it was likely to stay that way.

She finally decided on new jeans. A polo shirt like the one she'd worn to work. At least it wasn't the same shirt. She tried things with her hair. She undid a couple of buttons.

She did them up again just as the intercom buzzed. He was three minutes early.

They took the tube to Chancery Lane and walked up the Gray's Inn Road to an Italian restaurant, where Costain had booked a table outside. He couldn't stop feeling nervous. More than nervous. Why? There were high stakes, sure, but he was used to that. It wasn't as if tonight was definitely going to be the big pay-off, that she'd immediately trust him and tell him what he wanted to hear. No, this was an undercover job; this would take weeks of slowly earning her trust. Only then to betray that trust, if she did have access to what he thought she did.

He looked sidelong at her face as they walked. That betrayal would be a terrible thing, but he had to do it. He had no choice. He was trying not to notice how tight those jeans were. Being attracted to her made what he was planning to do feel a lot worse.

He was aware they'd been silent for a long time. No small talk, which seemed fine by her. They reached the restaurant and were welcomed and seated by staff who seemed very pleased to have paying customers. He looked at her poker face again across the table. It wasn't as if he'd actually been on many dates; of course, this wasn't a real date. He had an objective here. So. Small talk. 'I used to come here a lot,' he said. 'The food's good, it's an Italian family place.'

'Sure,' said Ross. It was almost a shrug.

The waiter arrived and they ordered wine. When it arrived it was very welcome.

Costain pointed to his glass, worried that she might have thought he was going to drink drive. The reflex to be good, every moment, was deeply programmed into him now. 'I can always take a taxi when we get back to yours.'

She frowned, and he realized that she thought he meant he was already thinking about what might happen at the end of the evening. He suppressed an urge to explain and decided to move on to other topics. 'So—'

'Do you mean you brought girls here?'

He closed his mouth. Then opened it again. 'No. Well, yeah. Maybe sometimes. Actually, it was usually just me. When I was undercover.'

'But sometimes?'

'Yeah.' He found he'd said it almost as a question, almost as if he was asking her if that was okay.

'Where are you from? What did your parents do?'

Oh. Okay then. 'I grew up in Willesden. Then moved out of London. I came back to the Smoke after I became a police officer. More opportunities down here. When I became an undercover, I went back up north again between jobs. Safer.'

'You didn't say anything about your parents.'

That level tone of hers. The way her eyes were fixed on his face. He felt as if he was being interviewed about his part in some unspecified crime. He took a sip of wine and carefully smiled. 'Are you analysing me?'

'You know all about me. You were *briefed* about my family. If you don't want to talk about—'

'No. It's just strange that someone would want to know.'

'Why are you being so weird?' she said suddenly.

'What?'

'This is a date, right? We're on a date. I was making small talk, asking about stuff that's not relevant to our jobs. Like your home, your mum, your *dad*. But you're getting all nervous. Haven't you been on many dates?'

He was now actually glaring at her. 'No, honestly. You?'

'Almost zero.'

'Because we both . . .' He made a gesture that attempted to include a ton of sadness and horror and all the world.

'We both . . .' She made the gesture back at him. 'Yeah. Thought so.'

He found he was smiling now and, amazingly, she was smiling back. With her tooth biting her bottom lip, just a notch. There was still something reserved about her, though; maybe there always would be. The way she'd underlined the word *dad* back there, as if seeing if that would get a reaction – had that been an indication that she suspected what he was really up to here, that she knew Costain would have found talking about her dad and his current situation difficult right now, because those were pointers towards what he was secretly planning?

It was entirely possible that she did suspect he was up to something. She was vastly intelligent, used to picking signal out of noise. Okay then. He was used to the possibility of those around him being suspicious of him when he was undercover.

It dawned on him that he'd been looking at her for a long time, and she'd accepted that calmly, looking straight back at him as if they were both sizing up the enemy.

He realized he was hard. Now would not be the time to get up from this table. What had they been talking about? He cleared his throat and looked away. 'You, erm, asked about my parents. Dad was a taxi driver, Mum did some cleaning. They split up; I went to live with Dad in Nottingham. They both passed away a while back.' There, he'd said 'dad' a few times without suddenly blurting out all his plans. Okay, he decided, two can play at this game. He reached into his jacket pocket and found the card. 'Listen, I just remembered, sorry to bring up job things tonight, but I found this in here earlier and, well, I didn't mention it to the team today.'

'What?' She was looking openly suspicious at him now.

He slapped the card down on the table. It was a business card with just a map that had a bit of the Sight about it and a date. 'I found a few of these behind the bar at the Goat, in a drawer marked "auction". What do you reckon that's about?'

Ross tried to keep her expression steady, but she was so angry – with herself and with him – that she wanted to leap up and throw this table over him. She had to wait while the waiter brought their meals over, and Costain made ridiculous small comments about the preparation of the dishes, as if he was still trying to impress her.

She'd thought she could safely see how much he knew, but he'd had that card. He knew it was an auction. He could either tell the others about it – and there must be a reason he hadn't done so already – or, worse, he could come along himself. If the object she was so desperately seeking was on sale there, as the barmaid had hinted it might be, then he would understand, if he didn't already, that he needed it as much as she did. He would bid against her. He might still have dodgy sources of cash that could go much further than an intelligence analyst's savings would. Or, if the auction was based on barter, on sacrifice, he was better placed with his life in the underworld to find terrible things to offer, when all she would have was herself.

That whole chain of thought fell like a row of dominoes as the plates were put on the table. If she was honest with herself, she'd been having fun watching his fumbling attempts to unlock her, enjoying watching him, until now.

What was she going to do? She couldn't risk him bidding against her, so she had to try to get him onside. It meant not showing him this anger and instead telling him what he wanted to hear. So he had won, damn it. For now.

She reached into her bag, found her own card and put it down on the table beside his. 'It's an invitation,' she said, 'to an auction, as you've realized. An auction, I think, of occult London objects.'

He smiled right across his face, as if appreciating her all over again. She'd revealed hidden depths. 'Why haven't you told the others?'

'Why haven't you?'

The smile continued. 'Because I'd like to see if there's anything on sale there that might help me avoid going to Hell.'

She took a deep breath and let her secret out. 'And I'd like to see if there's anything on sale there that would get my father out of Hell.'

'Interesting.' He wasn't pretending at all now, just going through the motions, giving her credit as a fellow player while looking at her as if he wanted to eat her. 'And do you think there will be an item on sale there that will allow either . . . or both . . . of us to achieve our respective goals?'

She paused for a moment, getting tiny satisfaction from keeping him in suspense. 'I've been reading up on an object called the Bridge of Spikes. There was a document about it in the hoard we found in the Docklands ruins. Very hard to translate, but I managed it. It talked about a device that resurrects a person to full, breathing, unharmed life, wherever their body is, and simultaneously wipes clean what you might call their ethical record.'

'A "Get out of Hell Free" card.'

'Exactly.'

'Is this a London thing?'

'No. It was used once, in medieval times, somewhere in the Middle East. I think it can be used once per century. And, yes, that means that this occult shit can happen in other cities. I haven't told the others that, either.'

He took a long drink of his wine, his eyes never leaving hers. 'Once per century also means that only one of us could use it.'

Her lips were dry; Ross took a drink herself. Her heart was racing. An efficient solution to Costain's problem now, she knew, would be for him to kill her and dispose of her card. She was pretty sure he wasn't capable of that. Pretty sure. But now he had the prospect in front of him of having all his sins erased, would he decide it was worth it? She examined his face again. No. At least not before he was sure he had it in his sights, there at the auction on the night. She would have to play him along, right up to that moment, then find a way to get the object and run. 'Right.'

'I knew you were thinking that.'

'I was.'

'You're also thinking I might bid against you. Try to nick it from you if you won. Worse.'

'Yeah.'

He paused, considering, then looked at her with a quizzical expression that contained an edge of hurt. 'Is that why you agreed to this? To see how much I knew?'

She shrugged. 'Maybe a bit.'

He seemed to accept that. 'What are we going to do?'

She found she wasn't angry any more. As he'd said, they both now knew what the game was going to be. 'Join forces. Go to the auction together. See what happens?'

He considered that. Then nodded. 'What about . . . this?'

'What?'

'Is this still a date?' He was trying to make her think he was actually still concerned about that – that it really did matter to him. She wasn't sure how she felt about it. If she was going to be stringing him along, waiting for a chance to take the object for herself, she didn't want to have to play the scarlet woman to do it.

That would only be the case if she wasn't also genuinely . . . okay, this was complicated. She looked him in the eye. 'If you want it to be.'

He looked like the cat that had got the cream. The size of his reaction, and the moment it took for him to conceal it, warmed her. Or fooled her, she thought, a moment later. He held up his glass. 'Cheers.'

She picked up her glass, satisfied that at least her hand wasn't shaking, and touched it to his. 'Cheers.'

It was around eleven when they got back to Catford. They had each made an obvious effort to talk about other stuff on the way, though when Ross started to weigh up various dead ends in the op, he had gently shut her down. Yeah, that was just normal. She should know when to let herself not work. She liked having someone tell her that, actually. It was seductive. It was probably quite deliberate on his part.

They walked to her place; the housing block loomed above them. They stopped by his car. She wasn't going to invite him in.

'Well,' he said, 'thank you for a lovely evening.'

She couldn't help but laugh at that. 'No, thank you.'

'So, neither of us is going to tell the others about . . . ?'

'No.'

Instead they were going to play out this game of theirs. He was looking at her very determinedly. She let herself look challengingly back.

'Well.' She put a little tired sigh in her voice. Time to turn in. She was going to see how far he was prepared to take this.

He suddenly stepped forwards and put his hands on both sides of her face, and with incredible gentleness and force at the same time, kissed her.

She realized that she'd raised her hands. What she did with them, what she did next, this was so important, she had just a second to decide . . .

She wrapped her arms around him and kissed him back. She let the kiss become passionate. She closed her eyes. She let his tongue into her mouth. Okay, so she was now the full-on scarlet woman. Damn it.

She had to stop this before it got too intense and in a moment he'd think they'd be going inside to—

He broke away. She opened her eyes. He was looking at her with the most gorgeous, scared, vulnerable expression. His hands dropped from hers.

'Good night,' he said. With a smile that again had just that hint of the cat that had got the cream about it, he got into his car.

She stood there while he drove away. After his car turned the corner, she dropped her head to one side, confused. 'Oh,' she whispered, 'well played.'

Quill woke from dreadful dreams that he couldn't now remember to find himself sweating in his duvet, and his phone once more ringing.

'Would you please tell him,' Sarah groaned, 'to kill people in the *morning*?'

Quill answered his phone. It was Lofthouse. 'A third murder, same MO,' she said. 'It's open season on rich white males.'

EIGHT

The bar in Hoxton was called Soviet, all sofas and low tables and big red projections of Stalin on the wall, so deeply ironic that Quill wasn't sure he quite followed it. It had been packed at the time of the incident. There were dozens of witnesses, who were now slouching around looking vaguely annoyed, glancing at their expensive watches, as uniforms and Scene of Crime Officers moved between them. There was a huge splatter of blood on the ground between fallen tables, from where a body had recently been removed. Only Quill's people could see that there was also a splatter of cold silver, which continued across the establishment, right to the window, where this time entry as well as exit splatters could be seen on both sides. An enormous dripping mass of it also covered the far wall. The name of the deceased was Rupert Rudlin, twenty-eight years old, worked for Challis Merchant Bank as an analyst. Parents in Twickenham, single, one sister living in the States.

'He kept looking over at this young girl, I mean, young woman,' said Jamie, who was, to give him credit, visibly shaken in his bomber jacket and necktie. 'He kept saying he was going to go over and talk to her, and everyone was, you know, laughing at him. She was sitting at a table with this guy; Rupert kept saying she was out of his league. And then there was a crash from the window. It was the protestors outside.' There had been, Quill had gathered, a major Toff gathering outside the bar that evening, something approaching a flash mob, swiftly brought together by Twitter. There were enough youths with those masks in this suburb to do that now, he supposed. 'They'd thrown a dustbin or something. So we all cheered and waved to them, you know? The bouncers – sorry, security staff – went out there and talked to them. Some of the lads in here – and I don't agree with this, okay? – they got out their wallets and started waving their cash at them, and pointing to themselves, and they got this chant going, "bankers" . . . "wankers" . . . pointing back and forth. Really stupid. Everyone was texting and tweeting about it and, you know, wondering if the police were even going to show up, what with this strike vote and everything.' Quill was sure that his expression hadn't revealed anything, but the young man stopped and looked awkward. 'Sorry. Anyway, that's when we started to hear the *sieg heil*s from outside, and we realized there were bloody skinheads . . . well, not real skinheads now but, you know, that lot, they were out there too, and they'd started to fight the Toffs. You could see them outside the window, laying into them, chasing each other across the square, getting into scuffles. There were cheers from in here, not *for* either side, really. Anyway, I looked back and Rupert had gone over to the woman at the table, had gone to chat her up. That was Rupert all over. The bloke she was with just got up, looked at his watch, didn't seem like he wanted to get in the way of that. More of a business drink than a date, I got the feeling. But I still thought it was a bit odd that he didn't want to make sure Rupert wasn't going to hassle her.'

'Did she respond well to Rupert's advances?'

'It looked as if he was getting somewhere. She was smiling, anyway.'

'What about the bloke she was with?'

'He headed off. I didn't see if he actually left.'

'What happened then?'

The young man paused, and Quill, through experience, knew that now he was at the point where the impossible had intervened. The boy was trying to navigate through what he could say that might be believed.

'Just tell the truth.'

Jamie hesitated, then gave in. 'I thought maybe I was on some-thing, that maybe someone had dropped something into my pint. That table –' he pointed – 'right beside Rupert and this girl just . . . erupted. All the glasses went flying. This guy that had been standing there was knocked down by it, got cut across his head, and he was screaming. The girl went to help him, squatted down to see what was wrong with him, and Rupert went too. I was thinking maybe some sort of bomb had gone off. And I think the security people started to come over.'

'And?'

'She went flying backwards. Like she'd been on one of those springboards stuntmen use. I mean, she shot upwards, I saw her feet off the ground, backwards, and she sort of flew, just a couple of feet, and hit the back wall there, and she stayed there, hanging there, and she was struggling, she was yelling, it was like she was actually fighting with something. She had no idea what was going on, no more than I did.'

'What was Rupert doing?'

'He went to try to get her down. But then . . . he spun round, and blood came out of his mouth. I thought he'd been shot. I ducked down. Really, I did. But then these . . . wounds . . . they just started to appear on him, up and down his body, across his neck, and he was staggering about, screaming. And then, then it was like something just burst out of him, like he'd been ripped open. There was this enormous spray of blood, more than you'd think there could be. He fell down. The crowd panicked, I mean, everyone just went apeshit, trying to get outside, running right into the Toffs and the skinheads, and then the police got here, thank Christ, and . . .' He trailed off. He was looking at Quill almost desperately. 'That's the truth,' he said. 'Is that okay?'

'Not many of the witnesses did tell the truth, actually,' said Ross, reading the report that had been thrust into her hand by an annoyed-looking member of Jason Forrest's staff. 'You can't really blame them. Our own witness statements tend to greater accuracy in cases like this because we let them know it's okay to say mad shit. We have statements here taken by the main operation, saying that both a skinhead and a Toff protestor did the killing. Which means, I hope, that Forrester will just regard the statements we've harvested, when we share them with him, as equally mad.'

Quill glanced through the big window at a hungover early summer morning. A police line was keeping an enormous scrum of press back from the scene of the crime. Forrest himself was now striding about the room, looking at where the body had lain, with Lofthouse at his side. There was no message this time, they were certain, having examined every inch of wall.

'It all fits the profile,' said Costain.

Ross was frowning. 'White men is a big profile. It's everyone who's not "the other".'

'*Rich* white men isn't as big,' countered Sefton. 'There's a reason why they're called the one per cent.'

'Was Staunce rich? Was Spatley *rich*?'

Quill recognized that Ross was sort of talking to herself out loud.

'Privileged, then,' said Costain.

'Usually means the opposite in our world,' said Sefton.

'Great,' said Quill, 'we're in a land of things meaning their opposites. What about the woman who was attacked?'

'She wasn't among those who stayed behind and were interviewed and processed,' said Ross, looking at her own copy of the notes. 'We have some descriptions – wildly varying, of course. There is, hooray, security camera footage of the whole bar.'

'Hooray indeed.' Quill looked up and grimaced. 'Gird your loins, here comes trouble.'

Forrest had arrived, Lofthouse beside him. 'It took us a couple of hours to sort out the scrummage outside before we could even get in here,' he said. 'Multiple arrests, protestors and now, dear God, rival right-wing protestors.' Quill recalled seeing graffiti about 'kikes' on buildings around the square. 'That's rare to the point of unique for round here. The hard cases in my cells are saying they're aiming to break up every Toff gathering.'

'Just what we bloody need,' sighed Quill.

'What, they're onside with the bankers?' Ross had a look on her face as if reality was lying to her.

'What we're getting out of their online forums is that they think the Ripper message indicates that these killings are all a Jewish conspiracy, and that by wearing that mask, the Toffs are supporting the secret powers that rule the world.'

'Which in previous decades would have been associated with the bankers themselves,' said Ross.

'Bloody hell,' said Quill, 'now it's like anything can mean anything.'

'The Ripper really should have been more specific with that message,' said Sefton. 'Then at least we'd only have one side to deal with.'

'So, DI Quill,' said Forrester, 'what can you bring to the table?'

Quill had prepared this report mentally over the last few days. 'We've placed undercovers in relevant communities and are already hearing useful chatter, though none yet of operational relevance.' He wished he could mention the silver, but couldn't think of a way to do it.

'So, you've got fuck all?'

'Yes, sir.'

'Fantastic. Keep up the good work.'

'Any fingerprints here?'

'No matches with the others, no.'

'May I ask, sir, if, given this, we're still building a case against the driver, Tunstall?'

'Of course we are. Logically, he *must* have been involved in the first crime, and it beggars belief that we won't have him for it in the end. When we've got enough evidence we'll rearrest him, and he'll eventually give us his accomplices. End of.' With an ironic glance at Lofthouse that looked to be about Quill's bizarre querying of that certainty, he was off.

'To be expected,' said Lofthouse, reassuringly.

'Yeah,' said Quill. 'He has someone he fancies for it. I'd probably see it like that myself. Let's check out the security camera footage, shall we?'

They had a few different angles to choose from this time. There was the young woman: white, late teens, five four, slim build, no visible identifying marks, long brown hair, here in a pony tail, dressed reasonably expensively and fashionably, sitting at her table. There came Rupert Rudlin, the victim, to talk to her. Standing up was the woman's male companion: white, late thirties, five nine, large build, no visible identifying marks, balding, dark hair, off-the-peg suit, glancing at his watch, saying goodbye to her and heading off. They followed him across the bar and out of the door, shaking his head at door staff, pushing his way through against their urging him to stay inside, actually going out into the riot. Then light arrived in the corner of the frame and the shining figure in the shape of the Ripper leaped lightly into it. The assailant had landed on the table, causing the drinks and empties placed there to fly off, wounding the bystander as the witness had stated. The young woman had tried to aid the wounded man and been slammed up against the wall, where the assailant indeed held her for twenty seconds, as Rudlin got to his feet.

'Look at how much silver gets spilled on that wall,' said Sefton. 'A bigger deposit than any we've seen.'

'Spilling fuel,' said Sefton, 'like something's going wrong.'

Rudlin had indeed gone to help and had been attacked as per witness statement. This was the first time Quill and his team had seen the Ripper at work. They watched the shining shape of a razor sweeping through the air, cutting and cutting. There was an unhinged rage to it, but also a terrible precision. There was a sudden hauling of the razor that made the victim scream silently on the footage like a slaughtered animal. Then the Ripper was bounding off and the young man had collapsed into a pile of his own bloody insides.

The woman had stayed put for a moment after the Ripper had dropped her, unharmed, then she'd hauled herself to her feet and run for the door. She also had got through the door staff, who were reacting to the violence now happening inside their establishment, and was gone into the night.

'I want a word with her,' said Quill. 'She's experienced that thing close up, and it let her off. And she saw fit to run, immediately, through more trouble.'

'The bloke who was with her too,' said Costain. 'Would you walk out into what was going on outside that bar?'

'I would need,' said Ross, biting her bottom lip, deep in thought, 'a reason.'

The team circulated the description of the woman and her companion among the witnesses. A few people had seen them, but nobody knew who they were. They weren't going to be able to get the main inquiry to put pictures of them onto the news, Ross realized. All Forrest would see on this CCTV footage was the sort of headache-inducing visual lie that she and her colleagues had experienced during the Losley operation before they'd got the Sight. To see even as much as he had – a young woman being thrown against the wall by something invisible – their witness must be somewhere on the lower end of the Sighted spectrum. Most of those working the main inquiry would interpret the same scene as her being thrown to the floor, or something like that.

Ross wished she could feel comfortable around Costain. His expression when he glanced in her direction, that shared secret, made her wince inwardly. She wished they could have had that kiss without having the prospect of the auction hanging over them. That look on his face, if she could ever think of any expression of his as genuine, said he wasn't feeling comfortable either, that maybe he was as vulnerable as she was. Yeah, maybe.

They found the woman's original companion, the balding guy, on CCTV camera footage from outside as he left the bar, skirting the edges of the clash between protestors, and then they managed to follow him, camera to camera, to Old Street, where he'd caught a taxi heading towards town. Ross noted down the registration number. Checking earlier CCTV footage from the bar, the man had paid only with cash, damn it, and not a card they could check for at the bar. They'd at least have a record of where he'd got out of the taxi. The woman's path from the bar was caught on a couple of cameras, but then she'd vanished into the backstreets. Ross knew from previous experience that the CCTV footage wouldn't be good enough for the facial recognition software used by the Photographic Intelligence team to be any use, but she sent images of both patrons to them anyway.

So now Ross was looking for links between this victim and the others. Rudlin had been pretty ordinary, not important like Staunce and Spatley: redbrick university, Lancaster; reasonably well-off family; nobody close to him worked in police or government. It was possible that the idea here was just to create terror in a particular group of people, but then why not kill loads of them? The presence of the protestors outside was interesting. The faces that had been identified in the crowd outside the bar didn't match any who'd been present at the Spatley murder, but that sample, among all the masks involved, was pretty small. It was perhaps indicative that the protestors just happened to show up in this neighbourhood and mount their first ever protest outside a bar on the night when the Ripper attacked someone inside it. That was a very attractive connection to make, now with three data points in a row, but it could still just be coincidence, given the prevalence of the Toff movement across London. Perhaps the Ripper was somehow the 'spirit of the protests' or being summoned by someone in the Toff crowds, or feeding on their anger or something like that.

Tired coppers from the main investigation had told her they'd found no sign of a pre-organized picket of the bar on Toff websites. But with an organization this diffuse – if it could be called an organization at all – there was usually little warning of anything. It was as if they were dealing with a flash mob as a culture. A bunch of tweets had gone out, giving the impression that something was already happening outside this particular bar, and other people had shown up to join in. The main investigation had asked Twitter to provide details of those accounts under the Data Protection Act, and Forrest's office had promised to share that with her.

'If our lot ever get something on *Crimewatch*,' said Quill, after she'd told him, 'they'll need a special effects budget.'

In the back of Ross' mind, as she worked the case, she was also working her other problem. She looked to Costain every now and then, and gradually she realized that there was something she could do to change things, perhaps to make things better. It would involve no risk on her part. It would be very hard on him.

That was all right.

She waited until he was on his own, staring into the fine detail of the silver splash on the wall. 'About last night . . .'

'What about it?' He was careful now, guarded. She could tell that he thought she was going to say it had been a mistake, that it was all over. He was worried either about losing the connection they'd made or about missing his chance to get hold of the Bridge of Spikes. Would she ever be able to look at him and make an accurate assessment of what he was thinking?

'I had a good time.'

She felt horribly pleased to see his sudden smile. 'Oh. Great.'

'So, we should talk about how we're going to go forward with all this. I mean, if we're going to go to the auction together, how we could maybe find, you know, some trust.'

He was nodding quickly. 'Absolutely.'

'So, I was thinking, second date?'

'Right. Right, yes.'

She didn't like the amount of power she had over him either because of her bloody *allure* or because he was giving it to her in order to flatter and deceive her. 'Do you mind combining business and pleasure? There's someone I want you to meet. My place at

2 p.m. tomorrow.' She walked off and looked over her shoulder: yeah, now he was the one watching her go.

Sefton lay awake in bed, listening to Joe snoring beside him. He couldn't help but keep seeing the blows the Ripper had struck. The news tonight had been about escalation, about far right groups starting to march in areas affected by the riots, starting to shout down Toff protestors. From what he knew about the Thirties, he didn't like the feeling of where this was all going. If people started to feel the establishment was failing them, that the police were failing them, they looked for order in terrible places.

He kept thinking about Barry Keel, about human remains. The two deaths overlapped each other in his head, to the point where he felt vaguely guilty, insanely, for Rudlin's death too.

He had to do something more than he was doing, he decided. He had to find some way to heal both himself and everything around him. He had to see if the centre was going to hold, to ask a greater power for answers.

At home, Quill stayed up late that night, looking at the documents of the case, wondering if there was any single thing more he could do. They'd gone out to the Spatley home that afternoon, after they'd got all they could from the new crime scene, and had found, even with their Sighted eyes, nothing the main op hadn't.

Forrest was starting to realize that Quill's team were bringing nothing extra to the operation. There seemed to be *no* connections between Rudlin and the other two victims. They still had very little in the way of access to an occult underworld that seemed to know nothing about this case. Nothing, nothing, nothing . . . and time was running out both for his team and for the next bloody unlucky man who the Ripper decided to randomly slaughter. Just as he'd finally decided to go to bed, his mobile rang. He saw it was Sefton, and answered.

'Jimmy,' said the voice on the other end of the line, 'I've decided.

We're not getting anywhere. So it's time for me to do something I've been putting off. Something a bit scary.'

'You know,' said Quill, 'Ross called five minutes ago, and she said almost exactly the same thing.'

NINE

It was Sunday morning. Sefton stood at the familiar bus stop in Kensington. Nobody else waited there. The streets were quiet, still calm, despite that now omnipresent smell of smoke. You could actually hear the birdsong. The occasional jogger or dog walker passed him.

He heard the bus approaching. He looked down the road and concentrated . . . and yes, now he knew what he was looking for, there it was: the number 7 bus, to Russell Square, as indicated by the display on the front. This wasn't a modern bus. It was a very old one. As Sefton knew from terrifying experience, you needed the Sight to see it, let alone board it.

He put his hand out. He tensed up as the bus slowed down. He could see nothing behind its dark windows. It stopped, and he got onto the rear platform. Brutus had said that each time he had to find a new, more dangerous way of coming to see him, but surely if he made it again through what had been an overwhelming passage, at least he'd get a hearing. He braced himself to encounter what was in this darkness, taking a step forwards as the bus accelerated away from the stop at—

He turned. This was different. They were travelling incredibly fast.

A force that he could not have argued with thrust every inch of his body at once towards the door.

He had time to yell and—

The bus vanished. He hit the road. There had been a moment in his head of knowing he was going to. That moment was the worst thing of all.

He bounced. He rolled. He missed the wheels of a car that swung suddenly out of his way. His body hit the kerb and he yelled.

He lay there, taking big, slow breaths. He was okay, but only because something had made sure he was okay. It wouldn't do so next time. That had been a warning.

Brutus had meant what he said. He'd been stupid enough to try it anyway. It would need something new. It would need something worse.

The middle-aged Asian woman who answered the door of what had been Ross' family home in Bermondsey was the same one as the first time Ross had come here. That had been months ago, during the Losley case. The woman seemed to recognize her, but then looked suspiciously at Costain beside her.

'I'm afraid we need another look upstairs,' she said. 'Police business. Nothing you need to worry about, but we'd really appreciate it. My colleague is a detective sergeant.'

Costain showed her his warrant card.

As she had last time, the lady took the offered documents inside and called the station to check they were who they said they were. She and Costain waited, looking at each other. She'd refused to tell him where they were going, in a teasing way, as if it was going to be something pleasant. By now he must surely have realized why they were here, that this was going to be much more business than pleasure. He was already looking tense and awkward.

The woman opened the front door once more, let them in and told Ross she knew the way by now.

This was only the second time Ross had been back to the house where she'd grown up. The look and smell of it filled her senses, reminding her of her childhood and how it had been taken from her. At least these days it didn't set off her allergies. She led Costain to the top floor without a word. There was the door where she'd looked through the crack to see Dad hanging there, seemingly having hung himself, but actually, as she'd spent so long proving, having been murdered by his own brother. She opened the door and this time walked straight in.

'So this is the place?' It was only a few streets away from where Costain had worked for Dad's murderer, Rob Toshack. He still looked awkward. It was good that she'd taken him out of his comfort zone. Now he surely knew what he was in for, yet he was still here. He must really want whatever he wanted.

'Yeah.' She stepped into the middle of the room, under the ceiling rose, and looked up. 'Dad?'

There was a moment when nothing happened. Ross feared, and kind of hoped, guiltily, that perhaps this time he wouldn't be here. But that would result in even more fear, wouldn't it? Because then she'd never know what had happened to him.

Then colours that weren't like any she'd ever seen started to unfurl in strange waves from the ceiling, and with them came the stench, the smell that came pouring down on them, the air feeling heavy with it, settling onto her shoulders, getting into her hair.

The ceiling opened and he burst downwards on the end of his noose with a cry, his eyes finding hers as he fell, his legs flailing, his hands trying and failing to hold on to the rope around his neck. For reasons he had never explained, he could only appear in the room where he'd died, so she could only ever see him again here. That beloved face. So terrible to see it in pain. So wonderful to see it animated with something that could be called life. Terrible and wonderful were still, for Ross, mixed up together in this room.

'Girl,' he said, his voice cracking on the rope, staring at her. 'It's been so long. Why didn't you come sooner?' She hadn't expected that. She felt absurdly guilty to have someone else here to hear that. But now Alf was looking across at Costain, startled. 'What's *he* doing here?'

'He's—'

'You're telling me that you and him—?'

Costain could only stare. He'd taken a couple of steps backwards, Ross realized. He was now almost flat against the wall. He'd put a hand up to cover his nose and mouth. His expression was terrified.

Ross quickly turned back to her father. 'We're not here about that.'

'I know you work with him, I keep an eye on you. But you know he was one of Rob's men—'

'Yeah. He was undercover—'

'But he really *was* one of Rob's men. Rob was like a dad to him. You haven't seen him – I have, girl.'

'I've heard the tapes—'

'You haven't heard everything.' Her father had actually started to cry. 'Don't *trust* him, girl.'

'She doesn't!' That had come from Costain, a shout from behind his hand.

She didn't know how to deal with all this. This wasn't what she'd come here for. 'Dad, I came here to ask about the case we're on—'

'The Ripper. I know, I watch you. You don't come to see me, but I see you.'

'Do you know anything about what it is?'

'I can see any bit of London I want to. You can see everything from up here. They like us to see what we're missing. But I don't have no bloody way of watching out for something when I don't know what I'm looking for, do I? I follow you. I follow you too, boy! But I don't see every time someone's murdered.'

'So—'

'But don't you go thinking I'm useless and leave me alone here! It's *all* up here! What's that they say, "Hell is other people"? The things I can't tell you! Don't you know, boy? You've had a glimpse of it.'

Costain closed his eyes and appeared to be controlling his breathing, didn't seem able to reply.

'What do you mean, Dad?'

'I'm saying I've *seen* Jack the Ripper. But up here. And when all this started to be something you were looking into, I checked out all the echoes of him down there and all. And this ain't nothing to do with him. This is something new.' Alf looked over his shoulder suddenly, and the tone of his voice changed into a high growl of pleading. 'They let you have a bit of hope. This is me getting my hope. They let me see you. But then there's more pain, and you can't stand it in the end – your brain just switches off and then you wake up in here again, ready to have it all crushed out of you again . . .' He was crying again, actually wailing. She was too, she realized, a low noise in her throat to match his.

'I'm working on it, Dad. I'm trying to get you out.'

'Hope again. You're part of it!' His face contorted as if he regretted saying that more than anything. 'No, I didn't mean that! Come and see me soon. Please!' Then he looked over his shoulder again, and started to scream abuse at something that was coming. He had been found out, she understood. 'Let me stay with her! Please! It's the only joy I—!'

Something hugely powerful heaved him back into the ceiling, all in one sudden and terrible movement. With a slam and the stench bursting again into the room, the ceiling closed.

'Dad!' Ross shouted helplessly after him. 'Dad!' She stopped herself. He wasn't coming back. Not this time. Now she knew that every time she came here she was contributing to his torture. That was why they, whoever they were, had let him talk to her. But now he'd been caught, she doubted he'd be allowed to give her any help that went against their cause. She allowed herself to shoulder the burden of having hurt him. She would not cry. Not here. She had tried to save him when he was first hanging here in this room, and she would save him again. She was doing something towards that goal. She would not let anything stop her.

She turned slowly to look at the person who might stand in her way.

Costain was shaking, a hand still over his mouth. He saw she was looking at him. After a moment, he composed himself enough to say something. 'That smell . . .'

She had thought about what this would do to him. She knew it would remind him of his own time in Hell. But she had thought that, beyond that, it would show him exactly what her dad was going through. A darker thought came to her. Maybe it wasn't that she'd hoped to persuade him to let her keep the object that could free her father. Maybe it was that she'd wanted to demonstrate why she'd do anything to keep it. Now he knew what he was dealing with.

She went to him and calmly took his hands in hers. 'Do you see now?'

He nodded. He licked his lips. His eyes met hers. 'I want to help.'

'I know you do.' Though she really didn't.

'He's wrong about me.'

'You don't know you're going to end up in Hell, not for sure, but my dad is in there *now*—'

'Rob Toshack would have given me to Losley. I *know* that.'

'I know—'

Costain suddenly shouted. 'I was planning to take it for myself, okay?!'

Ross stared at him, trying to see the truth in his eyes.

'But I won't now. I won't now. Okay? I want you to use it on *him*. I want you to get *him* out of there.'

Ross didn't know what she believed. She didn't want him looking at her in that moment. So she pulled him to her. Awkwardly, they held each other.

Quill only remembered to get his dinner suit back from the dry-cleaners because Sarah got Jessica to run into the kitchen and ask him if he'd done so. He was looking forward to this do where the staff of her paper were going to be shown what it meant to be part of the *Daily Herald* media group. It would be an evening out where he wouldn't have to think about being a police officer, or about London falling apart, or that two of his team had reported back from extraordinary experiences with nothing but a single negative between them: that whatever was doing the killings wasn't anything to do with the original Jack the Ripper. Of course, at this do, everyone Sarah introduced him to would be interested in his job and ask what he was working on right now, and he'd lie, probably. In the back of his head was the thought that idle conversation might uncover some journalistic titbit about the Ripper or how the *Herald* knew about that bloody scrawled message. But how likely was that, really?

He was hauling the suit through the front door when he got a text from Lofthouse telling him that his request to search Spatley's offices had been approved for tomorrow. At least there'd been some progress.

The reception was held, to Quill's surprise, behind a completely nondescript door, without even a letter box, in a tourist-packed street in Soho. Sarah, done up and smelling of some new perfume, had buzzed an intercom and told a receptionist they were there for the Vincent do, and they'd been let in to walk up a flight of stairs to a coat check. Another staircase took them to a surprisingly spacious bar with a stage and corporate logos everywhere. There was already a crowd; Sarah had insisted that they did not 'do the copper thing' and arrive early, as if this was a crime scene that might be disturbed. Quill gratefully switched off the demanding bit of his head that was a police officer and kept a step behind Sarah as she found her editor, Geoff, and some others from her work, who all looked equally out of place in evening wear and starry-eyed at being in this media nirvana, while forcing themselves to remain cynical in almost every utterance.

Quill recalled he'd enjoyed their company on the last few occasions he'd encountered them; he let himself relax further. He hoped he could get out of his head the news reports of which boroughs were burning. Had it been his imagination, or had there been fewer tourists on the streets? The journalists who didn't already know indeed asked him what he did for a living and what he was working on now, and he circumnavigated the truth. The room filled up a bit more, and a suit came onstage to general applause and thanked everyone for coming. He introduced, to Quill's pleasant surprise, the comedian Frankie Boyle, who did a highly entertaining routine that was unexpectedly harsh towards their host. Sarah nudged Quill in the ribs and indicated where the familiar figure of Russell Vincent stood among a gaggle of close advisers, all of them laughing uproariously at the jokes being told at his expense. A bit too enthusiastically, Quill thought. Vincent was in his early fifties, with saggy jowls, hair that was a bit uncontrollable and a twinkle in his eye. 'I bet,' Quill whispered to Sarah, 'if he suddenly stopped laughing, the whole room would too.'

'Yeah, Quill, except you.'

'Probably.'

Vincent happened to look over at that moment, saw Sarah's party and clearly pointed them out to his inner circle, who nodded along, looking approving.

'I hope that isn't "sack them all anyway",' said Geoff, who was a very balding man with a continual sigh in his voice. 'I've been warned he might come over. If he does, don't tell him you're a copper, Mr Quill. We don't want to scare him off.'

Boyle came to the end of his routine, and told his audience that now he'd got paid they could all fuck themselves, which produced another cheer. He departed with a jolly wave. Almost immediately, Vincent headed over.

Quill patted Sarah's shoulder. 'Here we go. Good luck.'

'I'm a professional,' she said.

'Don't spill your drink on him.'

'Now you've jinxed that.' She put her wine glass down on the table.

'You'd be Geoff Sumpter of the *Enfield Leader*,' said Vincent, holding his hand out to Sarah's editor as he arrived. 'Russell Vincent.' The voice was how Quill remembered it from the telly: that slightly puzzled, self-mocking tone, as if he was stumbling his way along, delighted by life. It was a public school voice, but a chummy, harmless one. Quill found it all very artificial, a deliberate attempt at being charming. He remembered the most famous moment of the Bussard Inquiry, when Vincent, in the middle of dealing with the charges of phone hacking that had been levelled against his newspapers, had had also to deal with his own mobile ringing during his testimony. His frantic, clownish efforts to switch it off had actually got the ministers laughing. Quill fixed a smile on his face now, hoping he wouldn't have to talk to him.

Geoff introduced his team, and Vincent shook each hand in turn. 'I'm not going to remember anyone's name, you realize; I have people to do that. Which of you is Sarah Quill?'

Geoff indicated Sarah, who was now looking flabbergasted. 'Er, hello!'

Vincent held up his hands. 'Don't worry, I've got a list here of one person on each of the acquired titles whose work I think is exemplary. Or rather, who my people think is exemplary. They want me to tell you it's me who thinks that – but oh dear, I've blown that. The rest of you are disposable!' He threw up his hands before they could even react and laughed. 'No, no, you all get to stay. In fact, yours is the title I think we're going to keep doing exactly what it does now. I think you lot might actually be able to win your circulation battle, once you're plugged into our distribution network.' Quill watched the smile on Geoff's face getting broader and broader. 'Geoff, you run a great ship. You all enjoy yourselves. I just need a quick word with Sarah and her husband here.'

Quill girded his loins as, without pausing, Vincent led the two of them off into a gap that automatically opened for him in the midst of the crowd. His people had not followed him, but had been left to carry on chatting up Geoff and his team. Quill was aware of everyone in the room wondering who they were to deserve such face time.

'We're going to be screening some of the new ads that are going out tomorrow,' said Vincent, as the screen behind the stage lit up, 'and I'd value your opinion, but mostly I'm doing this to let each of the talent I've picked out from all the papers look like they're going places, so the rest of the staff tune into that, and –' he plucked a card from his pocket and put it into Sarah's hand – 'you now have my personal contact details, so if you or I need to ask each other anything, we can both do that. Or, to not insult your intelligence, you're going to keep tabs on your boss for me.'

'Ah,' said Sarah.

'Standard practice. Geoff's an honest bloke, and I don't think he'll lie to me, but I always like to have another honest source in reserve. Oh, here we go.' On the screen now was a scene of a group of footballers all gathered around, engrossed in an issue of the *Herald* with the headline 'Invasion of the Immigrants'. The footballers were all black. A couple of them had their mouths open in extraordinary astonishment, gaping at whatever the contents of the paper were meant to be. The music that accompanied the clip was something Latin and trumpety. 'Do you think,' asked Vincent, as if he was asking for a second opinion about a corked bottle of wine, 'that this ad is a tiny bit racist?'

Quill looked to Sarah, who was obviously making a split-second decision about telling truth to power. 'Yes.'

'Good! Good! Why?'

'It makes them look stupid.'

'So you might be moved to complain to the advertising standards authority?'

'I don't know if I'd go that far.'

'We're hoping some people will. That's why that's the cheap one. The idea is that it gets banned, we make a great fuss about it, how we thought we'd made a very liberal choice to hire a bunch of black actors. The headline on the paper, that's to lure people into that way of thinking too. I think if the headline had been about bananas or something, then it would really be racist, not just pretend racist. I'm of Jewish descent myself, so . . .' He left that with a shrug. 'If it's banned it gets talked about in pubs, replayed on YouTube endlessly, it gets a sort of fascinating sheen to it. It makes us look young and rebellious, which is what our research tells us is what we're most seen as not being. It's called "outrage marketing".'

'Ah,' said Sarah, 'right.'

'Hmm. You're still against us showing the clip, though?'

'Yeah.' She said it as if it was just narrowly the best of no really good options.

He laughed. 'This is all good. I need you to be honest with me.'

'What's the music about?' asked Quill.

Vincent turned to him, and Quill found himself being sized up. 'Something with no relation at all to the subject matter: Herb Alpert. People will ask exactly that question. Again, it'll stick in their heads, but that effect fades quickly. If we kept doing adverts with that attached, it'd stop being jarring and start just being our tune. These days anything can come to mean anything. Sorry, you must be . . . no, don't tell me – James, yes, I recall. And you are a . . . police officer, are you not? A detective. Right, hence the question. It's your job to sort through a huge number of signifiers, many different people and events, and work out which of them means anything to you.'

'I suppose,' said Quill, slightly dreading what might come next, and already tired by how fast this man spoke. He hoped that at no point would Vincent ask him to give him the inside track on anything. Although this bloke was supposed to be the only newspaper proprietor who didn't do stuff like that, he was obviously a bit of a shit, and probably guilty of something. But then Quill thought that about most of the general public.

'What I like about the Met,' said Vincent, 'is that it's still a meritocracy.'

Quill suppressed a cynical laugh, and managed a tilt of the head that he hoped indicated nothing in particular.

Vincent seemed to notice the half-heartedness of the gesture. 'Well, that's what senior officers always tell me. I started out as a copy boy; I've been an editor all my life. Oh, here's another one.'

He looked back to the screen and started to narrate what he saw in this next advert. 'Handsome young chap, smart suit but not expensive, down-to-earth London accent but not faux Jamaican *youth* accent, more the sort of voice kept alive by soap operas, so he's doing what the audience *want* to do and *could* actually do, leading them into thinking that if they copy him and buy the paper, they'll be free and happy like him . . .' Quill noticed that the finely ironed copy of the *Herald* the man flapped open had the same headline as in the last advert. 'He's our aspirational cheerleader figure, he's in all the rest of these, which will actually get on telly and push the brand along in the spotlight.'

'Interesting,' said Quill.

'We're really in the same job, James. You notice meaning, I try to make it.'

Quill wanted to ask if a newspaperman's job shouldn't be to report the news, but, aware of Sarah's tight-lipped smile, contented himself with a chummy laugh.

'Well, I must go,' said Vincent, 'if those above you ever grind you down . . .' He took another card from his pocket and placed it in Quill's palm.

Quill looked at the card and his eyes widened. He looked up at Vincent. 'Tell me,' he said, lowering his voice, 'Mr Vincent, have you ever experienced anything impossible?'

Sarah's face was suddenly a. picture.

Vincent seemed to falter. Here, Quill was sure now, was someone who knew exactly what he was talking about. 'I . . . I don't know what that is, and I don't have time to get into it. Sarah, James, good evening.' He moved swiftly off into the crowd.

Sarah looked aghast. 'What the fuck, Quill?'

Quill took the business card from her hand and held it up beside the one he'd been given. To his eyes and his eyes alone, they were both spattered with freezing droplets of silver.

TEN

'How did Sefton end up with "severe bruises on his arms"?' asked Lofthouse.

Quill didn't quite feel able to share all the details of Sefton's experiment. 'He failed to see a man about a bus,' he said. The two of them were walking down a corridor in the Treasury, all polished wood and the smell of a carpet that was cleaned daily. Quill had asked her to come along to give him as much political clout as possible in what looked likely to be a difficult day. What they'd seen on the way in – protestors gathering in Parliament Square – had put them all on edge. This time the youths in the masks had been carrying an enormous puppet of the Toff character, held up by sticks. It held a bloody razor, doubtless made of felt. To Quill it felt as if this new Ripper was being elevated to the status of minor local god, a god that demanded sacrifice. Perhaps literally.

There was something else that was weird, too. As soon as they'd stepped into the precincts of the Houses of Parliament, he had felt a sudden lack of something, as if he'd walked into a recording studio and the ambient sound of the world had cut off. It had taken him a few paces to realize what was going on, then he'd walked back and stepped back and forth, oblivious to the glances he was getting, until he'd found a specific line where it happened. 'It feels . . . safe in here,' he'd told Lofthouse, who had raised an eyebrow at his performance. 'Like past this line the power of London doesn't work.'

'That has to be deliberate.'

'It does sound like the sort of thing those who laid down the law in past centuries might do: protect the centres of power from occult dodginess.' They'd gone out again and walked around the boundaries of the old buildings, Quill finding that the force field or whatever it was approximated to the walls in some places but not in others. The modern additions weren't covered. Everyone inside was lucky in ways that the vast majority of them didn't appreciate. He noted that this wasn't something that Lofthouse had known previously. When she said she knew less than they did, she seemed to be telling the truth. So why couldn't she tell them what she *did* know?

Finally, they'd had to head in again because it was time for their appointment. 'You're trying to get a meeting with Vincent?' asked Lofthouse now.

'I have a call in with him, as they say. He's obviously had an encounter with something from the Sighted world and, given that our suspect is the only thing we've seen so far that splatters, maybe even the Ripper himself. And Vincent radiates dodgy. The number on those business cards turned out to be just his PA, but that's closer than most people get.'

'Last time a fully armed parliamentary inquiry went after him he came up smelling of roses. Tread very gently.'

'Absolutely.'

'Did you find the taxi that picked up the male witness from the bar?'

'We did, but unfortunately he paid in cash, so we've just got a few extra lines of description from the foggy recall of a taxi driver. He bloody got out near Tottenham Court Road too, right in the middle of town, and we lose him on camera somewhere in the shops. So no indication of home address.'

'And you're pursuing Gaiman?'

'He's one of only two survivors from the Goat and Compasses

that we can definitely find. He's still in London, and in the face of a call from the Met, his agent was fulsomely cooperative, so our oomph is still respected in some quarters. Ross and Sefton, who insisted on getting right back on the horse, are interviewing him this afternoon.'

'The other survivor would be . . . ?'

'The surviving Keel brother, Terry, who we've left where he is. Sefton's been keeping a watch on the shop, and the individuals who were regular clientele seem to be lying low. For the moment.'

A door ahead of them opened, and a pleasant-faced, neat young man stepped out of it. 'Superintendent Lofthouse?'

They were taken to a rather more impressive door and shown in to see the permanent secretary to the Treasury, Sir Anthony Clough. He rose to greet them. A very guarded man, Quill thought: big smile on his face, but nothing in the eyes. He was large, had once been muscular, a big head with white hair around the temples. He'd served under both flavours of administration, was known to have an Olympian disregard for party politics and was, according to a senior Met colleague, 'cruel, but fair'. Having exchanged pleasantries, he addressed himself to Lofthouse and asked what reason her people had for searching Spatley's departmental and parliamentary offices, when they'd already been checked out once by the main inquiry. Lofthouse looked to Quill, who again trotted out that they were a special team with a special remit, and Lofthouse made the right noises to indicate that further questions, even from this level of seniority, wouldn't be advisable.

Clough paused for a significant time when Quill asked him whether or not Spatley had any issues in his personal life. Lofthouse and Quill exchanged glances.

'Michael Spatley was highly ethical. To a fault. But he'd recently been . . . distracted. He'd been delegating some of his parliamentary responsibilities to ministerial colleagues, often the sign of trouble at home.'

'What sort of trouble?'

'Oh, no, in this case, I don't think it was.'

'Sir,' began Quill, 'if you know of any dirty linen in, erm, the Cabinet . . .' He mentally winced at his turn of phrase. 'What I'm trying to say is, you can be sure of our tact, as far as it can go, and it'd actually be a service to the deceased if—'

'We don't, as a rule, let ministers with *things going on in their lives* get near the Cabinet. Though there have been exceptions. In Michael Spatley's case, the only thing I can think of that might possibly be relevant is that, at parties, he would chat a little too long to charming young ladies.'

'Are you saying he was having an affair?'

'Absolutely not. I'm sure, in fact, that he wasn't. But, and I hope you understand the subtlety and strength of our sensitivities in this area, I believe he might have *liked* to have been.'

Quill sighed. This man was sure he had powers in his own domain that equalled those of the Sight. Maybe he did. But it wasn't the sort of thing likely to produce evidence. 'Is there anything else about him you managed to . . . divine?'

Clough took a moment to find the right words. 'I think he had something on his mind. This is a *particularly exciting government*. The Cabinet don't share with each other as much as we've been used to. I have seen whips who were just one altercation shy of assault charges, whips confronting whips. That never happens. To be blunt with you, Detective Inspector, Superintendent, I'm privileged to serve within a government that at any moment might start fighting itself. If this is the brain of the country, that would be Britain having a stroke. So Mr Spatley was probably wise to keep his own counsel about whatever he was planning. Perhaps defection to the opposition, perhaps some uncovering of Tory misdeeds that might increase his own party's currently minuscule leverage within Cabinet – who knows? Actually, I do remember something. Just before he died, I asked him when he was going to pick a fight, meaning when was he going to start taking his own bills into committee again. He said he had a big one planned.'

Quill smiled in sudden appreciation. 'Interesting. Did you see any sign of this fight materializing?'

'Now you put it that way . . .' Clough seemed to be reassessing some of what he'd regarded as certainties before Quill had started asking him his simple list of questions. 'He displayed a certain paranoia. These days, that isn't unusual. He called in security on a couple of occasions. He felt the integrity of his office might have been breached, that it might have been searched. He said he'd put hairs across his desk drawers or something. I said, while sharing his concerns, that it was very unlikely that the place could have been turned over. He was also anxious that he might have a virus or bug on his mobile. Nothing was ever found. He was always changing phones.'

'Did you tell all this to our colleagues on the main inquiry?' asked Quill.

'Of course. They wrote down *everything*. But at that point we were all convinced it was an open-and-shut case of a protestor forcing his way into the car.'

Now here, thought Quill, is a diplomat. If Lofthouse went back to Jason Forrest and created trouble about that, she'd have something to work with, but if it made too many waves, Clough would have absolute deniability. 'So you don't think the driver, Tunstall, did it?'

'Well, who knows? But he and Michael were certainly friendly. Tunstall would come in to see him before they went home almost every day. They'd have a cup of tea.'

'Do you mean they were . . . *too* friendly?'

Clough sighed. 'I don't think their relationship was anything *that* out of the ordinary.'

'Bloody hell,' said Quill, as he walked into Spatley's office and took his first slow look around. 'We actually have a few tiny new possibilities to follow up.'

'A vague indication of possible motive,' confirmed Lofthouse. 'That Spatley was worried about being listened in on, that he might have been about to do . . . something.' The room they were in was clean and plush, all leather on the desk, panelling on the walls, wooden floors. Outside was a more modern cubicle space, where Treasury civil servants worked. Lofthouse, Quill noted, did what she always did when she entered a crime scene: went to touch the walls, as if measuring something. He found himself wondering if that had anything to do with her mysterious links to the Continuing Projects Team from the Docklands ruins. They were meant to be architects, weren't they?

She saw him watching her, and dropped her hand from the wall. 'What?'

Quill shook his head. 'Things I am not allowed to ask you about.'

'You know I wouldn't conceal anything that could harm your team.'

'Then—'

'But I'm really not going to go into it. I can't. Okay?'

Quill could only force a dissatisfied smile.

Lofthouse pulled on a pair of evidence gloves and threw another pair to Quill. 'All right,' she said, 'let's get started.'

They started by turning out the desk drawers, looking under them, tapping them for false bottoms. 'You know, when you said I didn't need to bring one of my officers—' began Quill.

'You thought you'd be doing this on your own?'

'Kind of.'

Lofthouse gave him a look of mock annoyance.

A young suit stepped into the room, saw they were there and reacted in shock for a moment, then obviously remembered who they were, made his apologies and left.

'That,' said Quill. 'That.'

'What?'

'Spatley felt this place had been searched. But even with him deceased, civil servants have to keep popping in here. No search that went unnoticed could have been very thorough. And it can't have been done by anything invisible and occult, because that couldn't have got in here.'

'We are in a Ripper-free zone.'

'A suspect still on our Ops Board – that is, Tunstall – came in here for regular cups of tea. Nobody would have paid attention to him popping in when Spatley wasn't about.'

Lofthouse stopped what she was doing. 'And do you know what I would have said if I was Tunstall and I'd just been accused of murdering someone I'd had regular cups of tea with?'

'I'd say I'd never do that, that we were friends,' said Quill, feeling as if he wanted to slap her heartily on the back or something equally inappropriate. 'But Tunstall hasn't seen fit to mention that, has he? It's as if he knows that drawing attention to his close relationship with Spatley, and mentioning that he popped in here for tea and sympathy, might implicate rather than exonerate him.'

Lofthouse nodded. 'You know, when coppers tell me they searched a room, I do tend to ask, considering how many times a second search is required in order to find the evidence we're after—'

'You reckon they just opened every drawer and read every piece of paper, and didn't, for instance, lift up those heavy bookcases and filing cabinets?'

'Of course, a normal human evildoer who was short of time wouldn't have moved the furniture in his search either.'

'So . . .' said Quill, taking off his jacket.

'I wish,' said Lofthouse, 'that I had come dressed for manual labour.'

They hauled every piece of furniture in the room out of its designated place. They revealed the remains of food, and a spider that must have felt they were hunting it down as it skittered from one hiding place to another. On the underside of a cabinet they found a cluster of obvious fingerprints in deep dust. Quill felt sudden copper glee. 'If you were doing this fast, you wouldn't bother with gloves, either.'

'If they're Tunstall's, he can probably explain them away. Dropped his keys or something.'

'Yeah, but at least it'll give him an awkward five minutes under interview. It'll be even better if we can find what he might have been after.' He continued to search while Lofthouse put in a call to get some Scene of Crime Officers over to record the prints.

It was under the last bookcase he hauled away from the wall: something white and dusty revealed between it and the skirting board. A business card. Quill picked it up. It looked as if it must have been dropped down there by accident. He showed it to Lofthouse. One side was blank apart from a mobile number written in biro. 'Relax in the Underworld' said the lettering on the other side, with an address in Berwick Street in Soho.

'A brothel,' said Lofthouse.

Quill laughed. 'I would have needed to look that up, ma'am,' he said. 'Excellent. We finally have some juice.'

'Politically, it might be an idea to give this to Jason Forrest.' Lofthouse said it as if she was sure Quill would say no, but she just wanted to put it out there.

Quill gave her her due, mentally rolled the dice, but finally shook his head. 'No, ma'am, I'm going to keep that from him for the moment. We're going to want to check the place out and I don't want the main investigation crashing through there, perhaps disturbing evidence only we can see.'

'James—'

'I know, ma'am, on my head be it.' He got out his mobile. 'We can use the old reverse phone book to look up the number and see whose phone it is, but best foot forward.' He dialled the number on the card. He waited a moment, then, without speaking, switched off his phone again. 'Straight to voicemail, just the auto-mated greeting.'

'Are you going to interview Tunstall again?' asked Lofthouse.

'I'll get that sorted for tomorrow,' said Quill. 'And this time we'll *all* be bad cop.'

Sefton and Ross found the hotel that Gaiman's agent had given them the address for. It was a simple three storeys, Victorian from the look of it, in the Seven Dials area, with the intersection of streets of that name visible from the door. Ross asked at the desk, and they were shown up to an ornate library, where armchairs were positioned in the sunshine and a breeze blew through the open windows. Nobody else was about. Sefton felt an ache in his legs as he sat down. He felt only half here, wanting to get on with finding the numinous in the world, but not knowing how. The Ripper, or rather his message, was exposing fault lines across London, and the bolder the rioters and rival groups of protestors became, the less the police seemed to be able to do to prevent them. His dreams made him feel as if he was being rifled through, and he woke with an urgent need to do something about all this. Still, he supposed, they were about to talk with someone who, according to Quill, might know more about occult London than they did. Background was always useful. But if Gaiman knew anything of direct relevance to the case, he'd be surprised.

'Hullo.' So this must be Gaiman, entering the room with a guarded expression on his face. He was all in black: a good-looking man, a long face, a lot of emotion around the eyes. Now he'd stopped and was looking startled at them. '*You two* are police officers?'

Sefton showed him his warrant card, and, as they all tended to do now, omitted to add that Ross technically wasn't an officer.

'I saw you both in the Goat.' Gaiman motioned for them to sit down at a table by the window, and he followed. 'Were you there undercover?'

'That would be an operational matter,' said Ross. She seemed burdened today, nervous about something. On the way over, she'd hardly replied to Sefton's attempts to start a conversation.

Gaiman frowned at them for another moment, then seemed to decide on a more friendly course of action and extended his hand. 'Neil.' They introduced themselves in turn. 'Thank you for blowing up my favourite bar.'

'Sorry,' said Sefton, 'not deliberate.'

'No, I think actually it was a mercy killing. You and your boss didn't see the place at its best.'

'Our boss?' said Ross, raising an eyebrow.

'The one who looked a bit lost there, stayed behind to help and looked like something out of *The Sweeney.*'

'Our boss,' Ross conceded.

'He's not an undercover,' sighed Sefton.

'Do you also have the Sight?' Gaiman asked. From the look on her face, Ross was about to say that was also an operational matter, so Sefton quickly confirmed they did. 'You're the first police officers I've ever heard of who had the gift.'

'Were you aware,' asked Sefton, 'of anyone before us who tried to bring law to the Sighted community?'

'People say there was someone, but I don't know who. Everyone seems to think that sort of went away a few years ago. I take it you're investigating a particular case . . . and now, of course, I realize, having seen the news, that it's obvious what that might be.'

'We're just putting together some background context,' said Sefton, wishing he could share more information with this man. He was, after all, the only friendly human being they'd met who saw the world the way they did. A waiter arrived, and they all ordered tea. Gaiman asked for honey with his, and, while they waited, all aware that their conversation would get intense again once there was no possibility of being interrupted, talked about the bees he kept at his home in the States. 'Each hive has its own personality,' he said. 'They have moods. You can't really call a single bee an individual. The hive will sacrifice it for a greater good.' Once the waiter had returned, he got them both to try a spoonful of the particular honey he'd asked for. It was, Sefton was pleased to discover, delicious.

When the waiter closed the door behind him, Gaiman put his hands on the table. 'So . . . the Ripper . . .'

Sefton had got out his special notebook, which by now was a very randomly organized grimoire of notes and diagrams concerning 'the matter of London'. Ross had got out her much more functional notebooks. 'Sorry to keep on about it, but we can't talk about operational matters. If you wouldn't mind answering a few questions . . . ?'

'Sure.'

'You told our boss that you'd been given the Sight via an artefact passed to you by a fan,' began Ross. 'We're interested in any information you might be able to give us about what could be called the occult community in London. How, for example, did you get involved with them?'

'I wrote a book called *Neverwhere*. It was a TV show first – you probably wouldn't have seen it. The novel version is very different, because in between the two I'd been given the Sight. So the novel was a rather more authentic, if still metaphorical, story about there being a hidden London. Some of the folk who live here and know about these things picked up on that, and they started to come along to signings. And I'd sort of know, whenever I shook the hand of one of them?' He had that American end-of-sentence question in his accent, Sefton noted. 'They'd very kindly invite me along to their get-togethers, and, whenever I could, I went. They're very set in their ways, but the odd thing is that London isn't.' He raised a finger and held it there as he seemed to want to completely explore a thought before he said it. 'Have you been to any of the other cities of the Sight?'

Ross sounded slightly defensive. 'No.'

'We've been a bit busy,' said Sefton.

'Paris is quite something. Cork I didn't really understand. Northampton is kind of . . . cute. Barnsley is delightful. New York is exactly what you'd expect.'

'Right,' said Sefton, hoping that he sounded as if he knew what New York was expected to be.

'Listen, you've heard of Jerusalem Syndrome?' Gaiman looked away as he continued, as if realizing there was the potential of rudeness here if he assumed knowledge they didn't have. 'When people go to Jerusalem, and within days, hours sometimes, they become convinced that they're not just a very naughty boy but are actually the Messiah? Well, I think that's sort of what the Sight is. That written large. Jerusalem, as far as I know, isn't a city of the Sight, though it has, as everywhere does, a handful of features only the Sighted can see, and no, I don't know why some cities are like this and others aren't. The Sight gives other cities the same superpowers over the human psyche that Jerusalem has. Both effects are about the buildings, about what the shape of individual cities does to the natural human heart. I don't mean *just* the buildings – that's only one of many layers. You've seen people make gestures now, use their voices? That's that layer. But if you place the buildings right . . .' He quickly moved the places of the cups and teapot on the table. 'That's another way to work with it.' He pointed out of the window. 'I met you here so I could show you this. We're at Seven Dials, the conjunction of seven roads. When you look at the pillar in the middle, using the Sight, what do you feel?'

Oh. Sefton reached out for the pillar with the Sight and found himself repulsed almost immediately. In a small way. That was probably why he hadn't looked at it like that on the way in here. It was like the thought of some small guilt that you got reminded of and skipped past. Like he felt about Barry Keel. He wouldn't have noticed it without it being pointed out.

'Yup.' Gaiman smiled. 'Seven roads lead here. It's said this was once the place in London with the highest crime rate because of that, by the way, with seven roads for a thief to flee down. But that pillar in the middle of them bears only six sun dials, because the pillar was designed before the seventh road was added at the last minute. So this is really Six Dials. London knows that and it drives it crazy. And so it also drives people who concentrate on the pillar crazy. Just a little. More or less depending on the time of day, actually. That's why those with the Sight call this place "the Severed Streets". They're aware something went wrong at the planning stage, and that it doesn't contribute as positively as it should to the occult power of London.'

Ross had an expression on her face that indicated she didn't want to be interested in this seeming irrelevance, but couldn't help it. 'Why did the number of roads change?'

'Money. They wanted to build as many houses as they possibly could. And that meant seven pubs, and so you put the pattern of the Sight and the pattern of money together, and you get one of the most notorious neighbourhoods in London, for a long time, until someone must have sorted that out. Probably someone who knew what they were doing.'

'So the power of money and the power of London are at odds?' asked Sefton.

'I've been wondering about that. I think it's more that the power of money doesn't care about the shape of London, and so sometimes people with money try to do things that go against the grain.' He smiled a warm smile at them. 'Being police among all this, you must find your world view gets . . . distorted by it. You must keep trying to find straight lines.'

'That's pretty much our job description now.' Sefton found himself wanting to go on a research trip to New York. To do that would give you such context. He also wanted to know which holiday destinations were 'cities of the Sight' before he went to any of them. 'Do you do any . . . practical work yourself?'

'A few youthful experiments. Now I like to live in places where that would be impossible, where I don't have to see unexpected things before breakfast.'

'What did you sacrifice?' asked Ross.

'You can always find something.' He poured the tea, looking away, as if distracted again.

'Such as?'

He stopped and regarded them seriously for a moment. 'Nothing that would get me into trouble with you. Am I suspected of something?'

'Not at all,' said Sefton. 'As we said, this is just background.'

'Who or what do you sacrifice to?' asked Ross, now firmly in interview room mode.

Gaiman sighed. 'London, as a concept, as is traditional, but . . . okay, I don't know how far you're into this—'

Sefton was startled. 'There's something else to sacrifice to now?'

'Yeah. You get that feeling now. I've been looking into this, and . . .' He stopped and considered again for a moment. Sefton wondered if that speech habit was really because his thoughts distracted him, or if he was being careful about what he revealed to them. From the look on her face, Ross certainly seemed to be favouring the latter interpretation. 'Listen,' Gaiman said suddenly, 'do you know about ostentation?'

'Please,' said Sefton, 'tell us.'

'It's a term from folklore, used there in the context of what are called "friend of a friend stories". You know, "there was this stoned woman who put her baby in the microwave" – urban legends. Well, sometimes, in cities that aren't Sighted, those stories come true simply because enough people have heard about them, and in a big population there's always someone mad enough to *try* it, whatever it is. But in cities of the Sight, I think that can happen a lot more easily. I think in London, to announce something is sometimes to take a further step towards that thing actually happening than would be the case outside. I think that might be what the phrase "streets paved with gold" in the pantomime means, to those in the know. That the streets of London are infused with—'

'That golden threadlike stuff.'

'Yeah. But I don't exactly know what that is. I've only ever seen it a couple of times.'

'When?'

'When my youthful experiments messed up. Unless the golden thread is preset to do something, I think you only see it when things go wrong. It's like lines of code in software. You're only meant to experience the effects. Have you seen the silver stuff?'

'The power source?' said Sefton.

Gaiman pointed at him with a little nod and pursed lips – an expression that made Sefton feel perversely proud of himself. 'These are visual metaphors for control and power that only the Sighted can access. Whether or not you'd say the gold and silver stuff is *real* . . . I'm not even sure that's a sensible question. I only ever saw either when something I did went wrong.'

'You never saw the silver splattered around?' asked Ross.

'Not especially. It's very valuable. It's actually the *definition* of value to those who are Privileged to work with the matter of London. It is the power they've sacrificed for. They tend to make sure it does what it's supposed to.'

'Are there any other ways of getting power, apart from making a sacrifice?' Ross was using the tone she'd employ in an interview room, which was making Sefton smile.

'You hear about people stealing power from others, or finding it or having it gifted to them, but those tend to be one-offs in specific circumstances.'

'Okay,' said Sefton, with a little look to Ross, who was now making notes at high speed. 'You were talking about how things happen more easily in London if they're talked about as being possible. Is that the start of London "remembering" something?'

Gaiman asked what exactly he meant by that, and Sefton tried to fill him in, without revealing operational details, about the conclusions his team had come to concerning, for example, the moment when Losley had been remembered by the metropolis and ghosts of her had appeared everywhere.

Gaiman finally nodded. 'I didn't know there was a name for it. But, yeah, when I'm here, I try not to talk about babies in microwaves. Try standing in Berkeley Square and reciting a poem about nightingales, over and over, for a day. My wife did that once.' He found a picture of her doing so on his phone and showed it to them. 'At the end, we were hearing their song, just faintly, but it was there. That's a quaint feature. It can become pretty un-quaint. I think you might find that very important.'

Sefton was remembering their own terrifying adventures in Berkeley Square and could see that Ross had made the connection too. That wasn't relevant right now.

Gaiman leaned forward. 'There's a question you want to ask me,' he said, 'but feel that you can't, because it'd give too much away about what you're investigating. So let me answer it anyway. No, I don't think this Ripper of yours is a product of ostentation. He's certainly been "remembered" by London, but—'

'That's confined to where it should be, in Whitechapel,' said Ross.

She got one of Gaiman's affirming nods too. 'But I have been wondering if the sudden appearances of these flash mobs *might* be a product of ostentation. In London, tweeting about something might be planting the seed of that thing happening—'

'So tweeting about a riot—' said Sefton.

'—could start one. If you knew how to do it just right. But also, imagine doing the opposite. What if you could seed the idea, especially right now, that everything was okay? That might start to make everything better.' He smiled hugely.

'Catching the Ripper would do exactly that,' said Sefton.

'It would,' said Gaiman.

'You seem,' said Ross, 'to be telling us a lot about what we need to do.'

'Do I? Sorry.'

They asked him all their detailed questions about everyone they'd seen in the pub, but he could only provide scant detail. They explored Ripper connections with him and asked if Sighted cities ever turned against the rich, if one could push the powers of a place too far. 'It is said,' he replied to that, 'that it's hard for a rich man to enter Jerusalem through the gate they call the Eye of the Needle. That's where the proverb comes from.'

Sefton for the first time wondered if Gaiman was making it all up; that didn't agree with what he'd read. 'I thought there was no such gate.'

'That's true,' said Gaiman, gently, 'unless you have the Sight. More honey?'

ELEVEN

Brian Tunstall had been shocked by his experience of being on remand in Brixton jail. He'd been on G wing, with a bunch of others awaiting trial, in a cell with, thank God, a very quiet man who had just shaken his head when Brian had attempted to introduce himself, as if he could deny the whole experience of being here.

Brian hadn't been able to deny it. While he was inside, and when he'd got past the shock of that terrifying, impossible thing that had happened to Michael Spatley, he'd started to mull over the idea that he deserved to be there. To his brief, because he didn't see how DI Quill's weird belief in what had really happened could help him in court, he'd maintained his other story: that a protestor had somehow got into the car. So to two different people he'd maintained two different fictions.

He'd started to feel he'd deserved to be there, and then they'd let him out. He'd gone back home, to Angela and little Alee. He'd spent a lot of time at night, woken by terrible dreams, troubled by his conscience, doing what he was doing now – sitting watching Alee asleep in her cot.

Tomorrow, DI Quill was going to visit to talk to him again. He must know something new, something that pointed to Tunstall's real part in Michael Spatley's death. Tunstall had been thinking all day about how good it would be to tell Quill everything. He didn't see how he could possibly face a charge of conspiracy to murder. Though there would, of course, be lesser charges, he might be able to do a deal. Quill had indicated that he'd believed the impossible bits. He would have to tell them about the money.

Yes, he thought now as he looked at his baby girl's face. Yes, I'll be a good example to her. I just want to be able to keep seeing her face, to be here for her.

He remembered the taste of the blood-soaked piece of paper as he'd put it into his mouth and chewed and swallowed. That was what they had made him do for money.

He would normally have watched TV if he couldn't sleep. But all you saw these days were news broadcasts about the protestors. He didn't want to see them. Even here in Hackney he could now hear the sounds of them. There were shouts from right outside the window. He hoped they wouldn't wake Alee up.

When the wall in front of him started warping, he wondered if he was dreaming, or if perhaps the stress he'd been under had deformed the shape of his eyes. It took him a moment to realize that something was really pushing its way through the wall.

He managed to grab Alee from out of the cradle before the first blow landed. He staggered to the bedroom door, shoved his way through it, one hand trying to fend off something he couldn't seem to connect with, his only thought to get the baby away.

He was suddenly aware of many terrible impacts happening rapidly across his body. He looked into the face of his screaming child. He heard what must be Angela yelling too.

He was so incapable of helping them.

Then he was gone.

Quill and his team stood looking at the remains of Brian Tunstall. No scrawled message this time, and, as far as Forensics could find, again no fingerprints. The adult witness, Tunstall's wife, Angela, had been too traumatized to answer any but the most basic questions, but it was clear that the MO had been the same. The Ripper had spared the woman and child.

So much for rich white men. Only two out of three for Tunstall.

The now-familiar silver goo showed the entry and exit points of the killer. Jason Forrest, unaware of them, stood glowering near one. As Quill watched, he just shook his head and walked away.

There came an alert from Quill's phone. He looked at it and found confirmation that the prints they'd found in Spatley's office had indeed belonged to Tunstall.

Back in the Portakabin, Quill said out loud what they all knew in their copper hearts. 'Tunstall must have *known something* about Spatley's murder and *we* didn't get it out of him when we had the chance. Gaiman suggested that if we catch the Ripper, we might turn everything around and save London. We might have fucked that up before we even knew it!'

They had gone over all the interviews again and had found nothing that spoke of Tunstall's complicity. The efforts to get Vincent to reply to their request for him to be interviewed were continuing. Billionaires, unlike authors, treated afternoons with the police as optional excursions. The reverse phone book the Met held online had revealed the mobile phone number written on the card found in Spatley's office to be that of a disposable model, known in the trade as a 'burner' – the sort of thing that organized criminal networks used to reduce the risk of being traced. At least it was still in use.

'The assailant,' said Ross, who sounded as tense as Quill felt, almost to the point of anger, 'also waited until the night before we were due to interview Tunstall again. I don't believe that's a coincidence.'

'Who, apart from Lofthouse and the four of us, knew we were going to talk to him again?'

'Tunstall himself might have talked,' said Costain. Quill thought he was looking well frazzled, as if sleep was eluding him more than the others, even.

'Or,' said Sefton, 'the Ripper might have supernatural means of learning about this stuff.'

'Has anyone got anything new about anything?' Quill asked.

'This morning,' said Ross, 'I heard back from Photographic Intelligence. As I expected, the images from the bar weren't good enough for their software to do facial recognition.'

'Fuck me,' said Quill. He went to the Ops Board and pointed at it. 'There is, as I have said before, *only* what's up there on that board. It is where the only salvation lies for such as us. Let us think. What could we add to it?' Already, the brothel business card had been attached to the corkboard with the number written beside it and an association line attaching it to Spatley. The card itself had revealed no clear fingerprints except Spatley's, but now they were at least sure that he'd handled it.

'But then he lost it,' said Ross, 'and that didn't worry him too much. Which means it's probably not a clue to him being involved in some sort of scandal.'

Quill frowned. 'Why do you say it didn't worry him?'

'As owner of that office, he could have locked the door, moved furniture about, found it again. It seems as if it meant more to the person doing the searching than it did to Spatley.'

'It's time we found out what the connection is, why someone might have wanted to search Spatley's offices for that card. You two –' Quill indicated Costain and Ross – 'take a trip to Soho and put eyeballs on the target.'

Costain had always found Soho's insistence that it was still naughty, almost because it had to be for the tourists, charming. It was actually calming to be back here. The sex-shop end of the business moving into the daylight across the way on Oxford Street had really taken the oomph out of the place, which now said gay and proud more than it said furtive. There was only one remaining peep show, and its signs sighed with the idea that this was the art of a lost age, like a freak show or a circus. Presumably because the area was still a popular brand, there were still over a dozen prostitutes working in walk-ups, stairwells with small advertising of their purpose that often seemed to lead to flats above independent television production companies (and there was an example of how rent levels created strange bedfellows). He assumed that meetings about new drama series were regularly interrupted by faked cries of encouragement. The TV people probably liked that. There was still a handful of men who made a living hawking to likely customers on the street and walking them to the stairwells. The prostitutes discouraged this parasitic trade. They preferred to have tips given to their 'maids', matronly figures who were, in effect, their PAs and lived in. There was a whole other industry of people who pretended to be prostitutes but were in fact thieves, and brothels that were actually high-priced drinking establishments which one was encouraged not to leave. There were also three or four genuine, surprisingly large, brothels in the area, including this one on Berwick Street, across from which Costain and Ross now sat, drinking coffee on a street-side table in the sunshine. The coffee was probably a bad idea. She looked as on edge as he felt. They had watched as a number of men had approached a completely nondescript door, had talked into an intercom and been welcomed up. Having established that the place was still working, in a while they'd take a wander around the map and work out back exits and boltholes.

'You're right at home here, aren't you?' Ross said to him.

He turned to look at her. They'd hardly talked on the way over. She was probably wondering if he'd meant what he'd said about helping her get her dad out of Hell rather than taking the Bridge of Spikes to save himself. He'd stared into the night worrying about that question himself, but the more he thought about it, the more he looked at her, the more he felt that, once again, he'd done the right thing; this time at least, the right thing felt good. 'I guess.'

'It reminds me of Whitechapel.'

'Does it?'

'I mean, all those dead women. Except here it's all kept behind closed doors. How many container-loads of Belarusian teenagers do you reckon get decanted here every week?'

On impulse, he reached out and took her hand in his. She stiffened, but let him. 'I meant what I said about your dad.' He wanted her to ask about that third date. Perhaps it would, by default, be tomorrow, the night of the auction. Or perhaps that was putting too many stressful concepts together for Ross. He wasn't sure she'd even recognize what 'third date' tended to mean in modern dating culture. She watched TV, didn't she? He found it odd, distantly, that he was so attracted to someone who'd reminded him so fiercely of his glimpse of Hell. Or maybe he liked the idea of being with someone who cared enough to keep him on the straight and narrow.

'I know you did.' He wasn't sure if that was a lie or not.

'We should talk about what we're going to do about the auction.'

'Yeah.'

He decided he was going to risk it. Just to see her reaction. 'You could call it our third date.'

She stopped what she was going to say, actually a little flustered, which was deeply pleasing. 'Technically,' she said.

TWELVE

The following evening, Sarah Quill watched her husband silently drink his coffee at the kitchen table. She never liked it when he was silent. 'So they didn't find an easy exit to the brothel?'

'Nah, but I'm not ready for Christmas presents in the middle of summer. We spent the day trying to find the woman from the Ripper attack on the Soviet bar and her male friend, but we don't really have enough to go on.'

'What are you going to do next?'

'Prepare to send Costain and Sefton in. Continue to pursue an interview with Vincent. Continue to search the victims' histories for some connection.'

'The announcement of the result of the postal ballot of Police Federation members is tomorrow.'

'Yeah.'

'If they have decided to take industrial action, coppers coming out illegally, won't it all contribute to how bad London is feeling right now?'

'And therefore to this ostentation malarkey. The thought had occurred to me. London will have been told it can do what it likes. And so it will. I don't want to think about what's going to happen.'

'The driver, Tunstall – you think he must have been in on it?'

'It looks that way. We looked over Spatley's two other offices, his constituency one and the one in the House, and didn't find anything there. We spoke to the chief whip, and he told us that, if anything, Spatley had been focusing himself, cutting down on constituency work.'

'To prepare for some sort of fight.'

'Yes, but in politics you'd normally need to gather allies, put a gang together – that was the feeling I got from every civil service bod we talked to. Spatley, paranoid as he was, hadn't told *anyone* what he was about to do, as far as we can tell. We got into the business of Spatley's phone with SO15, Counter-Terrorism Command. They have serious hackers, and they took his mobile apart. There was nothing.'

'And what about *your* phones?'

He smiled. He was always pleased when she worked something out. 'Them too. And again, a clean bill of health. We had SO15 sweep the Portakabin for bugs while they were at it. That caused a few raised eyebrows. Nothing found there, either.'

'So let me get this straight. You talked out loud about reinterviewing a witness while you were in the Treasury, a place which is, security-wise, presumably as safe as the proverbial Bank of England, and the witness you talked about interviewing is killed the next morning.'

'With us having only talked to each other about it, on phones which have definitely not been hacked.'

'But, dear God, somehow you're being listened in on.'

'It looks that way, yeah.'

'Maybe whatever evil shit you're up against this time is all seeing and all powerful?'

'Let's hope so. Then we can just retire and leave them to it.' He looked a little happier now. 'I always like it when we talk things through like this. We should have an Ops Board at home.'

'Really,' she said, 'no.'

Ross stood on her balcony, listening to the summer sounds of her suburb: the distant music, the cars racing by with conflicting tunes blaring from them, nearby laughter, the pubs, ambulances over the hill. Distant sirens spoke of continuing violence, which hadn't yet reached Catford. She'd stopped watching the news. It was all uniforms with shields and helmets and the surging of huge masses of people, and then fires and running kids with looted televisions. She'd thought there was a limit to how long it could go on; seemingly there wasn't. It was turning out to be a long summer. The Summer of Blood. Whoever had coined that phrase had – if what Gaiman said about ostentation was true – helped in a tiny way to make it happen.

She was dressed for the underworld again, in costume. The only advantage she had tonight was that, unless he'd looked it up – and he might well have done – Costain didn't know where her dad was buried. If she got the Bridge of Spikes, she'd have to get there fast and activate it, without Costain following her, she hoped. She didn't have any idea how the device actually worked. Presumably, if it was in the auction, it would come with instructions. She hoped Costain was also uncertain about that.

She would keep her knife on her tonight, in case she got hold of the Bridge and Costain tried to take it, in spite of all his promises. She was prepared to hurt him. She wouldn't back away from that possibility. She was doing this for Dad, and she wasn't going to stop now.

Alongside that, it was also going to be their third date. If he was being honest, if he was now genuinely on her side, they might end up together, might get to celebrate together. The possibility of that had turned her on all day, whenever she thought about it. She'd even gone out and bought some underwear.

It almost made her smile. Talk about all or nothing.

When he arrived, she opened the door to him and would have been happy to let him kiss her. But he didn't. He looked calm and serious and committed to her cause. The librarian look he once again sported helped with that. 'Let's get this done,' he said.

*

The map on the card had surprised Ross when she'd compared it to Google Maps. The location given hadn't looked promising when she'd checked it out in person, either. But she supposed it made a sort of sense.

How thin the Millennium Bridge across the Thames felt as they walked over it that evening. Perhaps it was because with every step Ross felt something enormous growing all around her. The sun was still a way above the horizon behind her, making her shadow sharp on the new stone. The full moon was in the sky ahead, the base of it still hidden behind the buildings. She found that Costain, beside her, had slowed his walk too. She looked over the rail, to the river itself. It was sparkling in the combined light, a reminder of the great river of silver and gold that lay beneath all things in London. Tonight it felt as if it was simmering with the million sparkles on its surface, preparing, flexing like a muscle. It was uniting with the sky above, creating this enormous sensation of a waiting, observing, presence.

She could feel London tonight as if she had her palms against the heart of a wild animal. She could sense it watching them. She supposed it was because she herself was on the edge of a precipice. Maybe all Londoners felt it at times like these. Maybe this was how some of the Privileged felt all the time. It wasn't the first time she'd thought of them as lucky. This was the truth that was under everything.

If she looked down into the detail at the water's edge, she'd see terrible things, but that would be the truth too. To be part of a city was to be a cell in a bigger animal, an animal large enough to have a conversation with the sea, which the river moderated, and the sky, which the river reflected. To be part of a city was to have an index of your mortal life right in front of you: as you got older you'd start saying you remembered when it was all different around here.

She understood why those who had the Sight felt the need to hang on to the past. She herself, she realized, was trying to get back to when her dad had been alive. It was as if she was trying to begin her life again, even when everything about a city said the world went on without you.

She slowed to a stop and Costain halted too. They were halfway across the bridge. Where they stood, people had attached padlocks to the horizontal wires, usually with the names of couples on them. It was a gesture that was supposed to be about eternal love, but it had always felt a bit creepy to Ross, suggesting that locks had anything to do with love. Every month, the City of London Corporation sent people along with bolt cutters to remove them.

She understood now that she had no idea about that sort of love except as something people talked about. She'd always hoped if she ever felt like that, it'd be free of the locks she'd made for herself, of the burdens of her own quest. That it would be freeing.

She felt now how small her mission was. Just one person – her dad. She was prepared to harm Costain, to do *anything*, for that one tiny being. She could give all that up and choose love instead, the river seemed to be saying to her.

No, all she knew about London said the opposite: that the actions of one person could be remembered. Saving her dad was who she was. Sorry, she said now to the glory of London, I am what I am and I will do what I am going to do.

The glory of London seemed to worry in reply, to flex its river muscles anxiously, to fret about what she was going to contribute to its history tonight.

'What are you thinking?' asked Costain.

She turned to look at him, and was sad for him because he was with her. 'It's beautiful,' she said.

They finally made their way to the end of the bridge, and thus to the enormous square and ugly building that had once been Bankside Power Station. 'The Tate Modern art gallery,' said Costain. 'Are you sure this is the right place?'

Ross got out the card again. The vortex on its surface was twisting, reaching forwards, the map distorting more and more as they got closer. 'Incredibly,' she said.

The art gallery was open late for a new exhibition: *Metaphysical: The Nostalgia of the Infinite*. The poster had made Ross wonder if, despite the occult underworld's problems with the whole concept of modernity, this might in fact be an exhibition that suited it. What she took from the accompanying leaflet: the concept of items or buildings being placed to overshadow and influence people – surely that struck a nerve with them? The Turbine Hall was packed with people queuing to get up to level three, where the exhibition was. Ross recalled seeing something about this having suddenly become one of those summer art ticket rushes London had, with staggered entry and sweaty groups of people craning to look at the paintings, even as the suburbs burned.

Thankfully, their destination was down in the Tanks, originally underground oil reservoirs, some of which were now used for exhibitions themselves, but not all. They saw more of the Sighted sort of people as they made their way through an installation where projectors would suddenly display random film clips of people talking about dead relatives. The Sighted they saw, in their ragged period costume, were sighing or walking quickly through or even sniggering at the exhibit. 'It's sort of like a half-hearted version of our lives now,' said Costain, standing in the light of a woman sobbing uncontrollably, holding up a picture of what must have been her dead teenage son. 'No wonder they don't like it.'

'I think maybe,' said Ross, 'they just don't like modern art.'

She found the side door she had located a few days before, which had now been left unlocked, and followed a furtive-looking group of the Sighted through it.

There was nobody checking invites at the door. To know where the auction was seemed to be enough. The room they entered didn't look as if it was part of the Tate – more as if it might still be a working part of a power station. Perhaps the pipes overhead did gleam a little too brightly, and the wall that seemed to be taken up with one big engine did so a touch artfully, but it was considerably more authentic than its surroundings. Right beside it, yes, Ross could feel it through the wall, they were up against the river here. It roiled and fretted just feet away.

She recognized several faces from the crowd that had been at the Goat and Compasses. Judging by the startled looks among those people, they were recognized in return. They had something to do with the death of Barry Keel. There were none of the wannabes here from the top floors of the pub; they were amid the serious people now. Among the crowd, though, were a scattered handful who looked a bit different: smart people in business suits finding quieter corners to talk on their phones. Ross glanced to Costain, who shook his head, neither of them had any idea what that different demographic was about. Ross felt a few attempts to 'read her bar code' and used Sefton's blanket technique to foil them. They died down after a few moments. If only Ross could read bar codes herself.

Ross saw that people were starting to look at the fob watches they'd pulled from their ancient pockets, and that a crowd was forming in front of a low wooden stage. In its normal life, this place must be some sort of lecture space used by school groups and the like. There was no sign of any chairs, so the crowd stood, or in some cases just sat on the ground, presumably ready to haul themselves up when an auction item they were interested in was announced. Ross and Costain got as far forward as they could, to a place where they could see the stage.

A door at the back of the stage opened, and without any ceremony, into the room walked an elegant elderly woman with long silver hair, dressed in a grey ball gown that was actually covered in cobwebs. Ross could see a couple of spiders on it; one of them was moving.

'Madams and Messiers!' the lady called. Her accent was pretend posh, not even an attempt at French, a music hall barker, playacting 'above her station'. The crowd applauded. 'Welcome once again to this high point of the Seen season, the place to be Seen, our quarterly quantifying of quality, your refreshment on the way to your revels, a palimpsest of prognostication, prestidigitation and parsimony!' The crowd went 'ooh' at every long word. The host leaned closer to someone in the front row, and put her hand to her mouth in a stage whisper. 'It's the stuff of London, on the cheap, dear!' Then she straightened up again. 'The truce is in place, so mind your fucking manners. I am your 'ost, Miss Haversham with an "er" as well as an aitch, not Havisham like that berk Dickens 'ad it.'

Ross heard the crowd chanting along with that bit, a mantra they'd obviously heard many times before.

'I can tell you good people are itching to begin. Bit hot out there, innit? Bernie the Bitch, distribute the catalogues!'

A very thin middle-aged man dressed as a waiter, with bicycle clips on the bottoms of his trousers and a hangdog expression, entered at that same instant through the door behind the stage. In his arms he carried a pile of papers, which were eagerly snatched up by the audience. When Ross got hold of one, she saw that this list of auction items had been printed very roughly, as if from some form of mechanical copier, the faded ink pink and purple. The pages smelt of chemicals. There were over fifty items listed. There were no descriptions and no pictures, just the name of the object beside each item number. She found herself desperately looking down the list. She looked once, she looked twice. Then she threw the piece of paper at Costain. 'It's not there! That barmaid said it would be. She said she had "a strong feeling". She said it like she *knew*!' Costain grabbed the paper, looked quickly down it himself, as if he might see something she hadn't. On the stage, Bernie had joined Haversham, carrying an enormous ledger and a quill pen in an inkpot, which he set up on a small lectern.

Ross looked at the crowd and the hosts as they prepared to begin. She couldn't just walk away. She marched up to the stage. Costain quickly followed. 'The item I'm after,' she called, 'it's not here.'

Miss Haversham looked at her, and Ross had, in that moment, to use the blanket harder and faster than at any time previously. 'We've had no withdrawals, have we, Bernie? Are you sure it was meant to be on sale tonight?'

Truly, she wasn't. She'd been caught out, she realized, by

assumption. It made her want to laugh and not stop laughing. But still she answered yes.

Haversham sighed. 'You aren't, you know. We get quite a few like you here, following one of the ways that happenstance and aim interact in the metropolis. They all find their just deserts.' She added a big stage wink, then turned away.

Ross wanted to yell at her. She could feel the crowd looking at her with pity, shame and – given what had happened the last time she and her mate were about – worry. Costain now had a grim look about him. Was he distraught for her, or for himself? She put that thought aside, because a new idea had come to her. It had brought the sudden pain of new hope with it. They stepped aside from the crowd to talk in private. 'That book . . .' she said, 'that'll be, what, a record of sales?'

'Yeah.'

'And it's bloody huge.'

'Yeah.'

'So maybe what I'm after has already been sold at one of these auctions, and the details of whoever bought it are written down in there. Maybe that's what the barmaid meant. Maybe she'd seen my future.'

'That warning we got during the Losley inquiry about someone close to us dying, that was as if someone had seen the future, so I suppose it's . . . possible.' With a lurch of her stomach, Ross knew from his tone exactly what that grim expression of his meant. He was thinking that she might have deluded herself, that she'd aroused false hope in him, put him through the emotional wringer for nothing. Was he about to walk away, to reveal that his attempts to be close to her were all a lie? No, even if that were true, he didn't quite have reason enough to do that, not yet.

'Look, even if the Bridge isn't there, that list would be a treasure trove of background sources for our team. If it turns out that I can't do anything for *myself* here—'

'Then we should do something to help our guys. Yeah, I agree.'

That would mean she could tell Quill where they'd been, make this secret excursion something the two of them had pursued of their own volition, like when Sefton had gone off after Brutus.

The crowd quietened. The auction was beginning. Ross fought down her fury and disappointment and tried to keep her hope in sight. The rushing of the water nearby spoke of power that was nearly hers, but might never be.

'Everything is allowed,' said Haversham, clearly reciting from a familiar ritual, 'anything can be dealt in here and, as I'm these days forced to add –' and she made a significant pause before adding it – 'anything can be *bought*.' There came grumbles from the audience, but angry shouts of support too. 'Although, for the first time in a decade, for obvious reasons' – was there a glance in Costain and Ross' direction then? –'the Keel brothers aren't present this evening.'

Again, there were both catcalls and cheers.

Bernie, having donned white gloves, held up what looked to be a small piece of tarred wood with splinters sticking in all directions. Ross felt the Sight swing to it, as if he was waving around a lantern in a darkened room. 'Lot number one,' said Haversham, 'a piece of the sign that was fixed to Tyburn Tree when it was first blooded by William Longbeard, declaring him to be a heretic. Is the provenance felt as well as signed for?'

'The provenance is felt,' called out a man in the front row who was wearing what looked like an ancient agricultural smock; a few others joined in.

'We start the bidding with small beer, small favours or . . .' again that hesitation, '. . . two hundred pounds.'

Ross watched, fascinated, as the crowd started to yell out the names of everything from material goods to body parts to immaterial concepts. 'A pinch of plague dust!' 'My last good tooth!' 'An hour of suicidal depression!' One of them, as if representing his faction as well as making a bid, insisted on that 'two hundred pounds!'

With what was clearly an extraordinary skill, or the power of some whispered word or subtle gesture, Haversham decided the money was outbid by the depression. 'With the man in the tricorne hat.' The demographic in the suits, she saw, had their phones out now and were listening to them, occasionally bidding themselves. So they were proxies, agents for buyers not actually present, people hired in who . . . well, who knew what they believed about what they were participating in? Ross wished she could make use of that version of the 'checking-out' gesture that could investigate a mobile phone. The identities of those bidders might well be good background info.

The bidding continued for three more rounds, with the lot finally going to the man with the money. Groans came from the crowd as he pushed his way forward to shove the notes into Bernie's hand. Bernie kept his gloves on for that.

'The movement of money around London must be like another force on the city,' said Ross. 'You'd think they'd be more up for using it.'

'Except money stays *modern*,' said Costain, 'because they change the designs every few years, and new notes are printed all the time.'

The next few lots showed the same pattern: items from the distant past of London being bid for by both this strange form of barter and by money. Haversham seemed to try to treat both systems equally. The successful bidders who had bought lots for intangibles were taken into the back room by Bernie, each for an illusionist's moment: the door opened again to let them back in at the very moment it had shut. Each item was handed to the successful bidder as soon as their business was concluded, and several people left early, having presumably won or failed to get what they'd come here for. Ross recognized a few of the items: there was a Tarot of London pack of a different design to the one she'd seen previously and an old hardback *Book of Changes*. Finally, the last item in the catalogue was accounted for.

'Why do you think they keep records of the bidders?' whispered Costain.

'Maybe they keep track of the provenance of each item, from

owner to owner, just in case someone manufactures something that only looks old.'

'Or contains a trap.'

'So that ledger of sales records is indeed the purest imaginable juice, the most valuable object here.'

'So, what? Are we going to try to nick it?'

'There's probably some fucking terrifying security in place.'

'Yeah, and we've no time to scope it out. Maybe we should find out when the next auction is, and—'

'No.' The path that led to a different sort of life for her was too tempting. She was shaking her head even as the thought struck her. She knew what she was going to do. It scared her. 'Haversham said anything could be bought.'

'But—'

'Does anyone have any further business?' called Haversham, returning to the ceremonial tone, clearly expecting that to be the end of the auction.

Ross stepped forward before she had time to think, shrugging off Costain's slight attempt to restrain her. This was her only chance. This was clearly what the barmaid had meant in sending her here. Or if it wasn't, this was her trying to tell her own story. 'I do,' she said.

'What do you offer or wish for?' Haversham sounded as if she sort of knew, as if she was willing her on. Was that real, or was it just for the sake of spectacle?

'I wish for . . . that book.' She pointed at it. Bernie raised his eyebrows in shock. There was a combination of amazement and amusement from the audience. Haversham raised a finger and they were silent. 'We've heard that before, haven't we, ladies and gentlemen and others? Please, young lady, before you begin anything you can't finish, understand the value of what you seek.' She went over and held up the ledger. 'This book is a cornucopia, a concentration, a concordance of what are known in the vernacular as right proper names. My own name, Haversham, is a nom de gesture' – she again pronounced the words as if they were

English – 'because I don't want this lot knowing what I was born as, in case there's a dispute and it's used against me. My real name is as valuable to me as my life. This volume contains more than a thousand such names. Do you really think you have *anything* to offer, girl, that could convince us to sell it to you?'

'No. Which is why I don't want to *buy* it. I know the object I'm after only arrived in Britain in the last five years. So I only want to see those entries. I want . . . the chance to read that book for fifteen minutes.'

Haversham let out a bemused breath. 'You'll still need an offer of enormous value. But . . .' Ross got the feeling she was making use of some internal power rather than merely deciding. 'It's *possible* you *may* have something worth it.'

Ross could see, out of the corner of her eye, Costain looking sidelong at her, wondering what she was going to offer. She glanced at him, asking him the question first, then back to the auctioneer. They were about to find out if he really did have any secret funds. 'What's the opening bid,' she asked, 'in cash?'

The crowd groaned. There were shouted insults at her, but also scattered cheers. She got the feeling this would be the furthest anyone had tried to push the imposition of monetary value on this community.

Haversham thought for a moment, her inner power doing the maths. 'Twenty million pounds,' she said.

Ross felt a hollow open in her stomach. She slowly looked to Costain, who was staring back at her. He shook his head. *Come on. As if.*

She had no idea what to do.

No, no, she did. The audience was laughing at their reaction to the size of the sum. Some of them were yelling about how absurd it was to put a price tag on such things, an obscenity. There was factional sympathy for her. There was outright cynical mockery too.

She had to find something else to offer. Something huge.

Haversham was looking at her like a judge. Not unkindly.

'All right,' she said. 'I offer . . .' She found herself breathing more quickly, wanting to be sure she knew the size of what she was doing, making herself accept it, for the sake of her father. 'My left hand.' She felt Costain beside her start to react and pushed her fist into his arm to make him shut up.

'My left hand and a finger from the right!' shouted a voice from behind her.

The crowd roared with laughter. They were laughing at both bidders. At them being so wide of the mark. She turned to see who else had bid so guilelessly, and realized, with a shock, that she recognized who she was looking at. He must have come in late and stayed at the back, and the truth was that they'd been concentrating on fitting in rather than examining the crowd. White, late thirties, five nine, large build, no visible identifying marks, balding, dark hair, off-the-peg suit, and, yes, she had previously been looking at him on grainy CCTV footage.

It was the man who'd been talking to the woman in the Soviet bar, who'd left before the murder of Rupert Rudlin. He was meeting her gaze now, unsurprised by it. They were competitors – that was all. Or perhaps they could both win this, if they reached the reserve price. There was nothing to stop him looking at it for fifteen minutes too. He wasn't pleased she'd led him into being laughed at. She glanced back to Costain, and saw that he'd recognized the man too.

So this was going to be difficult. Their duty was clearly to apprehend this person of interest.

'That's nowhere near what's required,' said Haversham, bringing Ross' attention quickly back to the stage. 'Are you wasting our time?'

She thought quickly. 'A year of depression and paranoia.' She could face that. Of course she could. There would be an end to it. Unlike Dad's time in Hell.

'Two years of that!' The man from the bar again. He was actually trying to keep up with her. He didn't care what the rest of the room thought. He would wait until she found the right level, if she ever did, and then make sure he matched her. Damn it!

More laughter, but it was dying now; the crowd saw both of them as merely hopeless, no longer even funny. Haversham didn't answer.

'Me,' said Ross. 'I mean, you know, a night with me.' This was surely much bigger than anything else she'd offered.

At least it made them laugh louder again. Among the laughter, Ross was actually pained to hear the man making the same offer, his voice breaking as he did so. She looked back to him again, and saw how desperate his expression had become. What was driving him, that he'd prostitute himself like she just had? In his case it looked more as if he was motivated by fear than by need.

'You can't offer yourself to London,' said Haversham, now starting to get annoyed at Ross' naivety and the way the man was parroting her. 'We've seen what happens. It's not allowed, which normally *goes without saying.*'

'You know who you might really be giving it up to,' whispered Costain in her ear, furious. 'That smiling bastard. Would you just think before you—?'

'No.' She stepped forward out of his ability to stop her and did what she had to do. 'I offer my future happiness. All of it. For a lifetime.'

There were actually gasps. Various members of the audience turned to look at her, some with new respect, some with a sort of vertiginous horror at what might be about to happen to her. They were shaking their heads, appalled by the harm she was doing to herself. This from people missing fingers and teeth. She was scared now to see those looks; she'd thought she'd be past that. It was too late now.

She and the whole room turned to look at the man from the bar. Ross could see now that he was shaking. That he was on the edge of tears. 'Sixty million pounds,' he said.

The room went silent. The audience had been startled by his sudden shift from one faction to the other. Ross looked back to Haversham, who was considering, using whatever hidden power worked out conversion rates for her. Her decision here might well affect the future of this community. 'I do not think,' she said finally, 'that a lifetime of happiness can be equated with such a small sum of money.'

The crowd exploded in anger and applause.

Ross looked to see what the man was going to do. He was looking right at her, imploringly, and now she saw that expression fade into fury and defeat. Abruptly, he shook his head. He walked quickly towards the door. She couldn't follow him – that would be against the rules at any auction, this lot would surely prevent her from leaving. She looked to Costain, because he had to get after him, but Costain was just staring at her, an agonized, empty expression on his face.

'Don't you care that he's leaving?' she whispered.

'I care about *you*,' he said.

Ross looked round, but the man had gone. She turned back to the stage. Haversham was looking horribly sad for her. She felt terror in her throat and stomach but she stood firm. She had done this. She would not retract it. Even if she could.

Haversham waited for a very long moment. As if she was hoping for an interruption. 'Any other bids?'

There was absolute, careful, silence.

'Going once,' said Haversham.

'Withdraw the bid!' hissed Costain.

'Going twice.'

'We withdraw the bid!' yelled Costain.

Haversham ignored him. 'Going three times.'

The moment stretched. Ross wanted to yell for her to get on with it.

'Gone,' said Haversham.

Silence.

Ross numbly stepped forward. She didn't want to look at Costain. She headed for where Bernie was looking sympathetically at her, beckoning her towards the back room. He led her through the door.

She was in an absolutely black space that felt roomy, with air blowing in from many directions. She suspected that this was like

Losley's tunnels between houses. Bernie closed the door behind them, but somehow Ross could still see. He reached into his waistcoat and produced a tiny brass item, something like a curled-up trumpet. He held it up to her. 'I'm sorry it has to be like this,' he said. 'It'll be easier if you don't struggle, but I appreciate that you won't be able to avoid it.'

She watched as he approached and lifted the object towards her face. It wasn't obvious what she was supposed to do. This felt like a dream, as if what she'd done couldn't possibly be as bad as it seemed to be. She wanted to protest, to say she hadn't meant it, but the whole difference between being an adult and a child was that she could do this, she could make this sacrifice—

The device suddenly sucked at her face.

She cried out. Bernie slammed a hand onto her shoulder as she tried to twist out of the way. He was strong, he was infinitely strong! That was good, because she couldn't help trying to pull herself away, and she couldn't stop what was happening. It was pouring out of her nose. It was forcing its way up out of her throat, and forcing her mouth open, and . . . here it came! It was like throwing up and drowning at the same time. It started squirming out of the corner of her eyes a moment later. It was being sucked into the metal shape. And now she could almost see it! It was—

It was happiness.

She couldn't quite see what it looked like, but she knew what it was. In this space it was mentally labelled for her, in the same way that something in a dream is instantly recognizable. He was pumping joy out of her. She had been full of happiness and she hadn't known it. She had been full of joy.

Losing it now, she suddenly realized, was much worse than the physical feeling of it being wrenched out of her. It took her back to a sudden, pure moment of horror from her childhood, when she'd let go of a balloon that her dad had got her at a fair. She'd grabbed for it and missed and it had floated higher and higher and she'd started to scream, because it was going and she'd never get it back! Never! Never!

Bernie held her there as the terror of loss became too much to bear.

Then it passed and was gone, into memory. The last bit of joy was taken from her.

He put the device back in his pocket, and took out a big crimson handkerchief of absolute cleanliness, and wiped her face with the care of a father as she staggered, leaning against him. Then he put the cloth away in the same pocket, and she realized that it would be taken to the same place as the device. Her scraps were to be taken to the table too. 'I'm sorry,' he said, 'but you asked for it.'

She walked back into the room to find the audience waiting for her. She had only been gone, to them, an instant. They wanted to stare at her. They parted for her, their gazes examining her. She could still feel. She'd expected to be utterly numb, had looked forward to it, even, during her sacrifice. Instead she could feel annoyance at them looking at her, fear at what she'd done to herself, even a sort of calculating hope for what this would mean for her plans for her father . . . and there was Costain, not angry now, just terribly worried for her, and she felt a swell of relief, even, as . . . there was a reaction in her to his expression.

Perhaps the device had gone wrong.

No. She wasn't that lucky. Perhaps this just wasn't so bad as it was meant to be. Perhaps 'happiness', for this lot, was very narrowly defined.

No, something inside her said, this is grief protecting you. The full meaning of it hasn't hit you yet. Relief is not happiness. Hope and lust are not happiness. Perhaps you are already losing sight of the thing you lost.

She went to the book on the lectern. Haversham took a fob watch from a pocket of the spidery gown. Ross found her own notebook, but Haversham raised a finger. 'You are not to take notes,' she said. 'That wasn't part of the bargain. You have fifteen minutes. From now.'

Ross opened the book and found the pages to be smooth with dust. The lists were written in a precise, looping hand, the scratches of the quill visible. There were, as with the catalogue, no pictures and no descriptions. She noted the dates on the pages and saw that the auction was four times a year, yes, on the solstices and equinoxes, so she had nineteen to search. She flipped back, started with the first of them, and worked forwards in time, running her finger down the lists. She knew what the thing was called in the translations she read, the Bridge of Spikes, and had seen a few variations. The familiar name of a person leaped out at her. There were sometimes celebrities at these auctions, then. At the winter solstice auctions in particular, there were a number of them. Four years ago, a famous singer had bought . . . something the name of which meant nothing to her. What he had offered? Oh, that was so terrible for him.

She stopped at the winter solstice of three years ago when she saw another familiar name. Oh. Oh, but that meant . . . !

It meant she had found something useful for the investigation. She had come here for her own ends, but here, in what she was staring at in amazement, she had found something new to go on for her team, some startling new leverage they could apply. What could she do about it?

She called Costain over.

'You can't show him—' began Haversham.

'I can tell him!' shouted Ross. She whispered the name and item and given address in his ear.

He stared at her, astonished, started to say something.

She pushed him away and quickly turned back to the book. She had to put that out of her mind now and get back to her original aim. The object she was after wasn't in the first two years of auctions she looked through, to the point where she started to panic at the thought that she'd missed it, because she wasn't going to get to the front of the book before the time ran out, but then—

There. Her eye had gone past it then instantly been drawn back.

She realized she was breathing more deeply, her fight-or-flight reflex set off just by seeing the words on paper. Anna Lassiter was the name of the purchaser, at 16 Leyton Gardens, with a postcode that put it in Kentish Town. Sixteen flowers, laid on, Leyton, she ran a mnemonic around her head a few times, piling associations on the address and the post code. She should tell Costain this too, have two brains remembering it. She looked over to him. He'd seen that she'd found something.

No. Still no. She still could not trust him.

She slammed the book closed and grabbed her notebook, ripped out a page, pulled out a pen and wrote the information down before he could arrive beside her. She folded the paper up and shoved it into her waistcoat breast pocket.

She had it. She knew the location of the object that could bring her dad back to life.

It made her excited. But it didn't make her happy.

She headed for the door; Costain followed at a run.

He caught up with her in the Turbine Hall. 'So what's the plan? Are we going straight there?'

She didn't want him going with her. She didn't want to tell him that. She felt emotionally exhausted, and she was aware of a terrible numbness that had taken hold of some part of her personality like an anaesthetic. Besides, though she really did want to go straight to the address and at least look at where this precious object might be, it did make more sense to use all the tools at her disposal to learn everything she could about the place beforehand.

She turned to look at Costain and saw that he was prepared for disappointment here, prepared to be disbelieved, as he'd been doubted all his life.

She put her hands on both sides of his face and kissed him.

He kissed her back. Then he stopped. 'Lisa,' he said, 'we have to talk about—'

'No,' she said, 'we don't.'

*

She took him home. He kept on kissing her as she slowly pushed him up against the wall, but he was not going to go any further. His expression said he wouldn't let himself unless she gave him some sort of signal. She took his hand and put it not on her breast as she'd thought to do, but on second thoughts, between her legs. They stood there awkwardly, him looking at her, still questioning, even at that, him cupping her. She found her body was moving unconsciously against him. She opened her mouth to say – God, did she have to give him permission aloud?

Something suddenly changed in his expression. He took the hand away and went to unbutton her, to start to undress her, quickly, roughly. She raised her arms to let him.

He manhandled her and turned her body and opened her with his hands. He spent so long licking her, expertly, but agonizingly too long, too precisely. He was still fully dressed, even. He needed to keep his control. She grabbed his hair, and looked into those deeply worried eyes. Wasn't he hard? Hadn't she made him hard for her? 'For God's sake!'

He looked at her as if he was convincing himself this was real. He was so unused to being wanted. Suddenly, he got to his feet.

She watched him, wondering if he was going to leave her there.

Slowly, he started to take off his clothes. When he was naked, he put a hand on his cock, showed her how hard she made him. He was shivering.

She reached into her bedside table and took out an unopened packet of condoms. She opened it; her eyes kept darting between her short-nailed fingers slipping on the cellophane, his face, his cock. She kept expecting to find laughter somewhere in all this, but, no, it was all deadly serious. She supposed this was what it was going to be like for her always now.

She had sold happiness for—

No, she didn't want to think about that now.

She took out a condom packet, ripped it open and reached out. She held him, pleased at how hot he was, at how steadily hard she'd made him. At the feeling of him pulsing in her hand. She rolled the condom over him, and pulled it to cover him, tight. She looked up at him again and took a deep breath.

'It's okay,' she said.

His lips bruised hers as he slammed her back into the pillow.

They lay there afterwards, feeling the cool through the open window, the sounds of summer and of distant violence still outside. Costain slowly ran a hand down her back as she lay on his chest. He felt that he should now show how gentle he could be. Here was a woman who'd just suffered a huge emotional loss, and he'd . . . *had* he taken advantage of her? He looked at her face. She looked calmly back. He already thought that perhaps she seemed different, not quite displaying all the emotions he might expect. But then she wasn't like the other women he'd been with, and he didn't know what was normal.

He still felt that this was . . . uneven. That he should somehow . . . pay for what he'd just done. Either guilt had become so much a part of his life now – living as he was with the prospect of Hell – that it had infested this moment too, or maybe this was something more natural, how he felt now he was with someone . . . for real. Maybe for the first time. Maybe this sort of guilt was what most blokes dealt with when they were in their teens.

God, they were both like children. 'I want us to be together,' he said. 'Do you?'

She paused for a long moment. When she said it there was no happiness in her voice. 'Yeah.'

'So we keep telling each other it's okay.'

'Okay.'

'And tomorrow we talk about—'

'We'll talk about everything.'

They slept.

In the early hours, Costain woke from dreams of being closely investigated, explored even. He got up to go to the toilet, and he walked over the pile of her clothes, the underwear that couldn't have been her usual choice, which she must have worn for him, and there was the waistcoat which had, in its pocket, that piece of paper with the address where the item that could keep him out of Hell was located.

She had left it there. She wouldn't have done that offhandedly. She had decided to leave it there. She had stirred as he'd got up and she was probably awake now. Watching him to see what he'd do. He had to prove himself.

He stepped on over the waistcoat, went to the bathroom, came back.

She was looking at him, sitting up, entirely awake. 'You didn't look at the piece of paper.'

'No.' He went to sit beside her on the bed. She lay against him once more. He looked at her. He could see that frown on her face in the darkness. He'd always found how solemn she looked kind of horny, now he thought of it. That seriousness had indeed extended to how passionate, how committed, she'd been. But the idea that she would now be like that all the time . . . the hurt she'd done herself felt enormous. That was the biggest reason he wouldn't look at the address: the high price she'd paid for it to be hers.

'I'm never going to be happy,' she said, as if reading his thoughts. 'I'm satisfied. Calm. Peaceful. But not happy. It turns out that happy is an active sort of thing.'

'Would even getting your dad out of Hell make you happy now?'

She shook her head.

'I'm sorry,' he said. 'I tried to stop you.'

'You shouldn't have. I don't regret it.'

'Okay,' he said.

They were silent for a few moments. 'Go and get the piece of paper,' she said.

'No.'

'You have to. We need to trust each other.'

He hesitated. Then he went over to her waistcoat and came back with the paper. She switched on the bedside light.

They looked at the address together: 16 Leyton Gardens. It seemed a small thing to base such trust on. He looked at her face and saw the intensity of her expression still. 'Thank you,' he said.

She looked almost angrily at him. As if she was already wondering if she'd made the right decision. 'We work a full day tomorrow,' she said. 'We don't put this before the job.'

'Right.'

'Then we go to this place, research the buyer, make them some sort of offer.'

'Or—'

'I don't want to think about that until we have to.'

'Okay.'

'Then we resurrect Dad. We go to where he's buried and dig him right out.'

He kept his voice even. He was amazed at such trust. He was going to be worthy of it, he *was*. 'Absolutely.'

'Right. So there's something else we need to do, right now.'

He found his phone and started texting Quill. 'You're sure about the details?'

'Yeah. I found in that ledger the name of an item purchased at one of those auctions two and a half years ago, a "scrying glass". The name of the buyer was Russell Vincent.'

THIRTEEN

The next morning, Rebecca Lofthouse opened her front door to find, standing there in a business suit, an extraordinarily beautiful young woman. 'Good morning, Superintendent,' she said. 'I'm here to drive you to Lord's.'

Lofthouse stared at her. 'I didn't order a driver, and I'm not going to Lord's.'

'Forgive me, but you are.'

The accent was very RP. One of the better schools, without the mockney they tended to produce these days. There had been no threat in her tone. 'I've got a meeting—'

'We've postponed that for you.'

'And you are . . . ?'

'I'm afraid you'll never learn my name.'

'Oh,' said Lofthouse, feeling both relieved and a whole different sort of worried at the same time. 'You're one of the funny people.'

Lofthouse kept looking out of the window as the woman drove her, making sure the car was heading for north-west London. The young driver had neither confirmed nor denied that she was an officer in what the older generation of the Met called 'the funny people', and what the younger generation, influenced as they were by the movies, called 'five', when actually it should be MI5, or, more properly, the Security Service. When she was sure the car was going where she'd been told it was, she checked out what else had happened overnight: Quill was reporting that his team had encountered the man from the Soviet bar once more, and that, by using the right words in a message to Russell Vincent via his PA, his team had finally got an appointment to interview him. They were also preparing to raid the brothel. The results of the postal ballot on strike action were due to be released today. Lofthouse felt something give inside her. It went against everything she believed in for police to strike, but she understood why they would. She looked back with fondness now to the couple of weeks of the Olympics. There had been soldiers on the streets then doing happy crowd control. They might be returning soon, and bloody private security firms too, and things would not be so happy.

She wished she could share with James Quill the burden she was bearing, the reason she couldn't tell him anything about why she believed him when he talked about the occult powers of London.

The car pulled up at Lord's, in a parking space in what seemed to be a private members' car park. It was the first day of a Test Match, Lofthouse gathered, and there was a mass of people in sun hats, carrying cool boxes, some in the distinctive striped blazers and ties of Marylebone Cricket Club, heading for the many entrances of the ground. No amount of riots would change that. She recalled the distraught emails of American friends during the London terrorist attacks of 2005. They been shocked by the everyday responses they'd got, how she'd ridden the tube the very next day with only a slight second thought, how she'd been polite but a little sighing with her replies. To Londoners, bombs and riots were just an extreme form of weather.

She was led through a door opened by a waiter at the rear of a bar, and then swiftly closed behind them, along a concrete corridor behind the stands, and then up a flight of steps into the light, revealing a view of the ground, the green of the pitch looking perfect and clean, and somehow too close and too small to be an area where people really played international sport. A sign said this was the Tavern Stand, reserved for members and their guests. The beautiful woman whose name she would never know led her upwards still, into a balcony with a sidelong view of the wicket, where, far below, the bell had rung, and, to rising applause, the teams were coming onto the field. To the right was Old Father Time, the weathervane in the shape of an old man with a scythe, taking the bails off the wicket for the end of a game. Lofthouse had never understood why the home of cricket had put death in charge. She allowed herself to be led along the balcony to where, sitting back in the shade, were two middle-aged ladies in summer dresses. One of them looked to be of Indian heritage, a walking stick propped on the chair beside her, very long black hair tied back. The other was white, with a fringe of blonde hair, laughter lines around her eyes. They were both smiling at her, pleased by this civilized abduction.

'We're just getting tea,' said the dark-haired lady. 'Would you like some?'

'Or hang on for an hour and we're planning on a bottle of rosé,' added the blonde. 'Bit early as yet for the lady petrol.'

'Tea, please.' Lofthouse sat and waited as the woman who'd driven her here took the order and departed.

'Now,' said the blonde woman, 'our apologies for the secrecy.'

'I'm Rita,' said the dark-haired lady, 'and this is Sue.'

'Not our real names, of course.'

'Because those I will never hear.'

'Exactly!' Sue smiled as if Lofthouse was a quick learner.

'We,' continued Rita, 'are, as you put it to your driver, Bob, the "funny people", which I've always thought is a really flattering bit of Met argot for such tremendously ordinary civil servants as ourselves.'

'It's really not,' said Lofthouse, not minded to be as gracious as her abductors.

'Well,' said Sue, 'let's pretend it is. Women were only allowed to become members here in 1998, you know.'

'Not that we *are* members,' added Rita.

'I know who I'm talking to,' said Lofthouse. 'I know you tend to get access to whatever you want. Why did you bring me here?'

'Well, your operation, Fog, isn't progressing as fast as it could be, is it? Oh, good shot.'

Lofthouse looked across to the pitch to see a ball rushing across the boundary, a cheer rising in the crowd below. She wondered how they knew anything about Operation Fog, but was certain she wouldn't get any answers, just a bit more 'charming' hand waving. Why was the Security Service interested in Quill's team? 'Did you bring me here just to criticize the activities of my unit?'

'We weren't criticizing,' said Rita. 'We're here to help. I always think the game of cricket sums up what we do.' Lofthouse grudgingly turned to see an Indian fast bowler she couldn't name start his run-up towards Alastair Cook. 'We try to anticipate what's coming –' Cook ducked as the ball sped over his head – 'in terms of the illicit activities of foreign governments and terrorists on British soil, and to react in the most appropriate way. Either defence, or, when it's safe to do so, attack.' On the big screen across the ground, she watched as Cook prepared himself for the next ball, the sponsor's logo on his bat front and centre. 'Every year, both this sport and what we do gets more influenced by money. Be it the Indian Premier League attracting those who'd otherwise choose to play for their country, or the non-localized nature of many modern threats to the stability of this nation.'

Lofthouse was sure she was being told something, but she had no idea what. The bowler completed his run-up, let go of another ball too fast to follow, and the crowd reacted before she saw what had happened. The wicket had been uprooted, and now Cook, furious with himself, was walking away from the strip in the middle, and the crowd were applauding. Oddly, it felt as if a lot of the applause was directed at the bowler. Strange that the English should have built here something so seemingly unpartisan.

'Every now and then something like that happens,' said Sue. 'And when the game is cricket we say, "Well played," to the other side. But in the game *we* play, there are other options.'

'You're saying you take direct action?'

'Of course not!' Sue pretended to be shocked.

'We don't blow things up,' said Rita. 'We let them explode of their own accord.'

'Because alongside the laws of cricket,' said Sue, 'there is also the spirit of the game, just like the unwritten constitution of Britain.'

Lofthouse didn't like the implication that anything in the UK happened beyond the reach of law. She was aware, though, that because of the allusive nature of the way she was being told this, it could all be very easily denied. 'Why are you telling me this?'

'You might at some point be searching for a solution to a specific problem and think of us.'

'I'm never going to reach out in that direction.'

'Of course not.'

'Why do you think I might need you now?'

The beautiful woman returned, with a tray upon which were three cups, sugar, milk and a teapot, all with Marylebone Cricket Club logos. She put it on a small table she erected for the purpose and left. The pause gave Rita and Sue the opportunity not to answer the question. 'The trouble,' ventured Sue, stirring her tea, 'is that sometimes we chance across some indicative piece of information that should rightly be dealt with by another service, but don't quite have complete faith in the service in question.'

'Especially when it's something . . . enormous,' added Rita.

Lofthouse looked between them. 'You don't trust the Met in general, because of the possibility of a strike.'

'The certainty of one, about three to one in favour of illegal action,' said Sue. 'That's how the vote will go today. But also because we have reason to believe that certain parts of it have started . . . not quite playing the game.'

'But you *do* trust me?'

'Because we know you're honest, and you're in charge of Quill's team, and they did so well on the Losley case. *Remarkably* well. *We* remarked on it, didn't we?'

'We *did*,' said Sue. 'We *noted* it.'

'What exactly *do* they do, by the way?' Rita said it quickly, looking back to the pitch, as if it was the most trivial question in the world and she had an absolute right to know.

Well, that was one of Lofthouse's questions answered. These two knew nothing about the Sight. She tried to keep the enjoyment out of her voice. 'That's an operational matter. Are you saying you know who our Ripper is?'

Sue laughed prettily. 'In the same breath, you won't give but you want to take! Tell me, what is it that you're getting up to that your superiors, your husband and your office know nothing about? Where do you go when you leave home and take such care not to be followed? We're sure there are no financial irregularities or you wouldn't be here, but please tell me it isn't just some dull affair.' She took another sip from her cup. 'Do you want to tell us about Quill's team, or about that?'

Lofthouse stood up. She hoped she wasn't shaking visibly. 'I'll be going now.'

There was a cheer from the crowd. A ball went whizzing up onto the roof of the stand above them and rolled down with an audible noise. Lofthouse looked back to Rita and Sue to see that they were at least bothering to feign being impressed. 'Sit down, Superintendent,' said Rita gently. 'We're only playing.'

Lofthouse, reluctantly, sat. She couldn't afford not to take anything they had to offer. How did they know about her excursions? She had been so careful.

'None of the above is as important as us getting this information to you,' said Sue. 'You ask if we *know* certain things. Not for sure, no. But we aim to clear our consciences—'

'Such as they are,' said Rita.

'—and send you in the right direction. Having stumbled across some information, the nature of which we're not going to divulge to you, we decided to use the unique capabilities of our organization to investigate the financial dealings of several people who are doubtless of interest to you.'

'Michael Spatley MP,' said Rita. 'Squeaky clean.'

Lofthouse felt able to risk a follow-up. 'Not even sexually dodgy? No payments to brothels, and so on?'

'Interesting,' said Sue. 'But no.'

'Rupert Rudlin,' said Rita, 'had his misdemeanours – actually paid for cocaine on his credit card a couple of times – but nothing to concern you. But as to the others—'

Lofthouse was amazed. 'You have something on the *other* victims?'

Rita handed her an envelope. 'This is our gift to you. Because of what we think is going to happen soon.'

'We're not going to tell you what that is,' said Sue in a stage whisper.

'Your Metropolitan Police Commissioner, Geoffrey Staunce, and the driver, Brian Tunstall,' continued Rita, 'both have a history of unusual payments being made to them, Staunce until a couple of years back, Tunstall only recently. But Staunce got another one . . . the day after Spatley was murdered.'

Lofthouse looked through the papers with growing interest. 'Thank you. This could be extremely helpful.'

'Not as much as it could be,' said Sue. 'The trails all lead back to cut-outs in the realm of offshore banking. Not even our reach extends that far.' She looked up suddenly at the sound of leather on willow. 'Oh, *lovely* shot.'

FOURTEEN

Quill's team had gathered in front of the Ops Board once more. Ross had told the others about the auction, but had made it sound as if it was something she'd found out about from the Docklands papers only on that same night. She'd managed not to mention that Costain had come along too. She'd thus established an honest context for having connected the man who'd left the Soviet bar to the big circle they'd drawn to indicate the wider world of the London occult underground. She'd mentioned getting a look at the auction ledger, and thus finding the record of Vincent's transaction, as though anyone could easily do that. She had made no mention of her ordeal.

Sefton had looked suspiciously at her as she'd told them all that, but had in the end accepted that he'd made solo jaunts himself; it was something their team did. 'Just bring me along to the next one, okay?'

'Absolutely.'

'Are you okay?'

Ross had needed her best poker face for that one. She'd managed to avoid looking to Costain. 'Yeah.'

Sefton had finally just nodded.

Now, Ross attached an association thread between Tunstall and Staunce. 'According to Lofthouse, Tunstall received six cash payments of ten thousand pounds each during the six-week period before his death. He was smart enough not to put them into his Barclays current account, but instead started up a deposit account with Mansion House, a bank based in the Cayman Islands.'

'The main investigation would have looked into his financials,' said Quill. 'But they didn't find that; it took the funny people to do so. So it was set up by someone with considerable knowledge of financial kung fu.'

'The payments made to Staunce,' continued Ross, 'which he put into a more traditional Swiss bank, Heinkemann's, are of the same amount and frequency, but happen in bursts, every few months, the first of which was paid ten years ago.'

'That'd be when he became commissioner,' said Quill.

'They cease two years ago, but then there's another payment, the day after the Spatley murder, and then Staunce is killed that same night. This gives us a clear association line between these two but we don't know what that association is.'

'We were given that on a plate,' said Quill, pointing at the line that connected Staunce to Tunstall. 'We didn't have to work for it. I don't like that. Kev, what have you got for us this fine morning?'

Sefton stepped forward and used a marker to add to the concepts part of the board. 'Scrying,' he said, 'means looking deeply into. A "scrying glass", the item Vincent is recorded as having bought at that auction, is something used in stories to answer questions or get info.'

'As in "mirror, mirror on the wall"?'

'That's the one. I say "in stories" because I couldn't find anything in my research that came from a real-world source.'

'There's nothing in the Docklands documents either,' said Ross.

'But this is one of those points where the shallowness of our research materials is obvious. I get the feeling, because it is so well documented in folk tales, that almost anyone at the Goat and Compasses would know what a scrying glass *really* is.'

'Assumption,' said Ross.

'Professional instinct,' said Sefton. 'But, yeah.'

'So did Vincent buy one,' said Costain, 'to see if he was still the fairest of them all?'

'Someone,' said Quill, 'is about to equate us with Grumpy, Sneezy, Bashful and Happy. No, don't sort out which is which – they were picked at random.'

'No they weren't,' said Sefton.

'At least,' said Quill, 'the mention of said object made Vincent suddenly very cooperative. I think we might shake some juice out of him today.'

Ross finally risked a look at Costain. He smiled back. She felt only relief that they'd sold their colleagues on her story. It was going to be difficult doing her duty today. After work, the two of them were going to set out on their own quest.

It was at least vaguely possible that, by tonight, her dad would once again be alive.

That afternoon, the four of them took an unmarked car over to Marble Arch, parked with Quill's logbook propped in the window, and looked around for the address they'd been given by Vincent's PA. It turned out to be a very plain door to a mews flat, with what had been a stable made into a garage beside it.

'It's the same address as he gave to the auction,' noted Ross.

Quill rang the doorbell. 'Hi ho,' he said. 'It's off to work we go.'

They were led up from an entrance hall by an assistant, and it became clear that this wasn't one mews flat, but a whole row of them knocked together. Some of the rooms were just bare repositories of empty bookshelves and unlooked-at art, but some seemed thoroughly lived in. They were taken along a corridor with carpeting that made their copper feet tired and were finally shown into the presence.

Russell Vincent immediately stood up from his desk and shook their hands. 'I'm sorry my office took so long to get through to me about this,' he said. Sefton saw Quill leave that one unremarked on. 'DI Quill, good to see you again. I'm glad it's you handling this, but, ah, gosh, exactly what *this* is . . .'

Sefton hadn't felt anything of the Sight on entering the building and he didn't now.

'What this is,' said Quill, 'is something many might find unbelievable, but I now strongly suspect you won't.'

Vincent looked awkward. He was clearly wary of them, trying to find a way to run this meeting on his own terms. Here, Sefton thought, was a man who didn't know whether or not he could trust these people who'd come asking questions. 'The sort of thing you were asking about at the do the other night, but which I was a bit shy of. Before your approach became . . . official.'

'Are you, Mr Russell Vincent,' said Ross, using the official-sounding language they'd agreed on earlier, 'the owner of a scrying glass?'

'Yes,' he said quickly, perhaps a little guiltily. 'Actually, that's why I wanted to meet you at this address.'

Vincent pulled a dusty cloth away from an object which stood in the corner of one of his many disused rooms. 'This is it,' he said, 'my "scrying glass". The romance of a name, eh?' It was a full-length mirror on a stand which allowed it to be turned on a vertical axis, the sort of thing you might find, Sefton thought, in a Victorian lady's boudoir. It certainly looked ominous: an absolutely smooth surface in which he could see the contents of the room reflected.

Sefton looked over his shoulder and saw that the PA who'd answered the door had followed them in. Maybe Vincent wanted a witness at all times? She was standing on the threshold here, as if nervous of what had just been unveiled. Sefton stepped forward and put his hand up to the mirror. Then onto it. The glass was cold to the touch but no more than you might expect. There was nothing that said 'London' about its appearance or manufacture. There was no feeling of the Sight about it.

'What does it do?' said Quill.

Vincent looked awkwardly at him and his team. 'I rather need to know how much you fellows know about . . . well . . .'

'The power of London,' said Sefton, adopting a confidence he didn't feel. 'Enough. Whatever you're going to say, we'll believe you.'

'So, you're police officers who know there are impossible things here?' Vincent seemed fascinated. 'My goodness. That must be so much help in your work. If you need to find a missing person or a suspect, you must be able to just make a gesture and . . .' He made his own fumbling turn of fingers in the air.

'You'd think,' sighed Quill.

'So you can't do that?'

'That'd be an operational matter,' said Ross.

'But at least you can defend yourselves against . . . against what we both know is out there. Please tell me you can do that.'

Ross raised her eyebrow at him. 'And again.'

'You were going to tell us, sir,' said Quill, 'what the scrying glass does.'

'You mean you don't know? Well, that makes this more awkward, in that I don't see why I should . . .' He trailed off, but seemed to make up his mind as Quill's expression became darker. 'I suppose you could find out from just about anyone in the community. Look, let me start at the beginning. I suppose it all began on the day I walked out of the Bussard Inquiry into phone hacking, having told them I'd run roughshod through my media business, found a few editors responsible for looking illicitly into the mobile phones of politicians and celebrities and sacked them all. I gave my word to those bastards – and, more importantly, to the public who buy my papers – that from now on mine was going to be the clean press corporation which didn't do that sort of thing.'

'How very ethical,' said Costain, a completely non-ironic look on his face.

'Not so much, actually,' said Vincent. 'I could see the way the wind was blowing – towards bloody government regulation if we weren't careful – and I wanted to be the one who could use being spotless as a unique selling point. Trouble was . . . how do I put this?'

'It's not easy being clean?' said Quill.

'Well, precisely. Politicians and celebrities these days aren't exactly soft touches. If you're pursuing stories in the public interest, which, yes, does indeed sometimes mean "what interests the public", you've simply got to cut a few corners. So I, erm, started to look for new ways to do so. I'd always had an interest in occult matters, always been aware of the whispers, knew there was something to it. So now I sent some of my people on fact-finding missions. They went incognito to a few pub nights—'

'Such as . . . ?' asked Ross.

'I think one was called the Goat and Compasses, I deliberately didn't keep records of this stuff. Never mind being a bit dodgy, my shareholders care if I've, erm, you know, gone bonkers.' He looked awkward again for a moment, as if wondering once more if they too would think he was mad.

'Understood,' said Quill. 'Go on.'

'Well, I finally went to one of those pub nights myself, incognito. I wasn't very impressed with the people involved. They seemed all over the place; they didn't know much, and, well, I can respect people who don't have time for money, but this lot seemed desperately conflicted about it, obsessed with what they claimed to despise. I got my people to dig further, to ask about . . . well, about devices that could be used to find out people's secrets. They came back with a suggestion: the scrying glass.'

Sefton looked at the others, and found they shared his shock. So a scrying glass might be what was being used to listen in on them, might have been what led to the leak that had got Tunstall killed.

'How?' growled Quill. 'How does it do that?'

Vincent looked reluctant. 'Well,' he said, 'I'm assuming this is never going to reach the authorities because, goodness knows, any new inquiry wouldn't believe you, but you've got me over a barrel here, just knowing I've got one of these.'

'We're after bigger fish than you, sunshine,' said Quill. 'Tell us.'

'The scrying glass is meant to be a device for entering people's dreams.'

Sefton wanted to punch something. How many times had he had that feeling in his sleep, of something rifling through his mind? He looked again to his colleagues and could see from their own expressions of horror and anger that this was a shared experience.

'And once you're in,' Vincent said, 'you can check out whatever's in their memory.'

'How did that go for you?' said Quill, advancing dangerously on Vincent.

The billionaire raised his hands in surrender. 'It didn't go at all,' he said. 'I've never successfully used the blasted thing. Wish I'd never set eyes on it. I bought it at this auction which took place under the skeleton of a whale in the Natural History Museum. Not wanting to be there myself in case I was recognized, I stayed on the other end of a phone line and had my proxy purchase this "scrying glass", which I'd been told was as rare as hen's teeth. I paid around forty thou for it and had it delivered to me here. I expected some sort of instruction manual, but there was nothing. So I decided that perhaps using it was just going to be a matter of instinct.' Sefton recognized his own blundering attitude to dealing with the power of London. 'The first time I tried . . . well, the only time . . . Maggie, would you please continue the story? Tell the truth.'

Sefton was intrigued by the idea that otherwise the PA might not tell the truth. They all looked to the middle-aged woman, who now had an awkward expression on her face. She'd been surprised to hear all this from her boss, Sefton felt. She was wondering if he was mad. But she was also very worried that he might not be. 'It must have been about two and a half years ago,' she began, haltingly. 'There was snow on the ground. I was downstairs making tea, and Mr Vincent had said that that night I could leave early, because he was going to be busy all evening. And then I heard him cry out from up here. There was the most enormous crashing around. It was like someone had got in here and was attacking him. I should have hit the panic button, but I didn't; I just ran upstairs and opened the door and found him staggering about. The room was smashed up. It must have been over in seconds, whatever it was. His shirt was ripped. Mr Vincent saw me standing there and yelled for me to get out. He ran out himself and closed the door behind us. He made sure I was all right, but he wouldn't tell me what had happened – just that I wasn't to tell anyone, and . . . well, he's never asked me to work in this room since, and I've been glad not to.' She looked as if she was now making some terrible mental calculations about how her perceptions of what was possible had changed since the start of this meeting.

'What happened?' Sefton asked Vincent.

Vincent went to a sofa and sat down. 'Something I now think you might be familiar with. Something I've been wondering about coming forward about since the murders started. How could I? When you asked me about the impossible at the party, Inspector Quill, I should have told you then, but I knew nothing about you.' He let out a long breath. 'I was attacked by Jack the Ripper.'

Sefton found his mind racing. So there was a connection between the Ripper and the scrying glass. That made sense. Whoever was spying on their dreams also seemed to be the one who chose the Ripper's victims. He stuck his tongue out and tasted the air. He found a metallic taste, a reminder of when he'd smelt the silver goo. It was very faint, but after two and a half years, perhaps it would be.

'That evening that Maggie describes,' continued Vincent, 'I'd been trying to activate the mirror, looking into it, willing it to do something. When something started to appear out of it – this figure, pushing slowly through the glass – I was intrigued, not even very frightened at first, because it moved so slowly. I thought I'd got what I was after, that this was going to be some sort of, I don't know, supernatural being who'd go and listen in on things for me. As it became more clear what was emerging, I got scared. It was what we'd now call a "Toff" protestor, though nobody had heard of them then, with the mask and the top hat and the cape and . . . this one had a razor. When that started to appear, that's when I started to yell. The moment I did, he leaped out of the mirror and attacked me . . . or he tried to. I thought I was dead the moment he started slashing at me. But for some reason the blows just seemed to cut through my shirt. After just a moment, he seemed to realize that, and fled.'

Sefton was now writing down details himself. What could have stopped the Ripper from killing Vincent? And why such an early murder attempt, then nothing for months after? Maybe it had needed to fix whatever the problem with this killing had been. 'Which way did it go?'

'I'm not sure. He just seemed to fly off and vanish, maybe . . . that way?' Vincent gestured vaguely towards the window. Sefton went to look, inspected the wall and window closely for any sign of the silver goo associated with a Ripper exit, but there was nothing. Again, a long time had passed. They had no idea if this stuff evaporated. He went back to the mirror, had another look for goo, found none and, with a glance at the others, put the cloth back over it.

They all relaxed a little. Maggie had to lean on a wall.

'Maggie found me here a moment later, in a daze,' said Vincent. 'I didn't let anyone else in here after that. I kept the cloth over the mirror, always half expecting it to happen again. I wanted to get rid of it, but I didn't see how I could do that without endangering someone else. It's not as if I could explain the problem. I thought about breaking it, but if looking into it had resulted in the appearance of that . . . ghost or whatever it was, then who knows what would have happened? Since the protests began I've always wondered if the man I saw was somehow . . . I don't know . . . leading them. And then, when the killings started . . . but who could I tell?'

'Can I take another look at your business cards?' asked Quill. Vincent looked puzzled, then took a metal case from his pocket. Quill took it, opened it, and showed them to Sefton. There was preserved a spatter of silver, faded but obvious. 'Do you keep a supply here?'

Vincent went to a little open box of them on the desk by the mirror, and pulled one out. The same silver deposits. Looking more closely, Sefton found signs of it across the top of the desk also, but the card seemed to have absorbed it in a way the wood didn't. He got down on his hands and knees and smelt the carpet, found the tiniest droplets still deep in the weave. Vincent's story checked out.

Vincent was looking perplexed at him, not able to see the silver himself.

'Can you think of any reason,' said Costain, 'why the Ripper might have attacked you?'

Vincent was silent for a moment. Then he seemed to decide that he might as well go the whole distance. 'I didn't just want to know people's secrets for personal gain. I wanted protection.'

'From what?'

'I'd started receiving anonymous death threats, left in places where nobody should have been able to go.'

'Did you report this to the police?' asked Quill.

'No, because when one is aware that one is involved in . . . questionable activities . . . one doesn't like to summon the law right into one's home, does one?'

'Do you still have any of these messages?'

'Well, no. They tended to . . . curl up and turn to ashes as soon as I'd read them, or vanish off my phone or computer. They had a sort of official tone to them. I think, having declared myself to be an honest newspaperman, I'd got on the wrong side of what the late Princess Diana called "the dark forces" in British public life. I was feeling the same sudden chill that Assange, Galloway and Snowden must have felt. I never found out why I was being singled out, or who was doing it. But, given the way the threats were delivered, I became certain they might have genuine supernatural power on their side.'

'What were the threats about?' asked Ross.

'They were quite vague. They just said they were watching me and that if I went too far out of line they'd punish me for it.'

'So you wanted the scrying glass to try to find out who was doing it?'

'Absolutely.'

'Your newspapers seem to do well enough without the use of this,' said Quill, tapping the mirror. 'Do I take it you've gone back to the old-fashioned sort of dodginess?'

'The oldest sorts,' said Vincent. 'The power of money and the willingness of people to tell on each other. Now, I've told you all I know. Am I off the hook? Have you had your pound of flesh?'

A thought had occurred to Sefton. It was dangerous, but his team had taken on worse. 'Mr Vincent,' he said, 'you may have gathered we're specialists in this kind of thing. You've been very cooperative, but I'd like to ask one last favour. Would it be possible for you to lend us this mirror, to aid in our current investigation?'

Vincent raised his hands, relieved. 'I would be *delighted*.'

They heaved the mirror back to the car in silence, all of them feeling as if they were handling a bomb, but, as Sefton was all too aware, also dealing with a different sense of terrible oppression. They got it into the boot, climbed into the car and closed the doors before they felt they could talk about it. Ross said it first. 'Fuck,' she said. 'Someone is bugging our sodding dreams.'

'They already know all we know,' Costain said. He had a terrible look on his face and Sefton could only wonder what secrets of his own he had to lose. 'And next time we sleep, they'll know we're on to them too.'

'We need defences,' said Quill, looking to Sefton. 'We need them today.'

Sefton took out his phone and started searching. 'I already have a few ideas,' he said.

'And I,' said Costain, 'need to text a man about a thing.' He had started to do it before he'd finished the sentence.

They listened to the news on the way back to the Hill: a live announcement of the result of the Police Federation postal ballot.

'The government had every opportunity to negotiate,' said the voice of Commander Stephen Marcus, the leader of the strike campaign within the federation. 'They still do. We do not take our duty lightly, and we will always be willing to return to the bargaining table. But the public should know that, even in the current situation, with disorder on the streets of London every night, this government have not seen fit to look to better conditions for police officers, nor for greater numbers of police officers, and put in place a cut in starting salary. They have seen fit to attempt to take operational control of police forces in London and have assigned them on occasion seemingly at random, without the knowledge and experience of professional police officers, leading to increased danger to the public and to the officers themselves. As such, unless the situation changes, our members have voted for, by a three to one majority, and will begin, in three days' time, this coming Saturday, a series of twenty-four-hour strikes . . .'

'Fuck a duck,' said Quill.

They got back to the Hill and, between the four of them, carried the mirror into the Portakabin. 'Not a lot in here to mess up if it, you know, activates,' said Costain.

Ross tacked a card with Vincent's name on it onto the Ops Board, in the Ripper victim category, with asterisks beside the line, indicating that he'd survived.

Sefton was very aware of the other three all looking urgently to him. He made sure he'd searched everywhere he could think of. He had a couple of leads. 'I have to visit some antique shops,' he said.

While Sefton was away, Quill got on the phone to Lofthouse and asked about her dream life. She felt she hadn't been spied on, which was a relief. She was worried as to why he might ask, so Quill filled her in as far as he could. The news came through that all police leave was cancelled until the strike. There was news footage of last night's, and to some extent this afternoon's, riots in Fulham, Brixton and East Ham. There were rumours of isolated incidents in leafy suburbs like Chesham and Rickmansworth. Quill wondered how they were going to keep awake. Every time he thought about it he felt a terrible sense of violation and wondered exactly what memories of his the intruder had spied on, thought about Sarah's privacy as well as his own. He saw the look on Ross' face and realized they'd all be thinking the same thing. He went to the tea station and pulled out the big jar of coffee. 'We are not,' he said, 'going to be giving this bastard the chance to have another look.'

Sefton finally returned with a small collection of objects that, he said, indicated both serious London provenance and the concept of things or people being kept locked out. There were keys from the Tower of London, boundary markers from royal gardens. He saw how unenthused Quill and Ross were and raised his hands. 'It's all I could do,' he said. 'I really have no idea.' There was nothing of weight about any of the objects. 'Before tonight, I'll write down some instructions about putting chalk lines and salt around our beds.'

'Sarah,' said Quill, 'is going to love this.'

Costain looked up at the sound of a car horn outside the Portakabin and bounded out. Quill went to the window and saw him talking to someone through the window of an ancient TR7 that looked more mud than car. The car had stopped on the road rather than come in through the gate to their makeshift car park. Costain turned, clutching something, and the car accelerated away.

'This is a bit more practical,' he said, coming back in with a carrier bag. He opened it up to reveal several packages of a grey powder.

'Methamphetamine?' said Ross.

'Bless you,' said Costain.

Quill looked to Sefton, who was staring incredulously at what was on the table. Had it really come to this, that they were going to break the law themselves?' 'Fuck, no,' said Quill. 'We keep that for when we just can't stay awake any longer. And we don't keep it in here.'

Costain nodded. 'Sure. There's a hidden compartment in my car.'

'Oh, that makes me feel so much better,' said Quill.

Sefton went over to the mirror and uncovered it. 'This thing feels so completely dead,' he said. 'It's as if, when the Ripper left it, it took all the power with it.'

'Maybe that's what happened,' said Ross.

'Do you reckon it could appear out of there again?' said Costain.

'Perhaps,' said Quill, 'it's like that movie, and you just have to say his name three times, like Ripper, Ripper—'

The others all yelled at him to stop.

Quill sighed. 'Like I would. I now work on the basis that things like that might actually be true.'

'Maybe,' said Sefton, 'the scrying glass needs some other form of activation. I'm wondering if the Ripper appearing out of it was some form of what Gaiman called ostentation, if the first stirrings of protest, two years ago, somehow summoned it.'

'That wasn't quite how he used that word,' said Ross. 'There has to be an existing story about something happening, which then becomes real. Just as we've seen. None of those protestors was expecting Jack the Ripper to come back and lead them. It would have been, I don't know, King Arthur or . . .'

'. . . or bloody Robin Hood,' finished Sefton. 'You're right.'

'Put the cloth back over it, anyway, eh?' Quill said.

Sefton did so.

'All right,' said Quill, 'if someone's eavesdropping on our dreams, we've got a few hours left with us still having one up on them. So we're going to follow up our major lead right now. We're going into that brothel tonight.' He went back to the board and pointed to the business card. 'Tunstall, or persons unknown, turned over Spatley's office looking for something. That card, an indication of Spatley having links with persons of ill repute, was in there to be found. We need to go into the brothel, find out if anyone in there knows anything about Spatley or any of our other victims, especially anything that could be a motive for murder.'

Ross went over to the wheezing PC and brought up her database about the brothel, showing photos that she and Costain had taken of prostitutes and their clients arriving and departing. 'Nothing unusual on the surface,' she said. 'We know all the exits. There'll be some muscle in there. There'll be something to prevent johns shagging and running.'

'So we do the simplest possible thing,' said Costain. 'I go in as a punter.'

'I should go,' said Sefton. 'I'm better with the Sight. I'm more likely to find any anomalies.'

'I'd recommend you both go,' said Ross. 'Having a look around isn't something they'll encourage punters to do. You'll have to find some way between you to break out of the routine of being introduced to women downstairs and then being led straight up to the bedrooms.'

'We're not allowed to shag on duty?' said Costain to her, with a raised eyebrow.

She looked calmly back at him, too professional to rise to that.

'I'll have to ask Joe,' said Sefton. 'I think he'll be okay with it.'

Quill went back to the board and drew a vague shape in the air with his finger. 'We have to move quickly, but we might suddenly run into something significant,' he said. 'It's like when we didn't know what Losley was, when the disparate things she did made no sense on their own. We keep hitting the outer features of a dirty great unknown. They're all connected, but we can't work out what the shape in the middle is. The elephant in the room, as encountered by a team of blind people, who each feel what they think is a different animal.'

'It's weird,' said Ross, 'how that expression's come to mean something everyone *should* see and doesn't want to mention, rather than something nobody could see. It's as if fooling yourself is standard practice now.'

'Except,' said Sefton, 'with the Sight, we're the ones who should be able to see it.'

'And ours,' said Costain, 'is going to be one sodding terrifying elephant.'

FIFTEEN

'Mr Stephens, Mr Dawson, please sit down. This won't take a moment. Thank you for choosing the Underworld. The first thing I'm going to need from you is a three-hundred-pound deposit, cash or credit card, against your tab at the bar. You leave that with me, and the girls who'll be attending to you this evening will let me know how much of that you've used in services; if you go over, you can top up with them. Anything left – and we all hope there won't be, I'm sure, because we're looking to provide you with a good time – will be refunded to you on your departure. Now, you're not on a clock; please don't feel rushed, and just to let you know the way we operate: after you've chosen the girl or girls who'll be attending to you, the first thing she or they will do is take a long relaxing shower with you. During that, she or they will just make sure that you're as healthy as you gentlemen appear to be.'

'She's saying they'll check us down for creepy crawlies, yeah?' Costain looked over to Sefton, sprawled beside him on the very Eighties sofa, their legs way apart, their clothing once again that of the small-time gang soldiers they'd spent a lot of their careers pretending to be.

'Let's get this done.' Sefton took out two rolls of cash and gave them to this businesslike middle-aged woman in an evening gown. 'You available?'

'Not this evening, though if you become regular customers, perhaps I might make an exception.' Her voice, thought Costain, was exactly what he was used to from hookers, just enough acting to let everyone stop worrying about what was real and what wasn't, but not the full commitment that might lead to doubt. He felt aroused at that familiar timbre and immediately guilty for it.

Ross and Quill sat in the car around the corner, parked in front of a newsagent, watching the young media folk and the tourists looking for nostalgic thrills pass by in the late evening sunlight. They were listening to what was going on round the corner, via the wires each of the undercovers wore. The two speakers were, at the moment, providing a weird sort of stereo. Now there was just the sound of the two men going through to some other room. Ross had rebuffed Quill's attempts at conversation. She could feel time running out, could feel tiredness rising inside her. She would take that meth as soon as it was offered. She was desperately wondering whether whoever had accessed her dreams now knew about the Bridge of Spikes, whether the address they had for the owner had already been raided by something with a lot more power than they had. Costain had promised to wait to check the place out until she could come with him. She believed him. Just about.

The sound coming over the speakers changed. 'Is that someone moaning?' she asked Quill.

'That's from one of our less private rooms,' said the middle-aged woman, having led Costain and Sefton into what Costain thought looked like the front room of a couple in their eighties, or maybe the stage set of one, because it felt hardly used. It smelt of cigarettes. From an inner door four women entered, all dressed in lingerie that looked as if it had been through the wash too often, all affecting a pose which was meant to be that of a fashion model, but was similarly dulled by repetition. They were professionally present, and that was all. Costain tried not to find that absence exciting. He should really be too worried about the current situation his team, and himself in particular, were in to be aroused, but the body did what it did. There were two white women, an Asian one and a black one. 'Gentlemen,' said the hostess, 'please pick one or more. Our rates obviously increase steeply for more than one.'

There had been a door leading off each room they'd been in. Through it, Costain was sure, would be one or more hard cases, ready to protect the investment here. The prostitutes would be on a percentage, but it would still be more than they'd get on the street. 'The one on the end,' he said, picking one of the white girls.

'You know what I like, Tone,' said Sefton, and nodded towards the Asian woman.

They were both led to rooms leading off a corridor; through a couple of other doors could be heard more, rather artificial, sounds of passion. Again Costain tried not to respond to the art of those simulated groans. The woman he was with smiled professionally at him and let him into a particular room, a rather bare bedroom with a double bed, a shower in one corner and a single painting on the wall, apparently sourced from the same sort of place that provided anonymous art for hotel chains. 'One hundred and fifty for a blow job,' she said, her voice retaining that businesslike composure, 'two hundred for straight sex, two hundred and fifty for anal, eighty for spanking, and I tell you when to stop, fifty for me using a strap-on on you, and if you want to look in the cupboard, there are toys in there, and I can tell you what each of them will cost to use.'

'Okay,' said Costain. 'I'll think about it.'

'But first.' She went and turned the shower on and, turning back to Costain, started to undress, with a series of practised movements. 'Please call me Lucy, and let me know what you'd like me to call you.'

Costain wondered how long he could ethically wait to do this, and decided that, especially given who was listening, now would be good. 'My name is Tony,' he said, 'and I'm actually a private investigator. No, keep the shower running.' He stepped between her and it, and took a roll of bills from his pocket. 'On top of your cut from what I gave your boss, I'll give you four hundred for the answers to a few questions, none of which will jeopardize your employer or put you or your job at risk.'

She thought about it for a moment. 'Money now, and I decide.' He handed it to her. She counted it, then put most of it in her bag. She put the rest on the duvet. 'You tell them you had a blow job.'

Sefton was also sitting on a bed, next to the woman he'd come here with, who called herself Mi Ling. He hadn't come out with any particular cover story. He'd just started talking, which hadn't surprised her. He supposed a significant minority of her clients did that.

'You're going to have to pay for the time,' she reminded him after a moment.

He handed her some money and gave his background as one of the people he'd been as an undercover once, adding that they must get all sorts through here.

She made a non-committal noise, alert to anything in that direction. More than her job was worth, to give away information. Sefton realized that this was going to take a while. He manoeuvred the one-sided conversation back onto safer ground.

'I don't think I want to tell you about that.' The woman with Costain was looking angry and . . . yeah, afraid. 'We never saw any politician, I don't know what you're talking about.'

Sefton and Mi Ling had finally found themselves laughing together at a completely safe conversation about recent celebrity misdemeanours. Sefton was pleased when she went from that to ones she knew about herself, because, as he'd suspected, she was sometimes at the sort of party that had paparazzi waiting outside. It was safe for her to talk about what her famous acquaintances got up to there.

After a while he took a risk and held up his phone to show her a picture of Spatley. 'Is that the bloke who got killed?' she said.

'What about this one?' He showed her a picture of Tunstall, then Staunce, but the only result was her frowning at him. These people meant nothing to her other than faces on the telly. 'Would you know if they'd been here?'

'Course I would,' she said. 'We all know when someone famous comes through. Are you a reporter or something?'

'Look at this,' he said, showing her a picture of Rupert Rudlin taken from CCTV footage.

'That's—' She stopped. She was looking at the phone intently. 'I don't know the man, but—'

'But?'

'The woman he's with . . . she's a mate of mine.'

Sefton realized that he was looking at her in shock. He made himself point to the image of the woman who, a few moments after this picture had been taken, would be thrown up against the wall. 'Her, you mean?'

'Yeah. She left here. I mean, suddenly. I mean she still owes them money. Nobody knows where she went.'

'What's her name?' The woman looked suddenly awkward, wondering again if she should get involved with this. 'Listen, look at me, look at me, I'm not after her to harm her, I'm trying to save her. You believe me, don't you?'

The woman considered for a moment, then finally nodded. 'That's Mary. Mary Arthur. She wasn't full time here. She did jobs on the side. When she disappeared . . . we all said she must have made it big, gone to Saudi.'

'Do you know where she lived?'

'Somewhere in Muswell Hill.'

'This is saving lives . . .'

'That's all I know.'

The door burst open and an enormous man in a Brazilian football strip, carrying a baseball bat, with a bar through his nose and a huge moustache, threw himself at Sefton.

Costain jumped back off the bed, his hands in the air. 'Mate, mate, I didn't touch her!'

His own assailant, shaved head and paunch, pretty designer T-shirt with a much-copied image of some Seventies model, hefty about the limbs, obviously used to dealing damage and carrying what looked like a specialist hunting knife, instinctively glanced at the woman.

Costain wrenched his arm over, made him drop the knife and dived for the door.

Sefton felt his bruised ribs as the Brazil fan made to smash him across the body. He danced out of the way, avoided the grasp and headed for the door. He saw Mi Ling carefully not reacting, then he was out of there, into the corridor, where he could hear a whole stampede of footsteps rushing up the stairs. There was Costain, dashing out of a door in front of him. They looked at each other. 'Window?' said Costain. They grabbed for it, and started to haul it away from its sealed, peeling paintwork.

'Fuck,' said Quill, panting as he arrived at the door, Ross beside him. 'Fuck.' He hammered on the door, rang the doorbell, and then kicked it for good measure.

The door opened and a woman he assumed to be the one who'd welcomed Costain and Sefton looked out. 'This is a private—'

Quill shoved his warrant card in her face. 'I know what this is. My name is DI James Quill, and the two men you're having a go at are police officers on an operation. So unless you want to be party to assaulting a police officer—'

There came a crash from behind the building. 'I think,' said the woman, her voice dripping with contempt, 'you'll find they just left.'

SIXTEEN

'Thanks for coming in for us,' said Sefton. They were back at the Portakabin, with very strong coffee and, if Quill himself was anything to go by, a feeling of both relief and new pressure at having found a fresh lead. The name Mary Arthur was now written under the victim photograph on the Ops Board. That was a precious data point that their mysterious enemy would become aware they knew of, if they went to sleep.

Costain stretched his knee and winced. 'We should have them for not keeping a fire escape in working order.'

'Mary Arthur,' said Ross, looking up from the PC. The others gathered around to see. 'Last known address in Muswell Hill, a landlord who called the police when she went missing . . . two months ago.'

'Way before she was in that bar,' said Costain. 'Looks like she went back to her freelance work.'

'Having cut off all ties with everyone she knew,' said Sefton. 'She deliberately vanished.'

'Is that her mobile number that was written on the business card we found in Spatley's office?' asked Quill.

'Not that's listed,' said Ross.

They went over to the board. Ross reached for an association line, then put it back in the box. 'I want to associate Mary Arthur with Spatley,' she said. 'But I can't quite do it yet.'

'Work it out loud,' said Quill.

'Michael Spatley MP handles a business card from a brothel he probably never frequented. He loses it in his office, so he obviously doesn't think it's very important. Perhaps he's copied down the info from it, though we haven't found that. Perhaps he's tried the phone number, like we did, and got no result. But Tunstall, or whoever was paying Tunstall, *does* think it's important, enough to search the place. Then Mary is attacked, but not killed, by the same entity that killed Spatley. And who's this fucker?' She stabbed her finger angrily at the picture of the man who'd been at both the bar and the auction. 'I think there are, in reality, association lines all over this lot. But I can't attach them on the board because we don't know what they are. Oh.'

She'd stopped. Quill felt relief at the sound that indicated an imminent breakthrough. 'Tell us, maestro.'

Ross put her finger beside the picture of Rupert Rudlin, the actual victim from the bar, and ran it in a circle right round him. 'I was talking about lots of associations for the others. Then I could see it: no associations for Rudlin, not with *anyone* on this board.' She pointed back to the picture of Mary Arthur. '*She's* linked to all this, though we don't know how. *She* was the one who was initially attacked in that bar. How about if the Ripper was there for her, and Rudlin just got in the way?'

Quill felt his relief wane slightly. 'But . . . he had a good shot at her. He had every chance to kill her.'

'And Rudlin *is* a rich white bloke,' said Costain.

'Yeah, we've been saying that, haven't we, that Jack the Ripper now just kills rich white blokes, but Tunstall wasn't rich, and as for them all being white, well, they've all been part of the establishment, so storks on roofs there, but, blokes . . .' She trailed off.

Quill waited for more insight, but she just hugged herself and sighed, unsatisfied. 'Okay,' he said, 'how would you sum that up?'

'I'd bet,' said Ross, 'and this is an assumption—'

'Marked as such,' said Costain.

'—that Mary Arthur was meant to be the Ripper's next victim.

That he had *motive* for killing her. And for some reason didn't, and killed Rudlin instead. If we can crack that motive and that reason, we might crack this.'

They kept looking at the board. They wanted desperately for something new to leap out at them. It didn't. Quill finally turned to an expectant-looking Costain and made his decision. 'I'm going to choose to believe,' he said, 'that our dream lurker already knows all we know. That he or she might actually get scared off by the idea that we know what they're up to in our brains. So tonight we try Sefton's protections, and if we feel we're being got at, we do our damnedest to wake up, and we don't yet resort to snorting bloody meth, all right?'

It was in the early hours by the time Costain and Ross got to 16 Leyton Gardens. Ross had asked Costain, as soon as they got in the car, to get out his supply, and he'd demonstrated to her how to sniff it. It felt good; the effect wasn't as extreme as she'd expected. But then, she'd experienced some extreme things to compare it to. The others could do what they liked; she and Costain had reasons of their own for staying awake.

She'd realized, spending the day with him – sometimes nearby, sometimes away, sometimes with his voice over a speaker – how strange it was for her to be with someone. They'd touched each other in passing, when nobody else was looking, just a hand on her arm. To have touch in her life . . . it was like a sense she'd lost the use of. There was comfort in it. It made her aware of where the happiness would be if she could feel it. It was like a currency she had none of now, none to pay him back with, none to reward herself with. She was trusting him, and that felt weird too, but he deserved it: every look he gave her, every word he said, told her that he did. Still, she planned to stay right beside him to make sure. If he betrayed her . . .

She didn't want to think about that. The meth might make her more paranoid. She had to guard against that.

Every now and then during that day he'd looked to her, as if

checking she was okay, as if checking for happiness, and had found
. . . his expression said he was slightly disappointed not to have
found it. Every time.

They'd driven past burning cars and heard the thunder of drums
and smelt the smoke. But for now it was keeping away from Kentish
Town.

The address of the owner of the object turned out to be in one
of the grottiest two-storey apartment blocks Ross had ever seen.
Every one of the flats on the lower floor had a garden, and all
but two of them were overgrown. The balconies on the upper row
were the same: window boxes stood empty and piles of junk sat,
inviting more disarray. The lights in the particular flat they were
interested in weren't on. 'I wonder how she paid for it,' she said.

'The same way you did?'

'Maybe.'

'Are you okay?'

'Yeah.'

'How are you feeling?'

'Speeding. I'm never going to be feeling *happy*. Could you stop
asking?'

'Sorry.'

You're never going to make me happy, she didn't add. *That's a
conclusion you might end up dwelling on*. She leaned into him for
a second, just headbutted his shoulder.

They went to the door of the flat and rang the bell. Nobody
was in. They asked next door, where there were still lights on.
Yes, the bloke in the Spurs shirt said, freaked out to have his
doorbell rung at this hour, but comforted by Costain's warrant
card, the young woman who lived there, weird she was, he'd seen
her about recently. She kept herself to herself. The only time he'd
spoken to her, well, he didn't think much of her, to be honest.

They got a description, which was as detailed as you might
expect from one meeting, generic, even. The small amount of
research Ross had done on this woman had found that here was
someone else missing from official records, exactly as Losley had

been. She wondered how common a trick that was among the Privileged. Ross didn't want to have to look through hundreds of records to find the ones where the Sight could reveal concealment again, not with the address in question in front of her and the owner in situ, but she would if she had to to find out more about her. They went and looked at the door again. It looked easy enough to break in but that threat assessment didn't include whatever occult nastiness might await inside.

'Do you reckon it's in there?' Costain asked.

'No idea. Can you feel anything?'

'No.'

'Me neither. I was thinking she might have . . . you know . . . used it.' She hadn't wanted to say that out loud. If one had bought the Bridge to insure one's own safety, her reading indicated that it had to be on one's person at the moment of death to do so, but if she'd bought it to return someone to life . . .

'I thought that too. Didn't want to say anything.'

They waited there for a while, not knowing what to do. 'Do you think everyone who dabbles with the power of London goes to Hell?' asked Ross. She could feel the drug surging through her brain, putting her above worries like that so she could say them out loud.

Costain shrugged. 'Toshack said all four of us were. But I never believed that. I thought it was just a threat, another way of saying the Smiling Man was going to kill us.' He was looking kind of hungrily at the door. He saw Ross looking at him, and his expression changed. 'So what do we do now?'

'We keep coming to this house,' she said. 'We do it in shifts if we have to. We meet this woman, and then we do whatever we have to to get the Bridge of Spikes.'

Quill went home to find Sarah already in bed, reading. She looked up in surprise at the bag of salt and carrier bag of clinking items he was carrying. 'Hello, love,' he said. 'I feel like experimenting in the bedroom tonight.'

She was horrified when he told her. She talked about getting all of them out of London right now, going to stay in a hotel in Reading or something. But Quill pointed out that, unlike with Losley, there was nothing to indicate that this intruder couldn't find them wherever they went.

The salt-and-chalk line on the carpet and protective items on the bedpost comforted her only a little. But she got to sleep. It took Quill himself a lot longer, but he finally did.

He woke in the morning to find Sarah looking at him interrogatively. 'Well?' she said.

'I don't think anything weird happened,' said Quill. 'I think the defences might actually have worked.'

On the way in to Gipsy Hill, while stuck at the traffic lights, Quill put in a call to Forrest's office, asking if the DCI had time after work tonight to compare notes. He'd emailed his team over breakfast, and none of them had reported incursions into their dreams, but Quill didn't entirely trust that. He'd been so exhausted and tense last night he suspected he'd have slept through anything. Ross and Costain sounded to have renewed energy. He'd told them the next thing they should do, while continuing to pursue the prostitute Mary Arthur, was start organizing a raid on the Keel occult shop, where they might find some more defences against dream incursion. That was going to need some seriously bogus justification, so getting the main investigation back onside was a priority. Besides, now Quill had a lead to share with them.

He got a call back a few minutes later saying that DCI Forrest would indeed be free and in central London this evening, and that the Opera Rooms was his quiet pub of choice. Quill was pleased to hear that. He could not only do the business he had to do, but he could also become more au fait with a copper whom he felt was much like himself and could try to begin the process of requesting backup for a raid that they'd have to try and squeeze in before a police strike, the purpose of said raid being one that might well escape the DCI.

So Quill entered the Portakabin with some slight hopes. 'Today is when it all comes together,' he said, 'when the elephant in the Portakabin reveals itself.'

'And shits on us all,' said Costain, laughing a tad shrilly, Quill thought.

The team spent the day concentrating on Mary Arthur, exploring possible further links, from geographical to financial, between her and the other victims, not excepting Rudlin, on Ross' insistence. Quill sent Costain back over to the Soviet bar to ask around about prostitutes using the place. This was not, Costain reported back, having been gone a bloody long time, something the bar staff were aware of, even on the sly. So Quill's prediction for the day failed to come true. But he knew this was the right line, that this was how they'd crack it. He had some hopes that they might have freed themselves from the problem of being got at when they slept as well, though Sefton looked incredulous at the idea that his defences had worked.

At six that evening, thinking that a bit of bonding with a superior officer might well take him over the limit, Quill headed for the railway station. He fell asleep, as he always did on trains. He realized with a start that he was doing so, but he had some of Sefton's protective objects on him. Finding them with his hand, he let it happen, and he started to dream.

He was backstage at a Rolling Stones concert, and he was talking to Mick Jagger, who turned out just to want to talk about money, while Quill was all about the music. 'Nowadays,' said Mick, 'the world is just as bad as it was in the seventies, but we've had all our illusions scraped off, and it seems people are willing to put up with that without, you know, revolution.'

Quill said something, he wasn't sure what. This is a normal dream, a wary part of him kept saying.

A nondescript figure was standing behind him. He had a hand on Quill's shoulders. Quill ignored him for a moment, then realized, with a start, that he was looking into the back of Quill's head. 'No, don't move,' said the figure calmly, like a doctor. Quill stayed put, with his back to him, but suddenly he had a gun in his hand, because a part of him was yelling that he really needed to have a gun right now.

Quill knew what this was. He spun round and tried to grab the figure, but he couldn't register any details of it. His hands went straight through it. Quill stumbled forwards into the figure, which was trying desperately to get out of his way, but now Quill had found that the figure was actually a hole, and in trying to grab it he was falling.

Quill lost his footing completely and fell into the void.

SEVENTEEN

FOUR THOUSAND YEARS AGO

Quill fell into the dreams of a mind much older and much bigger than his own. He screamed as he fell, but made himself stop when he saw how huge what he was falling into was. He wasn't sure he wanted this mind to notice him. The woman who was dreaming dreamed the same things, over and over. Quill had no idea of time, but he was inside her dreams long enough to understand everything. The sadness of it fell over him like a shadow.

The word 'kennet' meant three things to the people of the hawthorn bushes: a long low mound of soil with rock slabs cut by the ancients in a grove at its door; the entrance of a woman, from which came children; and something that was evil. That was why it was a swear word, something shouted by soldiers over beer in the round house.

In the woman's dreams, which were now his own, Quill found himself standing inside a kennet that she thought of as her home. He no longer had the gun he'd imagined into his hand to protect himself. He was here on the night when everything had changed, a terrible night. She kept dreaming about this night, over and over. Quill could feel that something dreadful was going to happen.

The air was dry as if he was in a library. The floor was impacted mud. The only illumination was moonlight, entering at one end of the kennet. The walls were made of piled rock slabs, covered in painted patterns, swirls and grids. Quill looked closely at them and saw handprints and fingerprints, thousands of years old, and wondered at them. This is what that terrible night had been like, the memories of the dream said to him, grabbing him and shouting it desperately in his ear like a needy drunk. The swirls had been drawn by those who'd brought her body here, many decades ago, when her flesh had died. They had drunk the rotten beer, and the swirls and grids were what they had seen. The fingerprints were her own, pressed to the wall when her flesh was dead, to mark her passing, before they carried her into the chamber where she slept.

Quill tensed at the news that the woman whose dreams he was swimming in was dead. He felt for a moment that he was dead too. He watched and felt a reiteration of what he'd seen already, and realized that, though she was dead, the woman kept dreaming because of the shape of the kennet. It was shaped like this so that her information was kept intact, so living people could talk to her. But not for much longer after this terrible night that was being remembered. This was the night when it had all changed.

The kennet, he saw in his mind's eye, as the woman's dreams remembered it, ran along a low ridge near where the people of the hawthorn bushes kept their sheep. It was many paces from the road. It took an effort for the hawthorn people to bring offerings here. They brought their questions with them. They asked the wise woman what they should do.

So what this lot called a kennet, Quill found his own word for: a barrow. He was inside a barrow, a real place, somewhere. His detective mind kept grabbing onto the concepts swirling around him and pinning them down: he was in a barrow somewhere near where there were hawthorn bushes.

He reached out, instinctively starting to ask questions, and recoiled in horror from what he found. She was right here, just a few feet away, at the darker end of the kennet, this enormous, hugely powerful mind! She roared forwards at him again, trying to grab him, needing to know what he was, this ghost from the future. He retreated, cowered, hid.

As her memory raced around him, searching for him, he saw that she lay on a bed of charcoal. Around her was a scattering of star shells, round lumps of rock that had been cracked open to reveal a five-pointed symbol, which seemed to be made of rock too, but also looked as if it had once lived. The fish traders some-times still brought star shells to the hawthorn people, saying the rocks came from the sea, and calling them 'nuts' or 'knots'. There was a counting rhyme sung to babies:

> *One is you, if you're lucky,*
> *Two is the mother, you on her breast,*
> *Three is the father, the words,*
> *Four is the chair, the world,*
> *Five is the knot, the knot that catches things,*
> *Six is the flies, the infected wound,*
> *Seven is the secret, the heart of the sky.*

Quill felt the power of the song getting stronger and stronger, reflecting from one end of the kennet to the other. The sound shapes of such old songs were made to be sung in the kennet. He hid from the power of the song, hid from her, as the song grad-ually faded in intensity and her memories drifted into those of happier times.

She had been happy here after her death. For a very long time. She had become a small god because of where she had been placed. She would share wisdom with her people who entered having made the right signs and sung the right songs and filled themselves with the rotten beer.

Quill wondered what had gone wrong, and instantly regretted it, as she shrieked the answer, the screams reverberating, trying to find him, to grab him so she could tell him and take some tiny comfort in the telling. She was so alone now, driven out of her dead mind by loneliness, in an afterlife of one.

The people of the hawthorn bushes had changed, her scream said. The men had stopped visiting her. The few women who still had, before this terrible night that was about to happen again, as it happened time after time in her dreams, did so secretly, and said awful things like, yes, she was still a small god to them, but they were being told that the sun and the moon were much bigger gods. The men had told their wives not to come here any more. The priesthood of the sky had said terrible things about her and had started to point out the kennet as it cast a shadow on the hillside, saying it scared the children, that it soiled the cloaks of the sun and moon whenever they rolled over it. They had a new name for her now: they called her a 'wight'.

Quill felt the slow second death she'd experienced. She'd gone from being the mother of her people to being more and more excluded, her existence becoming more sour every day as love was slowly drained from it. She couldn't move from here to plead her case. She couldn't leave the kennet because that was how the land was shaped. The shape of the land that had been chosen to give her a continuing presence also kept her here, because if she left it she would be powerless and would roll back here like a leaf being blown back into a hollow by the wind.

Men were now in control of the hawthorn people, the last few women who had visited had told her. Those women had laughed bitterly that at least it cost them nothing to come to the kennet, except the usual boughs and flowers and roots to burn. The sun and the moon demanded expensive sacrifice, of livestock and grain. The priesthood had started to make their own currency, of unpolished axe heads that could never be used. What was the point of hoarding something and exchanging it and never using it?

Quill felt the terrible night coming to its climax. Something bad was approaching from the direction of the village of the hawthorn people.

The new wooden circle had been made. He could see it in the

dreams: a better sort of grove than the stone grove around the opening of the kennet, the only place now from which to adore the only gods. The people, as instructed by the priesthood, whose actions they encouraged with every acceptance, had built ditches around the new circle, banks for the audience to sit on, a ceremonial way to progress into it, wooden trackways off in several directions for the spirits of the dead to leave it and join their fellows with the sun and moon in the sky.

The kennet was in the way of one of those tracks. They felt it might infect the path, that the terrifying wight in the kennet might snare the beloved dead and drag them in here with her. Why would she do that? How little they knew her!

He could feel the seething fear and hatred of those who were approaching. He could feel only tiny protests among them, concealed in the minds of a handful, not to be spoken aloud.

The existence of the kennet had become too much for the hawthorn people to bear. They had spent too much, gone hungry too often. They had made a final effort, staged a great collection. They had paid farmers and fishers and soldiers to suspend their duties and come to the kennet over several days with the longest light. Tonight was to be the last night of that process. Tonight was the last time a great column of people with torches had come up from the village. Tonight was the last time the woman in the kennet would have visitors at all, be talked to at all, be loved at all.

Quill looked back to the memory of moonlight at the end of the kennet and saw it as precious now, as some fondly kept remembrance, but now gone. Tonight, the terrible night that went round and round in memory, was when the light at the end of this tunnel had been cut off. The sleeping place of this dead woman was about to be turned into a tomb.

Over the last three long days the men had used levers and gestures to lift the stones of the grove at the kennet and brought them inside the opening, intending to seal up the wound in the ground that so alarmed them.

Quill needed to be close to her as the horror approached. The men with the stones were inside the kennet now, their shadows in the way of the moonlight. He wanted to comfort the dreaming woman as he comforted his daughter, as he sometimes had to comfort his old dad when he forgot something. He wanted to be the law for her, to do something about this terrible injustice, but he could not be anything but a fragment of her dreams, an observer. He made himself stumble into the darkness, his hands reaching out. He reached a chamber at the end, where a ridge in the mud at his feet marked the edge of the space where the woman was. He felt the fear radiating out of the darkness in front of him. He could sense that immense fury roaring around and around, anguished at the idea of being bottled.

She didn't know what he was. He tried to reach out to her. She was too big. He smelt male and new. His every gesture bounced off the roaring whirlwind that was her, a terrified animal rushing around and around.

The stones started to be placed against the end of the small enclosure. They wanted to keep using the rest of the kennet, Quill realized. They wanted to move their animals into it to shelter them from the cold, to make profit from it. By sealing her up in this part they would cleanse it and make it into just an ordinary place. Perhaps they could use the terror of her too: pray to the sun and the moon, or the wight will get you.

As the darkness was built across the entrance to the chamber, and the woman in here with him became more and more afraid, as she always did in this part of the dream, Quill heard a sudden high sound from outside.

A priest was singing a single note: a chant that was being repeated all down the hill, a straight track of sound that reached all the way back to the new wooden circle in the village. He sustained the note and made it resonate back to him from the end of the kennet. It was a last stab.

Quill felt it like a needle lancing through him.

It was to provoke her. It was to make her *feel* her imprisonment.

Then the workers slammed the last great stone against the chamber they were in and sealed it, and the note was cut off. The moonlight vanished. The great note of horror rebounded down the length of what was now absolute darkness, echoing and echoing, building and building into a great cry of rage.

Quill groped around him, overcome with sadness, trying to find her with his hands to comfort her. He reached out and felt bones. He had a hand inside her ribs, into her heart; he stretched out quickly with his other hand, intending only to steady what he'd found, and caught her skull, and she was falling apart in his grasp.

That was only her body. Her real self roared into his head. She was going to . . . to . . . she was trying to get inside him! She thought he might be an escape, a way to claw her way out. She needed a body, any body! She could form one if she was given the power, but if not she would take what was within reach. She was going to take his body and use it to get out of here, back to the world she needed to be part of!

Quill held up his hands and screamed.

EIGHTEEN

Quill looked around him and saw that people right down the length of the train carriage were glaring at him for screaming.

He lowered his hands. He made eye contact with the woman sitting opposite him, whose frown had turned into a laugh. He let out a long, relieved breath. Then he realized that he should record what he'd seen, that it had all felt important. He jotted down some quick headings in his notebook. Then he texted the other three to let them know that, at least with portable defences, their terrifying problem was still a problem. He'd give them all the details tomorrow.

The train pulled in at Victoria. He got to his feet and smoothed down his suit. There was something odd here, he thought. What was it? A strange sound in the distance, from the station concourse. The commuters around him were noticing it too as they all got off the train, looking in that direction, not hesitating to walk swiftly together towards it, but worried now, looking at each other. The sound grew louder as he went through the ticket barrier. There was noise echoing from the archway that led from the station. Slogans and chants and yells and drums. Those bloody protestors again. Near the tube entrance, the image of a Toff mask, now almost a logo, had been painted over a poster for *Les Misérables*, the paint still dripping.

He went into the underground, got out at Embankment, and

walked the short distance up the hill to Charing Cross. He was startled now to hear the same noises echoing across this concourse too, coming from the road outside. He went out there and took a look. Near the Charing Cross itself, disrupting the taxi ranks, with drivers hooting at them, a small party of protestors in masks and capes had assembled. 'Burn it down,' the leader was yelling into a megaphone, 'and start again!'

Yeah, he could understand the appeal of that. Sensible policies for a happier Britain. He turned to head towards his destination, but a sudden thought struck him. He took out his mobile and called Sefton. 'Here,' he said, 'what you said about . . . "ostentation" was it? Is anyone still keeping tabs on where Twitter says the next protest is?'

'Wait a sec, I'll check out my saved searches.'

'Only they seem to have split into different groups . . .'

'Are you around Charing Cross?'

'Yeah.'

'They were starting to say it's kicking off outside the station there about ten minutes ago.'

Quill looked behind him, and saw more and more protestors, many of them in the Toff outfit and mask, arriving from all directions. 'You can see how that works, practically,' he said, 'but in London, what you found out was that saying something's going to happen is also sort of encouraging it to happen, right?'

'Yeah, Gaiman thought that was how it worked.'

Quill turned, staying on the phone as he waited to head across the road, looking all over, hoping to see a uniform, but not finding any. 'We ought to get Lofthouse to get the Met in general on to this: watch Twitter, find out where there are rumours of protests and anticipate them—'

'I don't know how much that'd help; there are loads of small potential trouble spots tonight, by the looks of this. And, you know, with the strike coming up, every department's trying to get stuff completed before it starts.'

Quill crossed on the lights, a wave of tourists around him,

passing Toffs coming in the other direction. He was looking forward to the relative cool of the Opera Rooms, which was an upstairs bar with big leather sofas in a pub called the Chandos near the Strand. They kept the windows open in summer. 'Give me a call if any of them flare up. Okay, see you . . .'

Quill was looking dully ahead at one of the many Toff figures coming in his direction, but something inside him was yelling an alarm at him. At first he thought he'd crossed on a red, that he was hearing some oncoming car that was about to run them all over. He wasn't hearing anything, he realized; it was his new senses shouting a warning. Huge meaning was approaching, coming straight for him.

He looked into the face of the figure marching across the road towards him. It was masked and caped like all of the others. But in the moment he'd turned his attention to it, it . . . started to blaze with the potential of the Sight.

From the eyes of its mask were falling tears of silver.

In that second Quill knew what he was looking at . . .

The figure ran at him.

'Kev,' yelled Quill, 'he's here! He's—'

The razor sliced the air beside him. Quill ducked aside and ran. He shoved his way back through the crowd of tourists coming in the other direction. They shouted happily at him in Dutch or something. They couldn't see what was behind him. Or some of them half could and recoiled, doubting themselves, dreaming.

He burst out of the other side of them, onto the concourse in front of Charing Cross again, and ran straight into the mass of protestors, looking round and round as their masks surrounded him and parted in front of him, every hand holding the possibility of a blade, every mask blank with no tears. He picked a direction and heaved his way through them. He still had his phone in his hand. He could hear Kev yelling from it.

He broke through them and found a gap ahead. He ran down the shallow hill that led around the corner of Charing Cross, down towards the Embankment. He grabbed the phone to his ear again, looking desperately behind him. 'What can you do for me, Kev?'

'I've called for backup. Where are you?'

'Embankment tube.' He heard Sefton yell that to someone on another line. 'I'm not going to get into a cab, not here. With the traffic, I'd be a sitting duck like Spatley—'

'Marked cars converging on you.'

'You'll just get uniforms killed.'

'I don't care.'

Quill saw light blaze at the top of the hill. A brilliant figure, like something out of William Blake, had shot up onto the heads of the crowd, and now took one huge leaping step towards him.

He turned and ran. Down the hill. Not looking back. He didn't panic. He ran with purpose. He was totally unarmed against this thing. He had to use his environment. There was a crowd flooding into the space ahead—

Dear God, no. It was more of them!

The masks and capes were rushing out of Embankment station and down from the bridge across the river. They weren't looking at him, but past him, aiming to link up with the ones at Charing Cross. He ran through them, heaving them out of the way, aware they were slowing him down, that light behind him getting brighter, closer.

Quill elbowed his way through the crowd, then, on impulse, turned right and ran at the ticket gates. He vaulted them, making the ticket inspectors yell, and pounded for the escalators. 'Going underground!' he yelled into the phone and pocketed it.

He ran down the escalator, pushing his way past people. He was going to take the first train that appeared. It was a Bakerloo line train, going north. There was no light behind him. He slammed his way through people, ran up the platform, and then hopped into a carriage just as the doors were closing.

'Stand clear of the closing doors,' said the recorded announce-ment. There was an endless moment as he waited for the light to shine down the length of the platform. Maybe he just saw the shadows out there start to lengthen. He wondered what he could do, trapped in here. He thought desperately of Sarah and Jessica. He'd left no message for them. He had to get home for them.

The doors slid closed. The train started pulling out. It accelerated. Nothing came for him. The other passengers, locked in around him, tight as sardines in a can, weren't looking at him, sweating and panting, didn't care. Normality crashed back into him, sheer relief. He looked to his phone, hoping to tell Sefton what had happened. That he'd given the Ripper the slip. No reception.

The train stopped at Charing Cross. Quill tensed again as a masked figure made its way along the carriage . . . no, it was just another protestor. He pushed past Quill and got off. Quill let himself start to relax. Where should he get off? Baker Street, call Sefton from the open Metropolitan line platform there, get a taxi either back to the Portakabin, or home . . . ? No, the Portakabin: he was only going to tell Sarah about this when it was ancient history.

Why had he suddenly been targeted? What had changed?

He got out at Baker Street, ran up the stairs to the Metropolitan line platform, found phone reception after a couple of steps and noticed the flashing of a couple of voicemails – that would be Sefton, desperately trying to contact him. Before he could hit them, his phone rang. He answered it.

'Where are you?' said a voice on the other end that he didn't recognize.

'Who is this?'

'It's Neil.'

'Neil who?'

'Neil Gaiman.'

'What? How did you get this number?' Quill wondered if this famous person had picked the mother of all wrong moments to ask him about some detail of police work.

'Listen, there's something about what's going on right now that you need to understand—'

'Ostentation, yeah, we got that.'

'Never mind that now. There's more to it.' Quill suddenly realized that Gaiman sounded almost as tense as he was. 'I know what's going on, and only I can help you. I'm in a car, coming in from the north. I can get you away. Where are you?'

'Baker Street tube.'

'Right, I'll be outside in a few minutes. Call me back if you have to move.'

He hung up before Quill could ask him anything further. Quill was about to head for the exit, but stopped as he understood what he was looking at. From here he could see across several platforms. From trains at all of them were spilling, among other passengers, a number of Toffs.

He called Sefton. 'Where am I?' he asked.

'Baker Street?' said Sefton. 'If what Twitter is saying—'

'Right,' said Quill. 'They must have been prepared to form flash mobs in this general area—'

Again he stopped. Just slightly, the quality of light on the platform had changed. The weight of the Sight shifted within him, gravity turning his head like that of a prey animal smelling the predator, nausea and panic making him stare.

At the far end of the platform, light was leaping into the air above the crowd again. He turned, but the doors of the train had closed a moment before and now it was accelerating off. 'He's here again, Kev!' he shouted.

He ran down the platform, shouldering through people coming the other way, the Victorian vastness of the station vault above him; shafts of sunlight illuminated him as if he was a small animal running through the forest. He ran past the snack bar. He raced along beside a train that was just pulling in, that nauseous light throwing his shadow against the side of it, shining into the windows, making one old lady look up at him and glimpse something terrible and then lose it again and look away.

He shoved his way along through another group of people clustered at one of the doors, waited to make his move until the doors were closing, then he dived in as they did. He was between the doors, heaving against them as they closed on him like vices, and then he was through them, into the train, as if he'd fought to be born, to stay alive. They slammed behind him.

Quill staggered to the other side of the train as it rattled off.

He felt something wet hit him. He looked at the far door and saw his shadow cast there by sudden light. He looked down and saw silver.

He leaped forward up the centre aisle and felt the blow miss him.

He looked over his shoulder as the train threw him left and right. Passengers looked up from their seats, wondering what he was heaving himself away from, if it could possibly hurt them. Deciding that it couldn't, that he was mad, they looked back to their papers and books.

It came bouncing after him, leaping down the length of the train. It left dripping silver in its wake. The silver was pouring from it, not just from the mask, but from under the cape, from its limbs. Quill felt for an animal moment that he might survive this, because it looked wounded, because that looked like blood.

But it was flying at him now with all its strength.

He knew exactly what it was going to do to him.

He reached the end of the carriage, where cooler air was blasting through the window down the middle of the cars. He was damned if he was going to let this thing get him without every ounce of fight. He dragged open the connecting door, then the one after it, and threw himself through them and slammed the doors shut.

The darkness outside the train and the nature of the roar around it changed in that second, and he looked back again.

The Ripper was slowly pushing through the first of those two double doors.

This had been a long train, hadn't it? A bloody long train. He'd got on somewhere near the back. Thank God.

Quill ran up the train, going through every connecting door and making sure they closed behind him. Door handles were too prosaic for the Ripper, he thought for a moment. After three sets of doors he looked back, though, and there it was, two carriages behind him, now flinging open a door, obviously having started to use them. Of course it had. It had probably written that message in blood. It could use its fingers if it wanted to.

Quill sprinted, put another two carriages between them. He saw the train was pulling in to Finchley Road. He was in a nightmare. He looked to his phone. He found slight reception. He texted the number Gaiman had left. He stepped out onto the platform with a bunch of other people and stayed wary of falling under the Ripper's eyeline as he raced up the stairs from the platform.

He left the tube station, looking in every direction, half expecting to see the busy shopping street once more filled with Toffs. To his sheer relief, it was not. Nothing followed him out of the entrance. He waited half hidden in the doorway of a newsagent. He hit reply to one of Sefton's panicked voicemail messages. 'I'm at Finchley Road,' he said. 'I'm going to see what . . . oh fuck—'

That glow and the weight that came with it was somewhere above him. He looked up, above the level of the shops, and saw a new star appearing in the sky. It was like Tinkerbell dancing its way up out of the metropolis, heading round and round, on a circular course, a corkscrew that was heading right towards him. It took a moment for him to resolve that shape, once again, into the Ripper.

The figure was running in the air. It was jerking the razor in front of it, miming the action of what it still wanted to do to him. It would never give up, he knew. 'Over here!' A voice was shouting to him.

A big black car had pulled up at the kerb. From the driver's seat, Gaiman was urgently beckoning him. 'Get in! Quick!'

Quill ran for the car.

NINETEEN

Sarah Quill was waiting. She'd woken up that morning to find that Quill hadn't come home. This was unusual, but hardly unique. She'd called his phone, expecting to find him having a bacon sandwich at some crime scene or in that Portakabin, which he'd described to her so many times that she could almost see it. She'd left a message on his voicemail, that surprised-sounding identification of himself, with a little hesitation which said, 'Is this thing on?' She'd asked him to call and got Jessica to say good morning to Daddy as she got her ready for nursery.

Then she'd gone to work, where there were new computers, and Geoff was showing everyone three choices of new *Enfield Leader* logos. There'd been a series of phone interviews about the promises made by central government concerning wheelie-bin collections. So many parts of London were burning now that they might as well announce which ones *weren't* on fire. At lunch, eating a sandwich at her desk, Sarah called Quill once more, heard the start of the voicemail again, didn't leave a message. She called the home phone and was relieved to find an answerphone message there but then frowned to hear that it was from the undercover Quill often talked about, Costain. He was asking her to call him back. He sounded worried.

Her fingers fumbling, she called the number he gave, and, with a feeling like a stone in her stomach, asked what had happened.

He said he couldn't tell her much, but it felt more as if he didn't want to, as if he was sparing her from something. Quill hadn't checked in. They regarded him as missing. They were pulling in resources from everywhere to try and find him. They'd call as soon as anyone knew anything.

After she ended the call, she immediately wanted to call him back and demand to know what he hadn't been telling her. But she didn't.

At 3 p.m. she collected Jessica from nursery and said nothing about Daddy. She hoped that this would just be a day without him that Jessica wouldn't even notice.

At 7 p.m., when it was time for bed, Jessica asked where Daddy was. 'He's at work, sweetheart; they sometimes have very long days. He might be here when you wake up.' Jessica had nodded and, five minutes later, repeated it to Sarah: that Daddy might be here when she woke up.

When Jessica had gone to bed and had had her story, and was asleep, Sarah called Gipsy Hill again and asked to be put through to the Portakabin. She got Lisa Ross, whom for some reason Sarah had always imagined to be very glamorous. She sounded nervous to hear from her.

Bloody hell. Bloody hell, this was getting worse. She started to ask all the questions and felt as if she had picked at a loose thread and now everything was unravelling.

'We know where he was when he made his last phone call. There's no indication that he's come to any harm.'

'I know about what you lot do. Was he doing something like that?'

'Mrs Quill—'

'Don't you . . . don't you tell me it's an operational matter. You're the one that . . . you were willing to . . . please, would you just tell me everything?!'

She did, in that halting, washed-out, carefully blank voice of hers. She did her best to make what Quill's phone messages had said sound positive. She emphasized that nothing had been found at the scene of the last phone call, outside Finchley Road tube station. There was CCTV footage of Quill dashing off, as if certain of where he was going, but the view of the camera didn't stretch far enough to see what he was heading for. There were no further witnesses so far. Sarah knew what they were thinking might be found. 'We're doing everything we can. We've been on this since that moment. Mrs Quill . . .' Then her voice changed, and Sarah got an inkling of why Quill told her he had such faith in this woman. 'Sarah. This is all we're doing now. We're going to find him. I swear to you, I'll call you as soon as there's news. Okay?'

Sarah gave Lisa all her numbers and said goodbye too quickly and ended the call. Quill would turn up having finally come out from his hiding place, smelling of shit. She would be so happy to see him. She could see his face.

Was this what it was like when it wasn't a false alarm? Was this what it was like when the worst possible thing finally happened?

She could feel the first tug of something that felt impossibly big. If she didn't think about this yet, she could hold it off. It might go away as things turned out to be okay. Oh, she hated him for doing this to her; she was so angry at him . . .

That stone in her stomach again. She felt hungry, but she knew she'd just look at what she might make to eat and not want it, and it would feel bad to start making it. She felt desperately sleepy too, stupidly so, but she didn't want to sleep in case the phone rang.

She went to the door of Jessica's room, intending to go in and take comfort in looking at her, but then she stopped. She didn't want to bring the stone in her into Jessica's presence. She didn't want it to multiply.

She went to bed. She actually went to bed and fell straight to sleep, as if this was a normal day.

The sound of the phone on the bedside table woke her up. She told Quill to please answer that. When he didn't, she remembered.

She grabbed the phone and nearly switched it off in her scramble to answer it.

Her name, spoken by this professional, caring, careful voice of a stranger, as a question, was the most terrifying thing she had ever heard.

TWENTY-FOUR HOURS AGO

'Thanks for that,' said Quill, as Gaiman brought the car to a halt. They had stopped in a side street somewhere near Edgware Road.

'Please, don't thank me,' said Gaiman, turning to look at him. He had the oddest expression on his face: a deliberate solemnity.

'Well, you saved me, didn't you?' said Quill. He went to open the car door. But it was locked. 'You planning to let me out so we can go and get a drink? Or are you going to tell me what's going on?'

The author had refused to answer questions as he'd driven the car at high speed, presumably thinking the Ripper might be after them. He'd only been distracted by sending a text message when they'd stopped at traffic lights. Gaiman just kept looking at him, his mouth a straight line of tension. Then it suddenly dawned on Quill what might be going on here. 'Oh no,' he said. 'You're helping him.'

The glowing figure burst through the car door.

Gaiman made himself watch. Quill screamed as he tried to move, to fight, but the razor flew back and forth supernaturally fast, slashing into the man's torso. Quill kept screaming. Gaiman desperately wanted him to die quickly, but that was such a terrible, selfish thought. The slashes reached Quill's neck and the sounds suddenly stopped.

The Ripper flew from the car. Silver splattered on the window. The remains of Quill's body fell in a heap across the seats.

Gaiman took a deep breath to calm himself. Then he switched on the engine once more, checked the rear-view mirror and drove off.

TWENTY

Dr Piara Singh Deb, forensic pathologist, let out a long breath as he looked at these two young coppers and their intelligence analyst. He remembered the last time they had come to see him, when they had been driven, burdened, more passionately engaged with the Mora Losley case than was useful for them professionally. He had been pleased to hear the subsequent reports of them having succeeded in saving children from the fate of those whose skeletons he had examined for them on that occasion. Now they looked just as fraught, but in an entirely different way. The young woman had a terrible expression on her face as she looked at the body on the slab in the forensic laboratory. She kept her jaw tight shut as if she was about to explode with rage, and her eyes shone with it. He expected some variation: perhaps this was the prelude to tears, but none came. She didn't talk at all as they viewed the body. The stockier black copper had a more conventional grief, which was somehow reassuring. He was pale, he hadn't slept, you could feel the tension in his neck. Their DS did all the talking. He asked a lot of questions. He seemed determined to remain calm and businesslike – something Singh had seen a lot in the way police dealt with horrifying deaths. But he was talking a little too fast, there was a touch of desperation about him. He was playing host today, in these terrible circumstances, to a superintendent as well as the three of them. He suspected the deceased, James Quill, had also been a friend of hers. The last time Singh had seen him, he'd been suffering somehow, lost. Now he was lost completely.

'The body was found at oh-four-twenty-eight this morning, having caught in the moorings of a tourist vessel near East India Dock. Exposure to the water indicates he can't have been in there for more than about nine hours.'

'That's before when he was last seen alive,' said the DS.

'Various other tests concur that death might have occurred soon after he was last seen. You tell me these are the same clothes he left work in. He was dropped into the river from some considerable height. I wouldn't be surprised if I was told that was off one of the major bridges upstream from where he was found. Needless to say, he was already dead.' Singh moved to look into the dead man's face, remembering how it had looked in life. 'Cause of death: shock and massive blood loss due to repeated lacerations of the torso and gross injuries to the testicles and lower abdomen.' The body was white, even the wounds pale. 'These injuries are precisely in keeping with the MO of the suspect you are investigating in connection with the previous murders.'

'Does he seem colder than he should?' That was the other black copper, who had kept his eyes fixed on Quill's face, as if making himself not look away. He'd changed since last time Singh had seen him. More certain. Harder.

'That's interesting. My thermometer doesn't say so, but . . .' Singh ran his hand over the chilly surface of the chest. 'I *feel* he is. No, please don't write that down, that's ridiculous. Why do you ask?'

The DC just shook his head. So Singh had to move on.

'I do see some indications, such as traces of fibre beneath the fingernails, that the victim was killed inside a car. The hands seem to have clawed at a seat, and we see leather and other indicators of a luxury interior.' Looking at Quill's hands, he recalled his own, a couple of hours ago, pulling a sheet back from this same face. That had been when Quill's wife had come in. It never stopped being hard to do that. 'Is this your husband?' he'd asked then.

'Yes, it is,' the wife had said, very quickly. In order to be doing all she could. He'd heard that sound so often. He'd stepped back then and let her do all the other things they sometimes did: put a hand to the deceased's face; kiss his brow, and, in this case, his lips. Sarah Quill looked exactly like the other widows he'd met, yet each of them was unique. Death was the most common thing to human beings, and still enormous for everyone. Dr Singh had a young family and had never known the death of someone he loved. He hoped his job would prepare him. He knew it would not.

She hadn't started to cry. Some did, some didn't. She was one of those for whom it was going to take a very long time before it hit her.

Now he turned to these others who had loved James Quill, wishing he had it in him to be a minister of some kind, a coun-sellor. But he knew nothing of death. He said the same to them as he'd said to Sarah. 'I'm very sorry.'

Ross put a hand over her eyes as they left the lab. She didn't want people looking at her. She didn't want to look at people. Or at anything. She felt Costain put a hand on her shoulder, felt the years ahead of her without happiness properly now for the first time. How terrible Quill's last moments must have been. Now she would never see him again.

Unless. Unless. Unless . . .

She couldn't look at Costain. The Ripper might come for the rest of them at any moment. Costain would be considering the very real possibility of suddenly being sent to Hell, at any moment. If she was in his shoes, what would she do? Would she immediately do her best to go and take the object, right away, intending to use it to protect herself? Or would she use it to bring back their colleague and friend, not just because he was their colleague and friend but because, in dying, he might have discovered information that could save them all? Or would she give it to her lover, so that a dead father might be returned to life? Not that there would be happiness for that lover in any of these outcomes.

The meth pumped up every negative she felt. She couldn't look at him because she would always be looking at the calculations on his face now. But she also could not let him out of her sight. She made herself look. She saw him only looking back with concern for her. But she kept on looking.

Sefton was watching Costain and Ross. He wanted to ask what could possibly be going on between the two of them that they seemed *distracted* from Quill's death. But he was full of grief and guilt, and he couldn't be sure of anything he might glimpse around the edge of that. His ridiculous presumptions of occult defence had failed entirely. Quill had looked to him to be the specialist, and his so-called expertise had provided him with a few stupid trinkets. The Ripper might come for the rest of them at any moment, and there was nothing he could do about it. It almost felt as if he'd killed again.

'Listen to me,' said Lofthouse. They all turned to her. The expression on her face was all business. They were not going to see her emotions. She was toying with that bloody key on her charm bracelet. Sefton wanted to shake her and demand to know what she knew that they didn't. 'We have every reason to think,' she said, 'that you three will be the Ripper's next targets. Normally I'd say let's get you into protective custody, but I think if I did that the results might be bloody terrifying, for you and for London. You're going to need to look out for each other. Is that clear?'

They all nodded, numb. Sefton wondered exactly how they were supposed to do that.

'What could you see that Dr Singh couldn't?'

'The body is, Jimmy is . . . covered in silver,' began Sefton, haltingly, 'head to toe. More than any of the others were.' He'd felt the cold shining off Quill's body.

'Do we have a crime scene?'

'We've checked all the major bridges for silver,' said Costain, 'and haven't found anything. If we can find this car, the interior should be covered in it.'

'We went straight to where the body was found,' said Sefton. 'Everything Jimmy had on him – phone, wallet, notebook and so on – was missing from the body, which might be designed to make this look like a robbery—'

'But of course it isn't,' finished Costain.

'You will have everything you need,' said Lofthouse. 'Even when the strike starts at noon tomorrow there are plenty in the Met that'll still turn out for Jimmy Quill.' Quill's death was all over the media. The Ripper had struck at the heart of the establishment again. As if Jimmy was just that, a shape for a story. Lofthouse had provided what she'd called the usual quotes. 'Jason Forrest sends his deepest condolences. He says he knew something was wrong when James was late for a pint. The main investigation team are now busy looking into connections between him and the other victims.'

'Good luck with that,' said Sefton. He wanted the Ops Board in front of him right now, wanted Quill to be standing beside it too, but he couldn't see what good it or anything else could do. 'I followed the pattern of those flash mobs on Twitter. The original tweets about them are from a variety of accounts, but they all use similar language. The first one of them always said something's about to happen in a particular place – where Jimmy was – and then, minutes later, Toffs from nearby started arriving, ready for action. Nothing impossible about the distances travelled, and it might have been harder to do if it had been a weekday lunchtime, but it's definitely a phenomenon. And I think whoever was sending the tweets must have known where Jimmy was, must have been trying to provide cover for the attack, at least at the start, and on the occasions when the Ripper found him again.' He remembered the sound of Quill's voice on the other end of the phone, the desperation.

'I've put in a new Data Protection Act request asking for account information about the tweets,' said Sefton, 'but with the DPA backlog and the strike, I don't know how long that'll take.'

'All right.' Lofthouse closed her eyes for a moment, then opened them again, as if willing herself to keep going. 'You're our only hope of catching this thing that killed James. I doubt I have to give you a motivational speech about doing that.'

'No, ma'am,' whispered Costain.

'And if you do catch the Ripper, things might get better, am I correct?'

'That's the hope we've been given,' said Sefton.

'DS Costain –' she put a hand on his arm – 'I'd normally appoint a new commanding officer from outside your team, but I'm going to tell anyone who's interested that getting up to speed with your unit would waste valuable time. So *you* are now in charge of Operation Fog. Are you okay with that?'

'Ma'am,' Costain nodded. Sefton was pleased to see no triumph or annoyance in him. There was only the anguish they all shared.

Sarah Quill had woken a neighbour, asked her to stay in the house in case Jessica woke up, and then driven through the scarily empty streets of London into a building that was far too busy, where she had seen her dead husband's body on a tray.

She had expected him to wake up. That would have been terrifying, but then, a second after, it would have been wonderful.

It had occurred to her, in that moment, that perhaps he actually *might* wake up, because now she knew impossible things could happen. But he didn't.

She hadn't wanted to touch him, but she had: she had pushed her head down and made herself kiss him, fighting awful horrors in the depths of her about this being the last time she would see . . . the body. Him. Calm voices told her that wasn't the case.

There would be a funeral.

She was given a hot drink and asked if she was okay to drive. He was still in there, still just over there, in the other room. Still, incredibly, not breathing.

They hadn't wanted to say how he'd died, but she'd understood what was under the sheet. That hadn't hurt her at all. That was just a detail that her brain had gently put in a place where it couldn't yet hurt her.

But it would. That detail had joined a list. They were all coming to get her.

She drove herself home. She thanked the neighbour and shook her head when the neighbour asked what had happened. The neighbour said Sarah was as white as a sheet.

So Sarah had been there when Jessica had woken up, like on any morning.

Jessica had come downstairs shouting, which turned into singing something off the telly. Then she had immediately said, out of nowhere, as if it was a certainty, that Daddy had already gone to work.

Somehow, Sarah was still sure it was all a mistake, but that was just trying to keep at bay this awful thing . . . which was true.

She was tempted, just for a moment, as she got Jessica ready to go to nursery – while Jessica talked and talked about Disney princesses and how she wanted all of them and that they could afford it, a word she'd only learned this week – to tell her that, yes, Daddy had gone to work.

But no. *No.*

The weight finally reached her, for the sake of their child. A child in whom she was seeing Quill's face. She had to make herself not cry. She stopped dressing her, she had to tell her first. There would be no nursery today. There would just be the two of them.

She didn't want to scare her. She took Jessica's hands and looked into her face, forcing herself to smile. 'No,' she said, and found that she was going to tell the same lie that so many children had been told. Because she was such a coward. Because she didn't want to hurt her with something she would herself have to take on first. 'Daddy's gone . . . on a long journey.'

THE PREVIOUS NIGHT

Gaiman heaved Quill's corpse up against the parapet on the side of Westminster Bridge. Around him, the night-time traffic was absolutely still, as if in freeze frame. There was no sound except his own breathing and the scraping of the dead body being moved across the stones. Had whatever was doing this brought time around him to a halt, or was he moving very fast? He looked down the river; without movement it looked as unreal as a movie backdrop, the lights somehow no longer alive.

He looked back to Quill, and put out of his head, as he had so many times, the knowledge that this man had a family. They would suffer for a while, but everything would end the same way for everyone. That was the excuse he allowed himself. That justification had let him do all this. He had found Quill, he had anonymously texted the person who controlled the Ripper, telling them where his victim was going to be. He was doing this for the greater good. But that was what everyone who did terrible things told themselves. To take comfort in that would be wrong. Instead, he accepted his guilt. He was an accessory to murder.

He took everything out of Quill's pockets and found the detective's notebook. He had to follow specific instructions in disposing of that.

He took a last look into the man's empty face, to make sure he wasn't sparing himself anything. He grabbed Quill by the legs, heaved him up the parapet like a sack and used his shoulders to push him over. The body fell into the river. He watched it hit the water and could still see it for a moment as the current carried it away. Then it went under and was gone.

There was silver on him, and in the car. He would have to clean it all. He had been forbidden to give himself up. The deal outlined by the ghost that had been sent to meet him was very detailed, but it hadn't, curiously, made any mention of *how* Quill was going to die, only that Gaiman would lure him into it. Gaiman got the feeling that the details had been improvised, a reaction to events.

He looked up and saw that the man who had offered him the deal, who had stood beside that ghostly visitor, was now nearby, in the middle of the road. He was well dressed, powerfully built, with a receding hairline and cold grey eyes. Whenever Gaiman had seen him he'd had a broad smile on his face; that was also the case now.

'I did what you wanted,' Gaiman said. He was shocked somehow to find his tone was still reasonable, that he sounded questioning, merely amazed at himself.

The man inclined his head, still smiling. *Yup, I guess you did!*

'Everything I've read tells me you keep your side of a bargain. That you don't, in fact, twist deals to your advantage like the Satans of literature. I want you to tell me again that, in return for Quill's life, the people I named have now been freed from Hell.'

The man nodded. Perhaps, if he ever spoke, his voice would destroy all who heard it.

'I told Quill's team that if they caught the Ripper, they could start turning things around. There was nothing in your contract to say I couldn't offer them hope.'

The man shrugged. His smile remained untroubled.

Gaiman took a last look around the artificial stillness of the bridge. Once more he made himself feel the full weight of what he had done. Then he got into his car and drove off. After a moment, the lights of London started to move again behind him.

TWENTY-ONE

Costain drove the others back from the pathologist's lab to Gipsy Hill. Sefton kept trying to find something on the radio other than bad news.

'. . . *actually one of the detectives working on a related inquiry, with no other apparent links to the other victims . . .*'

'*That it's come to this, that a Metropolitan Police detective inspector can be stabbed to death by what certainly appears to be the very suspect he's pursuing, because he was the leader of a team of only four officers, working out of a Portakabin, with almost no resources. No, I am not using his death for political ends, whatever that means; I'm saying that with better funding he would have had backup, he would have had team members around him . . .*'

'*This vote to strike has no weight in law, but what it does is bring this government up short, faces them with the idea that they might actually, amid increasing riots and protests, have to declare that officers who mount wildcat strikes have taken illegal action and have them suspended or even arrested.*'

'*One less. That's it.*'

'*These people don't speak for us or our movement. We do not advocate violence. Many of us who were here at the start are desperately trying to discourage the use of the Toff costumes, which are now widely seen as a sign of violence. There is no leadership structure, we're not*' *a hierarchical organization, no, so . . . let me finish . . . no, we have no power to enforce that . . .'*

'Britons, Londoners, we implore you – the police won't protect you, the urban rioters seek to burn your honest businesses, the work of centuries – get out onto the streets and stand up for what is yours. What's the face behind that mask, the killer of police officers and those who've worked hard all their lives to make good? I think we all know the answer, but so few people are prepared to say the words out loud. International financiers are looking to see this city burn, and then step in to plunder what's left at knock-down prices. Don't let them. Secure your own streets.'

The riots were actually ramping up now, drawing in other police forces like a fire draws in oxygen. Those forces and the protestors were waiting for the day of the strike, when the Met and all the other police forces would retreat and, presumably, strike the spark of the inferno. The owners of small businesses had now taken on a sort of costume of their own, a towel wrapped round their faces, a cudgel of some kind over their shoulders, and were filmed in lines and marches. Drain the colour from the picture and you could be in the thirties, Sefton thought, looking out of the car window at distant smoke. The banks had now shut their branches in almost half the boroughs. People were talking about not being able to pay in their wages, economists about the possibility of a never-ending recession.

It felt as if now Jimmy had ended, the world was ending with him. Sefton had to do something. But what?

When they got to the Portakabin, they saw the mirror they'd brought back from Vincent's standing there, and as one went to grab it. They heaved it through the door and finally left it standing outside on the grass. Whatever Sefton had said about it seemingly being bereft of power, they all still felt better without it in the room.

They looked at each other, standing outside in the sunlight, and Ross felt the weight of how long she'd been awake, the need for more meth to keep her going. They'd kept working through the night to try and find Jimmy, then to go and see his body. On the way here, the Data Protection Act results had come back, forwarded from the main inquiry, concerning the tweets that led to the mob outside the bar and the later ones that had sparked off the crowds of Toffs near Quill. All of the Twitter accounts, and there were several involved, had been set up by anonymous webmail users whose chosen names looked to be deliberately random strings of letters and numbers. The contact details given were plausible-sounding street names, but uniformly fictional; the phone numbers all led to the monotone of unreal connections. Ross had Googled the words but could find no connection between them, except that some of them were actual streets in a random scatter of different towns.

Without saying anything, she marched back into the Portakabin; the other two followed. She went to the Ops Board. 'Adding the two big questions,' she said, picking up a marker, feeling numb and roaring at the same time. 'One: why did the Ripper kill Quill?' She wrote 'motive?' beside a victim line connecting Quill to the Ripper.

'It must be something we learned recently,' said Costain, 'between the last murder and now.' He paced back and forth. 'It must be. It must be.'

'Mary Arthur,' said Sefton, pointing to the CCTV camera still of her. 'Jimmy was sure we were onto something with her. She has a possible link to Spatley. Somehow she's the only survivor of an attack by the Ripper—'

'Ironic,' said Ross, 'her being a prostitute.' Then she chided herself. The choice that was looming over her was putting her off her game. She was letting Jimmy down. 'No, fuck "ironic", *significant*. Potentially.'

'She's the lead we've recently been pursuing. Fruitlessly, so far, because that bar is the only place she's been seen since she vanished.'

'She might have needed funds, decided to turn a trick again,' said Sefton.

'Hoxton nick hasn't laid eyes on her, despite the description doing the rounds,' said Costain.

'It's the same pattern,' said Ross, 'as with Tunstall's death: we discover something new, someone who can follow up on that is murdered. Now, question two: how did the Ripper locate Quill?' Ross wrote 'how?' beside the same line, and underlined it many times.

'I want a watch on Twitter,' said Costain. 'If anyone tries to start a flash mob of those Toff fuckers anywhere near us, I want some warning. I want to know, okay?'

'Already on it,' said Sefton.

There was silence. Quill would normally have said something to further shape the questions they should be asking. Ross listened to the silence, feeling the limits of where the board could take them. She felt the speed of her pulse making the emptiness stretch. It was as if the death of Quill had been just the first enormous blow, and they knew more were coming. The business of the Ops Board, of trying to turn such huge impossible things into simple data, of trying to control the world that way, felt ridiculous now. That they had won against Losley seemed like sheer chance.

On the way to Quill's autopsy she had looked again at her research on the object that could bring her father back from the dead. She had checked every detail. The Bridge of Spikes, her reading said, was one of a kind. She hadn't found anything else that claimed to be able to do the same thing.

She put the marker down. 'Fuck this,' she said, 'fuck this.' She ran for the door.

She managed to get into her car and start the engine as Costain ran down the steps of the Portakabin. She accelerated out of the gate and onto the road and just glimpsed Sefton in the rear-view mirror, stumbling out after Costain, starting to shout.

Leyton Gardens in Kentish Town looked just as grim in the early afternoon. There were a few kids playing in the street. Still a smell of smoke; it was everywhere in certain suburbs now. Music from open windows on higher floors. Ross walked around the block, checking for exits. The curtains were open now; she'd been home since last time, this Anna Lassiter.

Ross turned the corner to head back round to the door of number 16 and found Costain standing there. He raised his hands in surrender. 'If you really want to do this on your own,' he said, 'I'll go straight back to the nick.'

'You left Sefton on his own?' she said.

'It doesn't matter. The Ripper could take all three of us as easily as one. He could. Just like that.' His teeth were starting to chatter. She'd let her meth intake drop, but he hadn't.

'Was he okay with that?'

'He just stared at me. Then he started to ask me what I was doing, but . . . I got out of there.'

'He deserves better.'

'Yeah. So. Yeah.' Costain stepped towards her. 'Do you want me along or not?'

'You'd really go back?'

'Yeah. Yeah.'

She studied his face. It was the most obvious move, pretending to do her bidding. She could imagine him grabbing the object out of her hands and sprinting to his car, just as they'd both run away from Sefton.

She knew the meth was compromising the choices she made. Doing this felt like standing on the edge of a precipice; so did everything right now. Their only hope was to stay together, but she'd run off. 'Stay,' she said. 'Let's get this done.'

They went to the door of number 16. Ross knocked. No reply. The original plan when they'd first checked this place out had been that they would swap shifts, do some kind of stakeout, wait until they saw Lassiter leave, then go in.

'Did you decide?' asked Costain. 'Who you would use it on?'

She shook her head. 'I don't know.'

'Okay. Sure. Right.' Costain took a tyre iron from his jacket.

'We don't have a warrant,' she said. 'This is illegal.'

'I don't care. Okay? I don't care.' He checked out the area near the lock and looked around to see if anyone was in sight. Just at that moment there was no one, but that wouldn't be the case a moment later, and there were plenty of windows. He shoved the tyre iron into the gap between the door and the frame, took a step back and kicked it. He kicked it and kicked it, *bam, bam, bam*, the drug not letting him pause.

The door burst open, the lock splintering the wood. The lack of bolts on the inside might mean there was nobody at home. With luck, they could search the place. Ross stepped straight in and Costain followed her, pulling the door to behind them as far as it could go.

Ross had been in some dilapidated homes in her time, but this one was towards the worse end. There were full ashtrays spilling onto the floor, cans of food with forks in them. The place smelt stale – old beer and cigarettes. The windows were stained, the light inside was low.

Ross took a step towards what must be the bedroom, and froze. She put a hand out to stop Costain moving. She felt . . . what was that just ahead? It reminded her of the fortune-teller at the New Age fair.

'I see it, I see it, okay,' said Costain. He made his way forward and indicated, an inch above the carpet, a line of . . . of nothing . . . just a slight reaction of the eye to the grain of the worn-down fibres. A tripwire. The fortune-teller had set one for certain words, and this Lassiter woman had set it for people to walk across. Costain stepped over it, and then across another similar one a moment later. 'Damn it,' he whispered, 'they'll be between us and the door.'

They made their way towards the back of the flat, with him leading now. Ross marvelled at the idea that he was better at seeing these traps than she was, but she supposed that was his nature, to look out for what could bring him down.

They went into a bedroom with no decoration. Single bed. One table. Old magazines on it. As welcoming as a dentist's waiting room. But lived in: clothes on the floor, hanging out of drawers. They quickly searched, under the bed, in the wardrobe.

Ross realized that she could only feel slight traces of the gravity of the Sight about this place. That feeling put in her something close to panic until she reminded herself that that gravity could also be concealed, which was what you'd do if you were hiding an immensely powerful object in a place like this. The traps didn't show up much either – or what use would they be?

She half expected to find an addict's supply and paraphernalia, but didn't. In the wardrobes there was a row of ancient dresses, the uniform of the 'Londoner' when out and about. She whizzed through them, patting them down when there might be a pocket. Nothing.

They finished with the bedroom, tried the tiny kitchen. They went through all the obvious hiding places: the grill; packets and cans in the cupboard; the freezer drawer of the fridge. How awful must it be, thought Ross, to have such an immense power in a place with so little ability to keep it safe. If you were keeping it for yourself, if you were hoping for it to save you when you died, you'd spend that life always on guard, always terrified.

Costain found a few traps as they explored and stopped Ross from walking right into one, in the breadbin. They didn't seem to be protecting anything specific. This woman would have to live with these traps, having to remember all the time where they were.

Costain suddenly froze. Ross heard it too: the sound of someone outside the door. He motioned for her to be quiet. The best they could do would be to wait until the arrival had entered, then rush past her for the door. The best they could hope for was that she was unarmed. They would have to leap those tripwires.

'Come on out, you cunts.' The voice was familiar.

Costain looked at Ross, telling her to stay here. He stepped out of the kitchen. She let him. But the voice had used the plural. Maybe this was for the best. They hadn't found anything. They'd have to try to make this woman an offer.

She followed Costain. Standing there was the young woman

from the Goat and Compasses whom Sefton had spent so much time with, the one he'd said had sworn at him all the time. She was dressed more normally now, in a black T-shirt and jeans. She was looking at them with an expression of supreme disdain but she also looked hopeless, as lost as they were. 'You're too late,' she said.

'What do you—?' began Costain.

'Don't fucking pretend, nigger. You were after the Bridge of Spikes. The object that lets you come back from the dead. But you're going to go away empty fucking handed. 'Cos some other fucker broke in here yesterday and took it.'

Ross found that she could barely breathe. She felt as if rocks had fallen into her stomach. Costain spun and kicked the sofa. 'Who?' he said.

'Like I know!' The woman sat down and made a noise that was halfway between a laugh and a sob. 'You can tell everyone else it's gone and all.'

'Everyone else?' asked Costain.

'Two blokes came after it the night before. Most of my defences got used up on them. They finally got out, on fire, with me screaming at them. I should have legged it then; I should have taken it with me. I made all these fucking sacrifices, just so some—' She had to stop, looking away. She wasn't trying to fool them, Ross was sure. Someone had indeed looked inside their heads and seen what they were after, and they had come and taken it. Two lots of people, somehow, had known and had had a go. What did that mean?

Feeling almost a need to get close to someone with whom she shared such pain, she went to sit next to her. The woman looked puzzled at her, sure there was nothing more Ross could want from her.

'You're Anna Lassiter?'

'How do you know my name? How did you know it was *here*?'

Ross reasoned that the next time this woman was among her subculture she'd hear about the auction anyway, so she told her about the price she'd paid.

'Good,' said Lassiter. 'Your sacrifice was in vain too.'

Ross ignored that. 'Tell us about the two blokes and the burglary the day after,' she said. 'All the details, from the top.'

'Why should I? You only want to find it so you can have it for yourselves!'

Ross looked to Costain. He reached into his pocket and produced his police warrant card.

'Oh, what?' Anna Lassiter looked between them as if her week had, if that was possible, actually got worse. 'You have got to be fucking kidding.'

Ross listened to the woman's account of the unsuccessful break-in and the successful burglary, asking all the things Lassiter would expect a police interviewer to ask. She let Lassiter believe that the Met in general knew a bit about the hidden world that she was part of, that they wanted to find the Bridge of Spikes as part of an investigation, not for themselves. Thankfully, Lassiter didn't seem to pay enough attention to the modern media to have heard much about the death of Quill or to connect him to the man she'd seen at the Goat the same night they were there, otherwise she might have realized their real motive. Or what might have been their real motive; Ross still didn't know who she would have chosen to save. Costain paced as they talked, barking the occasional question. Lassiter started looking perplexed at that, worried that she was looking at a cop and a user, but it didn't stop her from telling her story.

Lassiter had come home yesterday, having gone out to get some items to replenish her flat's defences following the break-in attempt, to find the Bridge of Spikes missing, with only small signs of a burglary having taken place. This must have been done, she thought, by someone with the Sight. Ross was surprised to hear that these were the first such attempts. It had been secrecy, rather than anything particularly useful in terms of defences, that had stopped Lassiter being raided before now.

'It would make sense,' said Costain, when she had taken him aside, 'that it's the same person who made both attempts.'

Lassiter had bought the Bridge at one of the underworld auctions over the phone, through a proxy. She'd used what she called 'craft' to conceal her identity on the other end of the phone from what she called 'checking', or as Sefton had it, 'reading your bar code'. She'd trusted the auctioneers with her address, she said bitterly, because nobody had ever successfully paid to see the register before, but she didn't want anyone else to know she'd got the Bridge. Ross had started to ask if the individual who'd been her proxy was trustworthy, but the woman had laughed bitterly at that, saying he was long dead. Yes, she had been planning to use the Bridge to save herself from death. Why else would she have held onto it?

They took all the details. It wasn't much to go on. The burglar had left no trace of his or her passing. The raiders hardly much more. Costain and Ross took prints from likely surfaces, and Lassiter angrily let them have hers for comparison.

Before they left, Costain did something Ross admired him for. He called up a locksmith, talked and talked at him about what a good thing locksmiths were, and paid over the phone for him to come and repair the door.

They left Anna Lassiter glaring at them furiously, like the jackals they were.

Costain and Ross went back to their cars in the bright afternoon sunlight, and Ross felt as if she wanted to die. 'We're not going to be able to find whoever stole it,' she said, aware of how tiny her voice sounded now. 'We don't have enough evidence. We don't have enough contacts in that world.'

'There are the fingerprints. You never know.'

She had to lean on her car. She didn't feel like going anywhere or doing anything. She was starting to see the edges of grief, doubled for her, unfolding infinitely around her. 'Why are you so hopeful?'

'I'm . . . not. I suppose . . .' He rested on the car beside her. 'I suppose I just have to keep going. For Jimmy.'

'Right. Keep going.' She made herself say it, but she didn't feel it.

They went back to Costain's place, took some more meth, fucked. Ross took what pleasure she could from it. She found no happiness. She was thinking about her father and Jimmy in Hell.

Then the phone rang.

TWENTY-TWO

Kev Sefton had stood at the door of the Portakabin watching Costain's car roar off down the road. He felt, in that moment, too angry to breathe.

What was he supposed to do? Carry on on his own? What could he do?

Nothing. He was meaningless and had now been utterly deserted. Was all this happening to him because he'd taken a life? He'd felt wrong ever since. Was that why Brutus was still rejecting him, why his source and . . . patron, he supposed, wasn't allowing him access? He had no idea how Brutus felt about death. Or about anything, really.

He sat down on the floor. He let his head drop back against the wall. He felt desperately that he wanted to fall asleep, but he couldn't let that happen. He felt a dream welling up in his head, making strange sense of his thoughts, and fought it off. He wouldn't close his eyes.

He closed his eyes. He was on the verge of sleep. He was on the verge of giving in. 'Help,' he said, with no power in his voice.

Something moved over the Portakabin. The light against his eyes changed. He heard a distant sound. Distant music. Dance music. It was like a hand on his face. It was an echo of the joy that he and Brutus had shared in a kiss. Dance music that took him back to happier times.

The music offered him a way forward. A terrible way.

He opened his eyes again. Everything around him was normal. There was a moment when he didn't believe anything strange had just happened. He was stressed out and grieving and exhausted. But what was he if not someone who did mad things because of something that might be a dream? That was a definition of what he had to be if he was going to go any further into knowing the power of London.

Slowly he got to his feet. He contemplated what was being asked of him. It would be a sacrifice. It seemed to hold the potential to wash him clean of Barry Keel's blood. It seemed to hold the possibility of doing due honour to Quill. It was something right for him and how he lived. Finally, he had a way forward in his hands. He looked up, then down, because he wasn't sure where Brutus' 'outer borough' could be said to be. He said thank you, silently.

He went to his holdall, intending to see what defences he could take with him on his journey. As he looked through it, he realized there was something missing – several things. He emptied the bag out onto the floor, and found that a bunch of items he'd kept because of their potential as protective devices: a box of London-made matches with what seemed to be occult symbols in the trademark, some salt from an ancient source actually within the metropolis, a horseshoe used in the Trooping the Colour . . . they were all gone.

He looked around the Portakabin, wondering what could get in and do that. The same thing, presumably, that had entered their dreams.

He put down the holdall and understood that he should do this without help. He headed for the door. He knew where he was going. He wanted to call Joe, but, no, he decided, he didn't want to frighten him.

Sefton had known there were dance clubs in London that kept going twenty-four hours a day, seven days a week, but he'd never been to one before. He found it in Vauxhall, a small dark dance floor in the basement of a club, the ethos of which was all concrete warehouse and the smell of poppers. Even at this hour, on a weekday, it was packed with men, dancing and occasionally snogging, when, for fuck's sake, London was falling apart. He himself hadn't come here to escape, but to find something. He couldn't really look down on this lot, though, could he? There'd been a time when he'd have been up for this. The flavour of music was trance, shading into pounding industrial – the kind of music that had sounded distantly in his head back in the Portakabin. Not that he knew one style of dance music from another. He and Joe had once laughed their arses off at a club flier offering 'intelligent handbag'. There was nothing of the Sight about this place. Nobody here had any strange weight about them.

He'd turned down a covert offer of 'speed, trips or e' near the door, but now he wondered if he should have taken them up on that. His reading had told him about mystics who'd made risky attempts to connect with something beyond themselves by pushing their minds into an altered state of consciousness. Doing that by drugs, or at least by street drugs, seemed too easy and would involve someone else's designs for one's brain. This had to be his sacrifice. It had occurred to him that he could have gone to a gym and worked his way into the state he wanted to achieve, but there there'd be someone to stop him.

He walked into the middle of the floor, closed his eyes and started to dance.

He danced for what he was sure was hours. He had his phone switched off; there was no clock visible from the dance floor. His body didn't know what time it was. There were no clues from the light. He stopped only for visits to the water station, which he'd do at speed, throw it down, throw it over himself, go back.

At first he tried to concentrate on several repetitive phrases that he ran around his head, trying to switch off his thoughts, but found he couldn't. He let his mind wander. He found all the different muscle groups in his legs, in his arms, his stomach, all starting to ache, so he'd shift a little when they did, and work something else. He let the euphoric breaks lift him, keep him going, then knuckled down to work hard again as the bass slammed back in. Every now and then he'd become aware of a man deliberately dancing near him, and he'd turn away.

He got exhausted and pushed through it, found new energy from somewhere, then burned that away too. He started to feel the aches from where he'd been thrown from the bus. He started to feel that he had to be absolutely weak and helpless to get where he wanted to go. That wasn't going to be hard. He kept thinking of Jimmy, of how Sarah would be feeling now, of how he'd given Jimmy such useless things with which to protect himself, of how it didn't feel like an investigation now, but as if they were all just children stumbling towards something terrible and huge that could pick them off when it liked. He thought of Barry Keel, that the man must have had friends, relatives, people who thought he was decent and kind and who loved him.

Was he just hurting himself? That was a deceitful, seductive thought whispering in his ear. He was harming himself in order to let himself feel better about Jimmy, in order to feel that he was working, doing something to take his mind off Jimmy's death. No, he told himself, these were weasel words, to make him stop dancing. He needed more water. This time he ignored the thirst. He burned the doubt out of himself by keeping going. He needed to rip up all these signifiers of what he was, all these words, and find what was under them, what was real. To do that, he needed to break himself.

He kept dancing.

It began as a pain up his back and chest and into his neck, a pain he feared as the start of something serious, a stroke or heart attack. He'd been told he had to face fear to get to wherever he was going, so he embraced it, pushed at the pain, letting it rack him. He felt his teeth clench and his breath start to come in gasps, felt the air was entering him in a different way now.

He kept dancing.

The pain came properly; it was all through his body, and there were disturbances in his vision, like the start of a firework display inside his eyes.

He kept dancing. He felt a shadow fall over him. He realized he couldn't see clearly now but he could still see the lights dancing inside his head.

Soon he didn't know what his body was doing; he was only distantly associated with it. It would continue being alive or it wouldn't. The pain could be ignored now, because it was only happening to that distant body.

Perhaps he was lying on the dance floor having some sort of fit. An enormous smell rushed into his head. It reminded him of childhood, but he couldn't place it. It felt somehow like death too.

The lights in his eyes turned and resolved into one shape and locked into place.

They formed a tunnel. A smooth spin of vision showed him that it led straight down. There was a hole in the world. Oh. He was on top of it.

Sefton laughed in joy as he fell down it.

He fell into a wide open space. He couldn't see it, he couldn't see anything, but he could feel it. His giddy joy turned to fear. He had to reach out into the darkness with his senses, not with his body. He had to find a way to do that or he'd keep falling in darkness, forever. He was aware, distantly, of his real body, still moving, perhaps doing something different to dancing now, not as warm. In fact it was cold. He concentrated on the pain and the cold, solidified himself around grief and fear.

He felt his way into London and saw it slowly resolve into vision all around him. He felt all the people who made it. The buildings were incidental to the people. The buildings were like a bouncing line on a mixing desk, flying up and down according to the needs and wishes and secrets of the people who pushed and pushed at the metropolis around them. The people made the buildings. He stepped out into what they'd made. He walked along a thousand balconies, hopped from one to another, ran along a line he was making as he went, association to association, along a tightrope across libraries and post offices and spires, the line springing to the beat that he felt all around him. He stopped and looked down at the metropolis around him and felt the compass points, from the big to the small, to the infinity of minuscule ones in between them. He felt how roundabouts and temples of all kinds produced eddies, how big malls created deluges, all to the unconscious will of the people, all manipulated deliberately by those who knew how.

He could feel the orbits of the outer boroughs. He looked up and decided to see them. He found he could. There were lots of them, up and out of the plane of the M25, and down below it, all swinging about Centre Point at their different angles.

The Centre Point building itself wasn't at the centre, but a little off it, so the wheel of London turned with a continual pulse beat thump around that hub. It was turning the wrong way. Anticlockwise. It was turning as if it had been set in motion with one big push. It wasn't going in the direction it was meant to roll.

Sefton tried, just for a moment, to set his strength against it, becoming a chalk hill figure on the South Downs and heaving at it, but only for a terrifying instant before he realized that its accumulated momentum would crush him utterly if he tried.

He came out of that and steadied himself. He saw a new hopeful direction, walked the back gardens down by the railway, walked beside every train coming into every station. He felt the flow of people in and out of London. He heard on his own personal soundtrack a speeded-up version of one of those pieces of Fifties 'bustling people' music.

He felt for the pain and the cold and called for the patterns to form inside his eyes again. He breathed in the right way and found the fireworks starting to go off. It was like being able to see his own brain working. The lights wanted to form their pit again, but this time he wouldn't let them. He made them form in front of him, made the lights into a tunnel he could walk into. He felt his real body walking too, distantly, not dancing any more, but outside, somewhere cold.

The tunnel that had formed inside his eyes matched, actually, with a tunnel in London that his body was walking into, a railway tunnel.

He looked down. His bare feet were on gravel. Beside them was a rail. The rail was vibrating with the rotary pulse he could also feel from London behind him. He looked up from it. There were golden lights ahead, reflecting on the silver of the rail.

He was afraid.

Good.

He pushed reality, which was trying to assert itself, back down inside himself again. He just had to step forward. Although there was a roaring up ahead. Although it was roaring directly at him now to get out of the way.

He had to believe there was more to himself and the universe than what was being roared at him. Jimmy Quill had taken the longest journey for what he stood for. Sefton had to do the same.

He stepped into the tunnel and marched quickly towards the light that was coming much more quickly towards him. There was, indeed, light at the end of the tunnel.

All the signifiers he'd seen came together for him, and he was sure he was on the cusp of understanding everything about the universe and his place within it.

That was when the train hit him.

'No, stop, all right, got you.'

Sefton looked around as hands grabbed him and pulled him aside. For a terrible moment he thought he must be awake on the dance floor, having been dragged back to life. For another awful second he was certain he could feel a train rushing past him, feel the air pummelling him, close to his clothes.

Then he looked round. He saw that he was somewhere new. Somewhere divorced from both those things and from anything real. He was in what looked like a cave . . . no, some of the walls were rock, but some of them were polished, tiled, like an underground station. Only this wasn't a real tube station, but something like a stage set, with stark, powerful lights above . . . or was that him still being back at the club? He could hear the music still pounding up there, muffled. There was a hint of the railway tunnel about the arches above too. He could hear something through the wall, rattling past, carriage after carriage. He looked away from that; it felt as if death was very near. There were escalators at the back of the room that seemed to loop back on each other, in an infinite recursion. The floor looked to be made of newspapers, the headlines and type and photos changing as he looked at them, squirming out of his vision. He himself was standing on a slight rise, on a pile of objects. He shifted his weight as if he was still dancing, and some of them rolled down by his feet: a rotted gas mask; a banner for a coronation; a Victorian cartoon of someone he didn't recognize wearing a sash saying something he didn't understand; a skull with what looked like a spear point through it.

Someone was still holding him, he realized. He turned and looked, and the firm pair of hands released him, apparently now convinced he wouldn't fall. The Rat King stood there, looking bemused at Sefton. 'You have my attention,' he said. 'You've fallen here as so many other things have. You showed yourself willing to make the ultimate sacrifice. So I thought I'd do the decent thing: take you one step back in time and save your life. You're welcome.'

'Thank you,' said Sefton. He had to sit down on the rubbish. He was shivering, breathing hard from the close call with death that a few moments ago he'd barely been aware of. 'Where is this?' he managed to say after a moment.

'My home. Where all the detritus of London comes to rest. Where what was once significant,' he held up one of the newspapers, 'becomes mere panto.'

Sefton didn't know what to say. He felt lost and desperate. He might have reached one of the 'outer boroughs', but this 'Rat King' had told him back in the bar that he didn't know the answer to his most urgent question. He'd almost killed himself to get here – he could feel his body still suffering somewhere – and now it seemed that it all might be for nothing. 'I-I was hoping to see—'

'You were after someone else? Well, tough. You've got me. Cuppa?'

Sefton looked up and was handed a cup of tea, by . . . it was the barmaid with no face from the Goat and Compasses. She now wore a thin, bloody bandage across where her eyes presumably still were not, together with a crown made of a cornflakes packet, and she carried a sword and scales strapped to a belt around what looked to have once been a Fifties party dress. Her pale masklike face made her look like a statue. 'Hello Kevin,' she said. 'Good luck. We love you.'

The Rat King rolled his eyes. 'I'll be the judge of that.'

'How's your friend doing?'

'You mean Ross? I wish I knew.'

The Rat King put a hand to his mouth in a stage whisper as he took his own cup from her. 'I don't know why I took her on. She breaks all my cups.'

'Please,' said Sefton, not drinking his tea, 'do you know *anything* that could help us find the Ripper?'

The Rat King snickered into the tea. 'Oh, I'm afraid not. The major players know to stay away from *me*; they can't stand that I can read their intentions like a cheap and nasty book.'

'Well, then, okay, can you take me to Brutus?'

'What, the Roman bloke? *Et tu Brute* and all that?'

Sefton wanted to kick something. 'He's who I met the last time I visited somewhere like this.'

The Rat King sighed theatrically. 'I don't *know* everyone who isn't real. There isn't a *phone book*.' He suddenly seemed to recall, holding up a finger. 'Wait. Was there nobody about in his London? Big, empty place, with just him in it?'

'Yeah, that's it.' Sefton found hope springing up inside him again. Maybe the Rat King was meant to show him the path that led to the object of his quest.

'Oh. Right. You can't get there from here.' The Rat King saw the defeated expression on Sefton's face and laughed again. 'I know him by one of his many other names. You didn't go on the right path today to get to him. If you haven't seen him, I should think he's still got his back to you. You should be careful of him. He can be very *demanding*.'

'So you know what he is?'

'It's not for me to share the meanings of the others. I am only in charge of my own.'

'Then what are you?'

'Listen to this policeman!' The Rat King grinned at the woman with no face, revealing gaps in his stained teeth. 'Most of those who come here ask mystical questions full of allusions and get a lot of bollocks in return.'

'He seeks the truth,' the woman said. 'He should get it.'

'You're right. He should.' He reached down and hauled Sefton to his feet, finished his own cup of tea, then threw it down to smash on the pile of rubbish. 'I am for rebellion. I stand against order. I don't build anything. I criticize what's been built. I am never *satisfied*. I look for you people to *try harder*. A lot of people think of me as a villain. I often am.'

'So . . . are you what's making the riots happen?' Sefton suddenly wondered if he'd been trapped by an enemy.

The Rat King looked at him as if he was a foolish child. 'I don't make things happen. Too much like hard work. I am what those who are not satisfied look to; I am what they have in the back of their minds, pray to, sort of. I intercede with the power of London and send some of it their way. If I've a mind to. In roundabout ways. If I can be bothered.' He looked again to the woman. 'I didn't really like saying all that. Bit too concrete for me.'

'So you're . . . a god?' Sefton had been an atheist all his life, but he didn't know any other way to say it.

'There are no gods. But that's what all the gods say.' He looked again to the woman. 'That's better. More cryptic.'

'If that's what you stand for, why did you save me?'

'Because, while I don't know much about your case, I do know that things up there –' he pointed to the roof again – 'might be about to get a lot more orderly. This is the way the British do things, you see: too much chaos, then too much order, swinging from one extreme to the other, always giving them something to complain about. They say they want a happy medium. They really don't. If you lot manage to nick the Ripper, then things will continue to tick along, with chaos in the mixture. If you don't, then . . .'

'You're talking about the extreme right taking power?'

'The British always love to flirt with that nice Mr Hitler, but they've never quite decided to take him home. *Yet.*' The Rat King stared his off-kilter stare at Sefton, and he got the feeling that his mind was being searched again. There was no sensation to it at all, and for some reason, what was terrifying and intrusive in dreams was fine here. 'Yes, you've had similar suspicions. Someone is waiting in the wings to save you all. Someone likes chaos only up to a certain point, the point where they can march in and make it all better.'

'Who?'

The Rat King shrugged. 'I don't know. You're the policeman.'

'What's the Smiling Man's part in all this?'

'Ah, you've met the new boy?'

Sefton was startled at that word. 'New?'

'Most of us go back to before you lot could stand upright. He's just a kid, relatively speaking. But he's made himself very powerful, very quickly.'

'I always sort of thought he was, you know, the Devil.'

The Rat King burst out into a staccato laugh that became a wheezing cough. 'Oh, no, dear me, no – the delusions of a child.' He threw an arm theatrically around Sefton's shoulders. 'Everyone you've met or heard about during this case has had good and bad sides to them, correct? That's one thing that's getting in the way of your search for meaning: that these days everything's got a bit mixed up. Anything seems to be able to mean anything; all the signifiers have been thrown into a barrel and are being picked out at random and assigned to just about anything, and the choice of what means what, as always, seems to be down to those with money and power. You despair about making accurate judgements about anyone. Well, I'm here to tell you, boy, it was always thus. And that *doubt* of yours is the first sign of wisdom. I liked it when you pondered, on the dance floor, the loveliness of Barry Keel, not that I myself share that opinion. That doubt of yours must be why Brutus picked you.'

'He "picked" me?' Even though it had surprised him to hear it said, Sefton sort of knew it to be true

'My point is that what you call the Smiling Man isn't "a force for evil". He's a bloke who's not real, like me, with his own aims and plans and maybe even a good side.' The Rat King considered for a moment. 'Maybe. I don't know if the shape he's made in lets him have one.'

'The shape he's made in?'

'By you lot. Don't look so startled. You people make all of us. And that's all you're going to get about him. I've already said more than I'm allowed. But the shape I'm made in allows me always to do more than I'm allowed.' He sniggered at his own cleverness. 'Oh dear, since you have walked this path and unfortunately found only me, I am obliged to offer help. What would you like for Christmas? No, wrong holiday.' He started to look in the pile of rubbish, throwing aside items which ranged from things that looked rotten to things that looked like precious jewels. 'This is the rubbish of London,' he said. 'It all descends to my level. Ah, here we are.' He pulled out a water-stained police notebook, which Sefton saw was one of the 'special' notebooks Quill had set aside for the work of his team that a judge might find unbelievable.

Then he realized. It was Quill's own notebook.

Sefton put down his tea, took the notebook, opened it, recognized Quill's handwriting. He flipped to the most recent page. He looked to the Rat King again, amazed. 'This is brilliant.'

'Glad to be of service. You haven't drunk your tea.'

Sefton felt a little abashed as he put the notebook inside his jacket pocket. 'In everything I've read, if you go somewhere outside of the real world, you're not supposed to eat or drink anything that's given to you. Sorry.'

The Rat King laughed. 'Clever fucker. I nearly had you obliged to serve me. See, you made a judgement call. You can do it. Even in this horrible new world you people have made. Bye then.'

Sefton looked in puzzlement between the Rat King and the woman, both of whom were now bowing to him as if this was the end of a play. 'What—?'

The Rat King clicked his fingers and the lights above them suddenly went out.

TWENTY-THREE

Sefton woke up. He looked around. It was early evening. He was sitting on the pavement, just along from a bus shelter. People were walking past him without looking at him. He sniffed. He'd pissed himself. So much sweat as well. He realized he knew this place. This was exactly where he'd come back last time he'd taken a trip to the outer boroughs; he was near Cannon Street tube. Why this place? He had no idea.

He remembered what had happened and urgently looked inside his jacket. There was Quill's notebook. Incredibly. He'd brought back evidence from outside the world. Somehow. He was exhausted, beyond fatigue, but he'd done it. He'd done it. He felt . . . too tired to come to any conclusions about how he felt, but there was a kind of level playing field in his head now. He had sorted something out inside himself. He reached for his phone, but his fingers were too numb to dial. He felt his throat and was sure he wouldn't be able to say anything if he could.

A car pulled up beside him. The window slid down, and to his surprise, there was Superintendent Lofthouse. 'Get in,' she said. 'I put some newspaper on the seats.' She sniffed. 'Now I realize why.'

She drove him to Gipsy Hill. He drank strong sweet tea from a flask as Lofthouse let him know what had been happening with the others. He let the drink start to warm the terrible cold inside him. His legs kept cramping, and his stomach was tied in knots. Costain and Ross were waiting back at the Portakabin, Lofthouse said. She'd managed to call them and order them to come back in. She wouldn't say how she'd known where to find Sefton. Whenever they stopped at the lights, she'd toy with that key on her charm bracelet. Sefton finally managed a whisper, because he was so angry at her keeping secrets from them. 'Five is better than four,' he whispered, his throat aching. 'Told that. Meant to be team of five. Like the Continuing Projects Team were. Right now, there's just three. You could at least make us four.'

She was silent for a long moment. 'I can't,' she said. 'Not now. You're just going to have to accept that. If, that is, you want me to keep helping you.'

When Sefton stumbled into the Portakabin, Ross came straight over. 'Oh my God, Kev,' she said, 'I'm so sorry.'

'We both are,' said Costain. 'We had to go; we thought we were onto something.'

Had they really? There was that look on Costain's face that Sefton knew not to trust. He fell into a seat and Lofthouse asked the others to get him a blanket and a change of clothes and a cup of strong coffee. He wanted a shower, but didn't feel able to walk over to the nick to get one. Slowly, as he was provided with those things, his voice came back to him and he spoke about where he'd been. Ross added the notes to the concepts column of the Ops Board. Did she seem even more distant than usual? He was so unequipped to tell right now. With his hands shaking, Sefton took out Quill's notebook, was gratified by their astonished reactions. He read out the last page: 'Met the suspect in a dream. No clue who. Fell into the figure. Back in time. Longbarrow. Fingerprints on the wall. Dead woman. Locked up. Angry. Dreaming.'

'Oh, James,' said Lofthouse, 'what the fuck?'

'"Back in time"?' echoed Costain. 'Was it him who was locked up?'

'So Jimmy encountered whatever's been visiting us in our dreams,' said Ross, '"fell into it," and . . . went back in time? Or did he have to get back here in time to do something?' She made a few attempts at adding new entries to the concepts list, crossing things out a couple of times before she was satisfied.

'It *must* be important,' said Sefton. 'That's what I brought back. It was so hard . . .' He found he could hardly continue. 'The secret to *all* this is in *those* notes.'

'"Longbarrow",' said Ross. 'That limits what he was dreaming about to a set of specific places. Maybe he was trying to tell us where to find the Ripper.'

'With fingerprints on the wall,' said Costain. 'So that's something we can follow up on. I'll bet there are records of fingerprints found at prehistoric sites. We find out where that longbarrow he mentions is; if it's real, at least we can go and see it, maybe find out why it's relevant.' He did an image search on his phone for barrows with handprints and showed them three pages of results. 'Doesn't really narrow it down,' he said. 'Six of these are in London, and four of them are now buried under shopping centres and stuff like that.'

'Send the pictures of those prints to Forensics,' said Lofthouse, 'they've got databases of fingerprints going back centuries, maybe some connection will leap out at us.'

Ross did as she asked.

'I really want to go to sleep,' said Sefton. 'I should think you lot do and all. But now I know what Jimmy knew. Now we all do. If that's what got him killed . . .'

Lofthouse nodded. 'This better be on my head,' she said. 'I'm ordering you all to take the meth.'

Sefton found himself desperately wanting to say no. As an undercover, he'd always turned down drugs, plus he wasn't sure if his system could stand it. But what was the alternative?

Costain got out his packets and looked to Ross with a raised eyebrow. 'Orders are orders,' he said. She just looked coldly back at him.

They all sniffed the powder. Sefton erupted into a coughing fit and hated the sharp feel of it up his nose. But after a moment . . . yes, it did make him feel better.

Lofthouse didn't partake. 'So,' she said, 'James said your next move should be to raid the Keel shop?'

Costain nodded, a bit too quickly. 'Yeah. Okay. Okay. We can interview Keel about scrying glasses: if he's got one; who else does he know who has; if there's any defence against them.' He gestured to the mirror that stood outside the window. 'We can ask what that thing is – if it's just a fake that Vincent got stuck with, which just happened to have the Ripper come out of it—'

'Or whether the object itself was actually a trap,' said Lofthouse, 'using the Ripper, maybe set up by those "dark forces" Vincent thought were working against him. Either way, you might get a lead on who was trying to kill Vincent, why that was so long before the other attacks, and why, uniquely, that one failed. And we might find some way to protect you three.'

'The strike starts at noon tomorrow,' said Costain, looking interrogatively at her. 'Noon. Tomorrow. Do we do this off the books? Do we even have time to do it any other way?'

'Let me talk to my friend the judge. I may have to bend the vernacular a bit to find just cause, but I'll come up with some legal reason for the raid.'

Costain paused. Then he nodded, again a bit too quickly. 'Ma'am.'

While Lofthouse got on the phone, Ross stared at the board, hoping something would leap out at her. Once the prospect of a raid on the Keel shop would have made her wonder if there was anything there like the Bridge of Spikes, but the unique nature of the item had been emphasized by everyone they'd talked to, Lassiter included. If she'd been writing this story, then Keel would have bought the Bridge from whoever had stolen it from Lassiter, but

Ross knew coppers and their friends could never be that lucky. She'd started to appreciate the feeling of the meth keeping her pulse racing. That was a bad sign. It was like a distant echo of happiness. She would have to make sure, after all this was over, that she never got the chance to be tempted by it again. After this was over. It didn't feel as if it ever could be. If it was, what would she do with her life? Be with Costain. Be unhappy.

It took an hour for Lofthouse to find and persuade a member of the judiciary that she had an urgent lead concerning the murder of James Quill, that they had evidence to suggest that senior members of the organization behind the Toff mask protests, which had obvious connections to the Ripper, could be found at a particular shop premises, where the masks were on sale. No, she hadn't had reports of any, but it was obvious there'd be some there, wasn't it?

Ross thought she saw an admiring look on Costain's face as he watched Lofthouse deliberately venture into what was very dodgy territory for a police officer: making up connections that weren't yet suggested by the evidence but that you assumed would be provided by the raid yet to come. Except in this case – and she was surely risking her career to do this, even with the blurry distraction the strike would provide – she was obviously not even imagining that the scenario she was describing was true.

She finally put down the phone having gained a search warrant. 'I feel dirty,' she said.

'Is that really different from turning the place over without *any* authority?' asked Costain.

'It is, because we have a piece of paper. I decide the meanings here. Now, how do you propose to conduct this raid of yours?'

They worked through the night. They took a lot of meth. They managed to find an Armed Response Unit in central London who, while they didn't want to be blacklegs, were relieved to be rounded up for an operation that would be going down an hour before the strike. Lofthouse got her call to Forrest answered at 6 a.m.

'You're getting in under the wire,' he said. 'Are you sure you need to do this now?'

'I am. Operation Fog will of course report back to you with everything it finds.'

Ross got an email at nine o'clock that made her heart sink once again. The fingerprints that had been taken at Anna Lassiter's flat didn't match those of anyone in the records, and certainly weren't a match for those left at the murder scenes. There were some glove marks, but no DNA other than that of the resident. Ross supposed Lassiter didn't get many callers.

At 10.55, on a brilliantly sunny morning, where the light seemed only to illuminate how nervy and strung out the city felt, an unmarked van pulled up on double yellow lines on a side road near the Keel occult shop that Sefton had visited undercover. This was the place that a 'customer seeking urgently to sell some items' – actually Costain – had been told he could find Mr Keel. Costain had seen from the windows of the van as they drove through the centre of London how quiet the streets were, how many businesses were boarded up or operating through side doors or had private security standing there already. The strike had put fear into the metropolis. He felt that tension in his head alongside a thumping in his heart from where he'd partaken again of his supply. London seemed to be as on edge as he was.

A traffic warden banged his knuckles on the side window. Costain pulled down the window and shoved his warrant card in his face. The warden just raised his eyebrows and wandered off: strange to meet a copper on the streets these days. 'We cut them off from the back of the shop,' said Sefton from the back of the van. 'That's where the serious shit is.'

'Right,' said Ross. 'Okay. Okay.'

Costain didn't like her looking as focused as this. It was as if she was slowly getting less and less range of expression. She finally saw him looking and managed a deliberate . . . well, it wasn't quite a smile. It seemed that she was already forgetting how to do that. Sefton opened the rear doors and got out, headed off on his part of this mission. Costain leaned in and kissed Ross, then she too got out and headed off.

Dear God, the last few days had damaged them all so much. Costain got out of the van and locked it. He himself had a terrible choice to make. He'd done something terrible. Again. It kept going round and round in his thoughts. The meth meant he couldn't trust how he felt about anything. For the hundredth time, he put it out of his mind. He took out his Airwave radio and called the Armed Response Unit, who confirmed they were in place, and on a clock counting down to noon, when the strike began. He was certain that if they ended up in a fire-fight, the unit weren't just going to down tools on the hour, but still, their clock-watching didn't fill him with confidence. He waited for Sefton and Ross to get to their destinations then headed towards the shop. To walk felt too slow, so he started marching.

Sefton entered the small car park at the back of the Keel store, used jointly with a patisserie next door. There was a lower door and a fire escape leading up to an office level, as their research had indicated. He felt like death, he didn't like the fire of the meth coursing through his system, and he knew sometime soon he was going to crash. But he was doing his duty, working for Jimmy and Joe and everything he stood for in this town, and he was content with his own head now and would keep going. If London survived, he could just about glimpse a future for himself. He'd called Joe and shut down all his fearful questions, and re-assured him he was okay and then said he had to go. He couldn't help but look behind him to where the unmarked van containing the Armed Response Unit was sitting ready.

He made sure nobody was about and tried to steady his breathing, but failed. He got out the London Olympics branded water carrier with a picture of that weird cartoon alien on it dressed as a copper and, his hands still shaking, started sprinkling its contents around the frame of the door. The water he was dosing the door with was from the underground river Neckinger, which met the Thames at a point where criminals were hung. Ross would be doing the same thing to the front door at the same moment. He finished with the lower door and headed for the fire escape, aiming to climb it as quietly as he could, aware that his limbs were shaking.

Ross entered the store and went to the counter. She managed what she knew wasn't quite a smile at the young woman serving there. She managed to stop her teeth chattering. 'I would like to make a complaint,' she said.

'I'm sorry to hear that. What's the nature of your complaint?' The assistant was genuinely eager to please. They must get a lot of mad shit in here.

Ross lifted the cage she'd brought in onto the counter. 'It's about this.' She pulled off the cloth covering it and revealed the stuffed bird therein. It had been the weirdest London-related thing they could find in the dusty corners of the Hill's evidence room in the early hours, though it didn't actually have anything of the Sight about it.

'Is that . . . a crow?'

'A crow!' Ross was following through on an agreed-upon script, not feeling it herself. But what she did have flowing through her veins was the feeling that she was onstage and wowing the crowd. It didn't make her happy, although it clearly should, and that disconnect was yelling at her continually, but it was certainly keeping her awake. She thought she probably looked and sounded more like a homeless person than anything else. 'This, young fellow-me-lad, is a raven. One that has recently departed the Tower of London. Much as it has departed this mortal coil.' She glanced across the shop and saw that other assistants were already looking over, taking an interest, amused. She wished she could feel the same. If it had been Jimmy doing this, he'd have enjoyed it, part of the great Met tradition of taking the piss. The assistants were probably getting overtime pay to come in today, with the strike about to break; besides, this place was most likely something like a home to them, somewhere they'd run to rather than away from. Again, she wished she was part of such a community. They'd be up for a bit of light relief.

The shop girl had got the joke, was trying not to smile. 'And did you purchase it here?'

'Well I wouldn't be coming to you to complain if I'd bought it elsewhere, would I?' She realized she was trying to sound like Quill.

'So . . . what's the problem?'

'The problem is that when you sold it to me, you did so on the basis that it was a live *Corvus corax*, beloved of Bran the Blessed, kept by the Yeoman Warders to ward off the destruction of the British Isles. Does this look live to you?' She gave it a poke and it fell sideways off its perch. 'This is an ex-raven!'

The other shop assistants had come and gathered round, forming an audience to what they were sure now was a deliberate performance, and not an embarrassing or threatening one, for once. Despite the staring demeanour of the performer. Ross looked the assistant in the eye and hoped she'd go for it.

She did. 'But it's got lovely plumage.'

'I demand,' said Ross, 'to see the manager!'

Of course, her face then immediately clouded, because Keel wasn't going to be up for this. 'I'm sorry,' she said, 'he's not to be disturbed.'

'We'll see about that.' Ross got out her phone and sent her prepared text to Costain. It just said, 'He's here.' She didn't look around as, unobserved, Costain walked quickly in and headed for the back of the shop.

Costain was trying to keep his thoughts from racing, to keep his mind on apprehending Terry Keel. He walked swiftly under the CCTV cameras beside the expensive stuff without breaking stride, hoping that would get him past the owner's notice. Keel had no reason to be particularly on guard this morning, after all. He wasn't the sort to worry about the police's ability to protect his premises. He was pretty certain of doing that himself.

He walked straight through a door marked 'Staff only', found nobody there now that they were all watching Ross' show with the bird, and headed up the stairwell. He was breathing too fast. He got out his Airwave radio once more. On the floor above was a toilet and an office. Costain stepped carefully as he reached eye level with the top floor. He couldn't hear—

Terry Keel stepped out from the office, an expression of cold fury on his face. 'You fuckers!'

'Go go go!' Costain yelled into the radio.

The window beside Keel burst inwards. Two Armed Response uniforms were bringing their weapons to bear. 'Armed police officers!' But Keel was already running, yelling, right at Costain. Something in his hand glowed like a hot coal.

Costain didn't fall back as Keel expected him to, making himself an easy target when Keel got to the top of the stairs. Instead he heaved himself forwards and grabbed the man's wrist. He slammed the hand with the fire in it into the wall. But Keel was a powerfully built man. With a cry, he shouldered Costain aside, rebounding from the folded copies of the *Police Gazette* from the 1840s that Sefton had stuffed into Costain's jacket as an occult London version of body armour.

Keel threw himself towards the fire door. Costain kicked himself off the wall and followed, knowing as he moved that he was in the line of fire between Keel and the armed officers, knowing they wouldn't shoot.

The weight of Keel's body slammed the door open.

Sefton was ready as Keel sprinted out onto the fire escape. But even Keel was surprised as the fire he held in his hand burst into smoke and steam. Sefton grabbed him by the lapels and swung him up against the wall.

Keel kicked out with one foot, catching Sefton on the thigh, flinging him back.

Sefton jumped back at him inside his leg and punched him in the bollocks. Keel yelled and threw himself forwards again, and Sefton let him, kicking out the inside of his knee to send him falling down the stairs.

Keel struggled to his feet to see armed police officers moving out of cover to take aim at him from every corner of the car park, shouting identification and telling him not to move. But he was thinking about what he could do, his hands not going for his pockets, but moving in the air.

Sefton leaped down the stairs as Costain and Ross burst out of the door behind him, more armed police officers in their wake. He got to Keel first, grabbed his hands before anything could form in them and slammed the man down into the gravel, one knee in the small of his back. Then he rolled off so Costain could haul Keel's arms behind his back and snap the silver handcuffs on him.

Keel stared up at the circle of police closing in around him, incomprehension adding to his fury. 'What the fuck do you lot think I've done?'

'You've just added resisting arrest and assaulting a police officer to conspiracy to commit murder, mush.' Costain glowered at him. 'We're the law now. Like in the good old days. And we don't like your beard.'

Sefton made himself calm down to a point where he could speak and carefully started to intone the words of the caution.

The rest of the shop workers were taken to the Hill for questioning, in a couple of marked vans that rolled up outside on cue. Ross thought they'd probably get only some vaguely interesting general background stuff from these mainstream innocents.

'Do you want to go with your workers for a proper interview?' Costain asked Keel, in the privacy of the man's own office, with the armed officers stationed outside. Ross was aware of the time ticking down to noon. 'Or do you want to settle things here?'

Keel folded his arms across his chest. 'You lot really don't want me to call my lawyer, do you? What was this, just a fishing expedition?'

'You did the equivalent of drawing a gun on someone you knew was a police officer.'

Keel was staring at them, realizing they were all talking at high speed. Maybe he thought they were trying to get this done before the strike started at noon. He deliberately slowed his speech. 'The *equivalent* won't bloody stand up in court. And you bastards killed my brother.'

'You don't want this to go to court,' said Ross. 'You don't want your customers seeing you in the dock, hearing about you being cross-examined, wondering just how many of the community's secrets you've given away. I mean, it's not like they're onside with you *now*, is it?' She brought to mind the image of the barmaid's blank features, of how Keel had injured her. 'You don't want to *lose face*.'

Keel considered for a moment. Then he lowered his head. 'At least you're in the circle,' he said. Then he sighed, as if he was talking to children. 'I mean,' he translated, 'the M25. Used to be the North Circular.'

'The traditions change with the times,' said Sefton.

Keel looked as if he wanted to spit at him. 'What do you want to know?'

Ross slapped a printout image onto the table. It showed the mirror standing on the grass outside the Portakabin.

Keel looked puzzled at it. 'Ordinary mirror. Nothing of my world about that. And I've seen it all.'

Ross looked to Sefton, who nodded. That only confirmed what they'd already thought. The idea that the Ripper might have come out of it because of the nature of the object itself had been a long shot.

'What about the Bridge of Spikes?' said Costain.

Ross saw Sefton's expression change. He wouldn't say anything in front of the suspect, but he was obviously wondering why Costain was asking about something of which he had no knowledge. She and Costain had talked beforehand about this. They might never get the chance to be alone with Keel.

'What about it?' said Keel.

Oh, he knew about it. He actually knew! Ross felt the tension in her own chest and appreciated the way Costain was keeping his tone level. 'Have you ever seen one?'

'There *is* only one. And, no, I haven't. When that was sold at auction, the bidding went on all night. It went into some terrible fucking places. Too rich for my blood.'

'Is there anything else that does the same job?'

'Of course there fucking isn't.'

Ross felt her hope fall away and hit the next level down, like a ball dropping through a maze. Okay. They would just have to find whoever had stolen it from the flat. It would take time, but that would be her life now – the life of both of them, together. She could accept that.

'Have you ever seen a scrying glass?' asked Sefton, trying to get back to the plan.

'Yeah, once. They're not unique like the Bridge, but they're pretty rare.'

'Where did you see it?'

'At another of the auctions. This bloke on the phone, a proxy for someone, he ran me ragged, beat me to it. Back in those days, we were the only two paying in cash. It was the night the auction was underneath the whale skeleton at the Natural History Museum.'

Ross nodded. 'That was where our source said he got the mirror we just showed you. That was sold to him as a scrying glass.'

Keel frowned. 'I don't remember that. The scrying glass I was after was definitely the genuine article: smaller than a human head, red glass, a thread of blood from an old London family in a phial around the frame. You concentrate on the exact location of your target, and the mirror forms a connection between you and their sleeping brain. Nobody in the know would mistake the mirror in that photo for a scrying glass.'

A terrible suspicion was starting to form in Ross' mind. 'What did this proxy look like?'

'White, late thirties, balding, dark hair . . .'

Ross asked a few more questions, then exchanged a look with Costain and Sefton. It could be the same man who had bid against her in her attempt to find the location of the Bridge. It would make sense. The owner of the scrying glass was the one reading their thoughts; having discovered their intention to find the Bridge, and what the Bridge was, who *wouldn't* send someone to compete to get it? 'Do you know who was he working for?'

Keel smiled and straightened up, realizing he had something valuable. 'I do know, because I did the old –' he made the 'bar code reading' gesture in the air and they all automatically deflected it. But again their phones chirruped. It made him laugh. 'I felt who was on the other end of the phone and it made me think something big was going down. So. What's it worth?'

'We leave you alone,' said Costain. 'And we don't start gossiping at the Goat, or whatever pub that community settle in, about how delighted you were to help out the new law.'

Keel considered further for a moment, then nodded. 'All right. The buyer was Russell Vincent.'

In the clear summer air, in the moment of silence that followed, Ross heard a nearby church clock, and then others in the distance, all begin to strike the hour of twelve.

Russell Vincent put his scrying glass onto its stand on his desk. He had his iPad ready beside it. Soon it would all start kicking off in London. The Summer of Blood had reached its apex. The day of the Ripper had begun.

TWENTY-FOUR

Costain grabbed Keel by the beard and hauled him out of his seat. 'If you're lying . . . !'

Keel cried out. 'It's the truth! I don't want you coming back here, do I?'

'Names are worth something,' said Sefton. 'If you found out who Vincent was down the phone, you found out who the proxy was too. Who was it?'

'I wrote the name down.'

Ross watched numbly as Costain released Keel, and he went to look in his filing cabinet. They had been played by Russell Vincent. He had given them an ordinary mirror, while he still had a real scrying glass. More than that, he'd employed the man who'd been there when the Ripper had attempted to kill Mary Arthur, who'd bid against them for the Bridge of Spikes. The obvious reason for Vincent to lie was that he was the one who'd been looking into their dreams. The information gained from their dreams had been used to coordinate the Ripper murders and to send Vincent's proxy after the Bridge.

The overwhelming weight of circumstantial evidence was that Russell Vincent, one of the richest and most powerful men in the world, was, somehow, the new Jack the Ripper. How could they ever prove it?

Keel had found the scrap of paper. 'His name was Ben Challoner.'

*

They got out of there. They left Keel waving to them from the shop doorway, asking if the nice ladies and gentlemen could please return his staff as soon as possible, grinning at how he had obviously rocked them back on their heels. Costain felt like punching him.

The Armed Response Unit made their apologies, did the necessary in terms of paperwork and left, presumably for awkward afternoons at home or down the pub. The strike was on. London felt silent, waiting. Costain, inside it, felt wired to the point of exploding.

The three of them marched into the unmarked van and locked the door. Only then did they feel able to talk. It was as if Vincent was already listening. 'Everything about this operation,' said Ross, 'makes sense if the perpetrator is Russell Vincent. I say we now regard him as our number one suspect.'

'Agreed,' said Costain.

'So how does everything fit together if it *is* him?' Sefton was looking as strung out as Costain felt. They felt like ants who'd just glimpsed a human being standing above their nest. Mora Losley had had no worldly power, only what her occult abilities gave her. Russell Vincent seemed to have immense power in both spheres.

'If Vincent has a genuine scrying glass,' said Ross, 'he could hack people's dreams like a phone tap. That could be why the *Herald*'s so famously clean: they get their stories without breaking the law, from the minds of celebrities and politicians.'

'It's no wonder they got the Ripper message story first,' said Sefton.

'If it's him, he deliberately used that message at the crime scene to send us on the wild goose chase of Ripper lore. He would have known from our memories that we didn't know what a scrying glass looked like, and that even when we found out, we'd assume *he* was the one who'd been played. It all fits. He tailored the fiction precisely to what he knew about his audience.'

'Just like he does with his newspapers,' said Costain.

Sefton made a noise as if he'd suddenly realized something. 'That PA,' he said, 'Vincent had her be there when we visited him, so she could confirm his story about the Ripper coming out of the mirror. She never said she saw the Ripper himself or anything happening with the mirror. It was all over by the time she got into the room.'

'Still,' said Ross, 'I don't believe he was that far-sighted that he staged something to set up his story way back then. Something violent happened to him in that room.'

'And there were genuine traces of the silver goo,' said Sefton, 'which Vincent apparently couldn't see first-hand, only, I suppose, when he saw our memories of it.'

'He was cocky enough to try to play us face to face,' said Ross, 'when everything else about him says he's cautious. Why?' She suddenly pointed at the other two. 'Because *he* wanted something from *us*. What did he say to us? What did he *ask*?'

Sefton found his notebook. 'He asked whether or not we could . . . find a missing person using gestures, and if we had any defence against scrying glasses. He must have known we didn't have the answers right then, but . . . oh fuck, I know what this was: he wanted us to go away and *find out*, and then he could look into our frigging brains like we were his own private Wikipedia!'

'At least,' said Costain, 'we didn't take him up on those suggestions.'

'I would have got there with the defences bit,' said Sefton. 'And then he'd have known how to get round them, for anyone else's brain he wanted to look into, if they tried to block him. Shit.'

'So who would he be looking for?' asked Ross.

'You said you thought the man that was killed in the Soviet bar, Rudlin, wasn't the target, that it was actually Mary Arthur,' said Costain. 'If Vincent is the one controlling the Ripper or being the Ripper or however it works, she got away from him that night.'

Ross acknowledged that with a frantic nodding. She fell silent for a moment, no longer able to control the movements of her hands as they flexed in the air, the product of her ferocious thinking.

Sefton hauled himself up and paced the confines of the van, looking more horrified every moment as the implications sank in.

Costain didn't like the silence; it made him aware of the terrible fear that was rising up in him. 'How the fuck do we nick him?' he said. 'We're going to have to fall asleep sooner or later. When we do he'll know we're onto him, and send the Ripper after us. We can't go after him without some insane level of proof, and with his lawyers, it'd still take years.' Also, he thought but didn't say it – and this was the most frightening thing of all – Vincent knew about the Bridge of Spikes. What would such a powerful man be willing to do to avoid death?

'Oh shit,' said Ross suddenly.

Costain was scared again by the expression on her face. 'What?'

'Keel said, to use a scrying glass, you need to know the exact location of your target.' She looked between them. 'That bastard knows where we live.'

'How?' said Sefton.

'Fuck,' said Ross, 'fuck.' She leaned on the wall of the van, and her face contorted into an expression of anger, but also, Costain was pleased to see, comprehension. 'Staunce,' she said, 'dates . . . fuck, this meth is getting in the way, it's all getting jumbled up, I keep forgetting bits—'

'What?' asked Sefton.

'I need a table,' she said.

They took the van through the quiet streets, parked on another double yellow and, near Bloomsbury Square, spotted a pub that was open. They found a corner of the empty cellar bar, and drank their double Red Bulls as Ross constructed a mobile version of the Ops Board. She finally placed it on the table as four sheets of A4 and put down coloured marker pens beside it. Costain felt something once again give inside him at her continuing professionalism, found himself looking up into her serious expression, hoping as always now for a smile that would never come. He knew that something terrible might soon come between them. The fear of it was rising up in him, making his hands play a clatter on the table surface.

'Staunce,' said Ross, 'Commissioner of the Met, could find out our home addresses, easy as breathing. We know he was being paid by someone. Those original payments stop . . .' she slid her finger down a list in one of her enormous rough books '. . . one day after Vincent bought the scrying glass at the winter solstice auction three years ago.'

'Because, if you can look into people's dreams,' said Sefton, 'you don't need sources for secret gossip any more, including police ones, so Vincent could dispense with Staunce's services.'

Ross added an association line connecting Staunce to Vincent. 'But then suddenly Vincent *does* need Staunce's information again, because he needs our addresses. He can't just look into Staunce's head and find them, because Staunce doesn't actually know them offhand; he needs to be told what to go and find out. So Vincent pays Staunce one more time –' she looked again at her list of dates – 'at 2 p.m. on the day he died.'

'Why does Vincent get interested in us then?' asked Costain. 'What did we do that day?'

'We interviewed Tunstall that morning,' said Sefton.

'So somehow Vincent knew about that,' said Costain. 'No, never mind somehow, there's only one way this guy learns secret stuff: he must have used the scrying glass on Tunstall when he went to sleep after we saw him, and he'd have seen Tunstall's memories of Jimmy telling Tunstall we believed him, and that we had abilities other units didn't. Bloody hell.'

'Staunce always took an afternoon nap,' said Sefton. 'First Vincent pays him, then he checks up on his motives, discovers something amiss, has him killed that same night.'

'When do we start feeling shit going on in our dreams?' said Ross.

'From that night,' said Sefton. 'I think.' They compared notes. None of them could pin it down exactly, but the date seemed right. They swore and got up and had to talk each other down

318

from the fear, until Ross started shouting at them to let her finish. Quickly, they sat down.

'Why was Vincent listening in on Tunstall's thoughts?' she asked.

'Tunstall, like Staunce, was receiving under-the-counter payments,' said Sefton. 'If those were also from Vincent, maybe he wanted to make sure Tunstall wasn't going to tell anyone about them.'

'And he wasn't,' said Costain, triumphantly. 'At least, not at first.'

He was pleased at the puzzled look that got from Ross. 'How do you know that?'

'Because it took Vincent so long to kill him. If you're a gang boss, sometimes you suspect someone in your organization has grassed you up, and so you kill them, torture them, whatever. But if you had the power to *know* absolutely who was loyal and who wasn't, to know who was even *thinking* about betraying you—'

'You'd drop a lot fewer bodies,' said Ross.

'We were about to interview Tunstall again,' said Sefton, 'about the brothel business card. Vincent must have seen that Tunstall was wavering, that he might crack during that interview, and finally decided he wasn't worth the risk.'

'It's kind of humane,' said Costain, 'compared to what we're used to.'

'And he waited to kill Jimmy,' continued Sefton, 'until Jimmy encountered him in his dreams and made some potentially incriminating notes about long barrows. Whatever they mean, those are the most important things. If Vincent knew now that we'd seen them, maybe he'd kill us too.'

Costain suspected now that what had kept him and Ross alive had actually been their quest for the location of the Bridge of Spikes, the success of which Vincent would have had a serious interest in, but he couldn't share that with Sefton. Maybe Vincent had been interested in what Sefton's occult researches might reveal. To Vincent, Quill would have been the one whose dreams were least likely to reveal anything useful. 'So let's assume – assumption noted – that Tunstall was being paid by Vincent to, maybe among other things, search Spatley's office . . .'

'To find, we think, a card that had been *lost*,' said Sefton. 'So its location wasn't in anyone's memory that Vincent could search.'

Ross made a fist in the air at that one. She was drawing new association lines at high speed across her pieces of paper, pushing the pen down too forcefully, occasionally tearing the paper. She'd drawn Vincent as a big blue whirlpool in the middle. 'Vincent kills Tunstall because he's about to reveal their connection. He kills Staunce, well, we don't know, but we might imagine Staunce was thinking about coming clean too. Rudlin is killed by accident when Vincent is really trying to kill Mary Arthur. We still don't know his motivation there, and we don't know why he failed. We think Vincent killed Jimmy because Jimmy had seen something key to his power and written what turned out to be bloody cryptic notes about it. And we still have no idea why he killed Spatley in the first place.' She held up her piece of paper. 'This is getting beautiful. But it's so fucking useless. Oh God, we're going to die.'

Costain slammed his fist into the table, as much for his own benefit as for hers. 'We still have three leads,' he said. 'We need to find those two people from the Soviet bar: Ben Challoner and Mary Arthur. And we need to work out what the fuck Jimmy was on about in those notes. Okay.' He looked up Challoner's name on his phone and found there was only one adult of that name in Greater London. 'He lives at 56 Flaxton Road, Clapham. We need to get him. Right now.'

Flaxton Road in Clapham was a row of terraced houses which had once been smart little family dwellings, in the era when 'the man on the Clapham omnibus' was the standard phrase for the everyday Londoner. Now they had rows of doorbells on every porch – upper flat, bottom flat, basement flat – and the boards for estate agents were all the best kind of firm. This was the sort of place, Costain thought, where you found Pret A Manger wrappers blowing down the street. The street was silent in the summer heat, with only distant sounds of televisions from behind closed doors. The security bolts would have been slammed shut already. Costain thought of the team as little creatures running at high speed through the maze that Vincent, looming over London, had made of the place. He wondered if little creatures could do Vincent any damage. Even actually finding him, among all his properties, would be hard. Was there really anything they could offer or do to Challoner to change this situation? Of course, there was something that could be done. But Costain would wait until there was no other hope before he would consider that.

'This isn't the sort of place anyone with seniority in one of Vincent's companies would live,' said Ross.

'It's student land,' said Costain, 'young Toffland, more ways than one.'

They rang Challoner's doorbell. No reply. Costain then rang the other two doorbells and when the intercom went live said, 'Police.' A high window opened, and he showed a warrant card to whoever was above on this simmering afternoon, waiting for the evening to start boiling.

'He's quiet . . . keeps himself to himself,' said the stressed-looking young woman in the flowery dress. The team looked at each other knowingly, recalling, thought Ross, the number of times they'd heard that about various guilty bastards. 'Is he in trouble?'

She watched Costain limber up like a method actor, letting a troubled expression cross his features and then killing it, all a bit jumbled by the meth. 'We don't know what's happened to him,' he said. 'Are you sure he's not in his flat? Have you heard any . . . noises?'

'What sort of noises?'

'How thick are the walls in here? I mean, if he was shouting for help . . . ?'

'Shouting for—?'

'Listen, we don't have time for – I'm sorry – do *you* think he might be in immediate danger?'

'Well, he *might* be . . .'

Costain looked to Sefton. 'The lady here thinks Mr Challoner might be in immediate danger.'

Sefton nodded frantically. 'Right,' he said, 'so we have to do our duty and take a look.'

They went down the stairs to the basement flat, and Costain tried the door. It gave a little even as he pushed it. He retreated up the stairs, took a run down, and kicked at the lock, which left him lying there on his arse, and the door swinging open.

Ross led the way into the flat. There was a living room, clean, with a flat-screen TV, Xbox, a small sofa and a table at foot level. A bedroom: lived in, but tidied up. Man smell. Joop. No woman. A narrow kitchen that didn't look as if you could cook in it, microwave and fridge. Costain found inside it the contents of the Abel and Cole vegetable delivery box that lay in a corner of the lounge. A bunch of the more exotic fruit and veg had started to rot. A small back-room office, with a PC, shelves. No books, not even a magazine.

Costain picked up a pile of papers from on top of the printer. 'Challoner keeps it tidy,' he said, 'doesn't have a lot to clutter it up.' He nodded towards a camera on one of the shelves. 'Luxury goods, which he probably couldn't afford. The rent on this place looks to be a step up from the income level of the person who bought the furniture.'

Ross had taken a file of papers off the shelf. 'Private detective licence,' she said. 'Ran out last year.' The photo on it confirmed that this was indeed the man they'd seen at the auction and on the CCTV footage from the Soviet bar. He looked scared even in the picture.

Sefton came in, holding up elbow and knee pads, which looked weird to Ross, not the sort of thing a skater would use. Brand new, without a scratch. 'Always look under the bed,' Sefton said. 'No sex toys, but these, which is weird.'

Ross went through every drawer, too fast for her liking, then went back and double-checked. She found another folder, this one containing photos. Big prints. They looked as if they'd been taken at a film premiere. But they were from the back of the crowd, the arm and head of a celeb waving as they got out of a car.

Costain indicated the printer, which was indeed a serious piece of work. 'Failed paparazzi,' he said, 'hence the protective gear. Failed private detective.' He held up a greetings card still in a ripped-open envelope, blank inside but for a printed note pasted in it, with 'Congratulations!' in a jolly font at the top. The receipt stub for the anonymous gift that had been enclosed was still in there. 'Ticket for the proms tonight at the Royal Albert Hall,' said Costain. 'Someone's looking after him.'

Ross reached under the sofa and found a Moleskine notebook that hadn't been written in, but it had contact details written in the front. She held it up to show the others. 'Where have I seen that mobile number?' she asked. Costain found a picture on his phone, and compared the number in the image to the one in the front of the notebook. They were the same. The picture was the one he'd taken of the back of the brothel's business card. 'He's the owner of the burner phone,' he said. 'Someone wrote Challoner's number on the back of the brothel card.'

As soon as they left the flat, Costain called Lofthouse. 'Dear God,' she said, 'Russell Vincent?' Ross asked for the phone, and told Lofthouse she'd photographed her portable Ops Board and was sending it to her in an email. 'You know the lines we're following. We're pursuing the hottest one as we speak. As far as we know, Vincent isn't listening in to your dreams. So if we don't make it through tonight . . .'

'Understood,' Lofthouse said. 'I'm still at my desk; I know a few others who are too. The Special Constables have largely volunteered to break with the strike. If you need backup, we'll find it from somewhere.'

Ross winced inwardly at the idea of the part-time Specials coming to their aid and dying in droves. 'I don't think, ma'am, that if the Ripper comes after us, any backup you could find would help.'

'I know,' said Lofthouse, 'but I had to say something.'

It was evening by the time they reached the Albert Hall. On their journey they had to tack away from suburbs where the radio news and Sefton's continual searches of Twitter had started to say things were kicking off. Ross drove. They talked and talked about what might be ahead and had all sorts of plans to avoid it. They were all acutely aware, she thought, of the potential for ostentation to bring trouble suddenly upon them. But of course, since, up to a certain point, Vincent knew the contents of their minds, he'd also know they were keeping a lookout on the social networks.

Ross, Costain and Sefton strode together up the steps in front of the enormous domed building. They could hear the sounds of the orchestra inside, stark against the absolute silence outside. Or not quite silence. Was it Ross' imagination, or the workings of the Sight, that she could hear distant drums and shouts? There was definitely smoke in the air. Signs said that the Promenade Concert tonight was still on. 'I like that,' said Sefton. 'Keep calm and carry on.'

'The band playing on the *Titanic*,' said Costain. 'We know Challoner's seat number; do we walk in there and drag him out?'

'He might be armed,' said Sefton. 'Our kind of armed. Innocent bystanders.'

'Then let's find out which exit he'll be using, get him on the way out,' decided Costain. 'He's not expecting anyone. If we miss him, we go back to his place.'

'Would *you* go to a prom concert tonight?' said Sefton.

'From what we saw of his flat,' said Costain, 'I think he's desperate in loads of ways.' Ross saw what might almost be sadness on his face and wondered if, like her, he was thinking about a man who had offered parts of his body at that auction, on behalf of his employer. Ross wanted to hold Costain. Wanted him. Now, she thought, it was in moments of sadness, of sudden vulnerability, that she felt closest to him. If it all literally went to Hell tonight, if they couldn't find anything to pin on Vincent, if the metropolis started to collapse in flames, maybe the two of them could get away. To where? To no happiness for her, ever, and the burden of that for him.

A sound made them all turn. A convoy of military lorries was roaring along Kensington Road, the trees of Hyde Park dark against their camouflage. 'Peacekeepers for tonight,' said Costain. 'Going back and forth to every borough where it sounds like something's going down. Without police liaison, or with a very reduced one. Being run out of the Home Office. Fuck's sake.' Behind those lorries came white vans with company logos.

'Private security companies too,' said Ross. 'Shit.'

'If anyone gets shot by that lot tonight,' said Sefton. 'Ostentation could ramp up the anger about that, amplify it, and we could be on the verge of sheer hell.'

'Bloody London,' said Costain.

They explored the layout of the Albert Hall area at a fast pace, decided on their options and went looking for an early dinner at the only restaurant that was still open. There was nobody else eating. They all ordered two starters and a main course and a pile of dessert, and they must have given the impression they were making the most of things before the world ended. The noises from the kitchen were the only sounds apart from their frantic speech as they drank every mouthful of strong coffee. Costain felt he might collapse at any moment. He had no idea what that collapse would even involve. If it involved sleep, it might mean death – not just for him but all of them.

He wondered how the waiters would be getting home. Would London tonight change London tomorrow once and for all? Would the streets in the next few days be like something out of John Wyndham: emptiness and distrust, and everything rolling downhill with increasing ferocity? Was that the plan the Smiling Man had hinted at through Rob Toshack, months ago?

He kept looking to his phone for the rolling news: riots in Tooting, Lambeth, Peckham, Wandsworth, and now reports of it coming into the centre of town, fascist marches in support of shopkeepers with cudgels, the army firing plastic bullets at youths in hoods running with televisions down Oxford Street, where a sports shop had the contents of its window strewn across the bus lane, and private security staff running left and right, trying to stop the looters who were rushing out in all directions. The Toffs, changing tactics, were pictured standing arm in arm in Trafalgar Square, marching across Westminster Bridge. There were scraps of interviews with them yelling that they were out here because they wouldn't be intimidated, and there was safety in numbers. It seemed futile to Costain. Parliament was sitting in an all-night session. There were rumours of a vote of no confidence in the government, of all leadership dissolving before the morning.

He glanced at his watch, which seemed to be working so slowly, and was relieved that the time had arrived when they might do something about all this, even if it too turned out to be a futile gesture. 'Okay,' he said.

London was tense, waiting, as they walked up those steps once more. The summer air was still and warm. It took Ross a moment to figure out what had changed. The lights in all directions were now dulled by a fine veil of smoke.

They took up positions around the exit that someone in Challoner's seat would most likely use, and they waited as they heard final applause roaring from inside the building, and then that sound turn quickly into the noise of people moving, of doors banging open. 'They've made their gesture,' said Costain, 'now it's a race to try and find a taxi.'

Sure enough, very soon the first people started marching out of the exit past them. They checked out every male face, mentally comparing them to Challoner. Then—

Positive ID. There he was, walking quickly along, his arms stiff by his sides, looking all around. He looked scared and puzzled but, based on previous experience, Ross got the feeling that was how he always looked. She made eye contact with the other two, and they converged. Sefton got in front of Challoner, while Costain slapped a hand onto his shoulder. Challoner halted, and the crowd flowed around them, more and more of them every moment. It was going to be difficult for him to do a runner.

'Who are you?' He looked between them as if he was instantly guilty. Then his gaze locked on Ross and Costain as he recognized them.

Costain flashed his warrant card. 'Police officers. Come with us, please, sir.'

He did, but only a few paces, out of the way of the crowd. He kept looking back over his shoulder. 'Please, in there—'

'What are you afraid of?' asked Costain.

Challoner looked round again. 'They put the masks on right at the end. I think it's a protest.'

Ross heard murmurs and exclamations from further up the steps. She spun to look. There they were. Out of every door of the Albert Hall was bursting a horde of Toffs in masks, with placards and banners. The rest of the crowd were drawing back from them, afraid. There came more and more of them. An army of them. They filled the space at the top of the steps and then started marching down them, towards the group around Challoner.

'That was organized using something other than Twitter,' said Sefton. Either Vincent had decided not to alert them in the same way, or the demonstrators had known that the substitute security forces in London tonight would be keeping an eye on social media.

Ross turned quickly to Challoner, knowing they had no time for subtlety now. 'We know about Russell Vincent—'

'What?' Challoner was now looking seriously afraid. He didn't know whether to be more scared of them or of the Toffs.

'We know everything, sunshine!' Costain grabbed him by the lapels and roared into his face. 'We know why you're worried about that lot! He uses them as cover, doesn't he? Do you know how many of his employees he's killed?'

'I-I don't know what you're—'

'You just happened to be in that bar, just happened to be chatting to Mary Arthur – yeah, we know about her too! We know she was meant to be the Ripper's target.'

'We know you go to the auctions,' said Ross, 'as a proxy for Vincent. You've seen us there too. We're the coppers who know about the terrifying shit of London. We're your only chance.'

'You tell us fucking *everything* and you might get to walk away from this. You might get to live. Because is Vincent worth it?' Costain had dropped his voice and was looking the man in the eye. 'You have risked *everything* for him, offered your own body for him, and what do you get back in return? Just every day a sense of dread. You come and work with us, you know you're on the right side, *you* will make a difference. It'll be *you* that brings him down.'

He was talking so fast, improvising at high speed as the wave of Toffs approached them. Challoner was shaking his head. 'We need to get away from here.'

'How does he do it?' shouted Costain. 'How does Vincent send the Ripper?'

Challoner looked startled to hear the name. He looked over his shoulder again, and now they could all see it. The approaching crowd of Toffs were throwing long shadows down in front of them. They were being illuminated from behind, by an unearthly light.

The Ripper was among them.

Challoner made to struggle out of Costain's grasp, but Costain held on. He must be on the Sighted spectrum. Perhaps that was why Vincent had chosen him. 'Too late. Chicken run. You reckon he's coming for us or for you? Tell us something we can use!'

'He . . . he makes things happen in London!' yelled Challoner. 'He goes on social media, he has all these fake accounts! He uses the Toffs and the skinheads as cover! He starts a riot happening, and then he sends the Ripper to kill whoever he's after, and then he can blame the Toffs for it! He needs to know roughly where his target is going to be—'

'You assumed you'd be going to the Proms tonight *with* Vincent,' said Sefton. 'When he didn't show up, you started to wonder why.'

'Good little boy stayed in his seat,' said Ross. 'You brought Mary Arthur to that bar so that she could be attacked, didn't you? You kept her there. And then you got out of there, because you knew what was coming!'

'Yes, yes!'

'How does it work?' yelled Sefton. 'What *is* the Ripper? How does he control it?'

'I don't know. I don't know!' Challoner was squirming in Costain's grip now. The light was getting closer.

'You can see that, can't you?!' bellowed Costain. 'Will you testify to anything we can get a jury to believe?'

'Yes! Just, please—!'

Ross looked in the direction of the light again. One of the Toffs was emphasized to her by the Sight, was something extraordinary. It was coming slowly down the steps among the others, moving first to one side, then to another, looking right at the four of them, like a predator sizing up its quarry. She could see the mask clearly now, see the silver falling from its eyes like uncontrollable tears. Suddenly, the figure lurched towards them.

'Run,' said Costain.

They sprinted sideways, out of the flow of the crowd down the steps, around the curve of the hall, hauling Challoner along between them. They were aiming for the van parked nearby. Costain was planning to take the wheel, and they would see if the Ripper could match their speed along the empty streets.

But the light was already flaring around the corner of the building. Something shot over their heads.

The Ripper was on them.

It sliced the air with a razor that seemed to cause the air itself to scream and part, like lightning. The first blow cut Costain's jacket, and he let Challoner go. The man made to sprint away, back into the fringes of the crowd, but before Ross could even shout, the Ripper had spun, leaped up, and come down on Challoner like a cloaked bird of prey as his victim looked up and screamed.

They all started forward, but the flashing of the razor pumped faster than the eye could follow and blood burst from Challoner's torso and throat.

That was the end of their lead, of their hope, of the little man's life of service.

The crowd parted, yelling and screaming, leaving a clearing into which the body fell. There stood the Ripper. It turned to face Ross and the others.

Was that it? Was that all it was here for? Challoner had been a loose end to tidy up, a thread that could lead back to Vincent. But what about them? Had Vincent tried to access their dreams, never found them asleep, and started to wonder if they'd guessed his secret? Was the Ripper actually him or someone, something, he'd hired or created? The shape of the body didn't look right for Vincent, if that meant anything. If he was in communication with, or actually was, this assassin, he'd just realized that they'd found Challoner, that they were that close to Vincent himself.

The Ripper took one decisive step towards them. Then another. It seemed to be hesitating. Ross could see the silver pouring down its face now.

'He's losing a lot of silver,' said Sefton. 'Maybe he's not doing so well.'

'You reckon we could take him?' said Costain.

'With what?' asked Ross.

The Ripper launched itself forward. It had its arm raised, the razor ready to strike. It moved in a blur.

Ross found herself stepping into the way in reaction, like returning a tennis serve. She hadn't thought about it. She flinched, expecting an impact—

But the Ripper had stopped. It had no momentum. It had halted like a cartoon. It was poised above her, arm back, ready to strike. Its mask was a mass of silver. It looked contorted, almost expressing emotion. It slowly raised its left hand, as if balancing itself, willing itself to attack. The skin of the hand, Ross was close enough to see, looked desperately human, wrinkled.

Ross suddenly understood why it might have stopped. Why, like a character in a video game, it was slowly starting to work itself back and forth now, trying to edge around whatever prohibition was stopping it from attacking her, to get to Costain and Sefton. 'Tony, Kev,' she said, 'get behind me.'

They did so. The Ripper stopped trying to jerk forwards.

'It doesn't want to attack women,' said Ross. 'Not Mary Arthur, and not me.'

The Ripper seemed to vibrate with tension for a moment. Then, with a movement so swift that Ross couldn't see in which direction it had flown, it was gone.

They sagged together for a moment. They composed themselves. They looked around, making sure it wasn't going to come back from another direction.

It didn't. They were safe. For now.

What did they have now? Did they have anything?

'Thank you for that,' said Costain. He held Ross. She kissed his cheek, feeling his fear. She felt only professionally satisfied that she might have saved him. She was acutely aware of the missing emotion. She felt the shock entering her and being amped up by the drugs, and she knew there'd be no happiness in the future to balance it, that there was increasingly nowhere left for her, emotionally or, she was starting to feel, physically.

They went to look at the victim's body, around which a crowd was now hesitantly gathering. Costain looked through his pockets and found a phone: a brand new cheap one, the sort you could get from a market stall, with no contacts in the memory. 'Bet he was told to ditch the old one right before tonight,' he said, 'so there'd be nothing to associate the corpse with Vincent.'

The concert audience was shying away from those Toffs who had stayed, some of whom had now taken their masks off, to reveal students and a disparate range of mainstream London faces. Some of this lot would be coming forward in a moment to say that a Toff had done this. 'We need to find out if we can pin the purchase of that ticket on Vincent,' said Sefton, sounding as if he knew how little a thing that would be.

'Already put in the request,' said Ross, looking up from her phone. With shaking hands, she took her rough books and portable Ops Board from her bag. She sat down on the steps and drew some satisfyingly certain lines across the Ops Board, the only control over anything she could have now. 'It refuses to kill women,' she said. 'So Mary Arthur is safe. If only we bloody knew how to find her.'

They waited until the paramedics had arrived to deal with the remains of Challoner. Ross felt gutted at the idea of putting a body, a crime scene and evidence into the hands of people other than police and associated specialists. The medics looked surprised that coppers were actually here. One looked pleased, the other disgusted.

What could they do? What was left?

They decided to at least go and check out Vincent's mews flat, just in case he'd been foolish enough to use it again. Costain insisted he could drive and the others just nodded. He drove them through a London where something worrying could be glimpsed down the end of every side street. It was as if their own experience of having the Sight was starting to be translated into the mainstream world. The feeling of impending chaos was worse for them, because they all instinctively wondered what the wider implications might be, how London would react to amplify it, what the Smiling Man would make of it. They tried to keep talking to each other, shouting to each other, even, to stay awake. They took more of the meth. The intensification of the fear of London beat through them now too.

On the radio news, and on the police frequency, they heard reports of police officers putting on uniforms and turning out to help the army. There were rumours that the Police Federation was going to call the strike off early, point proven, themselves horrified at how the riots in the further boroughs had started joining hands, were becoming what the few news commentators actually out there rather than at home reading Twitter were calling a 'ring of fire', moving in towards the centre of the cities of London and Westminster. The schools would be closed tomorrow, the news was saying, the post offices and buses and underground too, as the people that ran these things decided that safety now meant staying at home. Ross wondered if she was watching a metropolis swiftly crumbling, a culture flying apart.

The news of Challoner's murder was fighting the riots for the lead on all the websites, as if the Ripper was leading the charge, the symbol of everything that was happening tonight. The *Herald* was going big on that version of the story, inevitably. Its editorial was demanding that the army flood the streets with soldiers and impose martial law, because the government was clearly incapable of restoring order.

'There's another one,' said Sefton, who was also looking at his phone. 'Another Ripper murder.' Ross went straight to the *Herald*'s site, because of course that would get it first. The new victim had been identified as a former stringer for various newspapers. Christ, here was another one: a private detective. As soon as Ross had started to read about that killing, Sefton shouted there was another, a financier.

'It's because of us,' said Costain. 'He's killing everyone that could lead us to him.'

'Does that mean we've scared him?' said Sefton. 'Or has he now got the luxury of tying up all his loose ends?'

Ross got an email and recognized the name. 'The first of those victims,' she said, feeling as if they were rats being pursued into a corner, 'that's the person the Royal Albert Hall say purchased the ticket for Challoner tonight.' She slammed the seat with her fist. 'No wonder the *Herald* kept pushing the "mob did it" angle about the killings. Vincent used them as cover for every murder. And tonight he's got that cover just about everywhere.'

They reached the mews flat and parked outside. It was silent and dark, and through the windows that didn't have curtains they could see only empty rooms. An estate agent's board indicated it was for sale. They could hear the distant sounds of chaos moving closer. Costain felt a helpless fury marching back and forth inside him as he looked up at the building. The billionaire had many properties, in London and round the world. He also had an organization which could keep the Met in general – never mind one small unit with a bizarre story – at bay forever. He'd had a good long look at the way Costain's team did things and had used tonight to make any possibility that they might get him into court recede into the distance at the speed of light. Even the phone number Vincent had given to the Quills didn't connect now. Mary Arthur might have gone into hiding, never to be heard from again.

Eventually they would sleep.

'There's been a Ripper attack in Manchester,' said Ross, looking up from her phone. Costain went over to see, while Sefton went across to try the door of the building. The story checked out, the MO just the same. As they'd suspected, Vincent could reach them even if they fled London. Their only chance was to hide, to give his vast media network, used to pursuing disgraced celebrities, no clue as to where they were. They might need to live the rest of their lives in fear.

Again Costain considered his options. As terrible as it was, as horrifying as the line of dominoes that would now fall would be . . . he now had no alternative. He'd made his decision.

'I'm sorry,' he said to Ross.

'What for?'

'I have to go.'

She had a look of perplexed horror on her face. He didn't let it get to him. He would see much worse soon. 'What? No! We can't split the team up now . . . !'

He kissed her again, against her words, held her tightly to him, despite her moving away, her needing to know what he was going to do. He drew comfort from her and desperately wished he could offer some in return.

'I'll come back, I promise.'

He wanted to say this wasn't the scene where the hero marches off to make a heroic sacrifice. Except in a way it was. He was also about to do the most selfish thing he had ever done. He looked again at the wonderful shape of her face. He remembered her passion. He saw how her character informed that. She was the first woman who'd ever truly allowed him inside. Even as she was now, without happiness, when even saving her father would bring her no happiness, still her whole being was something vast and meaningful to him.

He turned and headed back to the van. He looked back to see Ross staring after him, to see Sefton going back to her, wondering what was going on. He kept walking.

Ross' mind was racing, trying to work out what could take Costain off alone. She could only make puzzled eye contact with Sefton. Hadn't she and Costain shared every secret? Was he . . . was he just *fleeing*? She watched him drive off, making herself give him the benefit of the doubt. He had told her he'd be back. This was something their team did. She had to trust him.

An alarm came from her phone. She looked at it to find a note from Forensics. 'Your fingerprint search was one of the few tasks I was able to complete successfully in the current circumstances,' it began, 'so it went to the top of the queue, but I find the implications extraordinary . . .' Ross scrolled quickly through the message and got to what those implications were.

'Oh my God,' she said.

'What?'

'One of those photographs of fingerprints inside a prehistoric long barrow, fingerprints put there four thousand years ago, matched the prints found at the Ripper murders.'

Sefton stared at her in shock. Then he grabbed the phone. 'Where,' he said, 'is this long barrow?'

After a few minutes' driving, Costain pulled the van to a halt, breathing hard. He'd been going far too fast. Only the emptiness of the streets had saved him. He'd switched off his phone as soon as he'd turned the corner. He was sure Ross would leave him messages. He didn't want to hear them. He reached into his jacket. He found the secret inner pocket, closed his hand on the object. He wanted to see it, to make sure no secret power had taken it from him.

The Bridge of Spikes was a plain gold sphere, small enough to fit into his hand.

He'd stolen it from Anna Lassiter's house two days ago, before he and Ross had gone there together, when Quill had sent him back to the Soviet bar to talk about prostitutes. He had used several of Sefton's protective items, taken from the man's holdall, to get into Lassiter's flat. He doubted he'd have been able to do it without what he was now sure had been Vincent's men making their own attempt hours before.

He had done it because he couldn't handle the idea of someone looking into his dreams. Because of how vulnerable that made him feel. He hadn't previously decided what to do with it, although keeping it on him was some sort of decision. He'd had fantasies about staging a fake raid and triumphantly giving it to Ross.

Now he had made his mind up. He had sacrificed so much for this. He hoped it was worth it.

Costain replaced it in his pocket, took a deep breath, and drove off once more.

TWENTY-FIVE

Ross and Sefton looked up at the building above them, dark in the summer night, framed in the ruddy light of the fires from the riots in White City. Only a few windows were illuminated. The former BBC TV Centre looked like the corpse of the building from Ross' childhood memories. What once had been a broadcasting headquarters was now home to independent production companies, other businesses, apartments. The circular building with the courtyard and the fountain and the statue familiar from so many magazine programmes was now a listed building, a sort of monument to the idea that broadcasting should belong to the nation, to the people. The Sight revealed so much more, it made the building actually hard to look at. Its sheer gravity made Ross feel she had to stand straight, with her feet balanced, or she'd be drawn forward into it. They stepped forward slowly, both of them trying not to stagger, the weight of exhaustion and drugs making what was in front of them feel like a swaying dream. The round building was like an enormous recording device, a swirling whirlpool of visual and audible information, caught here to be replayed forever, like ancient video, fluttering and distorted, the light of childhood, the memories of the great national occasions, the hope for unity, the hope of meaning. The density of the information moving in front of her made it hard for Ross to pick out individual moments, but every voice she heard, every image that swept past her pupils meant something to her, tugged at emotions right down to the core of her, from scenes she'd seen on screen before she was aware of having memory. This place had imprinted itself into the consciousnesses of Londoners for decades. Even now, with this temple turned over to profit, the memory remained; the memory fought the building's new purpose. This was a place of a billion ghosts.

Across the country now, the Ripper killings were continuing, and here they were, pursuing a tiny hope.

'They're sure it's here?' asked Sefton.

Ross stopped herself from looking again at the email. 'The long barrow in the grounds was partially excavated in the fifties, before TV Centre was built. That's when the fingerprints on the inner wall were photographed. Then it was reburied.'

They stumbled inside. Sefton showed his warrant card to the security guards on duty, who were surprised, and, in the end, relieved to have coppers around tonight. No, they didn't want an escort. No, they insisted on not being accompanied. They talked fast and harshly and scared the receptionists simply by how they looked on this terrible night. They were allowed through the inner revolving doors, into curving corridors. Ross tried to understand what the Sight was telling her about this place. She put a hand to the wall and felt and saw the gold thread, layered and deep, fine like the grooves on a vinyl record. You could play TV Centre, she thought, if you had the right enormous and precise needle. The information that rushed down these circular corridors, around and around, all sang the same sad song, about a future that had not come to pass, a dream of modernity, of a world evolving into unity through communication. What this building had stood for was an attempt within London to solve everything, to tell the truth about everything. No wonder so many things had conspired to stamp it out, to break this recording and broadcasting device.

Sefton was looking at Google Maps on his phone. 'I think I can feel where the barrow is,' he said. He set off at a run which became a stagger which righted itself into a run again, and, making sure that where he was going corresponded to the map, Ross followed.

They made their way, falling sometimes into the walls or into each other, through the high, empty space of an unused studio, ancient flats standing under covers, lights still hanging from dusty rafters, enormous doors and props which were now without context, waiting to be moved to other facilities. They saw the sad faded ghosts of every meaning, beloved and lost like old school plays. They nearly fell down circular stairwells. They passed a bar on several levels, where a couple of people stood apart, looking out of the long curving windows at the fires which were now consuming the skyline, washing the ancient carpets with crimson. Sefton could taste dark beer and old drama and the tales of actors, worn into the surface of those tables and that bar. He was following, as well as his map, a feeling underneath all this, buried deep underneath the earth, something he was now experienced enough to isolate and pursue, but Ross wasn't.

It was a feeling of terrible, ancient, anger. 'Angry' – that was one of the words Jimmy had written in his notebook.

They fell out of a side door that led to a little dark lane around the corner, where trucks stood with silver boxes. They sped up, Sefton shouting and pointing, sure his goal was in sight.

They finally found, out by an annex, an undistinguished lawn, with a high wall around it. A children's mural still smiled from the building beside it. The grass had been allowed to grow tall. They saw weeds and odd rough ditches in the light of the fires and a single blazing lamp at the corner. A small sign on what turned out to be a weather station indicated that this had once been the site of –

'The *Blue Peter* garden,' said Ross.

Sefton recalled the presenters of that children's magazine programme going out and doing nature items here from time to time. He put down his holdall, and from it took the spades and pickaxes they'd brought along – looted, frankly, from the smashed open window of a hardware store. The fury was now broadcasting from the ground right beneath him. He wouldn't need a map to pinpoint it. They had no idea what they would find down there, knowing only that – in the absence of Mary Arthur – this was their only remaining hope. So he was going to fucking dig until it gave way or he did. He just hoped nobody wandered past and saw what they were doing. 'If anyone asks,' he said, sinking his spade into the ground hard and fast with his boot, 'we're looking for the tortoises, the time capsule and the skeleton of Petra.'

It took a lot of digging before the quality of the surface underneath their spades changed. They dug too fast, and their heads started swimming with the effort until what they were doing started to feel like a dream and they kept having to yell at each other to keep going. People did come past, but none of them saw fit to challenge what they were doing on this uncared-for land, not tonight.

They hit stone. Sefton grabbed a pickaxe and started working away at it, slamming and slamming and slamming the blade into the rock, and eventually there was a block that could be cracked away with a crowbar and lifted out. Muscles crying out, they prised it out to reveal a gap into darkness beneath that was big enough for a person to get through, just. Sefton waited, hanging over the edge, thinking that maybe his goal was complete. He'd half expected this moment to free some howling banshee, but no. The archaeological survey of this thing had reported an inner chamber that had remained sealed. Maybe it was in that. Whatever it was.

They looked into the dark.

Sefton felt the great weight of what was down there, the enormous anger, clear now. It still wasn't free. He looked to Ross. She was obviously feeling it too. One of them had to go down there. Him, because of his greater experience of dealing with supernatural beings? Or her, because if what was down here was connected to the Ripper and did somehow share the same fingerprints, then it had shown itself unwilling to hurt women?

Ross' phone rang.

She answered it, hands fumbling with it, and as she listened to whoever was on the other end of the line, Sefton saw the expression on her face become one of absolute horror.

Russell Vincent stood up from his desk and stretched. He wandered to the window of his upper-floor apartment in a tower block of one of his many subsidiaries in Wapping and looked out to see, in so many directions, London burning. Great palls of smoke were drifting across the summer night. Concentrations of fire. It was like looking at a volcanic landscape. It was all down to him.

He had worked nearly three-quarters of the way down his little list, cutting every trail that could lead back to him and going on to attack his list of enemies, slicing through employee and celebrity and politician alike. It was fortunate, actually, now he knew what the Ripper wouldn't do, that he hadn't used any of his female staffers to act as his proxies in occult London. He had done his research, confident that the night of the strike was coming, finding out where every one of his targets was going to be, checking in on their dreams. No reasonable evidence could point to him. Okay, someone might well say, one day, what a coincidence that all these people had grudges against Russell Vincent. But how *could* he have been responsible? What had happened was *impossible*! The social landscape of Britain was about to change, anyway, and would make such speculations in public much harder to make.

He was genuinely sorry he'd had to kill Challoner. The man hadn't even considered being disloyal, and it pleased Vincent to kill only when he had to, to show noblesse oblige to his employees. But Challoner was weak and might crack under questioning, and so, ever since Quill had found that business card with his phone number on it, Challoner had been on Vincent's death list for tonight.

It wasn't every man, he thought now, feeling the strength of his fifty-four-year-old body as he paced the room, who got to enjoy this almost Roman sensation of absolute power. The *Herald* had the best coverage of what had happened tonight – that's what they'd say tomorrow morning. He'd actually done what so many other newspaper owners had failed to do, and through the use of multiple anonymous accounts and by taking advantage of the nature of London, had actually imposed his own meaning on Twitter.

He had played the police, even those special ones who knew a bit about this stuff, at their own game, and he had won. If Mary Arthur dared show her face again, next time he'd just get some bloke to hire some other bloke to put a bullet through her head, then use the Ripper to get rid of both blokes.

Then the Ripper could take a holiday. For a while. When the Coalition disintegrated tonight, and his friends from a different sort of politics stepped forward with their plan to crack down, the Ripper would vanish in the light of their golden dawn. It could always appear again if some new nightmare was required to scare the plebs.

Maybe it was time to stop luxuriating and move on to the next name on the list. He slid his finger down the list on his iPad . . . oh, that comedy actor who'd made a fuss about invasion of privacy and long lenses and got an out-of-court settlement back in the day. Well, he was about to get a lesson in just how much power he'd poked at.

Vincent sat again in the comfortable chair at his desk and prepared to make the gestures that would activate the scrying glass and connect his mind with the entity he called upon for the power to create the Ripper. He clicked the joints of his fingers and licked his lips, willing himself to do once again what was necessary.

There came a knock at the door.

Vincent stopped.

He'd said he wasn't to be disturbed. His PA knew that. So something must have happened that was truly extraordinary for her to go against his wishes, for her not even to send an email or call him. He went to the door and opened it.

He gasped at who was standing there, but before he could call for help or slam the door closed—

The man had marched into the room, his hands grabbing the lapels of Vincent's suit, his strength turning him and slamming him against the wall.

'Yeah, you slag,' said James Quill. 'I'm back from the dead. And I haven't had any dinner.'

TWENTY-SIX

TWO NIGHTS AGO

Quill had felt all the signifiers, all the meanings of the world collapse at the moment of his death. For just an instant, it had been a relief, an end to the terrifying pain. He saw his old life fall away below him with his body, and suddenly it had been like when he was dying in Mora Losley's attic, except now there was nothing to hold him back from speeding higher and higher towards . . . what? To somewhere where mind and matter existed together in a different way.

He felt the heat and closed his eyes. He had hoped for Heaven. Hadn't he been good? But he already knew that the supernatural in London wasn't about good and evil.

Sarah and Jessica – the thought of them made him panic and try helplessly to shove himself back down towards his body. They would hear what had happened to him. The hurt they would suffer. He couldn't help them. It was too much to bear. He pushed such thoughts away and tried to control his non-existent breathing and concentrated on the now.

He was looking at a sign. He was passing under it. He was being forced to read it. He hated what it said. Could what it said be true? No, it mustn't be, it mustn't be. That lie was surely meant to be the first step towards breaking him.

Then he woke up. That's what it felt like. It took him a few moments to process what he was seeing. He was, bizarrely, standing up. He was standing on a muddy, paved street with dung piled in the gutters, between rows of houses that looked Gothic, imperious. He looked around. There were people in all directions, people and horses! Carriages and carts and cabs. He took a step forwards and a man in a cap carrying a tray of apples on his shoulder shoved him out of the way . . . then looked at him, afraid, doffed his cap and hurried on. He was in London, he realized. He heard the chimes of Big Ben somewhere in the distance. They sounded weird, echoing. It was hard to hear over the clatter of hooves and people, so many people, many more than in the London he knew. This was, what, Victorian? Was he in Victorian times? No, it didn't feel real, somehow. Certainly, this was nothing like the glimpse of Hell that Costain had reported, but had he really seen anything past what Quill had seen in those first moments? He saw his reflection in a shop window; he was dressed in bowler hat and waistcoat and long coat with tails. He put his hands on his clothes; he could feel. He had a body, but it felt odd, like after a visit to the dentist. There was a small pain in his arm. For some reason it reminded him of being in hospital. Then he noticed: there was something on his arm, where the pain was. He reached to touch it and found his fingers went through something that was only sort of there. He pulled his sleeve round to see. It was a kind of tag that hovered in the air. It was attached right through the fabric, to his flesh, by – he winced as he tugged at it – something like an intravenous connection. Gingerly, he pulled on it, then harder, tried to pull it out—

He reeled and fell against the window, suddenly full of sickening pain.

He waited until the pain left him. It took its time. The people continued to walk past him, amused by him, some afraid of him.

He looked again at the tag. On it was a tiny clock face, a segment of it ticking down to something, along with his name, and . . . it said he had a job. He was 'a police detective'. What was this game? It was almost comforting, being immediately given a function. He was sure it wasn't meant to be reassuring. He thought again of Sarah and Jessica and wondered how far away he was from where they were. It felt as if they were a billion miles away, or rather, an impossible distance; you couldn't get there from here. There was something, he thought, looking around again, about the squalor of here that said, implicitly, that one would never leave. It was one of many messages written into the shape of the buildings, the air he was breathing. This was a different state from being awake or dreaming. Who he was had been squeezed into a space that was too small. The shape of it was made to limit and control him and make him afraid. There was none of the comforting pantomime of a dream, the ever-present knowledge one could escape.

This was Hell. He knew it. It was telling him what it was.

Suddenly, he coughed. He'd been tasting the air, and the muck of it had slowly built up in his mouth: it was harder to breathe than it should be. He looked around once more and saw that many of those in the street had cloths or scarves across their faces. He could taste industrial smoke on his tongue, see the fog of it in the distance. The faces of some of the children who passed were spattered, as if they had freckles of tar.

There were children in Hell? He looked up and saw a mother carrying a baby. There were babies here? He shouldn't be shocked. This wasn't about good and evil. He knew that now. But it meant that the terrible words written on the sign over the gate might actually be true.

There came the sound of a scream. Behind the window he was looking in, there were . . . children, naked children, and they were being . . . oh, God! He went to the door, tried to get in, shouted he was police, and knew in that second that he'd done that out of habit but in doing so had submitted to the label this world had given him. The door was locked, so he tried to smash the window, but nothing would break it. The gentlemen inside looked out at him with smiling bemusement as they continued their abuse. Quill looked back to the street. He saw a uniformed policeman and ran to him. He started yelling, pointing out what was going on. The man was extremely deferential. 'I see that, sir. There's nothing we can do, I'm afraid, sir. Would you like to take it out on me instead, sir?'

Quill stopped at the look of genuine fear on the face of the officer. He backed away. He went back to the window. He kicked at it a few times. 'I'll be back for you,' he said, impotently. Those inside hardly registered his presence.

He looked away. He walked off. He stumbled across the street.

He'd been shown that because he was a parent. Hell now made him acutely aware that he was walking away and leaving those children to their fate. He tried to find some mental posture that allowed him to feel more comfortable about that. He could not. He thought about Jessica. Hell laughed at him doing that.

The throngs with their top hats and waistcoats and gloves and pith helmets and spats passed, and he started to see it everywhere now, such horror. Child prostitutes in lewd costumes pulled at the trousers of the men and were kicked away or had their hands grabbed and were led away. Beggars with horrifying ailments were lying in the horse shit, some of them just a head and an arm sticking helplessly up out of it, a hopeful expression on their gnawed-away faces.

Quill tried to haul one up out of it, dodging as carts rushed to and fro, but the beggar was screaming and complaining, urging him not to do it. Quill finally managed to heave him out onto the road surface, such as it was, both of them covered in mud, and found he'd rescued just the smallest part of a chest, with arm and head still attached. 'What did you go and do that for?' the beggar asked, tears streaming down his cheeks.

Quill pulled him to the side of the road, with the beggar all the while screaming, 'Put me back!'

He sat the man up against a lamp post. 'I'll find you something to eat,' he said.

'Fucking newcomers, trying to make themselves feel better! Fuck you!' The end of the sentence was cut off as a boot from a passer-by sent the beggar tumbling into the street once more.

Quill watched as the beggar was run over by the wheels of a cart and, still alive and screaming, was ground back into the muddy centre of the road. He wondered how deep it was there, if there were layers of them down there, some sort of peace to be found.

You couldn't die here, he realized.

He moved on. What else could he do? He had to see. Hell noted that he had to see. It would therefore enjoy showing him.

He saw the body of a child being thrown out of a house, covered in soot. Other children ran to the door, pounding on it, demanding to be given the work that had . . . killed . . . the boy. The boy's chest started to heave, and he began to cough, black tar bursting from his mouth and nostrils.

Quill moved on.

What could money mean here? Why did people need it? Quill started to realize that there was a pecking order here and, oh, the pecks were precise and they went deep.

In every window, in every building, at the end of every alley, there was something else that made him sick. By the time he'd fought his way to the end of just this street it felt as if he'd been here for days; he was tired to the core, moving through so many people. That would continue forever, said Hell, with interludes where things would get horrifyingly worse. When would one of those happen? Unexpectedly. By surprise.

He heard what sounded like a distant barking, coming from overhead, and looked up. There was something odd in the sky. It was hard to see, past the smog, but there it was, a band of some-thing, as if he was standing on a planet that had rings. Now he was listening for it, he could hear all sorts of animal noises from up there, and Hell, whispering in his mind, told him that was nothing but animals, that that was where most of them were kept. Quill remembered all the times they'd heard about animals being sacrificed, that those who'd done that thought they were making sacrifice to London itself. But what they killed ended up here. He wondered if the foundations of this place were made of all the teeth and fingers and blood that people had cut from themselves in return for power on earth.

He realized that Hell was telling him things in the place in his head where he normally had the Sight, that the Sight had gone from him now. He had no greater feeling for anything. He found he missed it as if it was armour he no longer wore. The lack of it was another thing that added to his complete vulnerability. He moved on. Ahead, there was a building with red curtains at its windows, looking a bit like somewhere official, a post office or something. People with no expression on their faces, looking as if they'd been here a long time, were trudging tiredly into it. Here came someone who was fighting, being dragged into the building by his fellow citizens, shouting and bellowing, and ripping at their clothing. Quill felt a surge of pride and fellow feeling to see someone putting up a fight, but already he knew that the emotion was only there to be pulled away from him, already he was flinching from the blow that was about to come, and he had been here minutes, and would be here forever.

The people going into the building had something in common: the tags on their arms were flashing like Belisha beacons. Their time, Quill realized, was up. What did that mean? What happened in there? Hell felt his animal fear, the way his new body – which was somehow more compromised and pathetic than his old body, as if all the worrying signs of age that Quill had ever felt were packed into it at once – reacted to the smell of the slaughterhouse. Quill felt something inside him start begging and squealing, and he had to clench his teeth to stop terrible pathetic sounds coming from his mouth. This was in the first few minutes, and he had forever ahead of him. Since the end of the Losley case, he had been blissfully without the depression that had occasionally beset him. He'd fooled himself into thinking that his new awareness of a greater purpose to his work had rid him of his 'black dog', but here he knew he still had that darkness in him, here he knew it would be forced back into him.

He turned the corner at the end of the street, at a point where many roads met, where the volume of sound actually increased, and he saw the other side of the red-curtained building, the back door, where people stumbled out again, their tags no longer flashing. They had on their faces expressions of new hope, of shattered emptiness, of howling, sobbing pain, sobbing like laughter. He stopped one of them and started asking questions. 'Ticking down to the next time,' the woman said, 'going to get a drink.' She shouldered past him.

Quill tried to look at his own tag, but he couldn't now quite bend his shoulder and neck to see how long he'd got. He'd been able to see it before. Things changed arbitrarily, said Hell. He needed to know the clock was there so he'd be afraid of time running out. But he couldn't see how much time he had left. He could ask others to look, of course, but that would take a negotiation. He would never know if they were telling the truth. That might be why there was money here, because of that horrifying force underneath this . . . he didn't want to think of it as a civilization; it was a continuing parody of one.

He walked on. He had nothing else to do. He couldn't quite believe he still existed. Why was all this here, instead of just simple death? Why cruelty instead of nothingness? He remembered Sefton speculating that the memories of the dead contributed to London 'remembering' a powerful being or location. Maybe that was why so many people had been shoved together in such a small space, to increase that effect. He'd got used to the idea of death as part of nature, or he'd got used to it more than he ever could this. He walked and he walked. He needed to see everything. As if, said Hell, seeing it all would make it better. He covered a lot of ground. Day became night, which meant the sky had just become a little darker.

He found that there were versions of buildings he recognized. The dome of Saint Paul's was now a basin, filled with steaming water. The Houses of Parliament were like a leaning row of dominoes against the tidal bashing of the Thames, over which bridges covered in shops – shops that were actually falling off – swung dangerously, everyone nevertheless swarming over them, having to get to wherever they had to go.

He'd noticed it earlier, and now he saw it in every detail: the people were fighting over every scrap because they needed to pay others to increase the time on their clocks, or even to see the clocks. It was an economy of fear.

His 'job' allowed him to explore, he realized. His 'job' let him see everything. Was he going to perform his 'job'? To do so would be another submission. How could it do any good? He decided to go along with it for now, to wait and see if it could. Hell was pleased at his acceptance and indicated that it was sure he was keeping some part of himself apart from it. It could wait. In an eternity of time, he would become the thing it had labelled him.

A street trader was standing outside a grand circular building, a comedy theatre, it seemed, judging by the mocking masks hanging from its over-decorated pillars. In a battered carpet bag behind him were a pile of the tags, and the crowd all around him were jostling for them, fighting for them, showing him how much money they had. 'Now then, lads and lasses. Everything's for sale here, and we've got all the time in the world! I don't want your money, little lady, it's a question, is it not, of what else you have for me?'

Quill moved on, wanting to make an arrest, but already wondering what use that would be, wanting to smash heads, but already seeing how meaningless that would be, wanting to keep a part of himself separate from all this still, undemeaned.

People talked about 'them' a lot. How 'they' would come, about what 'they' would do to them. It was 'they', he soon realized, who you saw when your time ran out. He was aware he'd been here for some time now and kept thinking that it had to be any moment now, kept feeling that fear, suppressing it, wondering if there was any attitude, anything he could do that would give him any control over this process, apart from participating in this terrifying market of time. He knew that everything about this place told him there was nothing he could do. His time would come. He would eventually have to go into one of the buildings with the red curtains. He couldn't think about that. He had to be strong. Didn't he? What did that even mean here? What would that be for?

He used his authority – hating to do it, because Hell underlined how it compromised him – to stop people and talk to them. He asked them what year they were from. Some of them said the year had been twenty-something when they died, some said fifteen-something. The earliest was twelve-something. Not all of them wanted to admit they *had* died. Some of them had strange explanations, weird cosmologies of their own. Some, particularly the children it took all his courage to question, expected to wake up. The sheer completeness of it was a new horror to Quill: it meant that the sign above the gate that he'd seen when he came in, that he kept trying not to think about, this also meant that it might be true. There were more people from later times, of course, because more people had been alive then. To some of these people, this was a futuristic city they were suffering in. For most, it was a vision of the past. It didn't change, he heard. Or he found nobody who remembered it being different.

A significant number of them said they felt that things had once been different, even after they'd died. They thought the place they were in had changed but they couldn't remember how. That made sense, considering what Quill's team had found out on earth about the point when everything seemed to have changed, the moment when the Docklands headquarters of the Continuing Projects Team had fallen. Perhaps this Hell was not eternal after all, but actually quite new, in terms of its rules and how many people were in here. In all his walking, he still had not found any limits to this generic metropolis. It kept telling him that it did have some, that it was growing every second. However, every street was packed with people, much more so than Quill had ever seen in the real London.

'They always come for us in the end, sir,' said one of the

constables in a police station he entered. The interior of it was like something out of Gilbert and Sullivan: a lot of men, and only men, from different times, judging by their haircuts, all squeezed into Victorian uniforms, performing endless slapstick comedy and making jolly comments. 'It is how you spend your time before that . . . I was about to say that it counts. It does not.' He would be paid, he was told, amid much laughter at the obviousness of the newcomer's question, with a certain amount of time on his clock, 'at the end of the week'. Whenever that was. That seemed to be something that could be moved or taken away.

He stopped on the threshold as he walked out. There was something here that did not seem to be compromised by Hell. It was surely a trap, a device to give him hope, but . . . 'What the Hell,' he said out loud.

He was still being paid to be a policeman. Those in charge of him were arbitrary and miserly. So no change there.

A number of persons of interest in the matter of the Ripper murders would almost certainly be in this most outer of outer boroughs.

He would do his duty and continue his investigation. It would, at least, be something to do until they came for him.

He found Spatley first. He was working as the director of a home for wayward girls. It looked like a factory, with enormous chimneys. He watched as parties of female children were herded out of police vans and through the doors.

He saw posters and heard that Spatley was going to give a speech. Quill went along and found he couldn't get through the crowd. He stayed at the back and watched. Spatley stood onstage with banners and complacent matrons and stern sponsoring men who looked proud to be there. Spatley himself was in a high collar so starched that Quill was sure it made him stand straighter. But Spatley was sweating, and his eyes looked desperate. 'If I was not here to hold the powers that control this world back, to moderate their policies,' he said, 'then things would be so much worse. I'm doing a good job here. What I do here is important.' The rest of it was drowned out by audience laughter.

Afterwards, Quill went into the dark factory, barged past a pair of stout yeomen at the door and marched into Spatley's office. The man looked up from his work with an admirable amount of poise. 'What is the meaning of this affront?'

'Listen to you, already going native.' Quill sat down opposite him, in what turned out to be a squirmingly uncomfortable chair made of . . . he stood up and didn't look at it again. 'It's not often I get a chance to ask this: why do *you* think you were killed?'

'I'm . . . not certain. I don't deserve to be here—'

'That's what they all say. What do you know about a prostitute by the name of Mary Arthur?'

Spatley looked suddenly, desperately, guilty.

'Mr Spatley,' said Quill, 'you're in Hell. Even if, for some unimaginable reason, you think you can mitigate this place, what further trouble do you think an admission of guilt could get you into?'

Spatley looked at him for a moment as if his world was crumbling. 'I . . . was lured to a hotel room,' he said. 'With an offer, an offer that very specifically catered to my . . . It was like someone had looked inside my head. But it seemed too perfect . . . I mean, I went because I wanted to spring the trap. Seriously.'

'I believe you, sir.' He actually did.

'I pretended to be outraged that she was dressed as a schoolgirl. Well, actually, I was outraged. Or I would have been, had I not been there, you know, deliberately.'

'Could we please get to the meat of this, sir?'

'I sent her into the bathroom to change and took a look in her bag. I found her phone, discovered that that was her real name, Mary Arthur. There was a text message on the phone that described what was supposed to happen as a "honey trap". She was meant to take photos of me, to compromise me. I wrote down the number of whoever had sent her that text on the back of a card I found in her bag. When she came out of the bathroom, I sat her down and told her I knew everything. I tried to get her to come with me to the police, to tell them all about the man who'd hired her, although I was sure he must be an employee, a deniable freelancer. She listened; I'll give her that, she was interested. I ended up telling her all about my suspicions concerning who was behind this trap, put the story together for the first time – the first time I'd told it all to anyone.'

'Who *did* you think was behind the trap?'

'Russell Vincent, of course.'

Quill frowned. 'Go on.'

'I was about to start assembling my forces for a major inquiry into how he was attempting to influence government. A certain number of ministers to the right of the Tories adored him, but some of the moderates seemed actually afraid of him. It was as if he had a hold over individual MPs. The attempted honey trap convinced me I was right, that he was blackmailing his way towards some enormous . . . coup.'

Quill didn't know enough to make a guess about how credible that was. 'I take it Mary Arthur didn't agree to give evidence?'

'No. She said, sorry, she already felt a bit threatened by how scared the man she'd worked for had seemed of a boss he wouldn't talk about. If she'd fucked up a job for someone as powerful and dangerous as that, she said, she was going to have to vanish for a while. I wished her well and felt worried about how I'd burdened her with so much of the truth. I decided to stop gathering evidence and move to acting against Vincent as soon as possible. I don't know how he could have known my intentions, because I'd told nobody, but I think, on reflection, that my plan was what got me killed.'

Quill was starting to wonder at how calm the man seemed. 'Don't you want . . . I don't know, revenge for what Vincent did to you?'

There was something a little cracked in Spatley's smile in return. 'Look at where we are. Here I am, making a difference. I don't think I'd better allow myself thoughts of revenge.'

Quill wondered at the plasticity of mind of this politician. 'I gather you lost the card with her employer's phone number on it?'

'Yeah, somewhere in my office, I think. Though I kept wondering if it had been taken, because I often got the feeling that the place was being searched. It didn't matter. I'd written down both the number and the address of the establishment.'

'Ah. We never found that.'

'I kept it on me at all times. In my jacket pocket.'

Quill frowned.

'Anyway, neither seemed likely to be useful going forward with the inquiry; the number always went to a blank answerphone, and if I wanted to have another go at convincing Mary to talk, I didn't have to go via what I presume was her brothel – I'd written her number down too.'

Quill failed to stop himself looking surprised. 'You wrote down *her* number?'

'Yes. On the same piece of paper.'

Quill put a hand over his eyes. He was pained by now having hope again. Hell told him he could have all the hope he liked, he was never going to get any of this information to his colleagues. 'I don't suppose—'

'Oh yes, I can tell you it. I looked at it so many times, and I've got a good memory for numbers. But surely, we're both dead now, so it hardly matters.'

Quill leaned over the table and pointed into his face. 'It matters to me.' He made Spatley tell him the phone number, and wrote it on the back of his own hand. As he went on his way, he started to repeat the number to himself, his own mantra, his own tiny hope.

Staunce was actually quicker to find, now Quill had got into the ways of this place. He was a retired grandee, working on endless charitable schemes that always came to nothing, all the Hell money spent on them frittered away in graft, as he always complained at many luxurious dinners. After those dinners he would suffer days of indigestion and acid reflux that would leave him gasping on the floor of his study, unable to reach for water. He could have paid for water, but it seemed he was unwilling to do so. Quill found him in that condition, but, even curled up around himself like a wounded animal, he wanted to be interviewed. He wanted to talk to anyone. 'He paid me to tell him things which only the police knew,' he said, 'back in the day. Particularly gossip about celebrities. They deserved what they got. And it was harmless. Argggghh!' He gasped and curled up around himself again. 'But I stopped! I stopped because I knew it was wrong! Is no one listening?'

'*Who* paid you?' asked Quill.

He was told the name, and about how Staunce had taken another payment, and what it was for. 'You sold us out,' Quill said, 'to Russell Vincent.' He looked up to see an enormous roast being brought in by Staunce's servants.

'But . . . but I *thought* about turning the tables. I *thought* about turning him in, taking the evidence to the cabinet office . . .'

Quill straightened up and nodded to him. 'Thanks for that. I'll leave you to it; I don't want to get in the way of your dinner.'

Tunstall was in a workhouse, walking on an enormous wheel that was slowly grinding a millstone. He wore a long coat made of weights. Quill wondered aloud if this was something he was doing to himself.

'No,' the man sighed, 'this is very much something being done to me by others.'

'What got *you* killed?'

So Quill was told about a working life spent making some extra cash on the side, necessary to keep a home for his wife and child. The man had, as Quill suspected, been the one who searched Spatley's office. 'Not very professionally, I should think, but pretty thoroughly.' Quill was amazed, distantly, by the idea that Tunstall might still take pride in the quality of such a job. Tunstall had been told to stop the car, when he'd been driving Spatley, in a specific place at a specific time. 'We'd already worked out where security might send us if a particular road got blocked up. I didn't know what was going to happen. I was so shocked after . . . well, I didn't even know if that had been what the bloke I was working for had planned . . .'

Quill asked for a description, and recognized the man who'd met Mary Arthur at the Soviet bar.

'So I said what I'd seen happen, straight off. I suppose part of me thought I might get off because it was all so mad, though I was being well paid to take any fall. We was sent a lot of money in a way so my wife could get hold of it. We needed that money. You don't know how hard it is; they expect you to live in town . . . But then you lot turn up, saying you actually believe me, and you get me off. And I go home and . . . and it's all shit. I couldn't keep Spatley's face out of my head, how scared he was when he was killed. I *did* like him, all right? But I'm holding on for my family, it's all I ever did. Until you lot want to interview me again, and I start thinking I'd feel better if I told you everything. And then . . . then the Ripper came for me.'

'You want to come clean about *everything* now, then?'

Tunstall seemed to understand what Quill was talking about. 'I did something else on orders. When he was lying there dead in the back seat . . . I reached into his jacket pocket, and my hands were shaking, I tell you. I took out this piece of paper I'd been told was there, and I . . . I ate it. I was told that was the only way to get rid of it without tipping anyone off that anything had been there. Burn it and there'd be, you know, the smell. They didn't even want to risk me crumpling it up and taking it with me. I can still taste it.' Quill could see the tears welling up in the man's eyes. 'I mean, my mouth's still full of it. It's all I *can* taste.'

Quill went on his way and left Tunstall to his walking.

He found Rupert Rudlin in the middle of a crowd that kept grabbing him and hauling him over to waterboard him in a barrel of beer. Quill spared him that for a few moments and asked him his questions.

'No,' sobbed the young man, 'I don't know why I was killed! I don't!'

The crowd grabbed him from Quill again and kept on with their torture.

Quill discovered, much more easily than he expected, that the real name of the final person he wanted to interview was Eric Wilker. He was something of a celebrity. Quill arranged to meet him in a pub. He was a small man with threadbare clothing – someone so average that it took Quill a while to pick him out in the crowd. 'People tell me there's all this kerfuffle about me,' he said, sipping his half-pint of mild and bitter. 'I thought it'd all die down when I did. Back in 1888, I killed them filthy whores as a public service. One of them they say were mine wasn't, I can't remember which. Two more they say were other people were me. All the time I was working as a draper's assistant. I just did what I felt like with them after, and I laughed when I saw what they all made of it. Didn't mean nothing. I never sent no letters to anyone, I never wrote no message on any wall, I ain't daft. I stopped when it got too hard. Every now and then I was tempted, but then I thought, no, I've done my bit. I died of a fever when I was in my sixties. Thought about telling my old lady on my death bed. Decided against. Ended up here. And younger, which is nice. And here I get to keep on doing what I'm most famous for. Only, every now and then, they get a chance to do it to me. We take it in turns, you might say.' He took a slow, sad sip of his beer. 'All a bit pointless, really.'

That was true of Quill's investigation as well. He'd interviewed everyone he could find who was involved in the case. He was aware of Hell laughing at him for how short a distance that small hope had taken him. Now that small hope was gone. He knew who was guilty, but he had no way to tell anyone.

At one point, as Quill was walking down the street, picking his way through the enormous crowds, someone grasped him, flung him to the ground and started kicking him. 'It's your fault!' screamed Barry Keel. He seemed to be an alderman now, smart in his coat and tails. But his eyes were lost to madness.

Quill grabbed his leg, rolled it over, and slammed the man into the shit, his hand in the middle of his back. He was aware of whistles and of suddenly efficient hellish coppers running towards him from all directions as the crowd helpfully shouted all the details to them. 'I don't want to find out what they'll do to you,' said Quill, 'for assaulting a police officer.' He let the man go and kicked him on the backside, off into the crowd.

Quill supposed that bloody Mora Losley would be somewhere in this lot as well, and Rob Toshack and Harry and Harry's dad and a bunch of others who might bear him a grudge, but he wasn't planning on trying to find them.

Quill walked to where he thought Bermondsey should be, and asked around for Ross' dad, Alfred Toshack. He was directed to a small park, where he found an enormous tree that grew to a tremendous height above all those around it. Putting a hand to his eyes to shield them from the dull glare of the sky, Quill looked up into its highest branches and found a noose there. But there was nobody hanging from it. Alfred had, according to the passers-by Quill stopped and asked, been 'sent to the Tower'.

Quill went to the Tower of London, but his authority wasn't enough to get him in. Walking away from it, though, he had an idea. According to Ross, Alfred Toshack had been able to see every detail of what was going on in the everyday world from his vantage point in Hell. It was part of his punishment. If Quill could find somewhere high enough that he could access – in his condition he didn't fancy trying to climb that tree – perhaps he could duplicate that. Perhaps he could find out, from Hell, things he wanted to know about the real world.

He was told the centre of London was where, in the modern version, the Centre Point building would be. He went to see what was there, and Hell anticipated that, enjoyed it. He wondered if it would be a tall building.

He felt the shadow a long time before he saw, over the buildings, what was making it. At the centre of Hell's London stood an enormous statue of the Smiling Man. There was an entrance at its base. Like the Statue of Liberty, it seemed, one could walk up inside it and, yes, he saw movement behind them, look through the eyes.

He discovered, when he got to the entrance, that to do so would cost him. Of course it would. But he needed to do this, so he paid. Hell had known that he would.

He climbed the stairs inside the statue, which took all his energy, emphasizing each of his pains – of course it did.

He reached the top and looked out of one of the eyes. Beside him, helpless, sobbing newcomers were doing the same from the other. They had come here, like him, in a vain search for hope.

Quill looked out over Hell's London. There it was: not just this outer borough beneath him, but, at an angle to the horizon, the real London. He was looking down on it. London in summer, a blissful aerial view that made Quill feel an agony of wanting and loss. He could see it in several different ways, he realized. There was the physical city, there was a sort of contour map of rushing energies, and there was . . . as if it had been built there, a great wheel, the structure of which was threaded through everything, that cut across everything. The wheel was made of ideas made by people, or imposed on them. It had gone wrong, he saw: it was moving the wrong way. Right now, there was nothing he could do about that, so eventually he looked elsewhere.

He could *see* Jason Forrest's limited point of view, the history of the historical Jack the Ripper, the warring viewpoints of the occult community. He could see whatever concepts he wanted to see. He found himself automatically thinking about Sarah, and then suddenly he was looking at her, and he knew where she was on the map as he pulled his attention away from her.

Oh, oh, that was too painful. If he stayed here he was going to have to do it again. Again and again. What could he look at that was more practical, that could give him a despairing hint of his duty again? He looked again at the back of his hand, at the phone number he'd written there and memorized through repetition.

He looked back to the real London to find all the places Russell Vincent might be.

TWENTY-SEVEN

EARLIER ON THE EVENING THAT QUILL
RETURNED TO LIFE

Costain drove the van into the car park of St Gertrude's Church in the part of Enfield known as World's End and parked. He composed himself for a moment. Then he got out.

The facade of the church was bathed in spotlights on this still not very cold night. They threw deep shadows across the porch. As he approached the building, Costain saw a figure standing there, then stepping out to meet him. It was a young woman in clerical dress, a worried look on her face.

'Reverend Pierce?'

'You must be Sergeant Costain. Okay, let's not waste any time.' She sounded like an Oxbridge graduate, calm and professional. She was somehow more modern than Costain had expected her to be.

'I was surprised when I read you did this.'

'I don't like the fact that one *can* do this. Very few people know. Priests who apply to be the vicar of this parish are warned off it, and only if they persist are they told the nature of the geography here, and only if they then still persist are they trained to make use of it. Turns out I'm rather pig-headed. We're told it's for the health of London. There used to be some sort of body

363

overseeing it, but for some reason no one now seems to know how to contact them. I'm quite interested to see whether it still works.'

'Me too.'

She led him not inside the church, as he'd been expecting, but around it, to a side of the churchyard where there were no spotlights and the shadow of the building cut a straight line between light and absolute darkness. There they stopped. 'Here we are.'

'Have you done this before?'

'Twice. My predecessor only did it once. Demand seems to be on the increase.'

He showed her the Bridge of Spikes. 'I thought this was unique, or at least just once a century.'

'It might be. I don't know what it is.' He quickly explained to her, and she raised an eyebrow. 'In every previous case I've dealt with, and in all I've read, these are only *visits*. You think that this object offers . . . a permanent solution?' She sounded not only dubious, but worried at the implications.

Costain found he was suddenly angry. But not at her. He could only hope he hadn't sacrificed so much for something brief and terrible. 'Whatever. Come on. Let's do it.'

'All right.' She closed her eyes, said some prayers under her breath and made the sign of the cross. 'If you know what to do with that thing, do it now.'

Costain took a deep breath. He only had a feeling for what had to be done. The sphere seemed to be telling him. If he was to use it on himself, this is what he'd have had to do at any point before he died. He supposed you could even do it way in advance. He put the sphere in the palm of his left hand, and then, decisively, crushed it in his grasp. For a moment, nothing happened, and then—

He stared in shock as he saw the spikes burst through his flesh. It was as if his hand had turned into a golden sea urchin, every spike dripping with blood.

Then the obvious agony of that hit him, and he had to fall to his knees. He grabbed his left wrist with his right hand, staring at it. Blood was gushing around the spikes now, surely from some major artery! He was panting. The meth both amplified the shock and deadened it, let him see past it. But . . . it was . . . only pain. He somehow knew he hadn't been horribly wounded, that the Bridge had prevented that.

He managed to open his hand . . . the Bridge had vanished. He was sure, though, because it was telling him, that it had done its work.

The reverend was crouched beside him, he realized, looking desperately at him, wondering how she could help. 'Do it!' he bellowed.

'It's done,' she said. 'Can I get a dressing for—?'

'Not until I know!' Costain forced himself to look up from his own blood splattering onto the gravel of the church path. He looked into the darkness. He could see something moving there.

'The Maori of New Zealand believe their dead leave a pohutu-kawa tree at Cape Reinga at the tip of the North Island for a journey back to Polynesia – actually back to where they came from, historically,' said the vicar, staring into the void as Costain was, now fascinated. 'There's a river in Japan which is also, physically, the border between this world and the next, so they say . . .'

Costain watched as the vague shape resolved itself into a figure. He wasn't sure now if the uncertainty about it was in the world or in his head. He'd lost a lot of blood to get him to the point of being able to see this. The figure wasn't stumbling. It was walking quite purposefully, marching, even. It was familiar.

With a determined look on her face, Pierce went to the edge of the light and held out her hand.

Quill didn't know if he could trust this. He had found, standing in the head of that statue, that he was being forced to close his eyes, and when he'd opened them he was elsewhere, looking at a strange figure. The ferryman was, depending on which side you saw him from, either a cloaked figure with skeletal hands or an

Asian cabbie with tobacco stains on his fingers. He was pushing
the boat forward across the river of silver which warped under and
around them, his staff of many wrapped dimensions made out of
the pink flatness of the Hammersmith and City line as seen on a
tube map. Or he was driving across a bridge that didn't exist,
going north across the Thames, the road lined with a million
spikes, the tarmac ahead red with blood that was flowing down
to meet them. 'I don't normally go south of the river,' he said.

Costain watched as the figure reached Pierce and grabbed her
hand. He willed its features into being those he wanted to see.
He hoped he had given enough.

James Quill woke up. He was in darkness. He was gasping for air.
He sucked in a great breath of it. He didn't know where he was.
He . . . okay, he knew who he was. But there were gaps. He was
naked. Was he . . . ? He panicked for a moment, his limbs shot
out and hit the sides of a container all around him. He cried out.
He found that his throat hurt desperately. He bellowed again. He
made himself concentrate and reached out . . . the sides he was
touching were made of metal. He pulled back his legs as far as
they could go, and slammed them forward again—
   Suddenly, he was rushed forward, and was being hauled out
into a light too blinding for him to see anything, amongst shouting
people. He tried to lash out, fell, howling, onto a freezing floor.
He was in a room. More and more people were rushing into it
and they looked as astonished as he felt. He looked down at his
body. His familiar flesh startled him. It was . . . as if he'd been
gone from this house. For so long. There had been changes.
Swathes of new pink skin across his chest and abdomen, younger
than his own, smooth. Between his legs . . . new there too. The
people were asking him all sorts of questions. They put water to
his lips.
   A morgue, he was in a morgue.
   He took their hands and helped them haul him to his feet. He

knew something terrible . . . but that didn't matter now. Dear God, that didn't matter now! He grabbed the glass and threw back the water. He moved his tongue, croaked and licked his lips until he was sure he could use this . . . unfamiliar . . . body again. Until he was certain he could form words. He knew exactly the words he wanted to form.

'I know where Russell Vincent is,' he said.

TWENTY-EIGHT

Quill called Costain from the morgue, having had a vague memory of seeing him on what already felt like a dream of one side of that bridge he'd crossed. Thankfully, the DS had been expecting the call and arrived an hour later in an unmarked van. His left hand was bandaged, but only to the extent of a minor wound. By then, Quill had been given some clothes by still-astonished morgue staff who had started to assume they must have made some enormous clerical error and were probably about to be sued. Quill immediately told Costain not to call Sarah, having already talked to the morgue authorities on that subject. He had no idea how he was going to tell her he was back, was desperately restraining his own urge to call her, to go immediately to see her, because he wanted somehow to moderate how big a shock that was going to be.

He looked at his hands. He kept wanting to touch his body. He expected to feel traumatized, but it was as if his time in Hell had been filed away by his brain as being something like a dream. He felt abused on some distant, deeply internal level and was aware that this might come out and haunt him at some point. But at least for now it was absent.

He asked about how he'd come back, what Costain had had to do with it. Costain told him: about the relationship between himself and Ross, about the details of the auction that Ross hadn't revealed, about him committing burglary to get the Bridge. He unburdened himself of all the terrible shit that he hadn't shared with his colleagues. Quill had to sit down. He couldn't imagine how this was going to make Ross feel. He felt angry on her behalf, and his own – actually infuriated at this man who'd just saved him from Hell. Dear God, that was Costain all over. 'Why did you choose me to bring back?'

'Ross' father coming back still wouldn't make her happy. She even told me that.'

'Why not keep it for yourself?'

Costain looked annoyed at being questioned. He looked as if he'd expected something more from Quill. 'Because I want *all* of us to stay alive, and you're our only chance to do that. If the truth behind what you wrote in your notebook is as important as Sefton thinks it is—'

'Well, I know who's responsible for the Ripper murders.'

'Russell Vincent?'

Quill laughed in pride at his team. But the laugh turned into a painful cough and he had to drink some water. He waved aside Costain's questions about his physical state. 'And I know where to find him. And I've got a lead on Mary Arthur.' Quill had looked at the back of his hand when he'd first understood that he had come back to life, and found nothing written there. So he'd grabbed a piece of paper and swiftly written down Mary Arthur's number, hoping that, having repeated it so many times to himself, he'd remembered it accurately. Now he showed it to Costain. 'Can you get me to Wapping? I'm going to make a house call on Russell Vincent. We can catch up on the way.'

As Costain drove at terrifying speed through the night that smelt of smoke, and after he and the sergeant had compared notes, Quill dialled the number he'd gone so far to get and spoke quickly and urgently to a voicemail service. 'Mary,' he said, 'this is Detective Inspector James Quill of the Metropolitan Police. I know you're going to think this is a trap. Mainly because you'll have heard I was killed, like so many people who have angered Russell Vincent are being killed tonight. But I . . . avoided that, and so can you. He isn't as powerful as he thinks he is. We know you might have seen something impossible, and we know what you were involved in.' He repeated everything that Spatley had told him. 'We have specialist knowledge of this field. We really *can* keep you safe. Be a witness for us. You can bring him down. I'm hoping you will.'

'Tell her you'll pay her expenses,' said Costain. He asked for his phone back once Quill had finished the call, and listened to his messages. 'The others have found something,' he said, and he told Quill about where Ross and Sefton were. There was a look of tremendous hurt on his face as he did so, as if he'd been the victim of an enormous practical joke, the truth of which was only slowly dawning on him. 'The long barrow in your notes, they found it anyway. Did I . . . did I bring you back, did I do that to Ross for nothing?!'

Quill shook his head. Having heard about Sefton and Ross finding the barrow, and having put two and two together with everything Costain had told him, he felt dangerously certain about a few things now. 'Thanks,' he said, 'for my continued existence being valued at "nothing", but no. I think we're now going to be able to finish this tonight.' He started to give Costain specific instructions.

They arrived at the skyscraper offices of a company that Quill would never have associated with Vincent. Costain used more muscle than the threat of the law to march them past the front desk. Quill got into an elevator as security guards rushed in with urgent questions, and the last thing he saw as the doors closed was Costain holding them at bay with his warrant card, starting to bellow at them. His part of this plan would keep him down there.

Quill wanted to do this alone.

NOW

'How did you know?' asked Russell Vincent.

'Because I've just come from Hell. Where, as part of my continuing investigation, I interviewed witnesses.' Quill didn't want to say that his team had come to the same conclusion before him. Vincent wouldn't know anything of what they'd been up to since the night before the raid on the Keel shop that Costain had described to him. Quill wanted to keep what they might be up to now well away from Vincent's thoughts.

'So the Bridge of Spikes worked.' He was staring at Quill as if he was a fascinating lab specimen. 'I assume that's how you did this? Damn. Maybe I could have got my hands on it.'

'Why didn't you?' said Quill.

'I thought it was still at a very well-defended property, and I was hoping to give my people a lot more occult knowledge before I sent them to have another go.'

'Occult knowledge gained from us?'

'Absolutely.'

Quill looked over from where he was still holding Vincent against the wall. There, on the desk, was the scrying glass – the real thing, blood red. It was small, quite insignificant looking, but the Sight gave it great weight. It was the centrepiece of a lavish private office decked out like something from the Fifties, all green leather and polished wood, but with enormous picture windows that, given what was outside, gave the place the feel of a palace that was looking down onto the many plumes of smoke of a besieged city.

There was something else in here too. The Sight indicated an enormous, mocking presence, with a feel to it that Quill found familiar. He couldn't pin down exactly where it was. As soon as he looked in one direction, it flitted out of the corner of his eye. He recognized it, though. The Smiling Man was watching them, letting Quill know he was here, but doubtless keeping his presence a secret from Vincent. 'Do you see that?' he asked.

'What?'

'Nothing,' said Quill. He flung Vincent to the carpet, and before the man could do anything, marched over to the desk, grabbed the scrying glass and smashed it against the corner of a table, again and again. The glass didn't shatter. It didn't even break.

'You won't have much luck with that,' said Vincent, getting to his feet. He went to the drinks cabinet, recovering his composure, and poured himself a whisky. 'I'm pretty sure it's not actually glass.'

Quill looked round for a window to throw the glass out of and realized that none of them opened. He looked back to Vincent. 'I could just run off with it.'

Vincent produced a small black device from his jacket. 'This is my panic button,' he said. 'If I press it, my security people seal the building and burst in here.' He put down his whisky and checked his phone. 'They've just asked me if I think your sergeant downstairs is really a police officer.' He hit two keys and then the send button. 'I've just told them no, I don't think so – an entirely reasonable response, given this evening's chaos. They'll probably hold him until there's someone at Gipsy Hill to verify his identity.' He looked puzzled at Quill. 'Where are the other two? They haven't slept in several days. Are they on to me?'

'They're on their way over,' lied Quill. He strode purposefully back over to Vincent and stopped when the billionaire held up the panic button, his finger poised. Quill was trying to control the fury he felt about what this man had done to him. He and Gaiman both. 'Do you know why I came here?' he asked.

'To attack me or arrest me.'

'To hear you tell me the truth.'

Vincent frowned and glanced at something under the level of his desk. 'You're not wearing a wire,' he said. Quill walked over and saw what looked like a radio scanner. 'I don't think you've got any occult way of hiding that.'

Quill opened his borrowed jacket and displayed its interior to Vincent. 'Nothing up my sleeve. Besides, even if we got a recorded confession, do you reckon something as surreal as this could ever make it to court?'

Vincent considered for a moment, taking a sip of his whisky. 'What do you want to know?'

Quill had been sure the great communicator would want someone to share his story. Afterwards, he guessed, Vincent would just hit the panic button, have him locked up somewhere downstairs and then summon the Ripper. No loose ends, but Vincent couldn't resist the chance to share.

'How about: how did you first learn about the supernatural powers of London?'

'It's something London-based entrepreneurs talk about after a few beers. It's kept at the highest levels. You know, those used to risking millions are the only businessmen mad enough to believe things like that. I got interested, found out about the auction, and, like I told you when you visited me at the mews flat, bought the scrying glass as an alternative to using the electronic methods of covert news gathering. It worked a treat. I'd sit up here, connecting my mind to a celebrity here, a politician there, finding out all their secrets while they slept and then tipping off my editors as to how they could credibly find stories they could print. Watch – what you do is this.' He went over, and, carefully holding onto the panic button, took the scrying glass from Quill's hands, then set it back on his desk. He sat down in front of it. 'You concentrate on a particular location, perhaps a building, and the glass sort of tells you if anyone's asleep in that vicinity. You can't see anything, so you can't use it as a spy camera, worse luck; you just get a sense of who each sleeping person is. You pick the one whose brain you want to leaf through and you get your mind connected directly to theirs. It's like suddenly having loads more memories. You can't keep them all, but, like you were trying to recall something you yourself knew, you can reach for whatever you're after. With you lot, I usually just felt around for whatever you'd been up to the previous day.' He leaned back in his chair. 'That US presidential visit was so frustrating: I could never pin down exactly where he spent the night.' He got up again to retrieve his whisky. 'As you may have guessed, I also used the glass to further my political agenda. I'm mounting a sort of coup, Quill. I'm tired of politicians who court public opinion. What this country needs is a few who'll *make* opinion, who'll *tell* the masses what to think. *That's* what the British really like. I should know. I've been telling them what to think for decades.'

Quill, with his generally low opinion of the general public, allowed himself a grunt of recognition.

'So I used the glass to make good things happen for the MPs I liked, bad things for those I didn't, and I gradually let the idea seep into Westminster that this would keep happening, that I had everyone's secrets, that I was starting to be in control. It was especially ironic, considering that I'd become the "clean" news-paperman. They couldn't understand how I was doing it.'

Quill found he was interested in something. 'Did you notice that you couldn't spy on MPs when they were in Parliament?'

'Yes, and that was terribly frustrating, because I'd see them there on TV, dozing off on the back benches, and I couldn't do anything about it. That barrier around the building would be something to do with those mysterious predecessors of yours, I should think. I wish you'd learned more about them.'

'Me too.'

'Meanwhile, I brought together the money and the resources to set up what you see tonight, what's going on out there –' he gestured towards what was outside the windows, making the ice clink in his whisky glass – 'and the response to it. I encouraged thuggery on the far right, and made sure the Met and the other police forces were antagonized to the point of going on strike. The *Herald's* been prophesying the Summer of Blood for months, and now here it is. You lot gave me the word for that: ostentation. Those I favour to take over will suspend government, step in themselves, order a crackdown, restore order with amazing speed. The army, thanks to what I know about several generals, is partly onside. I should think we'll eventually return to some form of parliamentary democracy, but on our terms. I will have changed the whole political landscape.'

Quill could hardly believe the scope of this man's dreams. 'That's why you're doing this, but how? What's the connection between the scrying glass and Jack the Ripper?' Quill was pretty sure he already knew the answer.

Vincent nodded eagerly, as if this was the most exciting part. 'I started to use the glass randomly to sweep important locations where people might be asleep, where I'd pop into a few minds, see what I could find out: the House of Lords; the Police Complaints Commission. In . . . one of these locations . . .' Quill heard him pause, being careful. He was presumably aware of what Quill had seen in his shared dream with the woman in the barrow, but couldn't know that Quill's team had later pieced together where he'd been. '. . . I found a sleeping mind whose presence lit up the mirror with its power. I connected my mind to it, and . . . bam! It was enormous, it rushed into my head, and I went staggering around the mews flat, breaking things, having some sort of fit as I tried to deal with all that power rushing around my brain.'

'That's when your PA came in?'

'Her doing so knocked me out of my trance, broke the connection. There would have been that silver stuff that only you can see all over the place. I felt angry at her, though I was careful not to show it, because right before she'd arrived I'd realized that I could control the power I'd encountered. It was ancient and confused and, above all, asleep, in some way which went beyond all our definitions of sleep. It was terrifying, but also completely vulnerable.' Quill remembered his vision of the stone being slammed shut, of the once-powerful wise woman now locked away. 'Later that night I contacted it again. I dominated it, learned how to shape the power that flooded into me, to the point where I could afford to give it limited freedom, like a horse I'd broken. I let it make a body for itself in front of me, an energy form that was spun together out of this golden thread in mid-air, deliberately a body I could see, that others would only see when I wanted them to. I thought then that it was going to be like Caliban out of *The Tempest*, that I'd send it flying around doing invisible errands. I tried a bit of that, actually, but it wasn't very satisfying.'

'But then someone started getting angry at the influence you were exerting over Members of Parliament. Someone started making plans.'

'And I knew that my servant could help with that, yes.' Vincent looked almost irritated, as if he was being misunderstood. 'But, listen, you have to believe me: Spatley really went out of his way to get himself killed. I'd been observing his dreaming mind for months, hoping his plan to come after me would stay in the realm of Lib Dem daydreams. But he started to put real work into it, to make a mental map of what I was up to. I had to do something.'

'And you didn't go straight for the fatal option, I'll give you that. This is where Mary Arthur comes in, isn't it?'

Vincent smiled, seeming to appreciate Quill's insight into his cleverness. 'I took a look at his sexual fantasies and set up a honey trap catering to them – a prostitute who did the full schoolgirl thing, who was, as you say, Mary Arthur. What I didn't expect was that he'd end up telling her everything he'd found out about me. And that then she'd be sensible enough to go into hiding immediately.'

'And you can only read people's sleeping minds when you know where they are. Given that you make use of the same device, I assume that you also need to know where they are to send the Ripper after them?'

'Exactly!' Vincent pointed excitedly at Quill. 'Spatley, in the wake of the honey trap, was going to move against me *immediately*. So he simply *had* to die.'

'Well, obviously!'

'Through Challoner, my freelancer, I paid Tunstall, the driver, to search Spatley's office for the business card Spatley had lost on which he'd written down information that could lead to the prostitute or, if Challoner started talking, to me. The card wasn't very important to Spatley, considering he'd copied the details elsewhere, but very important to me at that stage, when I wasn't utterly confident of my power and was contemplating my first murder. When the car was halted by the protest, I made the power I'd contacted once more appear in front of me. I took the shape it had made for itself, and then imposed my own meaning on it, changed it, added certain details. Then I sent it off to do its job.'

With, thought Quill, its, or rather, *her*, own fingerprints intact.

'My idea then was only to make it look like a Toff protestor. I knew there were people out there who might get glimpses of it, after all, even if the only person I was intending to fully see it was Spatley. The Jack the Ripper bit was because of you lot.'

Quill felt a dull pain on hearing that. 'Because of us?'

'When you told Tunstall you believed what he was saying, I wondered how that was possible. When I realized you understood more about the secret side of London than I did, I must admit I got scared. If I was going to get away with what I'd done I would need a cover story. I had to sell you an alternative narrative, a meaning. Hence Jack the Ripper.'

'Why not just kill us all?'

'And shut off such a wonderful source of occult information?' Vincent shook his head. 'I decided to send your team on a wild goose chase instead, into the morass of Jack the Ripper legends, hoping I'd get you to try to solve all that nonsense. And I saw that the Ripper guise would act as a good cover if I located Mary Arthur, because then I would actually have to murder a prostitute. Reading up on the original Ripper murders, I came across that wonderful message on the wall, about the Jews being to blame, or not to blame, or whatever it's trying to say. It being so vague creates such a mass of conflicting meanings. An excellent motivator, for example, for my lovely skinhead boys.' He moved around the room, gesturing in mid-air. 'When I direct my supernatural servant to go and kill someone, it's me in the driving seat, willing it to move, controlling the individual movements. But when it's travelling or doing something mundane I just point it in a particular direction and let it do the work. Exactly like riding a horse. Fiddly stuff, like writing that message, or opening the doors on train carriages –' he gave Quill a wink – 'making those fingers do precise work – wow, that takes concentration.'

Quill realized something which gave him some small satisfaction. 'And being a former copy boy and subeditor, your version of the message just *had* to have proper spelling and grammar.'

Vincent looked astonished for a moment. Then he started to laugh. 'Oh! Oh, I hadn't realized. But you're right. That's tremendous. You have to give me credit for the intelligence of the wider scheme, though. As well as being of practical use, the Ripper icon became just what I needed to lead the Summer of Blood. I'd found the greatest outrage marketing brand of all time. The greatest aspirational cheerleader figure also, free and happy in his work, encouraging people to copy him. The Ripper gets people furious and interested and aroused all at the same time, and it can mean *anything*.'

Quill understood that Ross had been right when she'd said that the most important indicator was the Ripper's new MO: killing rich powerful men, and that Costain had been right about the scrawled message being just a load of front. 'And you being Jewish yourself, as you went out of your way to tell me when we first met—'

'Led you off into a whole different briar patch of conspiracy theories.'

'But so many of your people must have been hurt in the riots—'

'My "people"?' Vincent actually laughed. 'I don't have a *people*, Quill, I have *shareholders*. My mother just happened to be Jewish, it's not like I regard myself as one. Oh, hey, and you also bought that bit about the anonymous death threats, about me being worried by "dark forces"! I do believe most people actually think those are out there, that there's some sort of . . . controlling evil under everything. Or, hey, perhaps because of ostentation, now there actually *is*.'

Quill wondered if Vincent might have a point there, but he didn't let his face give anything away. The invisible presence in the room shifted, as if reacting to the notion, whether in pleasure or apprehension. 'You were there before us with ostentation – you must have been.'

'Well, I had rather got the idea that something like that must happen. When I tried to use Twitter to get together a few Toffs in Staunce's neighbourhood, to make it look as if they were connected to the Ripper, who was due to make his full debut that night, I thought it was a long shot. But they arrived much more quickly and in greater numbers than they should have. I started to see that they felt somewhat compelled to. Though, if you asked any individual Toff, I doubt they'd realize that.'

'So you used Staunce to get our home addresses, then killed him when he started to think of turning you in—'

'Then I had a lucky break. Mary Arthur contacted Challoner, who'd originally employed her. She'd figured that after the death of Spatley she couldn't still be in trouble, or at least that's what she told him. I suspect she wanted to find out if she'd been let off the hook. Of course she had no idea that I knew what Spatley had told her. I had Challoner pretend to offer her new work, to set up a meeting at a specific place and time. She was careful; she chose somewhere crowded – that Soviet bar. Bless. Once she got there, I had Challoner keep her talking, then "pop out for five minutes to meet someone higher up". Of course, he went straight home. He knew enough about occult London to guess what was coming.'

'But that time your Ripper wouldn't play ball, would she?'

Vincent smiled. 'I keep forgetting, you know it's a she.'

'Yeah. My team kept underlining their assumptions, but that was a huge one they ended up making, that the Ripper was a bloke. You led us into that too, when we interviewed you at the mews flat. We kept saying "it", you kept saying "he".'

'I'm so pleased you noticed that. Well, now I am, I mean.'

'Maybe we should have realized the truth when the Ripper refused to kill Mary Arthur.'

'I tried so damn hard to make her do that.' Vincent sounded as if he was sharing an anecdote about a difficult mount. 'But she just bucked and bucked. In that bar, she swerved aside at the last moment and suddenly I was stabbing just some random bloke! She was fine with letting me do *that*!'

'I think she's got a problem with men,' said Quill. 'A feminist Jack the Ripper. Anything really *can* mean anything these days. This is why she's leaking silver, isn't it, because you're forcing her into a shape she doesn't want to be in?'

'Yes, and I do wonder if she'll last much longer. Again, I only know about the fuel thing thanks to you lot. At any rate, she's probably done her bit now, but I'll keep using her. I've got a few more people to kill. I'll wear her down to the point where there's nothing left. Safer that way. Of course, if I'd known she wouldn't kill women, I'd never have started all this in the first place.'

'I presume this was when you decided, since Mary Arthur then went back into hiding, that getting us to find out about supernatural means of locating people was a good idea.'

'I'd already bought your wife's newspaper, and a few others at the same time so it wouldn't look odd, with a view to meeting you, looking you in the eye, eventually planting the seeds that would send you after whatever occult knowledge I might want to know. You surprised me by seeing that silver stuff on my cards. I only knew about that once I saw your memory of our meeting. When you came to interview me, I was prepared; I dropped a few hints about the sort of thing I wanted you to look into. Didn't work out. Perhaps I was too subtle for the plod mentality.' He grinned, enjoying Quill's reaction to that. 'Mind you, I did fob you off with that fake scrying glass. Just like with the Bussard Inquiry, I admitted to a little guilt, and this time got away with something much bigger. The detail of the ripped shirt, that's just the sort of visual image that sells a story, that makes people swallow a narrative.'

'Then you killed Tunstall because he was about to talk to us—'

Vincent sighed. 'Only because he was *definitely* going to implicate me. He'd done everything I asked, including finding that piece of paper with all the contact details on Spatley's corpse. Really, he got so close to having a happy life with his family and a big payoff.'

'If only he hadn't had a conscience.'

'Well, exactly.' Quill couldn't tell if Vincent was being sarcastic or literal.

'What about me, then? What did I do that drove you to . . . ?' Quill mimed stabbing himself repeatedly.

Vincent wasn't put off his stride in the slightest. 'Two things. You got hold of the name Mary Arthur, and you had that meeting of minds with my power source while I was looking into your dreams. I decided I could still use the other three, but that you had to go.'

'I nearly got away from you, though, didn't I?'

'Yes, and you would have done, I grant you, except . . .' Vincent seemed to consider for a moment, then smiled again, chancing his arm. 'Well, okay, perhaps there's something *you* could tell *me*. Perhaps something you found out in Hell has given you a lead on this.'

'And I should answer your questions because . . . ?'

Vincent held up the button. 'Because then I might let you live.'

Quill made an expression as if he was weighing up that promise. 'I've seen how you err on the side of caution with that.'

'If you don't, I'll definitely send you back to Hell, okay?'

Quill nodded. 'I'm convinced by your argument.'

'Who first called me anonymously, to tell me you were at Baker Street, then again to say you were going to be at Finchley Road, and finally texted me to say you were parked near Edgware Road? When I got to the car, I saw through the Ripper's eyes, and . . . I think it was someone you'd recently met, but I can hardly believe it . . .'

'Gaiman,' said Quill, amazed. 'I thought he was working for you.'

'Not at all. I want to know how he knew my number. Why he got involved.'

'Presumably you don't want to send him a thank-you basket of muffins.'

'Indeed not. He's another loose end.'

Quill looked again to the presence in the room that Vincent couldn't perceive. Was it his imagination, or did it seem to be gloating? The Smiling Man was the other power in London who might use a proxy like Gaiman to achieve his ends, but what were they? Had he just wanted to make use of Vincent to get Quill killed? There had to be more to it than that. He could surely have done that in a million different, far less ornate, ways.

Vincent put his finger back on the panic button. 'You know,' he said, 'if you're none the wiser about all that, then it's time I brought this conversation to an end anyway. You've heard everything. You can't stop me using the scrying glass, and – come on – you'll *never* successfully bring me to justice. So I assume you're now going to launch yourself at me in the vain hope of stopping me pressing this button?'

'Oh no,' said Quill, shaking his head, 'definitely not.'

Vincent seemed puzzled by Quill's matter-of-fact tone of voice, his finger hovering over the button. 'So you really did come here just to hear the truth?'

'No,' said Quill, shaking his head again.

'Then, what . . . ?'

Quill looked to where a strange and familiar light was appearing through the wall. He grinned. 'I came here, mush,' he said, 'to keep you *talking*.'

TWENTY-NINE

A FEW MINUTES EARLIER

Ross listened to what the familiar, tender voice on the other end of the phone line was telling her. He was saying what he'd done. He was calling, he said finally, from a room where he was being held by security guards, and Quill – Quill, who was back to life, who was back in this world instead of her dad – was about to do something which was informed by where they were, and so now she should listen, because . . .

She held the phone out towards Sefton while Costain was still talking. 'You should listen to him,' she said. 'It's important and I can't.'

Sefton was astonished; his eyes interrogated her. He hesitantly spoke into the phone, and listened to what Costain told him, and put a hand to his face in amazement.

Ross looked back to the hole in the ground. She listened, unable to stop the analytical part of herself from becoming involved as Sefton got all the information Quill had told Costain and his plan for what they should do next, relayed it to her, finished the call.

She looked down at the hole. Now she knew what Quill had encountered in there. What she was looking at was what, in the end, always seemed to be under everything: the thread of abuse that had wound its way through Whitechapel. She'd been right about something she'd said. It seemed a long time ago now: the Ripper really was just blokes and desperation for money. The meaning of this story truly was the killing of women.

She had no meanings left and no hope.

She picked up the pickaxe, stepped forward and dropped into the dark.

She landed inside the long barrow. She could hear Sefton scrambling after her. She felt the mighty presence at the end of the chamber, shut in, desperate to be awakened. She shouldered the pickaxe and ran at the rock wall.

Sefton got inside the barrow just in time to see Ross land the pickaxe against the stone, the scene barely illuminated by the lights through the small opening they'd made in the roof. She struck once, then she cried out, and started striking the rock time after time after time, screaming at it. Sefton watched. He wanted to say something. But anything he might say would be too like her scream. This was what Quill had just ordered them to do, but he was pretty sure that Ross would have done it anyway.

Light sprang from a sudden crack in the rock.

The interior of the barrow was revealed in every detail. Sefton had a moment to see those fingerprints.

Something burst from the rock at the end of the chamber. It still looked like the Ripper. Silver was hissing from its eyes and mouth.

Sefton wondered, in the instant he got a good look at her – for it was very clearly a her – if she would be able to make it out of the barrow and across London. But, as well as the coldness of the evaporating silver, there was in the atmosphere all around them a sense of enormous willpower, of something awoken. The barrow-wight opened her mouth and made a sound Sefton would never forget: a single note that banished the tattered remnants of what had been put here to keep her imprisoned.

Ross was looking up at her, empty, clearly wanting to be pleased that she'd freed her, but finding no meaning.

With a splatter of silver against the rock ceiling of the chamber, the being sped upwards and in a blur of motion she was gone.

NOW

Quill was relieved and awed and once again scared to see the figure of the Ripper walk purposefully through the wall of Vincent's office. He found himself flinching at the possibility that she would once more rush to attack him. She looked at him, considered him. Then she turned to look at Vincent.

He was backing away, looking to the scrying glass, but the figure in front of him felt different now, silver hissing from her, her Ripper guise only a garment that she could throw away if she could be bothered. This woman was awake. She made a noise that went beyond sound, and the scrying glass shattered, the pieces of the mirror embedding themselves into walls and furniture, the valuable ancient bloodline from the frame splattering across the desk. Quill lowered an arm and found himself miraculously unharmed.

Vincent managed to stagger forward, bleeding from a gash across his brow. 'Go back,' he said, and he still sounded commanding. 'I didn't call for you.'

She took a deliberate step towards him.

Vincent considered for a long moment. Then he bolted for the door.

The Ripper waited, and Quill got the feeling she was considering the other presence in the room, the phantom Quill was sure was the Smiling Man. Quill could feel that being's pleasure, his sense of completion. The Ripper despaired at that feeling.

The Ripper met Quill's gaze again. He felt himself noted, distantly approved of.

Then there was a blur of silver, and the Ripper was gone through

385

the wall. Quill looked around for that other presence and was thankful to find that he was alone.

Down the night-time side streets of Wapping ran Russell Vincent. His suit was sweaty from him having spent all night in it. It clung to him like a second skin, outlining the contours of his buttocks and thighs, his ragged breaths pushing his muscular chest tight against the silk of his shirt. As he ran, he saw people who were boarding up their doors or looking down from their windows or just doing what they always did and taking shopping from their cars, stopping to point at him as they recognized him. He could imagine the huge web of commentary, of tweets, people saying that a famous media tycoon was running down their street, that he looked afraid. That he would soon be in Whitechapel. In moments, all London would know where he was, that he was being pursued by something. He hoped someone with secret knowledge might see that, might help him, in the hope of a reward.

He saw the light behind him change as his shadow lengthened in front of him. At the same moment he heard the sound of drums coming closer, of shouts and now sirens from the crossroads he was running towards, and he saw people dashing away from him into their houses, slamming down windows, closing their doors rather than helping. The message they were sending out was that the chaos was arriving here.

From the crossroads ahead they came, just a handful of them, provoked from their nearby houses by the tides under London: skinheads and Toffs and a bunch of hopeful local kids, ready to go whichever way the wind blew.

They were all staring at him as he ran desperately towards them.

No, he realized, they were staring at what was behind him.

He turned to look at her. She was in the sky, walking down towards him. She was surrounded by a cloud of evaporating silver. He imagined the razor slashing him, penetrating him, making him helpless.

He turned back and looked around. He wasn't helpless. He'd

made his empire, damn it! He still had a few tricks! He feinted left
and then suddenly sprinted right, down an alley between houses.
She couldn't keep going forever, not losing that much silver. It
occurred to him that she must be showing that to him deliberately,
that seeing her like this was the first time he'd *seen* the silver. But
still, it didn't change the fact that was just her putting on a front.
She was fast, but he knew that she needed to see him to find him.
Assuming he could find a place where bystanders weren't reporting
on his every move, he could actually hide!

He kept running, turning left and right at random, using the
narrowness of the streets, always shying away from a light in the
sky behind him. He was in Whitechapel proper now, and wasn't
that ironic! A great story was building here. He wondered how
he'd tell it. He'd be the potential victim, obviously. 'I Faced the
Ripper . . . and Lived!' The story would help him if anyone started
wondering about his connection to the deaths tonight.

He ran out into a municipal open space, a playground with
nobody in it, with narrow walkways between houses in all directions. Perfect! He chose one at random and ran for it.

A second before he reached the corner, the illumination washed
over him like a searchlight and he felt his breath and adrenalin
pump again. He flattened himself around the corner. Had she seen
him? The light had stopped. He dared a glance around the wet
brickwork.

She was just standing there, in the playground, silver now
streaming from the eyes of the mask. It was billowing off her, up
into the sky, lit up by the street lights. She looked like a crashed
aircraft. The suit looked as if it was hanging on a stick figure. The
hat fell from her head. She dropped to her knees. She made gestures
to try to rise. He heard faint sounds from her mouth.

He stepped out from his hiding place. She looked up at him
and he flinched, ready to run again. But she made no move towards
him. A great pool of freezing silver was slowly spreading out around
her like blood. The melting snow woman. She was still following
his programming for her, to allow the victim to see everything of

his pursuer, even now, when the victim was meant to be him. She was jerking, trying to make anything work, and with every movement she lost more fuel.

He took a step closer to her, relishing his victory. He was panting with exertion and relief, alive with the blood pounding in his veins, every muscle feeling it. He was even erect. He felt the sweat between him and his shirt, felt his muscles fresh from a workout at the edge of vitality, felt the arousal of the chase, of having survived it. He silenced a laugh of relief.

She was subsiding, the material of her body dissolving. She was trying to say something to him, it seemed – some last curse. But the volume was so low it sounded almost gentle.

Now all that was left was a mask and a bagful of bones in some discarded clothes, swimming in a pool of silver. As Vincent watched, the mask and clothes began to dissolve too.

Vincent stepped quickly through the silver liquid, aware of how cold it made his feet through his shoes. He'd have to be quick. He took a handkerchief out of his pocket. If the mask would stay together, he wanted it, wanted to get himself photographed with it, the image that would sell the story that he too had been hunted by the Ripper tonight.

He squatted, reached down towards the puddle of silver, his handkerchief wrapped around his hand. He was just about to touch the mask when he saw something moving in the liquid silver in front of him.

A hand burst up out of it and grabbed his tie. It was an old woman's hand, covered in some sort of dye.

He was about to wrench himself back in panic when her other hand rose up out of the silver. This one held the razor he had made for her.

'No!' he shouted. 'No!'

The rest of his words became a long scream.

Costain and Quill looked down at the butchered body of Russell Vincent. He had been slashed many times across the chest and neck, and the space between his legs was torn open. His dead eyes looked up in horror and lack of understanding. He was surrounded by a pool of his own blood and by a pool of gently billowing silver. They'd followed the Twitter trail here and, in the absence of any other officers, would surely fail to create any sort of barrier between the crime scene and the news teams that were bound to start arriving shortly.

'Was that what you wanted?' Costain asked Quill.

Quill couldn't find an answer. What he wanted was for there to be a law that applied equally to Vincent and to himself, to those who saw themselves above it, and to those who enforced it. He'd had no other ideas of how to bring this to an end. His only consolation was how empty it left him feeling. He hoped he hadn't done this as the result of a cycle of abuse. 'If only this had been a Ripper we could have caught, that we could have shown to London in handcuffs. There's no reason now for Londoners to think the killings will stop. And when the media hear the Ripper's killed Russell Vincent, it'll increase the sense of chaos exponentially. How do we prove that the law still works and turn this shit around?'

There was a noise from behind them. Lofthouse arrived. She was staring in amazement at Quill.

'Yeah,' he said. He wondered if she'd hug him or something.

She looked him up and down and finally nodded. 'Right,' she said.

'Indeed.'

'Good,' she said, then seemed to decide she had to put a stop to this unseemly outpouring of emotion. 'There's been a vote of no confidence. There's going to be a general election.'

'What about Vincent's allies in the military?' said Costain.

'The military are actually containing a lot of the far right protests,' said Lofthouse. 'The death of Vincent, which has now hit the media as the biggest headline of the lot, means that a lot of people who were thinking of acting rashly have now thought better of it.'

Costain's phone rang, and he answered it. He suddenly looked urgent when he heard who was on the other end, held his hand up for silence. He seemed to be deciding what to say. 'No,' he said, speaking carefully. 'I'm another police officer, but DI Quill is right here beside me. I'll hand you over.' He mouthed the name of the caller as he handed Quill the phone.

Quill took it. 'Hello Mary,' he said.

They waited at the corner of the street, underneath dripping arches, watching dawn make its way into the narrow streets. Costain, because Quill didn't feel he could call up any police yet and announce he was still alive, had found some National Crime Agency staff who'd stayed at their post at the Hill, and so a car with a driver stood ready round the corner to take their guest into what they now were sure would be safe protective custody. Costain was trying only to think of the moment, though his thoughts kept leaping back to Ross, just as, with the chemicals draining from his system, his brain kept reaching out for dreams. He wished he could see her. He desperately wanted to hear news of her, though he couldn't bring himself to text Sefton and ask. He wanted to touch her. He'd never get to do that again. The Lisa Ross of his dreams and the real one were, for several moments as the sun rose, mixed up. He felt he'd been told something reassuring by her. Then, a moment later, he knew that wasn't true.

A taxi pulled up. Out of it stepped someone he had never seen in the flesh before, only on CCTV images – Mary Arthur. She looked very young and very scared. Costain showed her his warrant card and told her his name and rank. Quill and Lofthouse did the same.

'Is Russell Vincent really dead?' she asked.

'Yeah,' said Quill. 'Which makes it a lot easier for us to protect you. If, that is, you're willing to give evidence in the matter of your dealings with Michael Spatley MP, and what happened on the night of the death of Rupert Rudlin.'

That, thought Costain, might begin to sell a new narrative to the public, one which might indeed send London stumbling off on a different course.

Mary seemed to consider for a moment.

'There won't be any reward involved,' said Lofthouse, gently. 'There can't be.'

She looked suddenly angry. 'I'll tell you all about it,' she said. 'Money isn't everything.'

EPILOGUE

Sarah Quill was startled to see the name appear on her phone. She felt dizzy, felt the blood come to her face, felt anger rising. She was standing in the hallway, having just stood up from buttoning Jessica into her coat. She answered the call. 'Who is this?'

'It's me, love. No, please, don't hang up!'

She stopped herself swearing. 'Who *is* this . . . ?!'

'If someone else had called you, I knew you wouldn't believe it—'

'*Who is this?*'

'It's me! It's me! It's because of . . . the stuff about me only a few of us know. Okay? Nobody else would believe this. But you can. You can, love, you can!'

She found a terrible hurt inside her. She was dreaming, wasn't she? She'd had dreams like this in the last few days. This was hurting her with hope. 'But—'

'I didn't want you just to open the front door and see—'

'Where are you? Are you outside my house?'

'It's me, love. I've been waiting outside, wondering how to do this. I didn't want you to open the front door and see me and be shocked by—' But she'd dropped the phone and was grabbing at the chain and bolt on the door and she flung it open—

There he stood. In someone else's clothes, but it was him. She reached out, threw a hand at him, expecting somehow to find nothing there. He grabbed it. He pulled her to him. He let her look into his face. He made her look into his face.

All the ability dropped from her lower body and she fell into him. She was . . . so furious at him. So enormously angry. This was too big . . . this was too big an impossibility.

'Daddy!' said Jessica, coming out to see them, pleased that he was home and nothing more.

Sarah looked to her, and then back at Quill's face. He was still there.

Quill held out a hand from holding Sarah up. Jessica took it.

'I went on a long journey,' he said to her. 'I came back.'

Sefton had one and a half days of solid sleep. Joe took time off work to look after him. He woke with the smell of a natural, early autumn coming through the window. 'The centre held,' he said, his voice a croak.

'What?' Joe had entered the bedroom with two cups of tea.

'You said that was what crime fiction was about.'

'Did I? It's W.B. Yeats.'

'Okay.'

'They've found the Ripper's body,' said Joe.

Sefton hadn't managed to tell his boyfriend anything about the ending of the case before collapsing with exhaustion. Now he frowned, unable to process that. 'What?'

'Bloke dressed in the costume, left a suicide note, a full confession. All the murders were on Vincent's orders, he hid among the ranks of the Toffs but he hated them, and when the guilt became too much he killed Vincent then himself. Nice handwriting, apparently. He includes details of the murders, which the police – not your lot – are saying indicates it must all be true.'

Sefton sipped his tea and could only shake his head again. He had no idea what that meant.

Three days later, Quill's team sat in the Portakabin at Gipsy Hill, watching Quill put an X of black tape across the photo of Vincent on the Ops Board. They were silent, washed out, exhausted. Sefton hadn't expected Ross to come, but she'd entered right on time at the start of her shift, here to do her duty or face the consequences of her actions. She hadn't made eye contact with Costain, who hadn't tried to speak to her. Sefton was even more surprised that he was here.

He'd last seen Ross when the two of them had found Quill in a Whitechapel pub that had a lock-in of shift workers going on. They were scared shitless of the chaos on the streets and glad to include coppers. Costain had already gone home; that had been a condition of Ross coming to see Quill. She'd stared at him then, unable to believe it, unable, Sefton now understood, having heard everything from Quill, to feel happy at his return. Sefton, on the other hand, feeling as if he was about to die and needing to fall asleep, had just taken Quill in his arms and hugged him. Quill had hugged him back. Ross had managed only a few halting words to Quill. She'd managed to say it was good he was alive, but it had sounded almost like a guess. Then she asked if she and Costain were going to prison. The two of them had, after all, kept information from the investigation, committed offences. Ross had also lied to them about what she'd found in the Docklands documents.

Quill had just shaken his head. He looked as perplexed at what had changed in her as much as she was at him. 'Condemned man – me, that is – gets a last request, and I choose to let you off. We can't afford to lose you. What you've done to each other, to yourselves . . .' He looked at her interrogatively again, as if hoping she'd suddenly smile. 'I think that's punishment enough.'

Ross had looked angry at him for that mercy. Then, with Quill calling after her, she'd turned and left the pub.

Sefton had thought about it and decided he might, given the same circumstances, have done the same things. His colleagues had been only human. How terrible that was.

'We survived,' said Quill now. 'Well, you lot did, and I caught up.' He indicated the list of operational aims on the Ops Board:

1: Ensure the safety of the public.
2: Gather evidence of offences.
3: Identify and trace subject or subjects involved (if any).
4: Identify means to arrest subject or subjects.
5: Arrest subject or subjects.
6: Bring to trial/destroy.
7: Clear those not involved of all charges.

'Aims one to three . . . achieved, just about. The "Summer of Blood" is over. Everyone's lapping up Mary Arthur's story and this new revelation about the Ripper, fictional though it is. Vincent's rival media barons have seized on it.' The riots were dying down, and every party in this exhausted general election campaign was falling over itself to say it would negotiate with the police. Gaiman's guess that the mood of London had been linked to solving the Ripper murders seemed to have been correct.

'Where did that fake Ripper corpse come from?' asked Sefton.

'Lofthouse says she's asked for a meeting with those she feels are responsible and will report back. It's done some good for London, anyway. I don't know if that wheel you and I saw on our adventures is turning the right way again now—'

'It's not.' Sefton anticipated Quill's question and shook his head. 'I just know.'

Quill looked back to the list. 'Aim five . . . I'd like us to go after Gaiman, but he seems to have vanished. Besides, since the man he successfully conspired to murder – that is, me – is now alive again, and because of the difficulties we'd have in walking a jury through that, I'm tempted to say let's wait until he pops up again, then lean on him as a source rather than arrest him. And aim six . . . was achieved. But . . .'

'But look at us,' said Costain.

There was silence. Sefton looked again at the faces of his friends who'd betrayed and been betrayed and exhausted themselves and grieved and been to Hell, and remembered his own taking of a life and his own sacrifice. They had been pummelled by their experiences. They were so changed, once again almost strangers to each other. He didn't see how they could continue to function as a team. Even Quill, who'd been trying to jolly them along with procedure, couldn't seem to find the words to continue.

'There is hope,' said Ross. They all turned to look at her. She wasn't looking back at them. She didn't want to look at Costain at all, Sefton got the feeling. Her voice had sounded very small, very calm. 'The Tarot of London,' she said, 'when that fortune-teller consulted it for me at the New Age fair during the Losley case, she said that the Hanged Man, who was my dad . . .' She had to stop for a moment. 'He was supposed to bring hope for us in summer—'

'He did,' said Quill, 'during that case, and it was where he normally was in Hell that made me think of getting to a higher vantage point.'

'—but,' she said, 'he's meant to bring hope in autumn too.' She shrugged, slowly. 'So there's that.'

Sefton wanted to go over there and hold her. But the shape of her shoulders said she really didn't want to be held.

As soon as Quill told them they could go home and get some more sleep, to report back next week, Ross bolted for the door. Costain went after her. He couldn't help it. He could feel the other two willing him not to, but he couldn't stop himself.

He caught up with her before she got to her car. A muscle memory of how she'd felt made him put a hand on her shoulder.

She rounded on him, disgust on her face. He took his hand away. 'I just want you to know—'

'I sacrificed my happiness so I could free my father. Or maybe Jimmy. Maybe I'd have made that choice. You took it from me.'

'I could have used it to protect myself!'

'You brought him back because you got scared. You did everything to save yourself and keep fucking me for as long as possible.'

'No! Listen to me. If you got your dad back, nothing would change for you, that wouldn't make you happy!'

'That was my choice to make.' She took a moment to hold herself back. 'You think you're going to Hell. I'm *in* Hell. I won't forgive you.'

She went to her car and drove away.

Costain watched her go. He understood what he'd done. He had been surprised by a chance at happiness. He had stamped that chance into the ground until it was dead, and all the time he'd said to himself he was doing the right thing, the only thing.

'I know,' he said.

Rebecca Lofthouse wasn't entirely surprised when one morning a different but equally beautiful young woman rang her doorbell, refused to identify herself and announced she was here to drive Lofthouse to a picnic. She'd spent the last few days explaining to Forrest, and to many other incredulous parties in the Met, how Quill could still be alive. She'd told them his team had faked his death in order for him to go undercover, the details of which she would not share. It was only the fact that Quill obviously *was* alive that allowed her to get away with such a thin deception.

The picnic turned out to be by the Thames, down Henley way, in a meadow so perfect that Lofthouse wondered if it had been constructed for this purpose. Rita and Sue sat with a hamper and an ice bucket containing a bottle of champagne. Lofthouse felt they hardly needed the ice. There was a slight chill in the air, and the shadows were getting longer, but summer had not yet ended. There were still a couple of rounds of the County Championship left to play. Another group of picnickers sat at a distance, obediently picking at caviar. The beautiful driver went to join them.

'My team are a bit perplexed,' said Lofthouse, sitting down.

'What about?' asked Rita, a look of mock innocence on her face.

'They wonder why Jack the Ripper so conveniently committed suicide, having written such a specific note, incredibly, if accurately, incriminating the late Russell Vincent.'

'Oh, I saw that in the papers,' said Sue. 'Very neat, I thought.'

'It does give Londoners the feeling that things are back under control,' said Rita.

'Let's say that the still-unidentified corpse wasn't really Jack the Ripper. Hypothetically,' said Lofthouse. 'Where would someone get such a corpse?'

'I would imagine, said Sue, 'assuming whoever did this had the interests of the great British public in mind, it would have been ethically sourced.'

Lofthouse considered all the ways in which an organization with the Security Service's resources could find and doctor a fresh corpse and decided that she was willing to believe her. But still she was angry. 'You worked out early on that Russell Vincent had something to do with the Ripper—'

'The list of victims was indicative,' said Rita.

'—and you let my team get mangled as they tried to figure out what.'

'We picked right,' said Sue. 'They did a great job.'

'They even, though we're still not sure how, arranged for Vincent to be hoist by his own petard,' said Rita, 'fatally.'

'They're not pleased about that,' said Lofthouse, amazed. 'But you are, aren't you? You're happy he ended up dead.'

'Russell Vincent,' said Sue, reaching for her knife to butter a piece of bread, 'was somehow learning other people's innermost secrets.' She grinned hugely at Lofthouse and dropped her voice to a stage whisper. 'Only we're allowed to do that.'

Lofthouse took a taxi home. At least now she had something to tell Quill's team. She wished she could tell them everything. She looked to the key on her charm bracelet. There were times when she wanted to throw the damn thing out of the window. But the consequences of that were too terrible to think about.

Gaiman looked down at London at night as the aircraft he was in banked to begin its climb westwards over the Atlantic. He hadn't known Quill was going to come back, had been surprised to hear, from the same friends that were now also suddenly alive and well, that the policeman was too. He was glad. He had stayed in hiding, got out of Britain when it felt safe to do so. He didn't want to face any more questions. He believed he had managed to do as much good as anyone could, in circumstances which few people understood.

But, he thought, as London vanished under the clouds below, *that's what they all say.*

Quill lay in bed with Sarah. She'd been looking at his new body parts, pink and tender. He'd told her everything, though he knew she'd be horrified. Everything, that is, apart from one thing – that sign he'd seen on entering Hell. That would make too much of a difference to her life, to everyone.

'I don't know where to begin,' she said. 'I don't know how you can deal with it. I don't know how I can help. But I want to.'

'It was harder on you. I learned a lot by being absent. I'm fine.'

'Of course you're not . . . *fine*, Quill!'

'I've just got some odd memories, which seem a bit like a dream now, and a new cock. Thought you'd be pleased.'

The phone on the bedside table rang. Quill looked at the display and recognized the number. He hesitated. No, he had to answer it. He took it out into the hall and closed the door behind him before he did, so she wouldn't hear. There was, as he'd expected, only the sound on the other end of the line of something big and far away, breathing. Quill knew he was connected to the Smiling Man.

'So you're calling me to try and scare me,' said Quill, 'to remind me where I've been. I think you're hoping I might tell someone, even just Sarah, what was written on the sign I saw over the gates of Hell.' Silence. Had the breathing paused? 'Yeah, I've been thinking about everything that's happened, and I'm pretty sure that's what you want me to do. That's why my time never ran out in Hell, because you didn't want me coming back here a gibbering wreck. Maybe you planted the document that set Ross off on her quest for the Bridge of Spikes. Let me walk you through it.' He went down the stairs into the kitchen and started to make a cup of tea, the phone clamped to his ear, aware he was doing this to hold off with sheer domesticity the idea of who he was talking to. 'Gaiman was working for you. He made sure Vincent killed me. But I wonder if he also made sure my notebook ended up in Sefton's hands. He could have burned it, couldn't he, or just kept it? But no, he disposed of it somewhere in London, so it fell into the Rat King's clutches. Of course, he could have just left it at the scene of the crime, but then it wouldn't have seemed so important, would it? It took Sefton such a lot of work to find it that it was obvious those ridiculous few words of mine must contain some major clue. That was what got Sefton and Ross to the long barrow, and opening that finished off Vincent. So why would you want to let Vincent nearly complete his plans, and then get rid of him?' Quill watched the kettle boil. 'I think you like chaos in London. So you liked what Vincent was doing, but not what he was planning for afterwards: all those jackboots, all that *order*. If anyone gets that done, you want it to be you. Am I right?'

Silence again. The breathing had definitely slowed. Quill wasn't sure he wanted to hear the Smiling Man speak. But he was going to keep daring him to do so. 'I suppose some other people must have come back from Hell, or know what's written above that gate, what the secret is. But you've seen that I've got a thing about doing my duty. You were sure I'd *have* to tell everyone who'd believe it. That gradually that message would sink in to them. That it'd grind them down even more than they've been ground down now.' The kettle finished boiling. He poured the tea. 'So I'm not going to do that. I'm going to find a way to heal my unit. I'm going to wait until I'm sure they're able to cope with what I know. Then we're going to find some way to change it.'

There was a click from the phone. He'd hung up.

Quill found that he was actually smiling. He took a slow sip from his tea. He thought about Sarah and Jessica asleep upstairs, and what the words on that sign over the gate of Hell meant for them and for everyone else he knew. The sign had read:

It's everyone who ever lived in London

Acknowledgements

This book could not have been written without the permission and cooperation of Neil Gaiman, to whom I owe an enormous debt. He read through all the relevant sections and gave his approval. He is, of course, an honest and lovely man.

Others who aided enormously in the writing of *The Severed Streets* are: Simon Bradshaw, Dave Clements, Judith Clute, Simon Colenutt, Andrew Englefield, Kieron Gillen, 'SJG', Simon Guerrier, Lynn, Harry Markos, Jamie McKelvie, Cheryl Morgan, Chief Inspector Andrew Smith and Mark Wyman. Thanks are also due to Steven Moffat and Sue and Beryl Vertue, for old times' sake.